The
Lords
of the
West End

The
Lords
of the
West End

A London Fantasy

PETER W. BLAISDELL

THE LORDS OF THE WEST END. Copyright © 2024 by Peter Warren Blaisdell

Cover design by Damonza Book Cover Design
Interior book design by Andrea Reider

ISBN: 978-0-9992205-8-0
E-ISBN: 978-0-9992205-9-7

Library of Congress Control Number: 2024911256

To the pop bands that made the 1980s danceable.
Their music still echoes.

And to Samuel Taylor Coleridge's fragment, "Kubla Khan,"
packed with opium visions of imaginary realms.

London's West End is an attitude, not a neighborhood.

—Anon

One earth.

—Anon

I took it—and in an hour, oh! Heavens!
What a revulsion! What an upheaving,
from its lowest depths, of the inner spirit!
What an apocalypse of the world within me!

—Thomas De Quincey, *Confessions of an English Opium-Eater*

NOTE TO READER

This novel references alcohol and drug consumption and depicts violence in fantastical and real-world settings. Also, despite the author's admonishments, the characters liberally use vulgarity in both British and American English.

The Lords of the West End belongs to a modern fantasy series including *The Lords of Oblivion, The Lords of Powder,* and *The Lords of the Summer Season.* Though the main character, Bradan, an almost immortal magician, and his companion, the wolf Tintagel, appear in all of these novels, each of the books is independent of the others and can be read on its own.

The
Lords
of the
West End

CHAPTER 1

A Revel Amid the Stones

Winter Solstice, 1986

"I'm supernatural, not superhuman," Bradan told the wolf. "And I'm barely supernatural."

The wolf was disdainful. It had jumped an eight-foot-tall chain link fence in a single bound while Bradan clambered over the barrier tearing his jeans and gashing his thigh.

Climbing down the far side, finally confident, Bradan let go and dropped down to land lightly on Stonehenge's grounds.

It was utterly frozen, and clear—rare for the winter solstice—with the setting sun illuminating Salisbury Plain's snow.

From a distance, Stonehenge was small, a playground for a giant child with boulders tumbled carelessly about like toy blocks. Up close, the megaliths were enormous and their mass made them appear permanent.

However, time had shifted them.

Despite the disorder, the monument preserved its purpose and two pillars framed the setting sun. Bradan believed the builders intended this; Stonehenge had been their connection to nature's seasonal changes and alerted them to the solstice's exact date, letting the ancients know that over the next six months, the days would get longer and spring would eventually come.

Bradan touched one of the pillars. It was cold, but he didn't withdraw his hand, penance for sins committed over fifteen hundred years.

Mea maxima culpa.

He appeared youthful, but he was a timeworn soul in a young body. He was used to being the oldest thing around, older than cities, older than cathedrals, and far older than any living human. Here, he was an infant. Being virtually immortal didn't mean much on Salisbury Plain where even ghosts had vanished into time.

He was at Stonehenge to make a video promoting his band, though this was inconsequential, inappropriate even, in a primeval place that linked nature and man.

Besides, he risked arrest. As he and the wolf had approached the stones, he'd lain flat in the snow to hide from police patrols. The constables were here to prevent a mélange of neo-pagans and solstice tourists from invading the grounds, and the temporary chain link fence had been erected to keep intruders out.

Now Damian and his cinematographer, Martha, arrived and stood on the far side of the fence.

"Get your gear ready," Bradan said urgently. "We don't get this shot for another year."

Besides the cinematographer, the director brought along makeup and lighting techs—overkill, in Bradan's opinion. He just wanted them to make an edgy video showcasing his band's music and photogenic looks. If the footage looked gritty, good; if the band was grimy, brilliant. Keep it simple: get in, play, flee back to London before the police discovered them.

Bradan's band, Silicon Saturday, arrived and clustered shivering by Damian and his film crew. The crew was bundled up against the weather, but the musicians had all dressed for a club gig, not a frozen sunset by a prehistoric monument. Damian wanted shots of them with Stonehenge in the background, and having a fashion-forward band swaddled in winter clothing would kill the image. Suki and Liam wore leather jackets. They were warmer than their fellow musicians.

"Hadn't counted on the fence," Damian said. "It wasn't here when we scouted the location last week. That wrecks the shot. You read me? We're here to make musical history."

"We're here to make an MTV video, mate," Bradan said dryly.

"Besides, we need the Sillies—"

"Silicon Saturday," Bradan corrected.

"—we need the band close to the stones, read me?"

Damian snapped his fingers for emphasis, startling the musicians.

Bradan thought the lean director played the role of auteur to the point of absurdity with Ray-Bans and chain-smoking French Gauloises cigarettes. Going completely over the top, Damian wore a long silk scarf over a Burberry trench coat. The scarf's ends trailed in the snow.

He turned to Bradan. "How do you want to play this? I can film some rubbish any amateur could do complete with a blurry fence in the shot, or I can do something special. Your band is special. This place is otherworldly. I want to shoot something that will make MTV cream their pants."

He snapped his fingers again.

"Film us by the pillars," Bradan said. "Hurry. We're losing the sunset."

"How do we get over the fence?" Constantine asked.

The drummer wore shorts and a Motörhead T-shirt. He rubbed his head trying to keep it warm. He'd shaved it to hide his receding hairline.

"I'm not climbing. I don't even know how you and your dog got in."

"It wasn't that hard, Tiny," Bradan said.

"Doesn't seem easy," the drummer pointed out. "You're bleeding."

"How do we avoid the police?" Suki piled on.

"We're all outlaws tonight," Bradan said. "We do one song and go before anyone notices."

"They'll notice if we tear the bloody chain link down," Suki replied. She flipped orange hair out of her eyes.

"I've got no amp," Liam said. His accent was Irish. "You want the sounds of silence?"

No support from that quarter. Bradan faced a mutiny. None of his band looked keen to breach the fence however cool the video would be with the musicians playing Stonehenge.

Bradan addressed them from his side of the fence, "We *could* tape it on a London sound stage, but it'll look cheesy. This place works with our sound."

"I brought two practice amps along," Anuradha told Liam. "Plug into one of them. They're small, but they kick out good noise for their size, run on batteries, too."

Bradan nodded thanks to Anu's positive voice. The keyboard player was the group's diplomat.

"There's a generator in the trunk," Martha said. "It'll power our cameras and the band's mics."

"That still leaves: How do we get in?" Constantine said.

"I'll think of something," Bradan said. "Get your instruments."

"My synth's in the car," Anu said. Her hair blew about in the cold air.

"Liam, help me lug it here. We'll bring your guitar, too."

"Anyone have some blow?" Damian asked. "Not to rhyme, but I can't do a proper shoot without a toot."

"In the van," Martha answered. "We've enough to fuel a club rave. Molly, too."

"Skip the drugs," Bradan said. "You play better clean."

"Too late," Constantine said. "We got high coming up from London. Except Anu."

"No surprise," Bradan said. He remembered Tiny's capacity for narcotics from playing together in San Francisco years ago.

"Bring the gear," Bradan said. "You too, Damian."

The director stuffed his hands into his pockets and sullenly moved off with the rest of the group to their cars and a small lorry parked discreetly down the road.

Bradan watched them go. He needed privacy. It was small magic, but magic nonetheless, and he'd kept that part of himself secret for fifteen centuries. Now, excepting the wolf, Bradan had Stonehenge to himself and the wolf knew how to keep secrets.

He studied the fence. It would be taken down once the authorities felt the danger of Stonehenge being inundated with solstice celebrants had passed, but the barrier was firmly embedded into the ground, and he couldn't push it over with just physical strength. He'd need enchantment.

Bradan spoke half a dozen stanzas in Latin, feeling oneness with nature as he tapped into the power of the winter breeze blowing past and the vegetation under the snow waiting dormant for spring with water moving sluggishly through their liminal spaces.

The craft in magic was knowing what words achieved the desired effect; the art lay in leveraging those words with poetic cadence to harness nature's power. However, even for an adept, enchantment was irrational and unpredictable, and he'd never used this spell.

Spell-casting could be as good as sex, but when it went wrong, it was a missed orgasm.

Tonight, everything worked. The section of fence nearest him sagged to the ground as if its metal posts had melted. Nearby snow liquefied and grass beneath the fallen fence turned brown.

Immediately, Bradan paid the penalty for deploying even a small spell: fatigue. Nature taxed magic, exacting a price proportional to the outcome.

He doubled over gasping for breath. Still, he was proud his spell had worked and, from experience, he knew the weariness would pass.

"How'd it just collapse?" Anu had returned carrying her Roland synthesizer. Liam was at her side pushing a dolly with two amplifiers and his guitar case. Both eyed the fallen fence.

"I pushed it over," Bradan said. "It was temporary, not built to last."

"It seemed sturdy," Anu said.

"You look ill," Liam said.

"I'm fine," Bradan snapped. He didn't feel fine, but he gradually recovered his energy and composure.

The rest of Silicon Saturday and Damian's crew came back hauling instruments, cameras, and sound recording gear. Someone brought a case of cosmetics. They'd be actors as much as musicians tonight.

"They're all young and pretty, right out of *Vogue*," Damian said to his makeup woman. "Except the drummer. He looks long in the tooth. Lots of foundation for him. And let's give them all an edge. Make them look like they stepped out of a gothic novel."

"Couldn't carry my whole drum kit," Constantine said. "I've just got the tom and one snare cymbal."

"We'll dub your full kit when we're back in a studio," Bradan said.

Anything to keep this argumentative group of musicians happy. Now that the idea of shooting a video here had taken hold, he'd become obsessed with doing it right.

"Do a simple beat," he told the drummer. "Keep the rest of us on tempo."

Led by Constantine, everyone walked over the fallen fence and amid the huge blocks, feet crunching through the snow and frozen grass, tentative about being around such age. Liam ran his hands over a megalith. Bradan guessed the guitar player absorbed its power, though he didn't think any of them had a clue about the site's history.

In the fading light, Bradan watched the band set up as Damian fussed about camera angles and where to position the musicians by the pillars. Coke, Ecstasy, and marijuana made things chaotic. One of the sound guys tripped and fell sprawling. Bradan guessed that, excepting himself and Anu, no one was straight. Damian stopped to snort coke off one of the huge boulders through a rolled up ten-pound note, sending leftover crystalline powder swirling into the wind. Bradan hoped the film crew would keep enough of their motor functions to capture the scene, and he prayed the band could play through the dreamy haze of narcotics bathing their neurons.

He waved aside a small blond woman, one of the director's minions, trying to apply kohl to his eyes.

"I'll make you look like a pharaoh, luv," she said. Her accent was French.

"I'm just a musician, *chérie*," Bradan said.

Speed was critical, but he paused to take in the weird scene, a new wave pop band making music amid the relics of a five-thousand-year-old civilization.

Had the ancients made music? Had they danced?

Those long-gone tribes had built to last forever while he and his band would be thrilled if anyone remembered their melodies in a few months.

He pulled his Martin twelve-string from its case. It created incandescent tones. He'd been through a lot with the guitar including fronting a San Francisco acid rock group two decades ago. The bitter cold played havoc with the strings' tension, so he tuned it gently before strumming a chord. The guitar's shimmering notes floated out over Salisbury Plain. The sound hung in the evening, challenging the wind.

What would they awaken in this ancient place?

On the solstice, anything could happen.

"We have one take, I reckon," Damian shouted. "Let's make cinematic art. Do you read me?"

"I read you, Truffaut." Constantine had taken to mocking the director.

The drummer hit the first beat, Suki sent a bass note rumbling off the stones, and the rest of the band locked into the tempo. Since Constantine had only a minimal percussion kit, the rhythm was primitive and elemental. The drummer couldn't apply his usual complex jazz flourishes. To Bradan, the music was better for it, raw and simple; he imagined Neolithic tribes swaying through the monument in forgotten rituals, reaching out to touch one another.

"This isn't how we rehearsed it," Suki shouted over the music and wind. "It's out of control."

"It's magic," Bradan called back. "Go with it."

The Saturdays played a song that Bradan hoped would bring them attention in a musical scene packed with other chart-topping groups. He'd built the tune around a danceable, overdriven synthesizer riff and his lyrics spoke of timeless love in a transient world. Liam's guitar added edge and sent searing, elongate notes off to the far corners of the galaxy. Blended with the surging keyboard and guitar, the song had a South Asian theme that deepened it and set it apart from other pop songs. Anu's contribution.

Martha and camera techs flitted between the Saturdays like strange dancers, moving in for close-ups, then pulling away to pan across the whole band as they serenaded the stone blocks. Sound techs maneuvered to capture the music with overhead boom mics trying to stay out of camera range and away from the wolf who lounged atop a boulder.

It was all ad hoc, but Bradan was stunned that their sound was this good; brilliant, even. It was also loud, reverberating off the megaliths. He imagined they were communing with other times, other places—but did history want that conversation?

At Stonehenge tonight, past, present, and future coexisted in mutual suspicion.

Bradan pushed his guitar to the side like a gunslinger and stepped beside Anu to share playing her synthesizer, their hands crowding together on the keyboard and joining to create elaborate melodies and counterpoint. The song was supposed to last five minutes, but inspired by the setting, the band stretched out and Bradan lost track of time as he improvised a melody using the setting as a muse. It was a place for flights of fancy and the music was radiant, cold, and pure like winter in this primal place.

"I'm so high, not drugs, but we're making something great," Anu yelled over the volume. "This is way better than in a studio."

"Magic," Bradan answered.

The sun sent a last ray between the megaliths that framed its departure. Twilight took the stage and made Stonehenge a place of shadows and patches of moonlight.

Silicon Saturday sang for the cameras, but there was another audience.

They gathered, the audience: the Fae Folk, more sensed than seen. It had happened to Bradan before, but only when he'd played alone, to clear his mind, and circumstances had to be right—a setting remote from human affairs, a particular time of the year. There weren't many secluded spots anymore as mankind inexorably encroached on what had once been wild.

Bradan thought that made them angry.

The Fae judged. Bradan knew that, but he never knew what verdict they came to. Just that they didn't murder him; he supposed that was a passing grade.

The Fae arrived in two groups who stayed far apart using Stonehenge's blocks to demarcate their respective turfs; they manned rival forts using the massive stones as their ramparts, perching, sitting, or standing on the megaliths. Some carried spears tipped with pennants fluttering in the wind, green for one side, yellow for the other. Bradan sensed a very fragile truce.

The film crew and band played on oblivious to their supernatural spectators. Bradan thought he could sense the Fae when others couldn't because he'd survived from olden times when the human world and the Faerie kingdom had intersected more frequently and people weren't declared mad if they saw visitors from other realms.

Or maybe the band and crew were so wasted, nothing registered except their music's strength.

He knew the Fae weren't the clichéd, little winged creatures from fantasies who floated among daisies with mischievous, but essentially harmless, designs on humanity; there was nothing childlike and innocent about them and they weren't Barbies with wings, or Camelot fairies in gauzy, pastel gowns. Instead, they were from an eerie netherworld, connected to but altogether different from civilized spaces. They didn't conform to human norms because they despised them, and they wouldn't be sanitized into pale, safe caricatures to populate children's fantasies.

The wind picked up. Bradan looked up. Clouds encircled the half-moon and then blotted it out. The diminishing light made the Fae Folk fleeting retinal images, imagined rather than seen, on the edge of his sight and perception. Their features were shadowy, though he saw that there were scores of them capering about in the wind, cartwheeling through the night air, dancing to the band's melody. The original two groups now melted together as if rivals—or maybe hated enemies—had momentarily put aside their weapons and their feud to party, stretch out and touch fingertips, and dance together.

They were young, beautiful, and hard.

A few lounged amid the ruins catching their breath before rejoining the revel.

A tall, slender fellow in a broad-brimmed hat relaxed on the snow, stretched full length, indifferent to the cold, and saluted Bradan casually, touching his brim with a forefinger. He clapped along to the beat. Some of his companions arced through a little tornado of cocaine that spiraled around Damian after he carelessly upended a baggie of the drug onto a fallen pillar. Bradan wondered what effect this would have on Fae.

"Sun's down. We've lost our light!" the director shouted. "Put some spots on the musicians."

Bradan watched the director's assistants scramble to position portable lights on band members. Improvising, one of them pointed a flashlight at Bradan. The scene became even more dreamlike with wildly waving lights casting the musicians in abstract black-and-white patterns against the megaliths while supernatural beings darted about.

Suddenly, one of the Fae dancers, lithe and agile, swept down, slapped Bradan's hand aside, and pressed her fingers onto the synthesizer's keys, creating discord and cacophony where there had been grace and melody. The gesture was at once playful and menacing, letting him know that he was here at their sufferance and whatever dispensation he'd been granted to compose music in this spot sacred to long-vanished heroes could be rescinded in an eyeblink. Bradan pushed her hand away to silence the instrument's dissonance.

Sensing something unseen, but not right, Anu lost her place and stopped playing. Her glasses fell off.

"What's happening?" she shouted. "I can't see. There are shadows around us."

Ever the tease, the Fae woman flew over to the wolf, sitting on the edge of a stone block, aloof from the film shoot. It had disdained to notice the fairy dance, but she circled above the animal and reached down to caress its fur. The wolf's eyes blazed orange and, lightning-fast, it erupted off the megalith with a snarl audible even over the wind and instruments, snapping at this intrusion and grasping after her. Bradan knew the beast didn't tolerate unwanted touching. Just beyond the wolf's jaws, the Fae zipped upward toward the clouds. Bradan saw her panic—as well she should, since the beast was a descendent of Fenrir, the Norse wolf-god. The animal was as old as the hills. The Fae Folk—except for a few tricksters—respected that pedigree and gave the wolf his space.

Rage replaced the Fae woman's fear.

This risked becoming a battle between demons so Bradan stopped playing to sprint over and interpose himself between the wolf and the Fae woman now descending to retaliate.

The band stopped playing; their instruments guttered into silence. Damian's crew halted where they stood.

"The fuck?" Constantine yelled.

Ignoring his bewildered band, Bradan confronted the Fae woman. This had started as a fight between her and the wolf, but now transformed into a duel with Bradan and, for an instant, it was just the two of them with Stonehenge as their arena.

In her fury, she dropped any effort to hide from human sight. Damian shouted in alarm.

The Fae's appearance was fluid and fearsome. A tangled mane of hair, contained by a silver tiara intertwined with flowers, shifted color from black to pine green and then to dark brown, shades from a nighttime forest. Her rainbow-colored eyes should have been wondrous, but they registered wrath. She grabbed a pendant-tipped spear and flung it at Bradan. No time for a spell; he leaped aside, feeling a rush of air as the missile zipped past. It buried itself full length in the frozen ground.

Suddenly, Bradan had allies; other Fae, including the fellow with the hat, flew into the fray inserting themselves between the combatants, blocking escalation. Bradan intuited that cooler heads prevailed as some of them recognized that slaughtering a mortal in a spot as prominent as Stonehenge with witnesses—even drug-addled witnesses unable to comprehend what they were seeing—would bring unwanted attention.

As quickly as the fight had started, its energy faded. The Fae woman gave Bradan a parting glare—this wasn't finished— she'd shown fear of the wolf in front of her tribe. Then she arced into the sky. He knew Fae were quick to anger and slow to forget and he'd made a lasting enemy.

The rest of the fairies gathered. Then they too dissipated into the night, separating into two rival groups. Any musically inspired conviviality vanished.

The slender Fae man tipped his hat regretfully to Bradan as if to say this all could have been avoided before following the other fairies. He was the last to go.

There was an ever so brief pause when everything was still and Bradan tried to get his heart rate under control. He held his guitar so tightly he thought it would snap.

Someone giggled.

"I saw things, I don't know what," Suki yelled.

"Thought it was the weed, but we weren't alone," Liam said. "And your dog went crazy."

Can music connect worlds? Bradan wondered. *Tonight, I've accidentally summoned darkness.*

An intercom squawked and he saw police moving through the snowy grass toward them, backlit by headlights from their vehicles. Blue and red lights washed over the scene.

"That's a wrap," Bradan shouted. "Get your stuff and run for the cars. Damian, you have enough for a video?"

"I don't know what I've got," the director yelled back.

"Something remarkable if you edit it well," Bradan said. "Something otherworldly."

"Otherworldly is right. Who did you fight with? She floated!"

"What fight? You had too much nose candy. See to your crew. I'll distract the constables. Anu, your glasses?"

"Found them. What about you?" the keyboard player called, yanking cords out of her synthesizer and shoving them into a backpack.

"I'll manage," Bradan shouted. "Run over the fence. Constantine can help." He pointed where he wanted them to go.

"See you back in London," he yelled.

The disoriented musicians and film crew beat a scattered retreat. Constantine had fled many police raids in his time and had an instinctive feel for the best escape routes, so he coordinated with Anu to shepherd Silicon Saturday away from Stonehenge.

Bradan looked around. It was dark and confused, but he made out a dozen police surging across Salisbury Plain in a rough picket line toward him. Flashlight beams probed among the megaliths, but they hadn't figured out who or where the trespassers were.

"Stand where you are," a constable shouted through a megaphone. "Hands in sight."

"Tintagel, a little help," Bradan called to the wolf.

On cue, the beast let loose an unearthly wail. The howl reverberated out of a Norse hell to echo within Stonehenge. Bradan watched the police freeze where they stood. An appropriate spell would add to their confusion.

He recited eight rhyming stanzas. This time he spoke Celtic instead of Latin. It was instinct. Celtic wasn't the language of Stonehenge's builders, but it was the oldest tongue he knew. Some enchantment worked in one language, some in another. He'd never used modern English. Maybe that day would come.

Inspired by the setting and the band's music, he conjured images of Stonehenge's builders dancing by torchlight amid the megaliths celebrating the passage of seasons. There were men and women barely wrapped against the winter. They swayed around and between the megaliths, but didn't notice modern notions like chain link fences, and so moved outward passing through the fence like the imagined beings they were, beyond the stones toward the line of police who watched the approaching wraiths and called to each other in alarm. Bradan knew that in the moonlight, the constables weren't sure what they saw.

The images seemed intent on including the bobbies in their carnal dance, and constables' flashlights probed about madly with beams passing through the diaphanous figures until one of the lights settled on Bradan.

He felt a tug at his sleeve. It was the wolf telling him to use the uncanny distraction to escape, but Bradan was so exhausted from his spell he could barely move. Tintagel yanked harder and Bradan stumbled after him, over the fallen fence and away from Stonehenge. His guitar weighed hundreds of pounds, but he carried it. He'd never leave it behind.

He glanced back once to admire his handiwork.

Vanity was a magician's vice.

For a moment, his imaginary dancers mixed with the real constables in a sensual reel, inviting participation in ancient ritual, but the sensuality was one-sided as the police stood frozen in place. Then his images faded away, leaving the constables with no trespassers in handcuffs but in full command of Salisbury Plain. The dancers had done their job and weren't supposed to last. Flashlight beams reached after Bradan. The police would track him.

CHAPTER 2

Almost Camelot

Bradan was high on the only drug that counted: adrenaline. He jerked around to check the street behind him. Did he have the little town to himself? Nothing followed him, not constables, not Fae. Fae weren't always visible, though.

Amesbury, on the River Avon, was a world away from Stonehenge and the megaliths and moody plains that Bradan had fled. Unlike the big stones, eerie on the solstice, the village was no different than on any other on a cold, wintery night, shut up and not looking forward to the morning and another day of drear routine. With few tourists this time of year and a bleak economy, there wasn't much to be cheery about.

Bradan wondered if that made the townsfolk angry.

He'd support local business by getting a hotel room to sleep in before driving back to London—once he found his car.

Bradan shivered, wet from running across snowy grass. His shoes squelched as he walked. They'd once been nice. He needed to find a warm spot or risk hypothermia. He was almost immortal and immune to disease, courtesy of Merlin, but he could die as easily as anyone from violence or the elements. Amazing that in his youth, he'd survived winters in patched wool cloaks, thin leather boots, and cold chain mail.

Untroubled by frigid weather, the wolf paced along beside him looking about, missing nothing. It seemed to know pursuit would come.

"Hide when police show," Bradan said. "I'll pretend to be a hopelessly lost London musician on the way to visit friends in the area—the Martin helps my story." He hefted his guitar case.

"So does the Yank accent—but you don't look like anyone's idea of a house pet. For starters, you've got no tags; you've never had a rabies shot in your life."

The wolf's eyes blazed orange at the notion of a veterinarian's unwanted care.

"They'll take you into whatever animal control facility they have around here and, if you tear someone's arm off, they'll put you down."

The wolf seemed untroubled.

A half-moon presided over the small hours of the night and brushed the town's modest houses and shops with dim light, allowing him to navigate the main road's sidewalk. In the west, rain clouds moved toward the town, and it was dark enough to make his passage unobtrusive. He stayed close to the walls and windows, trying to fade into the background.

In winter, Amesbury was shades of slate gray and off-white that matched the lowering skies. Bradan saw Christmas decorations in shop windows, but their jolly red and green colors were bleached out in the gloom, and the plastic holly and empty gift boxes didn't bring to mind festive holidays.

Coming to Stonehenge had been a mistake. He'd conceived the idea of playing there as inspired marketing. However, he'd cheapened a sacred spot to make a silly video promoting his band. Further, he'd wanted to use the setting to stir his soul, but instead he'd agitated forces best left alone and surfaced memories better left stowed in his mind's far reaches.

Shame.

Merlin's legacy was for Bradan to use his long life and magical skills to honor nature and further art, but he'd done nothing for nature recently and Silicon Saturday wasn't really art, much as he'd like to think otherwise.

Lost in thought, he realized a police car had materialized at his side. After dealing with Fae, he didn't need this. The car rolled over the curb and onto the sidewalk with a crunch of rubber on pavement, trapping him next to a shop window. He'd have to clamber over the car to escape, but he had no intention of running. He doubted that he could be identified as a trespasser at Stonehenge since the police who'd interrupted the film shoot—probably still shaken from the wolf's howl and images of prehistoric tribal dancers—had only glimpsed him in the darkness. Even if he had been visible, he was guilty of nothing more than unlawful trespass—he wasn't the first visitor to want to touch the megaliths.

The wolf had vanished.

"Bad night for a stroll," a constable said. He'd rolled his window down only halfway to keep the cold out of their car. Bradan recognized the West Country accent. Both policemen stared at Bradan. They weren't overtly hostile, but they weren't friendly, either. Probably their colleagues had alerted them about mad events at Stonehenge.

"Lost," Bradan said. "I've been driving around in circles, so I parked the car and thought I'd orient myself better on foot. Zounds, didn't work, as you can see. I'm still lost."

Bradan realized he'd slipped and inserted a Renaissance-era oath into the conversation. One of the hazards of near immortality was keeping his speech current. Occasionally Celtic, old English, or Classical Arabic words and phrases crept in unintended, the relics of other times, other places.

Probably the constables would simply think him eccentric if they noticed at all.

"You've an odd accent," one of them said. "Sounds kind of English, but then again, not so much, outdated words and whatnot, like something out of an old play."

"Misspent youth," Bradan said blandly.

He remembered when Britain had been called Albion. No one would recognize it as such today.

Sometimes, to amuse himself, Bradan hinted at experiences he couldn't possibly have had if he hadn't lived for fifteen centuries, but always with a ready mundane explanation if someone called him on his intimations. He likened this to a cat keeping its claws sharp. The biggest challenge to near immortality—besides not being eviscerated by natural or supernatural enemies—was boredom. Tiptoeing up to the edge of revealing who and what he was helped him fend off tedium.

Sensing ridicule, both constables stared at him.

Careful, Bradan thought. *Let's not let things escalate.*

"Driving license?" one of them asked.

Bradan fished it out of his wallet and handed the license through the window.

"What part of America are you from?"

"Miami most recently as the license shows," Bradan said.

"You kept your American license. That legal, Colin?"

The constable's partner shrugged. "If he's got an international driving permit. You have that?"

"Yes indeed," Bradan said.

"Florida's a damn sight warmer than here," the one with his license said.

"Anyway, you're far afield from Miami. You one of the pagans that hang about Stonehenge?"

"Christ, no," Bradan said. "I'm Church of England."

"Hear, hear," Colin said dryly.

Ironically, it was true. Bradan was a Christian, but he also kept to his old pagan Celtic practices and saw no inconsistency in doing so. However, he wouldn't complicate the tense situation by debating theology with the police.

"I'm doing business in London at the moment," he said to change the topic.

"Whereabouts?"

"Mayfair."

Bradan saw the constables exchange looks inside their car.

"Posh," one of the men said noncommittally, but Bradan caught the undercurrent of scorn the English working class reserved for upstarts.

"The West End," the nearer constable said to his partner. "Oliver, ever take Emma to a show?"

"It's a drive into London," his partner replied.

Bradan didn't bother to tell the constables that no theaters existed in Mayfair. The residents would have come down with the vapors. The big theaters were in neighboring Soho. However, displaying too much city lore would confirm their opinion that he was an effete prick.

"Besides, Emma hates London," Oliver continued.

"As do I," Colin said. "It's all rubbish. Can't think what it must be like policing there. Drugs everywhere. Coppers must be armed."

"The dodgier part," Bradan interrupted, trying to insert humor into the questioning. "I live in the dodgier part of Mayfair."

The jest fell flat. There was a long silence between the officers. For the second time tonight, Bradan felt like a complete outsider.

"Didn't think Mayfair had dodgy parts," one of the constables finally said. "Think that buys credibility with us?"

In his long life, Bradan had been questioned by countless officials, inquisitors, priests, soldiers, police. As much as possible, one tried to control the direction the questioning was going. He needed to pry their attention away from his upscale digs in London.

"I don't know what buys credibility," Bradan said. "Mostly, I'm trying to get warm. I'm an art dealer—and a musician." Bradan held up his guitar case.

"In a band?"

Bradan nodded.

"Which one?"

Suddenly, he *had* credibility.

"Silicon Saturday. One record so far. It's a side thing. Won't pay the bills, but it's creative and it's a change from my gallery work."

"Heard of them vaguely, new wave pop stuff," Colin said. "There's no one to play for out here."

"You'd be surprised," Bradan said under his breath. Louder he said, "Ever visit Stonehenge?"

"Piles of old stones," the constable said. "Brings tourists. That's good, I suppose. Were you there a few hours back?"

"Just old stones, as you say," Bradan said.

They were pushing for information, but he wasn't going to cooperate.

"We've reports of trespassers," Colin said. "And a party or rave with dancers."

"Why would anyone be there on a cold night?" Bradan asked with as much innocence as he could muster. It was hard to talk with his teeth chattering.

While one of the constables examined his license with a flashlight, the other stared up and down Amesbury's deserted roads. The town looked desolate. Weak moonlight made the town resemble a black-and-white photograph, the scene reduced to essentials. "Seen any dogs?" Oliver asked.

Clearly, they'd been alerted to stories of demon creatures wailing in Stonehenge.

Bradan shook his head. "Why would I?"

"Someone reported howling after sunset."

"Haven't heard a thing, constable."

"You've got quite a wound on your leg," Colin said. "Something bite you?"

"Gashed it when I tripped," Bradan said. "I'll see a medic about it in the morning."

Bradan heard Oliver radio in information from his license to a dispatcher.

"Where's your car?" the other constable asked.

"Your central car park. I'm not sure where that is."

"Colin, anything from the desk on our friend Bradan?"

"Arrested for demonstrating at the Sizewell nuclear plant construction site earlier this year."

"Nonviolent," Bradan said quickly. "More of a sit-in than demonstration. They released me immediately after booking. I paid a modest fine."

"How reassuring," Oliver said, deadpan. "I was never fond of nukes. Colin, can we let the bloke sit in the back? We've sorted him and we've a dozen other things to do tonight. We can't let 'im walk about our fair town lost. Besides, it's raining. You a risk to civic order, Bradan?"

He knew they were toying with him on an otherwise dull evening, but he'd play along to get out of the cold.

"Officer, I'm only a danger to myself from getting frostbite and winding up in your local infirmary."

"Then we'll take you to your car, fair enough? Otherwise, what would they think of Amesbury hospitality in upscale Mayfair?"

The backdoor popped open and Bradan bundled himself inside, grateful for the warmth, but then was immediately appalled by the stench in the police vehicle. It smelled of bile and a Victorian morgue.

"Anyone die back here?" he asked.

"Nope. Last one didn't die. Threw up. Drugs probably, who knows? Happens all the time, unfortunately. Our garage doesn't clean it. Colin and I do the best we can to manage things as the mechanics can't touch the mess. Union won't allow it."

"Just a sec, officers. Let me get some air." Bradan lurched out of the car, doubled over, and vomited on the sidewalk, breathing in the cold, fresh night to clear his lungs. He guessed that the police intended to do him a favor to avoid him getting more lost than he already was and freezing, but riding in the car was a nonstarter given the stench. He decided he'd try something, uncertain of the outcome. He recited six rhyming stanzas. They were in Latin and quietly spoken so, even if the constables overheard him, his spell would sound meaningless.

Staggering from exhaustion post-enchantment, Bradan slumped back into the rear of the police car.

"Bloody hell," Oliver said. "Smell's gone, Colin, like it never was."

"By chance, I had some air freshener with me," Bradan said. "I used it. Now, can we drive to the car park?"

"A night for odd events," Oliver said.

CHAPTER 3

A Jaguar in the Rain

"The cops chauffeured you here? That means you were in trouble. You look awful, too."

The voice came from no particular place in the Jaguar E-type, but Bradan heard it clearly.

"Hello, Connie," he said. "At least I'm not in jail. Turn on the heat, for God's sake."

He wedged his guitar into the car's tiny rear luggage space, settled into the driver's seat, and slammed the door on a night gone wrong.

"The constables were impressed," he said. "They ran your plates to see that I hadn't stolen you."

"I'm flattered."

Rain beaded his forest-green Jag. It was a beautiful car just sitting forlornly in the dark, deserted parking lot. The E-type's flowing, sensuous lines promised fleetness standing still.

And it was haunted.

Connie was its resident shade. Bradan remembered meeting her when he'd bought a Volvo station wagon in Miami several years ago. She came with that car, but somehow she'd transferred to the Jag when he'd moved to London and, aside from relentless complaints about the steering wheel being on the wrong side, she'd made the transition smoothly from a Swedish daily driver built like a tank to a vintage English sports car with a bad electrical system. Bradan wasn't quite sure how a carefree spirit migrated across the Atlantic from one vehicle to the next, and Connie could be coy when describing the rules that bound her behavior, but the ghost was good company, she got on well with the wolf, and her sardonic humor kept him grounded.

Bradan also loved the phantom's Southern accent, which sounded like it came straight from the mud and muck of a Mississippi swamp and was entirely different from the London elite's crystalline speech inflections.

The wolf lounged in the passenger seat next to him. Somehow it had located the Jag while avoiding the police. Even curled up against the cold with its tail covering its nose, it was too big for the car. Bradan reached over to scratch behind the wolf's ears. The beast seemed irritated at this affectionate gesture, but tolerated it without a warning snarl. Hanging out together for fifteen tumultuous centuries gave Bradan privileges—a few.

"Did you get your video?" the ghost asked.

"Not the way I hoped," Bradan said tersely. "Hostile locals. I've seen the last of them, I hope."

"The police?"

"They're the least of my worries. I'll tell you about it later."

"You'll get to it in your own time, sugar. Don't let it bother you. Whatever it is, we've seen worse."

Bradan sensed a sympathetic, ghostly shrug.

"Yeah, I don't know about that," he said. "This could have gotten out of hand. I'm almost immortal, but that doesn't make me invulnerable."

He exhaled, venting his tension.

"Out of the night into the darkness," he said.

"Shit, what happened back there?" Connie asked.

"I stumbled onto an old war."

Bradan gripped the Jag's steering wheel.

"Ouch, you're hurting me, hon."

"Sorry, Connie."

In some eerie way that Bradan didn't understand, the ghost possessing his car felt physical damage to the vehicle as her pain. He'd always assumed ghosts were beyond the pale of mortal hurt and injury, but Connie had become one with the Jaguar. Being a bit supernatural himself didn't provide any insight into the rules that bound other supernatural entities. He wondered if any rules bound Fae.

"Maybe they'll forget about me," he said.

Bradan loosened his hold on the steering wheel. He remembered the Fae woman's parting look and wished this wouldn't turn into a lethal vendetta. Over his long life, he'd had little to do with the their realm and intended to keep it that way.

"What next?" she asked.

"I'll set up my Christmas bash when I'm back in London. The guests are already invited."

"Total shits," the ghost said. "Why bother?"

"My sentiments, too, but they have money and they buy art, so I'll play the proper host. It'll be a quiet affair."

"Back in the day, your Miami parties weren't so quiet, darlin'."

"That life's in the rearview mirror."

"Memories," she said.

"I live in the present tense," Bradan said.

"Sensible," the ghost said. "It's good not remembering too much."

"I can't always do that," he admitted. "Life's a dialogue between now and then."

"Least you don't show your age, sugar. You don't look a day over thirty."

"Thanks—always a kind word." If Connie were still alive, he would have hugged her.

"So, on to happier thoughts," he said. "Christmas merrymaking in Mayfair: mistletoe, holiday lights, a tree, and pretentious partiers."

"The band?"

"They won't fit with this crowd, but I've invited them anyway, not to play, just to get a kick out of my other guests. Also, they'd be mad if I didn't include them."

He shivered, still wet. The Jag's anemic heating system simply wasn't up to snuff.

"Want me to drive, darlin'?"

Bradan was tempted. Connie could drive anything thanks to her childhood on a Mississippi farm working with tractors and combines. She piloted the E-type beautifully when he let her, though she pushed well past the speed limit while somehow evading speed traps and tickets.

"We'll stay here and go back tomorrow," he said. "The biggest hotel around is the Holiday Inn. Maybe they've got a suite I can use for what's left of the night. Wonder if their bar is still open?"

Winter night went on forever in England. However, Bradan saw dawn lightening the east.

"Probably not," he said, disappointed.

CHAPTER 4

Fairies on Angel Dust

Mayfair, London, Christmas Eve, 1986

Bradan stood on his top-floor balcony looking at Green Park, which wasn't green tonight. Bare, black trees made the park larger and starker than during its leafy, summertime prime; it seemed to be a limitless space in London's center. Lamps in the park illuminated paths in straight lines that stretched off forever in a peculiar geometry between the trees.

Wind pushed the branches about, arms imploring heaven.

Despite the Christmas holiday, Bradan didn't find the vista festive. If anything, it was more austere than Stonehenge three days ago.

The park, normally the tamest of spaces, was wild tonight, deserted, left to spirits—and the wolf.

Bradan heard his beast's howl, a sound that hadn't reverberated through London's environs in over a thousand years. He'd set the animal loose ahead of his Christmas party. The creature was cunning enough not to be caught, though it did love spooking his neighbors out for a walk. Hopefully, it would stay away from nearby Buckingham Palace. Having a Dark Ages monster stalking the Palace grounds would provoke horror.

No living soul was out in the dismal weather, but there were plenty of soulless beings about.

His memories mixed with the specters; he couldn't tease them apart. He didn't try.

The wolf howled again and the sound bounced between the trees. Bradan guessed now the wolf didn't vocalize to frighten people; it warned him, perhaps about Fae. Were they planning to settle scores after the Stonehenge altercation? Fae hated human cities, but maybe they felt at home in the desolate park. It was otherworldly enough to resemble their fairy realm.

He shoved aside dread.

The park was eerie tonight, but his memories of it were good. He'd lived in London long ago and recalled summers long past. Two and a half centuries back, before the city engulfed the space, it had been rustic, though the fashionable, titled set frequented it on afternoons as ladies promenaded along the Mall's broad footpaths in silk dresses with bodices showing enough cleavage for passersby to admire the sight, but not so much that decorum was offended. Their dresses brushed the dusty ground.

Sometimes gentlemen walked arm in arm at the lady's side. Unattached males gathered nonchalantly to take in the passing crowd and tip their tricorne hats to acquaintances. They wore their hats over wigs white as snow and sported embroidered weskits, coats, and britches.

It was a moving outdoor party, and those of a certain class greeted one another courteously; if they weren't of a certain class, they were ignored.

And all classes sweated in the heat, whether wearing silk or cheap cotton.

Off to the side of the main promenade, farm maids sold udder-fresh cow's milk at a penny a mug, drawn from a herd that lazed in the heat in a fenced pasture.

At night, it was a different story as highwaymen hunted the careless, and lovers escaped—at least momentarily—passionless marriages by conducting assignations in the grass, pulling up skirts and shoving down britches. If these affairs went badly and scandal threatened, Rosamond's Pond was handy for suicides.

One July night, out for a stroll, Bradan had intervened to convince a young lady that the married earl who'd dallied with her, and then abruptly withdrawn his affections for another mistress, wasn't worth dying for in a muddy pond. Drowning was a bad way to go, and he'd told her that no one would care—or even notice—if she died. Besides, she was alluring enough that another aristocrat would court her soon enough. His reasoning worked and, a month later, he'd seen the woman, radiant, on the arm of a marquis. She'd smiled discreetly to him, acknowledging his support. He supposed this was success of a sort and Merlin would have approved, though Bradan wondered if her new beau would treat her better than the last.

Bradan wasn't sorry when the pond was filled during George III's reign. It stopped impulsive suicide. Some bodies from the lovelorn had never been found before it was covered and they still moldered beneath the modern, manicured park. Tonight, their phantoms were free to stroll and seek passion again.

A few centuries before the promenades, when the area was mostly open fields and far from London's center, it had been a cemetery for plague victims buried in haste with shovelfuls of quicklime tossed over the corpses lest whatever contagion had struck them down proved catching enough to threaten the gravediggers. He remembered the sounds of the metal spades biting into dirt as pits were dug for the bodies.

Thanks to Merlin, Bradan was blessed with immunity to pestilence, so when a friend died of smallpox and had been left to rot, Bradan had buried the body himself in the fields and read words of scripture over the grave. No one should pass unmourned and untended to. His bravery in the face of disease elicited fear from fellow Londoners, who'd assumed that he was a warlock or demon. Bradan's companion, the wolf, only added to his supposed supernatural status, so he'd departed for the continent for a generation until London forgot him.

Tonight, this Christmas Eve, Bradan knew that the dead were nearer than usual. The dim lamplight showed him specters in clothing from past eras walking alone or clustered in groups drifting through the dark tree trunks unhindered by physical barriers or modern concerns, lost in reflections about unwelcome death or opportunities missed while alive. Sometimes the phantoms interacted with one another, maybe they were familiar in life. Sometimes they passed one another without acknowledgment.

Snow swirled about, intensifying to blizzard force before tapering to flurries that meandered past his face and through the open French doors behind him into his townhouse. The weather couldn't settle on exactly how to celebrate the holiday.

His louche guests had no such uncertainties, and their volume and hilarity had soared as the night roared into the small hours fueled by ethanol and whatever narcotics they consumed. The titled partiers were intent on fun as if nothing bad could ever happen to them.

Blinking lights and the scents of peppermint and pine wreaths created a veneer of innocent Christmas frivolity over the bacchanal. Bradan smelled aristocratic sweat and dope, too. He'd open the French doors wider to let winter air in.

"Bradan, whatever are you peering at out there?"

The speaker was Lady Adela Leah Alexander pushing past other celebrants and up to his side. She ran her forefinger along his arm in greeting. They leaned on the balcony railing together, congenially looking out at the night.

He saw ghosts, she didn't.

"Lost in memories," he said.

"Pretty deep memories by the look of it. You're far too young for that. Come on. Play host to your shindig. You've invited the cream of young London society."

Bradan heard languid disdain of her peers. However, she was self-aware enough to direct some of the mockery toward herself.

"There are that many?" he asked. "I hadn't counted."

"Not so many anymore. The older families are dying. New money is replacing them."

"New or old, money's why I invited them. They're all potential buyers. My motives are entirely mercenary."

"Everyone's mercenary in London," she said. "That's forgivable, but not mingling at your own bash is a sin. People notice."

Her accent was matter-of-fact and modulated, befitting a member of the upper class in good standing with a hint of a refined drawl reinforcing her belonging to the right family and receiving the right schooling.

He looked at her. She wore a short, charcoal-colored skirt and dark-blue silk top that set off her black hair. The ensemble seemed pricey. It was also tight. It all appeared tossed together, suggesting she'd pulled it heedlessly out of a closet, but he knew that impression was artifice, and, instead, she'd carefully considered how to present herself. Most times, she was measured about her appearance and behavior, but not always. Del's lust ran hot when she let the reins loose.

He brushed a strand of windblown hair off her forehead.

"We were good together last night," she said. "We tried a dozen positions."

"A veritable *Kama Sutra*," he said.

"Where did you learn them all?"

"Misspent youth," he said. "I have favorites."

"Me too," she said. "If we keep at it, I'll need to make further amends to the neighbors about the noise. I've done it twice already."

"My fault as well," Bradan said. "Maybe a bottle of good wine will get them to ignore us. Or you could visit me here. The walls are thick."

"What a gentleman!"

Two and a half centuries ago, one of Del's ancestors, decked out in eighteenth-century finery, would have promenaded along the Mall, perhaps with her husband, probably not, certainly exchanging a glance with a duke or court favorite. Discretion allowed anything including quietly meeting with a lucky peer of the realm later in the evening for sex before both parties returned to their respective spouses and dull propriety. However, he couldn't imagine any of Del's forebears drowning themselves over love gone bad; they'd been made of sterner stuff, and she'd inherited this fortitude.

She was titled, but he knew she did something in corporate law at one of the big firms in the city, so she was making her own way. And, though her paternal lineage had owned manor houses and country homes since Renaissance times, her mother was of Iraqi-Jewish descent whose family had managed, despite all odds, to immigrate during the Second World War into less than welcoming British society, so Del's lineage wasn't entirely one of age-old privilege.

He respected that.

She was also active in Europe's growing green movement.

He respected that, too.

They'd marched together through London streets for environmental causes, though recently she'd pulled back to focus on her career. He didn't think that made her happy.

"A penny for your thoughts," she said.

"I was remembering last night."

Standing close to Del was distracting. Consciously, he shifted topics.

"They used to sell milk there." He pointed into the dark park. "Still warm from the cow, you couldn't get anything fresher."

"Is that what you're pondering?" She sipped a martini. "You're the strangest sort, though your artwork's fab."

"Don't know why milk came to mind, Del. Thanks for showing up tonight and bringing your set. The Sloane Rangers are well represented."

"They're attitudes with nice lipstick, but one of them wants to make an offer on the Hockney in the corner by the tree, probably more as an investment than because she likes or understands Hockney."

Del waved over the crowd to a group of young women standing by the painting. They waved back. They were as cute and as sleek as Del—if a little harder.

"I'll introduce you. Any milk on tap?" she teased gently. "Maybe they'd think you're being ironic if you offer it."

"That lot, they'd think I'm odd," he said. "So, no milk, just plenty of gin, Scotch, and excellent Burgundy in the bar, champagne bottles too scattered around my digs. Someone is passing around PCP-laced cigarettes and bugle. I need to stop that."

"Not in favor of angel dust and cocaine?" she asked.

"Nope. I brushed up against that side of life in Miami. I'm not going there again."

She regarded him. "You've lived other lives," she said.

"Perceptive," he said. Let her think his other lives were in the last decade rather than spread over fifteen centuries.

Hide big secrets with small lies.

"Mysterious," she said.

"Just private. And with no interest in making the same mistakes twice." He needed to change the topic again. Del was getting inquisitive.

"It's a rare night to host a Christmas Eve party," he said. "The weather is utter crap."

The wolf wailed again, this time nearer to his Mayfair flat.

"Christ, what's out there?" Del asked. "Sounds primeval. Are we being stalked?"

"Lost dog," he reassured. "As you say, time to play host."

He peered into his flat and saw a wall of tuxedos, cummerbunds, and gowns. Damian had wangled an invite and stood near the Christmas tree boring other guests. The Saturdays lounged nearby looking out of place but too smashed to care, except Anu, who took it all in soberly, a glass of white wine untouched in hand.

By then, everyone was fashionably and carelessly disheveled. It wasn't so different from eighteenth-century park promenades after the day's activities had wilted the dresses and weskits and the lords and ladies retreated to their townhouses to continue festivities.

Tonight, at his party, everyone was either titled or entitled, just out of school, coming into inheritances or prosperous careers, the world at their feet. They were young, too, but that would change as life, disappointments, drugs, and drink etched their features and corroded their bodies. From the vantage point of extreme longevity, he felt lacerating melancholy at watching friends and lovers wither. Detachment muffled sadness a bit. Detachment didn't make him a sterling human, but he needed it to survive.

He pushed aside morbid thoughts. This was a party after all. He strolled through the crowd making whatever witticisms came to mind to engage with people. Bradan knew many of them, but unfamiliar faces mingled with the crowd.

Several guests were becoming belligerent. The Christmas tree he'd had his gallery staff decorate and string with lights had been cheery and seasonal a few hours back, but it was now in danger of being knocked over by staggering guests. A red-haired fellow had tossed his jacket aside and looped Christmas lights over his shoulders like a bandoleer. He grabbed after a woman next to him who deftly sidestepped his advances with a laugh.

Bradan wondered if his artwork was threatened. Beside the Hockney, his staff had chosen the best work from his downstairs gallery and mounted it around his home, including sculpture by Jeff Koons, paintings by Edward Hopper, and mixed art by Yayoi Kusama. Now he doubted the wisdom of exposing several million pounds' worth of artwork to a pack of out-of-control boors; they wouldn't know quality art if it bit them in the ass, but perhaps they'd buy it.

"God, it's good to be British!" someone shouted.

"God, it's good to be fucked up," the red-haired man replied to general hilarity.

The firm that insured his gallery's art had insisted he hire guards, but the muscle was nowhere to be seen, so Bradan would have to play bouncer himself—a royal pain, as he'd rather be schmoozing with the crowd to promote his gallery's wares.

Across the room, he saw two bartenders plying their trade vigorously with no attempt to cut off the obvious drunks. He fought his way toward the bar to tell them to back off.

In front of him, two men shoved each other hard. Instantly, fists flew and other partygoers stepped back to watch a savage fight. They egged the brawlers on. Bradan bulled between the two, ducking thrown punches, and stiff-armed them apart. He'd drunk nothing and had the advantage of sobriety. He'd also been in so many fights over his existence that he could predict what they'd do next and duck or punch accordingly.

He threw a flurry of uppercuts and one hook. He hit hard, connecting with noses or stomachs. In seconds, both men were on the floor in a tangle of limbs, expensive clothing, and ice cubes. One of them tried to lurch upright to come at Bradan, but a member of the crowd planted a foot on his backside to send him sprawling again onto the slippery floor. A friend of Del's upended a wineglass over both fighters, mixing expensive Burgundy with their blood. Bradan wasn't surprised. This crowd would eat its own.

He'd made it clear to invitees they could bring along whomever they wanted in the spirit of the season and in the interests of broadening awareness of his art dealership five floors down on Half Moon Street. However, with 2:00 a.m. approaching, he doubted the wisdom of his open-door approach. So far, he hadn't sold a thing.

The fracas's conclusion garnered a sardonic round of applause from the crowd. One of the combatants realized he'd get no sympathy from his friends and levered himself into a sitting position to gamely hold up his hands in surrender before gingerly regaining his feet. Several people slapped his back. The other fellow still sprawled on the floor, cursed the crowd and threatened lawsuits.

Bradan's laugh cut through the noise.

"Seb, no one cares. Grow up, for fuck's sake. No solicitor will take your case—right, Del?"

"Not a chance."

"Gigi—you came with him, right?" Bradan asked Seb's girlfriend. "Get him to the bathroom to clean up."

One issue sorted. He spotted a group inhaling coke by the window, his next challenge. He elbowed his way through the press toward them, wishing he'd kept the wolf around. Tintagel would have chilled the festivities, but the beast intimidated troublemakers.

Near the balcony doors, he'd positioned an exquisite seventeenth-century oak refectory table. A tall, dark-haired man stooped over the surface and used a razor to arrange lines of cocaine on the tabletop. The white crystals on the dark oak wood were zebra stripes.

He glanced up incuriously at Bradan, mildly irritated at the interruption.

"Mind the wind. Don't want the bugle going out the window, do we, lovers?"

A couple hovered next to the tall man completely intent on the preparatory rituals of drug consumption and ready to inhale once he'd organized the blow. They weren't even trying to be subtle about it.

"Not at my party," Bradan said.

"Wherever and whenever I want, pet," the tall man replied. This time he didn't deign to look up.

Bradan's anger boiled up. He vaguely knew the couple, but he didn't recognize the drug dealer though he acted like Bradan was here at the dealer's sufferance.

"Good with the fists, mate," the dealer said. "I'll give you that, but I don't like being interrupted when plying my trade, so slag off."

The dealer hadn't bothered with a tux, and his one concession to raffish elegance was a sport coat and a scarf tossed about his neck. As he was wall-eyed, Bradan couldn't tell exactly where he stared. He would have appeared demented even without the weird eyes. A gold tooth and once-broken nose didn't help.

"Ply your trade elsewhere," Bradan said. Had the dealer's razor marred his antique?

"Tam, Nick, stick to liquor or get out, too," he said to the couple who were inhaling lines directly off his tabletop.

A mound of a different drug kept the cocaine company.

"PCP too, a real smorgasbord," Bradan said.

"You got that at a glance, mate, like a pro," the dealer said. "I hear it's no accident, dear. Still have friends in Miami? You were in the business once, though I understand it was transpo, not street-level stuff, well up on the pyramid in Pedro Schneider's organization with the Columbians. Tellin' me to shove off, a bit like the pot calling the kettle black, wouldn't you say?"

"Now it's just art," Bradan said.

A huge young man materialized next to the dealer. He was at least as tall as Bradan and fifty pounds heavier. And it was muscle. Tattoos covered exposed flesh on his arms and neck. He took in the situation with a dead expression. If there was any intelligence behind the stare, Bradan couldn't find it, but there *was* a flicker of recognition. He knew Bradan from somewhere.

"Meet Marco. He sorts things for me," the dealer said. "Maybe he can sort you. He's on loan from an American group I do business with. They want their product looked after."

Now Bradan remembered the big man from his time flying narcotics up from the Bahamas into South Florida, one of Pedro's crew. He couldn't shake past sins.

Bradan finally spotted his security crew busy chatting up pretty women near the tree. He needed to get their attention. A fight with these two criminals wouldn't be the hapless brawl he'd just stopped; somebody could die, maybe him. He needed his own muscle on hand. Bradan quietly, quickly spoke a spell. The unopened champagne bottle's corks suddenly popped, showering most of the room with foamy bubbles. It sounded like rapid gunfire. His partygoers yelled with delighted surprise, or irritation at getting soaked, or they were too wrecked to notice.

Using the distraction, Bradan gestured at the three security men. After the spell, he could barely lift his arms let alone throw a punch. Dealing with the two thugs would be up to his security team. One of them finally noticed and began forging through the crowd. The other two followed.

"Bad move, mate," the dealer said. He pulled aside his jacket to flash a pistol jammed into his waistband.

"Anything you can do, I can do better," he said, harmonizing to the old Broadway showtune's lyrics. "It's from *Annie Get Your Gun*. See, that's my cue to get my gun."

He pulled out his pistol and pointed it at Bradan. Still humming, he slowly extended his arm and pushed the muzzle into Bradan's forehead. The gun felt cold against Bradan's skin. Vaguely he was conscious of nearby partiers freezing and gaping at the scene.

Bradan didn't want to die like this, not at the hand of a cheap thug. His universe shrank to the diameter of the semiautomatic barrel pressing into his skull.

Then, like at Stonehenge, Bradan sensed that he had an audience, but it wasn't the dealer, or the partiers. It was otherworldly, predatory, and avidly interested.

Outside a gust of frigid wind blew inside in a cloud of snow-flakes, which swirled about partiers near the open French doors and antique table. The coke and angel dust lifted from their neat lines to mix with the snow in a spiral of natural and unnatural crystals. The whole peculiar cloud whooshed out over his balcony into the night.

Bradan thought he heard tittering laughter, pitched so high that a bat or hummingbird had uttered it.

"What?" the dealer screamed.

For an instant, Bradan thought the dealer, enraged at losing a small fortune in narcotics to a random gust, would unload a magazine of bullets out the French doors and into the wind, but then he centered the pistol on Bradan again. At this distance, he couldn't miss.

A shard from a broken champagne bottle sliced through the dealer's neck effortlessly, chopping through the man's spinal cord and flesh. Bradan saw the ivory-colored vertebrae poking up from mangled flesh. For the barest instant, the dealer stood upright, then he melted to the floor, sending a fountain of blood everywhere. His severed head bounced out the French doors like a hairy soccer ball.

Absently, Bradan noted blood dappling his antique table. He had no idea what was happening, just that he was somehow alive. Guests screamed and surged back from the decapitated corpse. Bradan tackled Tam and Nick. The floor was the safest place to be. The three of them fell atop the dealer's headless corpse. The couple shrieked and scrabbled to get back to their feet and only succeeded in completely covering themselves and Bradan with blood.

Can I take back my home from whatever is doing this? he wondered.

He pushed the dealer's body aside and shoved Tam's leg off his arm.

"This is real drama," Bradan heard Damian shout from across the room.

The drama isn't over, he thought.

Another blast of arctic air powered into his flat and lifted the heavy table off the floor to hurl it into his panicked guests. It almost brained him, Tam, and Nick before hitting the crowd with a crunch of broken bones, blunt force trauma, and screams cut off on impact. Then the glass panes from his French doors shattered and blew into his flat in a million glittering shards, lacerating those closest to the windows.

Whatever force created the chaos was unearthly.

Then it was gone.

Bradan knew this, but he didn't know how he knew it. He pushed off the floor and stood up, trying to take in the carnage.

I'll get help!

He realized he'd thought this, but hadn't said it, so he shouted it to the crowd.

CHAPTER 5

A Head Short

"**W**hat happened to his head?"

It was all Bradan could think to ask, but the chief inspector didn't care about his questions. He and two dozen other detectives, constables, and assorted emergency medical staff asked the questions here, not the host of this disaster zone. Bradan guessed they'd all been pulled away from Christmas festivities or putting kids' presents under the tree to face his horror.

Everyone wore latex gloves, and the disagreeable smell of whatever chemicals the forensics crew used in their crime scene workup replaced pine and wine fragrances.

"Construction scaffolding across the street," the chief inspector finally answered. "It's stuck on top of one of the metal supports, five floors up—on display, head on a spike as it were, like medieval times. Someone'll take it down in due course after we've got more pictures. Know him?"

"Not at all," Bradan said.

He tried to organize the bloody images bouncing about in his brain. Simultaneously, everything around him happened too fast and too sluggishly.

Were the police aware of the narcotics? Or had all traces of the drugs blown out of his flat? No one had asked him about cocaine yet.

"You're rather closed-mouthed about circumstances here," the inspector said. "That's not helpful to us. You were near the fellow that lost his head?"

"Right next to him, in fact," the policeman answered his own question. "Closer than anyone else. You must have seen what happened."

The inspector smelled of catsup and fast food. And he'd baptized himself in sandalwood cologne. Inappropriately, Bradan thought of spa treatments.

The cop had reddish muttonchop sideburns like a character in a Victorian print, which he tugged at from time to time as if to pull out strands of gray.

"I'm being open," Bradan said. "I'm in shock, trying to answer your questions, don't know what, why, or how this happened."

Bradan gestured at his destroyed flat.

"You were holding a knife, ax, or some cutting tool?" the cop asked.

"Christ, no. I was chatting with guests."

"Odd situation." The inspector let the understatement hang suspended.

"Could have been a chainsaw that done for him. The bloke's head didn't just pop off."

Bradan didn't like policeman who thought they were wits. The observation was stupid.

"I don't own a chainsaw," Bradan said, trying to keep anger out of his tone. That would feed the detective's suspicions.

He tried not to look at the corpse nearby with the tip of the spinal cord protruding from the neck's remnants. Someone had thrown a tarp over the corpse a while ago, but that had been pulled back as various forensics experts examined the dead man. The blood had stopped freely flowing, but a bit still oozed onto his hardwood floor. Crime scene personnel prepared to load the body into a long, rubber body bag and then onto a gurney. They couldn't remove it fast enough for Bradan.

Among the other personnel, a man Bradan took to be one of the chief inspector's associates stooped near the body staring at it. Then he stood up to mutter something in the inspector's ear. "My colleague here knows about him," the inspector addressed Bradan. "Detective Sergeant Hughes works the narcotics side of things. I brought him along because situations like this"—the policeman swept his hand about encompassing the carnage in Bradan's flat—"often involve drugs. A deal goes wrong or somesuch."

Bradan kept his expression neutral. "How did you ID him without his head?"

Both policemen frowned. Bradan assumed they didn't like argumentative witnesses. Hughes pulled a black-and-white Polaroid photo from his shirt pocket.

"One of the men took this," he said. "Had to climb the scaffolding."

"Your man must be quite a gymnast," Bradan said.

"Cyrus Fitzpatrick was the bloke's name," the detective inspector prompted.

Bradan glanced briefly at the ghoulish mess. Blackish blood coated the steel pole where the neck would have been. The impaled head reminded Bradan of executed traitors he'd seen in feudal times. Exhausted as he was, he wouldn't sleep easy with that image in mind.

Bradan shrugged. "Not a very photogenic fellow."

"You say you don't recognize him," the chief inspector continued. "But maybe you *do* know what he was doing, providing narcotics to your guests?"

Sarcasm soaked this comment.

"I don't know anything about him other than that he's dead and now you tell me his head's across the street," Bradan said. "I'm an art dealer."

"So you keep saying." The policeman stroked his whiskers.

"Our departed friend, Cyrus, had a 9mm handgun on him. Hughes found it under the Christmas tree. He threatened you?"

Bradan thought quickly. Other partiers had seen the dealer stick the pistol to his forehead, so he couldn't deny its presence.

"He had a gun. I told him to get out."

"Brave fellow, you are, confronting an armed man. Three of your guests said the dead fellow pointed the weapon right between your eyes. *That* spark a memory?"

"Things happened fast. If I'd thought about it, I probably wouldn't have ordered him to leave. I would have called your lot for help."

"That you should have," the inspector said. "Self-defense is as good a motive as any for killing someone. He had a gun on you. Somehow you cut his head off. Problem solved."

"He threatened me, but there's no way I could have done that." Bradan glanced at the body. "I can't even look at him."

"It's like someone did you a favor, taking him out."

"This isn't my idea of a favor." Bradan pointed about them at the carnage.

"No, I suppose not." The policeman chuckled amiably, inviting Bradan to share the jest. "Still, you survived."

Someone had set his antique table upright to free injured partiers from beneath it. Other than that, his furniture wasn't too disturbed—if he ignored the blood, broken glass, and smashed Christmas decorations. Amazingly, the Christmas lights over his mantelpiece still blinked. Bradan didn't like thinking of his home as a violent crime scene, but that's what it was.

The interrogation proceeded.

Bradan answered more and still more questions until morning Christmas Day. He'd hoped to exchange presents with Del, everything very thoughtfully wrapped, but that wasn't going to happen. Eventually, the detective inspector wandered off to be replaced by Hughes, who asked essentially the same questions over again. They finally let him sit down, but wouldn't let him help his guests as they were ushered to waiting ambulances or cabs home. They also wouldn't confirm who was hurt. Maybe they didn't know yet. He wondered if his band mates were okay.

Bradan examined himself. He hadn't thought to do it earlier, but he was intact. His clothing looked like he was a horror film extra who'd been on the wrong end of an ax, but it wasn't his blood.

The tux, a cleaning bill, he thought. *Is there blood on my art?*

Finally, the police finished, though he'd been assured he needed to be available for follow-up interviews, "to assist with our inquiries." Given the nature of the crimes, there were bound to be more inquiries. Was he a suspect? They wouldn't say, but there was no talk of charges, so he took that as a promising sign. He was warned not to speak to the media on Half Moon Street below who by now outnumbered the constables, medical staff, and shaken guests still stumbling out of his flat after being interviewed by detectives.

The chief inspector huddled with Hughes and several other policeman, then approached him.

"Here's another mystery for you: know anything about a rabid dog that seems to be out and about in the park? My men kept hearing it howling while they processed your flat. It had them jumpy."

"Inspector, I didn't hear wolves," Bradan answered.

"Wolves? Who said there was wolves about?"

"I'm rattled. I meant dogs. You asked about howling. That's wolves to me, not dogs. Regardless, I saw nothing, heard nothing."

This wasn't the truth, but there was no way introducing Tintagel into the conversation would improve his situation. The beast could fend for himself until the police left.

"Got a place to stay?" The detective stared down at Bradan sitting on an ottoman, one of the few items of furniture not covered in gore.

"My gallery on the first floor below," Bradan said. "Or I'll get a room in a local hotel. Can't stay here, of course."

"Indeed, you can't. It's ours until we're finished. If you've a solicitor, you can negotiate with us for access. Can't imagine that you'll be able to sell your pictures here anytime soon. They're all bloody, need a good scrubbing."

The policeman looked him up and down. "So do you, for that matter."

"I'll find a shower." Bradan didn't hide his irritation at the man's condescension.

"Well, we've got your contact information. Here's my card, Chief Inspector Young. Don't stray from London until this is sorted. By the way, what sort of name is 'Bradan'? Seems quaint."

Bradan stood up. He was considerably taller than the policeman. Now it was his turn to look down.

"My name is Celtic. I like it. And I won't run off if that's what you're suggesting. Also, I'll keep my guitar."

For a moment, the detective's expression signaled he'd make something of Bradan's truculence, but decided against it.

"Whose hat?" Young asked.

Bradan stared where the policeman pointed. He hadn't noticed it before, but a broad-brimmed hat perched atop his Christmas tree.

"That wasn't there earlier," Bradan said. "One of the guests must have left it."

"Daft-looking, wouldn't you say, sitting atop your tree?" Young said. "Velvet, expensive, like something for a costume party."

Bradan thought he recognized it, but he was still shaken and the slaughter jumbled his memories.

"Take it," he said. "As evidence or whatever. It's not mine."

Young pointed at the hat and one of his men tried stretching to retrieve it, but even though the constable was tall, the hat was beyond his reach. He grabbed the ottoman and stood on it to finally snag the hat.

"You throw a rousing party," the inspector said.

"Happy Christmas," Bradan said, matching sarcasm for sarcasm.

CHAPTER 6

Brilliant Bash

"Del, you okay?"

"Bradan, is that you? I think so. I'm back home, door bolted, a few cuts, glass of brandy in hand, ruined clothing—too bad, I liked that skirt and top. Others made out worse and that creepy drug guy was decapitated. I saw his head roll across the floor."

"Yeah, I had a front row seat."

"You didn't do it?"

"No!"

Bradan was aghast that Del would think him capable of brutal slaughter. He'd lived through tumultuous times in the past, but now he led a boring, civilized life selling expensive art to London's elite. Playing part time in a synth-pop band was as extreme as he got.

"Then how?" she pressed.

"No clue," Bradan said. "What I thought I saw was the sharp edge of a broken champagne bottle take his head clean off. It's mad. No one held the bottle. Of course, I couldn't tell the police."

"Uncanny."

"Everyone keeps saying that. Who else was injured?"

"I don't know," Del said. "But I'm sure others are hurt, hopefully not dead. Folks near me were cut by windblown glass."

"I'll call the people on the guest list including my band, check in with them," Bradan said. "It was my party; I'm responsible."

"It all went tits up," Del said. "What the hell happened?"

"I don't know, but I don't think it's over."

"Why?"

"I may know who did it."

The hat atop his Christmas tree was identical to that worn by the Fae man who'd languidly enjoyed the Saturday's performance at Stonehenge and then mockingly waved farewell after the rest of his tribe had departed leaving chaos in their wake. However, Bradan couldn't tell Del about insanity among the Fae.

They talked at and over each other for the next hour, comparing what they'd seen or thought they'd seen, their memories already distorting events. Finally, he calmed down enough to think about pragmatic next steps.

"Del, I think I'll need a lawyer. I don't know where the police will take this, but I'd like consul. Death, injuries, peers of the realm in a bad way. Can you help? I'll pay."

"Yes, I can help," she said.

God, he loved her! There was no hesitation. She was solidly behind him.

"We'll figure out payment later," Del continued. "If this goes criminal for you, there are people in my firm who I can refer you to, though I don't know what the police can charge you with unless they can somehow show that you did the dealer. Have drugs come up?"

"They know the dead guy peddled narcotics," Bradan said. "They recognized him. I don't think there was anything on him when he died; his drugs all blew out the window, bizarre as that sounds."

"I can't advise you to lie or withhold information. But—and you didn't hear this from me—unless you're directly asked, I wouldn't volunteer anything about narcotics. They may suspect the dead fellow was a dealer, but right now they're focused on murder and mayhem. Let them stay focused. If some of your guests took drugs, how were you to know?"

She paused, then giggled madly. Bradan wondered if events had unhinged her.

"Del?"

"Bradan, I haven't lost it. You mentioned distraught peers. This will amuse you. Gigi—you saw her at your party—she's the daughter of a baron of something or other. Anyway, she still wants to make an offer on the Hockney."

Bradan was shocked.

"She knows fuck all about art," he said. "And there's blood on it."

"That's its charm! The piece has a story now. She can tell her friends and she'll pay above market for it—whenever Scotland Yard allows you access to your place again."

Bradan laughed at the absurdity.

"There's more," she said. "Tam and Nick want the table they snorted coke from. They'll have it shipped to their place in Hampstead. They didn't have your number, so they called me. Others want to make offers on your stuff, too. We're all in shock, of course, how could we not be, but this wasn't the usual dull Christmas thing. In fact, your bash was a brilliant success."

CHAPTER 7

All Apologies

Mayfair, London, Christmas Day, 1986

Bradan walked from his gallery toward Green Park. He looked up at the construction scaffolding across Half Moon Street. Its skeletal metal frame supported planks for workers refurbishing Victorian-era brickwork.

He didn't see heads.

He did see an unobtrusively parked police vehicle apparently monitoring his gallery's main entrance, but he'd exited via a basement back door and didn't think they'd noticed him leaving. At any rate, no one challenged him.

It still snowed in little gusts that eddied about trees, but the blizzard had abated and weak sunlight shone through the flurries. Opalesque haze blurred the morning light, and ground mist rose to meet diffuse clouds smudging the boundary between earth and sky.

Last night, the park had been otherworldly and shrouded in history. Today, it was otherworldly, but innocent and white, in keeping with Christmas Day. A few bundled individuals walked along paths like characters in a Dickens holiday story, leaving dark, slushy tracks in the snow. Those close by called out season's greetings though they were strangers. He responded cheerily; it was Christmas in London after all.

Bradan had been barred from his flat, but he didn't want to return anyway. It would be a while before it felt like his home again—if ever. Instead, he was holed up in his gallery five floors down in the same building. Normally, his art was inspiration and comfort. Not today.

Anxiety ramped up as he walked deeper into the park. He almost turned back, but struggled with his fear and managed to keep going. He had a purpose beyond escaping memories of last night's carnage. Something had attacked him—or saved him, he couldn't decide which. He was sure it would be back, so he needed to know who or what he faced to fend it off. He believed the answer to who'd instigated the slaughter was in the park: the Fae. The wolf's howls last night indicated they were about.

The savagery visited on Bradan's party had been orchestrated by invisible forces and Fae were capable of incorporeal rage— if provoked, though there'd been no such wanton destruction in centuries. So, had his confrontation with the Fae woman at Stonehenge incited them? The insult seemed trivial. Whoever had started things, he'd happily apologize to dial down the animosity. But how did one make amends to magical beings?

Tintagel fell in beside him, leaving huge paw prints in the snow. The beast peered about alertly as if aware that it trespassed on someone else's turf. Bradan was happy for his company, though whether the creature would instinctively attack any Fae they came upon was an open question given the wolf's tense relations with some of them.

"Not much of a weapon," he remarked to Tintagel. He hefted his guitar case.

"But it's not supposed to be a weapon. We'll parlay if I can find them. They like my music. Maybe they'll come listen. Or they'll kill me."

Tintagel snarled.

"You think I should have brought a gun, but in Miami, sometimes guns were the solution, sometimes they weren't. Let's not go down that path again."

The beast appeared dismissive of his fear and ambled over to pee on a tree, leaving a brown splotch on the bark and marking this territory as his, Fae be damned.

"Are you afraid of anything?" Bradan asked. "Probably not, but you're a Norse demon. I'm simply Merlin's apprentice—former apprentice."

Bradan reflected that bravery was what was left when he was out of other options. He didn't see other options, so here he was.

They veered off the path and into a stand of trees. Their bare trunks bunched together and he no longer saw other walkers. London's sounds, already quiet on the holiday, grew quieter still, muffled by the snow. His surroundings weren't sinister, but he felt removed from the city and isolated. He supposed Green Park and adjoining Hyde Park were as natural as things got in central London—not very. However, if Fae congregated anywhere nearby, it would be here, though it didn't resemble their preferred haunts: wild groves far from humanity.

"Time to apologize," Bradan said.

Tintagel bared his fangs. Apologies were for losers.

Bradan stopped to pull out his twelve-string and slipped off his gloves.

It was so cold Bradan had trouble fingering his guitar, but he played the tune he and the band had performed at Stonehenge a few days back. He missed several of the chord changes, but it was recognizable. Then he shifted to other songs, accompanying himself with his voice. Aside from the wolf, he had no sense of spectators, supernatural or otherwise.

After singing and strumming for an hour, Bradan gave up. He was frustrated and freezing and his fingers could barely move over the frets. The wolf looked relieved as they headed back to his gallery.

The police car was still parked on Half Moon Street.

"London's finest believe that I'm a demented slasher and they've heard your relentless vocalizations. We couldn't look more guilty if we tried. So, we keep on sneaking in through the back door."

After he'd bought the row house at 2 Half Moon Street containing his gallery and home, he'd investigated its basement, revealing a rusted iron door, perhaps for maintenance access, at its far end leading to a still lower passage below street level. Carrying a flashlight and donning rubber boots, he'd led the reluctant wolf splashing along a descending brick tunnel to a smelly, larger subterranean stream beneath the neighborhood, the Tyburn. Bradan recalled it well from centuries ago for providing the best trout in the region before it had been encased and relegated to Stygian gloom. Now it resembled the Styx and carried sewage.

London was full of lost tributaries that had once flowed into the Thames, the inconvenient waterways covered with pavement and housing as the city refashioned itself over the generations. They were a legacy of a different era for humanity when slowly flowing water matched the area's bucolic pace of life and the roaring city hadn't yet subsumed the landscape's natural features. Modern, frenetic London lived its life, walking, driving, and building over these rivers, oblivious to their existence. He remembered them, but almost no one else did. Despite the Tyburn's current malodorous state, he was happy for his home's connection to an older London.

Back in the gallery, he propped the guitar case next to a Modigliani painting and collapsed on a modernist Oscar Niemeyer lounge chair. He knew his notion of playing to an empty glade in the park had been built on slender logic. He didn't understand Fae motivations, and he had no standing in the supernatural world.

Maybe there would be no further incidents.

~

For the Christmas noonday meal, the punch and food came out, good Rhône varietals, too; the hosts had outdone themselves trying for a traditional vibe with English holiday staples including mince pie, roast beef, Yorkshire pudding, and port cranberry sauce. They'd also thrown in sushi and vegetarian dishes for their more health-conscious guests.

With intentional irony, the hosts had strewn their townhouse with mistletoe and holly. Of course, someone had put Christmas carols on the high-end sound system. These started out light and saccharine, barely impinging on the guests' minds with comforting tropes about giving presents, but as the party progressed, the songs became darker, from holidays long gone; they'd been composed in bleaker times when the boundary between sacred music and damnation's hymns was permeable and not much separated God from his fallen angels.

The perfect digestive, cocaine, followed the food and wine. A mound of the crystalline narcotic was heaped on the table. The hosts wanted to make the point that no expense had been spared.

"Heard about the violence in Mayfair?" one of the guests asked conversationally as she inhaled two lines, one for each nostril. "Not much detail, but apparently some art dealer hosted a soiree, and things went pear-shaped."

"Saw it on the telly," the host replied. "Home invasion or drug hit. On Christmas Eve, no less."

"London's becoming more dangerous by the day," another guest noted. "But nothing of that sort happens to us in Chelsea."

"Because we're too well policed?" the host wondered.

"No, luv, because we're too boring."

A fire snapped and popped in the hearth, sending out a surprising amount of heat, so they'd left the windows open.

Then the murdering started. Some partiers escaped, most didn't.

∼

It was a simple transaction. The players knew one another; they'd done it before, though everyone was still armed, of course. Familiarity didn't breed trust, but they were comfortable enough to exchange gossip, while getting on with business. Demand for product was booming in Manchester. The London crew had more than enough to fill that need thanks to a strong Columbian connection.

One of the London sellers popped his Mercedes's boot lid so the Manchester buyers could inspect the goods, everything laid out neatly, rows of taped, plastic-wrapped keys. It was a bit of a ritual and the count was perfunctory. It wasn't good business to stiff a regular buyer. Things could get nasty.

"Shitty 'bout Cyrus. He weren't a bad dude," one of the Manchester crew observed.

"Wonder who'll take 'is spot? I wouldn't mind," the Mercedes driver said.

No one responded. It wasn't cool to talk of replacing someone the day after they'd been killed. Give the body a chance to
cool, *then* make your play.

"Marco will sort it," someone else eventually said. "Can't
leave no holes in the organization."

"Competition heating up," the Mercedes driver said, working to recover credibility after his faux pas. "Too many London
groups in this line of work, makes for a crowd."

"To business, mates," one of the Manchester gang said, peering into the trunk. "Don't got all night in this bloody cold parking garage in the middle of fucking nowhere."

That's when another buyer—taker, actually—showed up.

A street-cleaning crew a block off heard screams.

Later, when police forensics arrived, they noted lots of gore
and traces of coke in the Mercedes's boot.

CHAPTER 8

Official Inquiry

"**M**ore of the same," Chief Inspector Young said. "You see the similarities, I'm sure. A man 'lost his head' at your party and many others were badly hurt, and now this disaster in Chelsea, nine dead and counting. Then there was slaughter in a car park in Brixton. They came to bad ends, bodies mutilated—eviscerated, cut to pieces. It will be closed caskets at the memorial services. Some of that was on the news this morning, though many details weren't disclosed. No reason for more panic than we've already got."

Young had "invited" Bradan to his office to "assist the police with their ongoing investigations" of the pattern of killings afflicting London's West End neighborhoods.

It was the day after Christmas, but someone several offices down was playing carols. Bradan had heard enough carols for this season.

"The common denominator appears to be narcotics," the chief inspector said. "Someone really wants to get a load of them and they have no scruples about taking them forcibly."

"You've obviously collected the head," Bradan said. "I didn't see it on the scaffolding yesterday. Must be in your morgue?"

Bradan watched Young narrowly. The policeman had been bantering, toying with him, keeping him guessing about whether he was or wasn't going to be charged, but now Young's expression hardened and became opaque.

"Judging by your reaction," Bradan said, "Cyrus's head has gone missing from the Yard's custody." It was a shot in the dark, but intuitively he thought whatever supernatural agent had lopped it off might seize it as a macabre souvenir.

Young eased himself back in his seat. He wasn't going to engage on the head's fate.

"I'm obliged to tell you that you can include your solicitor in these conversations," he said. "However, I'm all ears if you'd like to share anything—just a chat, really."

When Bradan had gotten the chief inspector's call, it wasn't clear whether he could have refused Young's invitation, so he was here, sitting across from the chief inspector, but he already wished he'd included Del or one of her associates. The detective was trying to leverage ambiguity to keep Bradan on edge, but Bradan had nothing he was going to share. Instead, the London police had something to conceal, having bungled their evidence processing by losing the dealer's head—though the chief inspector hadn't admitted this.

Bradan studied Young's office. Though it was noon, the room was dimly lit by fluorescent fixtures and, if there had ever been any decorations, they'd come down a day after the holiday. Sepia tones painted the bureaucratically functional desks and offices. The police personnel sitting at their desks around Young's office were similarly drab. Bradan did see a Christmas card propped open on the inspector's file cabinet. It was from his car insurer and not signed.

"Do you wish to hold off on further inquiries until you've retained a solicitor?" Young pressed. "Judging by the crowd at your Christmas Eve party, you'll not be at a loss for legal guidance. Your friends must know someone."

Bradan caught the contempt in the implication: If he had to bring along a lawyer, he'd be that much closer to admitting guilt.

"I'll do that, ask my solicitor to sit in," Bradan said. He stood up to go. "Though I'm in no way connected to this madness. You had a car watch my gallery. You know my whereabouts."

"Well, that's the thing; my man in the car can't seem to account for you while the murders in Chelsea were occurring. You tried to be unobtrusive, but he nonetheless saw you walk into Green Park yesterday around noon carrying a large case."

"My guitar," Bradan said. "Not a very deadly weapon. I strummed a few chords in the park."

"Playing in the cold? Odd, wouldn't you say? Singing to the swans? Chelsea ain't all that far from Mayfair. Actually, it's an easy walk."

"It *is* an easy walk, but one that I didn't make."

"You have a very large dog," Young said. "My constable saw it accompany you into the park. An animal like that could do some damage. Yet when I specifically asked on Christmas Eve if you knew of a dog running about, you denied any knowledge of that."

Bradan shrugged. Fifteen centuries of contending with authorities of one form or another meant that he knew Young was trying to shake him into a damning revelation. But that wouldn't happen.

"I said that?" Bradan asked. "I don't remember in all the commotion."

"I've alerted animal control," the policeman said.

"Best luck. They'll find him elusive. Others have tried to catch him over the years."

"Who?"

"Various royal game wardens."

Young first looked baffled, then irritated. "Poor jokes won't make you friends in this building. There've been no royal wardens for the last six hundred years."

"Then my animal will be out of practice at hiding," Bradan said. "But spare yourself the effort of trying to catch him. He's not your culprit. Neither am I."

"Prove it."

"That's how justice works around here: guilty until proven innocent?"

"In my experience, the guilty are eventually found guilty," Young said. "Among the many things you haven't been truthful about is who all was at your party. The fellow that was decapitated was accompanied by another man, a rather large fellow. Some of your guests thought he was the dead man's bodyguard and described him to my colleagues. Detective Sergeant Hughes—you chatted with him in your flat—thinks he might be a cartel representative from South America or Miami. We understand they plan to expand into the U.K. and try to push aside the London gangs. Perhaps you've somehow gotten yourself embroiled in a turf war."

"I'm not part of any drug cartel. I deal in art."

"We've checked your background," Young interrupted. He rocked forward in his chair, pushing into Bradan's space.

"A few years ago, the Miami police questioned you about transporting narcotics from Columbia across the Caribbean into South Florida using large cargo planes. Quite a sophisticated operation, it seems. You were associated with a certain Pedro Schneider."

Young looked down at notes on his desk.

"Schneider is a Columbian national, one of the big boys from Medellín. Though it seems there may have been a falling out among their leadership recently, perhaps because Schneider is himself a coke fiend and no longer a reliable partner. He also appears to have ambitions that don't include his former cartel mates."

Bradan sighed inwardly. Inevitably his past had caught up, given the notoriety of the slaughter in his Mayfair flat. He'd put the Atlantic Ocean between smuggling in Florida and a quietly prosperous life in the West End. That was all at risk now.

"Never arrested, never charged," Bradan said.

"But suspected, like you are now."

"Oh, I'm guilty based on suspicion?" Bradan let mockery permeate his tone.

Bradan would be damned if he'd flee London, chased out by either natural or supernatural forces. If he left eventually, it would be on his terms for better opportunities elsewhere—and because of shitty English weather.

"I've seen you before," Bradan said.

He saw that this startled Young. "I've never set eyes on you until these recent crimes."

"All the same, you're a type that hasn't changed over the generations."

"And what type would that be? Someone that catches perpetrators and locks them up?"

"Nope. Someone who uses their office's authority to bully the innocent into admitting to crimes they haven't done."

"Whatever it takes," the inspector said. "That's not bullying; that's justice. And what past generations are you speaking of that make you so familiar with my type?"

Careful, Bradan thought. *I'm angry at being tricked into voluntarily coming to this interrogation, but I don't gain a thing by revealing my history and he won't believe the truth anyway.*

"I spoke of all the past generations where small men believed they weren't small."

That was a good note on which to leave Young.

As he left the office, he said, "Here's my lawyer's contact number. Do let her know if you want to 'chat' with me again."

He put Del's business card next to the detective's Christmas card.

"Happy New Year," Bradan said.

CHAPTER 9

Apex Predator

Miami, January 1, 1987

I'm afraid of my dreams."

"All the killing scars your mind."

Pedro stared at Marco like he was crazy. "No! You misunderstand completely. Killing is part of business, another day at the office. I'm afraid of my dreams because I fail in them."

"Dreams are just dreams, Mr. Schneider," Marco said. "Visions that don't mean nothing."

"My dreams have meaning. I'm not sentimental, but sometimes one has to believe unreasonably in a dream."

"Dreams don't buy me a cool set of wheels like a Lambo."

The drug lord regarded Marco. It was clearly time to clean house by getting new subordinates. He anticipated little intuition or strategy from them, but he did expect a modicum of sensitivity to his moods. However, at the moment he had bigger things to address than organizational changes to rid him of empty-headed underlings.

"Speaking of killing," Pedro said. "We've lost Cyrus, our very good London sales representative. Also, my product is vanishing under unusual circumstances."

Cynically, he noted that Marco seemed relieved that the topic had turned from dream symbolism to marketing narcotics.

"Actually, *we* didn't lose Cyrus," Pedro corrected himself. "*You* lost him—at a party, no less. You were supposed to keep an eye on things given all the competition we face."

Marco shrugged massive shoulders, refusing to engage. He was too big for the chair he sat in. The drug lord reflected that his crude underling didn't fit with anything at all in the office.

"Cyrus is—was—middle management," Pedro said. "Why was he selling at a party? That's *street level*. I taught him to delegate."

"Wasn't any party," Marco responded. "Lots of high-class people, lords and ladies. We was making connections."

Pedro sighed, left his teak desk, and walked over to floor-to-ceiling windows overlooking Biscayne Bay.

"He connected with the wrong people. That's poor judgment."

His office was on the top floor of a condo situated where the bay merged with the Miami River. Nothing was in his name, of course, but he owned a big stake in the building along with Cuban traffickers. He'd buy them out. He hated sharing control.

It was dusk and the view was phenomenal with the skyline bleeding light of every hue into the ocher-colored water below. In his office, a single lamp lit the desk. Otherwise the room was dark, making for a spectacular contrast with the view outside. It was easy to think of himself as a god from this vantage point. A yacht swept past beneath him with a party raging on deck. The revelers were no doubt inhaling his coke. He needed to get a yacht. Then he'd really be a god.

"Come over here," Pedro said.

"Why?" Marco asked. Nonetheless, the big man lumbered over to stand beside him.

"What do you see?" the drug lord asked.

"Water."

"Of course, but what else?"

"A boat."

"What you see is a vision from a dream. We can own that dream. To do that, we need to grow. And to grow, we need London first and then the rest of Europe. And to make London work, we need to find out who took out Cyrus and stole my product."

Pedro pointed Marco back to his chair and regretfully turned away from the view. He returned to sit behind his Danish teak desk and faced his subordinate across an expanse of fine wood. Discussing strategy with this gorilla was a waste.

He supposed it was winter somewhere, but that season never touched South Florida. He hadn't seen ice in the years since he was in an upstate New York prison. Probably, London was arctic. He hadn't intended to visit, instead leaving daily operations to Cyrus and his crew of dealers with Marco providing muscle when needed, but with things going to shit, he wondered if he should go himself.

Narcotics markets were saturated in the Americas, and unhealthy competition between suppliers left piles of bodies and eroded profits—all pointless. Medellín and Cali never got along and neither cartel had a strategy for where to go next. So, he'd filled the vacuum. London was the perfect bridgehead for him to expand into Europe with disorganized, local gangs that they'd easily shove aside. Now, Pedro wasn't sure expansion would be so easy.

"Have old colleagues in Columbia determined to intrude on my plans?" he asked Marco. "Or maybe that group in Amsterdam has designs on our activities? The Albanians and Jamaican Yardies are also coming up in the world."

He was dancing in a minefield.

"Don't know," Marco said. "It was weird."

"How so?"

"Dude lost his head. Blood ruined my suit."

The drug lord was mildly surprised that Marco's vocabulary included "ruin." Pedro used a razor to precisely arrange two lines of cocaine on his desktop. The white powder contrasted elegantly with the teak. The desk was spotless except for the long, twin traces of white powder. This symbolized order in a messy world and something he controlled.

He inhaled one line per nostril through a hundred-dollar bill and congratulated himself. That was discipline. He felt like more cocaine, a lot more, but he resisted. He'd reward himself once he got to the bottom of what had occurred in London.

"Besides your suit getting ruined, what happened?"

One needed to be patient or he'd never get a sensible story out of this cretin.

"His head was there, then it wasn't," Marco replied.

"Somebody hacked it off with a knife or ax, maybe?"

"That wasn't what I said. We was arguing with a tall guy, kinda long hair. You remember him—Bradan. Used to handle transpo for us. Had a bunch of two-engine planes. Lost us a load of product over the Bahamas."

"No need to remind me," Pedro snapped. "I've tried to find him for years. Now, it seems, you've stumbled on him in the U.K. I'll eliminate him there. Why's he even in your wild story? Did Bradan kill Cyrus?"

"Bradan's party," Marco answered. "Hot women, not Miami hot but pretty. They must work out. Nice tree, too."

"What?" The conversation was veering wildly off course.

"Christmas tree, nice decorations," Marco added. "It was holiday merrymaking."

Pedro pointed at a poster on the wall behind his desk. It showed a favorite business quote. Others bought art as decoration; he collected and framed pithy management maxims.

"Read it aloud," Pedro said.

Marco was utterly confused, but he gamely recited: "Your focus determines your reality."

The big man shrugged. "So what?"

"So, stay focused and tell me what happened, just the important things. Forget the women and the tree. Who killed Cyrus?"

"All the champagne bottles popped at once, sounded like an AK, bottles broke. Then the wind came inside and all the coke and angel dust blew out the window. Cyrus was about to shoot Bradan—it was in his eyes, but an edge of a broken bottle chopped his head clean off, through skin and bone. Blood everywhere, that's how my suit got ruined. I wasn't packing, so I ran. Thought it was competitors trying to take us out, but I didn't see no one doing the killing. Not Bradan, not anyone. Weird."

"Your story sounds impossible," Pedro said. "The police came?"

"They came, a flood of 'em. I waited on the street with other people from the party. Then I saw it. There was his head."

"Bradan's?"

"No. Cyrus's. Stuck way up on a building, like a warning. Weird."

"A warning to who? Us?"

Marco shrugged.

Pedro was tired of being shrugged at. He needed another line of coke to extract information from his subordinate.

"It didn't stop at Bradan's party," Marco continued. "Someone hit another party the next day, saw it on the news. Same story, a good time until lots of blood, bodies, drugs. Another thing happened at a parking garage the next day."

"Thing?" Pedro asked.

"This one wasn't a party. It was a business deal, group from Manchester that we worked with before was buying, two of our people was selling, lots of product about to change hands until it was interrupted. Dudes kept their heads this time, no one's noggin got mounted on a spike, but they got chopped to bits, all of 'em dead. Lots of drug stolen, our product *desaparecio*."

"Are we dealing with competitors or serial killers?" Pedro wondered aloud.

Thinking about it further, he said, "Parties, deals, bloodbaths, the common denominator is drugs. Someone wants coke—they want it badly."

"What are you thinking, Mr. Schneider?"

"I think that nothing about what you've told me makes sense. We need to know more about who's doing it."

"Who cares?" Marco said. "We find 'em, we take 'em out."

"We may do that. However, even an apex predator benefits from allies."

Pedro saw that this was lost on Marco.

"We're not well established in England yet," Pedro elaborated. "Yes, we've got a sizable crew, but we need associates. If we can find a way to work with whoever is doing this shit, they might be the partners we need."

"They killed Cyrus. He'll be buried with his pistol, but not his head. Don't seem fair."

Now it was Pedro's turn to shrug.

"Chopping someone's head off with a bottle of Moët, that's style. And they seem to evade the police without much effort. On the downside, this group is a bunch of complete, fucking psychos. Can we work with them? Let's find out. We'll remove them if we can't reach an accommodation."

Pedro poured cocaine out on the desktop. The crystals embodied purity and clarity.

"We need replacements for those we lost, people more professional. I've got ex-military and security services from Russia, South America, and Israel on the payroll here in Florida. I'll send some over to London."

"Bring in an army, if you want," Marco said. "How do we even find whoever is hitting us? They never showed themselves."

Pedro did two more lines. His cognition began to fray at the edges, but he knew what needed to happen.

"Someone must have wielded the bottle that took Cyrus's head off even if you claim you didn't see them. Have our people ask around. If it's another organization trying to push us aside, someone will have heard. Then there's Bradan. He must have some inkling of who turned his Christmas party into a slaughterhouse. He's resourceful in his own eccentric way. I know that from working with him a few years back. In fact, he has the same problem we do: Who's behind this? It doesn't sound like he's in the business any longer, but they threaten him nonetheless. It happened right in his home. So he'll investigate. Fine. Let him do the work. We'll watch him until he leads us to these mysterious murderers."

"He hangs out in a place called Green Park a lot for no good reason," Marco said. "I had one of our guys watch his place after Cyrus got iced."

"That's unexpectedly clever of you," Pedro said. He walked back over to the window.

"I've decided I'm going to London. Can you show me exactly where in this park he spends time? Maybe he's trying to meet them."

"Thought you'd want to kill Bradan for fucking us on that shipment out of the Bahamas."

"I haven't forgotten—it took me months to make up the shortfall—unforgivable, but we use him first, then remove him. That's simply good business strategy."

CHAPTER 10

Sylvan Glades

Green Park, London, Twelfth Night, 1987

"Let's knock harder on the doors of Faerie," Bradan said.

The wolf growled skeptically.

"I know, didn't work on Christmas Day."

It was midnight and the beginning of Epiphany, and he was back in Green Park with his guitar. Bradan wasn't sure whether the date had any significance to pagan Fae, but some holidays had pre-Christian origins, so it was as good a time as any to try again to negotiate a truce with the Fae.

And he'd brought cocaine.

As the chief inspector had recognized, the feature common to recent slaughter was narcotics. Silicon Saturday's Stonehenge shoot had been awash in drugs, as had his Christmas Eve party and the other scenes of holiday killing.

He'd sworn off anything stronger than Scotch after Miami, so it took a bit of effort to procure the blow, but Tam and Nick from his party had agreed to share from their stash in return for a discount on the antique table they were acquiring from his gallery.

Bradan periodically stopped and scanned the path behind him. He felt an animal awareness of danger. He didn't fool himself that he'd spot a professional tailing him—or anything supernatural. Still, he'd do his best to avoid being caught unawares.

"We need to stop the butchery," Bradan said quietly. "I didn't provoke it, but I'm the one person who knows just a little about what's behind the carnage."

They cautiously approached the same stand of bare trees he'd visited on Christmas Day. Plainly, his music alone wouldn't gain him a hearing. However, drugs and song in combination with a hallowed date and the deployment of magic might bring him to Fae attention though, if he did make contact, they might murder him just for kicks.

Bradan set his baggie of cocaine on the ground in the center of a small glade among the stand of trees, an offering. Then he created a spell for a bonfire's image. He wasn't a powerful enough mage to give the image actual heat, but ruddy light splashed over nearby trunks. If late-night park visitors were about, this would be a seriously weird sight.

When he'd recovered from the fatigue of casting the spell, he played.

"Let's party," he told Tintagel.

He didn't feel inspired tonight, just persecuted and miserable. As on Christmas Day, he struggled to strum his Martin twelve-string in the cold, and maintaining the fire spell was draining his mental energy.

He was about to quit when he heard clapping. The sound was as intimate as moth wings by a candle, but it carried across the glade. It came from a single pair of hands and the cadence was slow and measured, giving their approval a scornful quality.

Tintagel leaped up, eyes blazing orange, fur rising on its back, and glared at something among the dark tree trunks.

Bradan looked in the direction where the wolf stared and saw a seated figure relaxing on a stump.

"Steady," Bradan said. "We're here for a ceasefire, not a fight."

Tintagel readied for war.

Keeping his eyes on the figure, Bradan placed his guitar in its case and snapped the lid shut, but the clapping continued for a space.

The moment stretched out awkwardly.

Is he insulting me? Bradan wondered.

Then the clapping ceased, leaving the glade silent.

At first, Bradan registered what the man didn't have: wings, and, as far as he could tell in the shifting light from his imaginary fire, he wasn't a miniature version of a human; in fact, the being was the same size and shape as a slender man.

He was clothed, but the raiment's color fluidly transitioned to iridescent hues before settling back to cinnamon brown and then changing all over again.

Bradan had seen this Fae near Stonehenge's standing stones when his band played. He'd also seen others like him at dusk on the far edge of abandoned meadows reverting to an uncultivated, wild state, or in his peripheral vision among Britain's few remaining old forests. They were creatures of history and privacy, and probably contempt for men's depredations against nature.

Bradan worked to discern the being's facial features. Shoulder-length jet-black hair framed his sharp and intelligent visage and he sported a pencil mustache, but a broad-brimmed hat shadowed his face too deeply to allow Bradan to make out other details.

"I owe you a hat," Bradan said. "But it seems you've already replaced yours. Or did you steal it back from the police? Why leave it on my Christmas tree? As a calling card?"

He'd been flip until now, but dread replaced his cool humor and he wondered if this Fae had decapitated the drug dealer.

He also remembered the Fae woman who'd flitted down to interrupt his playing at Stonehenge and then tormented the wolf. She wasn't around tonight.

"Do you want my head?" Bradan asked.

But there appeared to be no threat. Instead, the entity before him levered itself lazily off the stump and sauntered over to the fire, its movements more a flicker than a man's deliberate gait, like a silent-era movie skipping frames. Respectfully, it gave the wolf a wide berth. The being reached out to heat its hands over the flames with an exaggerated display of warming itself on a winter night, seeming to share in the joke that this wasn't a real fire after all, but merely a mirage manifested by Bradan's modest enchantment skills. Indolently, he waved a hand over the imaginary blaze and instantly the fire became real. Bradan stepped away from the heat. Trying to form some connection—however tenuous—with the Fae, Bradan moved back closer and held his own hands palm out to the fire's warmth. He was freezing and the unnatural fire felt good.

For a moment, Bradan and the Fae stood in sociable silence. Then the magical entity glanced down at the bag of cocaine. His expression became unreadable, but Bradan intuited that lust for the drug battled with disdain for human weaknesses. Disdain won and the Fae reached down and threw the narcotics into the fire where the plastic blackened and merged with the crystals leaving an acrid smell in the glade.

Then the being yawned and stretched elastically, elongating itself to the height of the tree tops, before returning to human stature and gesturing for Bradan to follow him through the snow into the trees. It left no tracks.

A shimmer of violet light formed between two trunks and the Fae nonchalantly stepped toward it. Bradan stopped. He guessed this was a gate between modern London and whatever netherworld the Fae inhabited. He'd wanted to negotiate a truce with the supernatural entities, not visit their world, but he'd have to do one to accomplish the other. At the precipice, he paused before committing to the passage. The portal was opaque and Bradan noticed that London's common-place, nighttime city sounds were now muted as if they were being sucked into Faerie. The city's roar, civilization's cacophony, was muffled, almost indiscernible. Plainly, normal rules didn't apply at this border between realities. What lay beyond? Would his modest magical skills offer any protection whatever on the other side? Would his senses even be able to comprehend a radically different reality? And could he get back to his own world or was this simply some malign Fae jest with the outcome being his sticky end once he made the passage? However, the fairy realm had shown itself more than capable of reaching modern London. If they'd wanted to kill him, they'd had plenty of chances already, so maybe he was at no immediate risk if he made the transit.

How do I communicate? Bradan wondered.

The Fae reached out and touched Bradan's forehead like it was the most natural thing.

Instantly, Bradan peeked into the Fae's psyche and understood that the creature intended him no harm and indeed might want to exchange favors if a suitable bargain could be negotiated.

Then, the Fae inserted himself into the violet shimmer, but apparently realized that he wasn't being followed and stretched his arm back through the portal to London and beckoned peremptorily to Bradan, who stared at the disembodied arm for a moment.

"Now or never," Bradan told the wolf, who looked even less certain than him about entering. Suppressing fear, Bradan gingerly stepped forward, hands outstretched. He didn't feel the violet portal on his palms, and it was anticlimactic to simply stride from one world into another. The first thing he noticed was that it was twilight on a mild summer evening. The Fae realm's trees were leafy, though the foliage didn't always look green. In the dim illumination, the leaves glowed as if this world's color spectrum allowed Bradan to perceive the ultraviolet and infrared extremes of the light spectrum. The foliage radiated peculiar energy; every leaf had its own aura.

The scene surrounding him was unnatural nature, but nature nonetheless, exuberant, untamed, and untrustworthy. The forest stretched endlessly. It was far too expansive to be circumscribed by London's boundaries. Civilization had vanished and the terrain was primordial. Humans had never set foot here, and the very notion of humanity and its industrial pollution was inconceivable—except Bradan saw a Skol beer bottle nestled in the moss and brackish, oily pools among the trees. He smelled gasoline. The Fae man avoided the pools with an expression of revulsion.

The fairy world was vividly aromatic with both floral and herbaceous scents. Fertile smells from meadow grass, fallen leaves, and soil blended together in an overpowering mélange with an undercurrent of rottenness as if things had gone too far, grown too much, and begun the gentle slide along the downward slope toward decay and death.

A keening wail floated out of the trees. It was feminine and as ethereal, as longing and shameless, as he'd ever heard. Some of the fair folk were more demon than angel. Gossamer shapes flashed among the trees and up into branches and leaves. They weren't birds and moved too quickly for him to discern their character.

Bradan whirled around to see if the portal was still present. He needed to know that he could retreat to bland, prosaic normality if need be. Confirming that he could see an escape was like clinging to the edge of a pool if one couldn't swim and the water was deep without a visible bottom.

Reassuringly, the portal's faint violet haze lingered.

Bradan saw a condescending smirk on the Fae's face. He'd noted Bradan's panicked search for an exit.

Working to suppress his fear, Bradan surveyed his surroundings. He was here, so he needed to understand how to survive.

He saw a sinuous rill meandering through the trees lit by moonlight. For stretches, the water ran uphill unconcerned by gravity's logic. Water lilies in kaleidoscopic colors drifted with the current, a vision out of an opium dream.

"Glad you decided to come along," Bradan murmured to the wolf, who now stood at his side. It sniffed about. The creature was uncharacteristically tentative. Normally, it would have roamed widely to explore a new environment, but Tintagel kept so close Bradan felt him against his leg.

Their Fae guide—for that's what Bradan had come to think of the entity who'd ushered him into this world—turned and held a finger to his lips. The gesture for silence was universal enough to cross worlds.

Bradan heard melodies among the trunks with notes stretching endlessly and aimlessly from instruments he didn't recognize in a cadence he'd never heard.

The guide had a destination in mind and they crept forward silently toward an opening among the trees where Bradan could hear high-pitched vocalizations. These were words, but in an inhuman timbre. As quietly as he could, Bradan followed. The wolf moved with ghostlike ease beside him.

The three of them came to the edge of a glade and stood far enough within the trees not to disturb the convocation before them. The clearing was lit by moonlight and the stream drifted through its midst, flowing upward and over a small hill. It was like the revel Bradan had seen at Stonehenge a few weeks ago with a huge gathering of Fae, but the mood here didn't seem festive. If he'd expected frolics among the trees and magical creatures coupling midair or amid soft moss in an idyllic forest, he'd have been dead wrong. Instead, there was discord and acrimony with face-to-face confrontations between individuals and groups as fairies periodically lifted off the ground to swoop down on one another or grapple midair, their fighting sending off sparks.

Apprehensively, Bradan noted that the fairy woman who'd wrecked his band's performance at Stonehenge presided over the gathering. He didn't know whether the description "queen" applied in Faerie, but she fit this role based on the deference the group paid her. The woman's regal authority was emphasized by her languid pose. There was sound and fury around her, but she hardly stirred; the hurricane's eye.

The beings swirling about her might be subjects. However, she didn't appear interested in controlling them or mediating between adversaries; instead, she moved her arms gently to a musical rhythm only she heard and orchestrated the dissension, now pointing to a couple screaming at each other, now smiling benignly at a score of Fae, dryads, and nymphs deploying enchantment to eviscerate one another. Some held spears tipped with green pennants, others' weapons bore yellow banners.

Bradan noticed that the moonlight illuminating the clearing now had a bloody, reddish tint.

It wasn't a party.

The queen sat on a wooden throne set on a dais festooned with vines and leaves. Shocked, Bradan noticed skulls randomly scattered about her throne that had been inverted to act as planters for herbs and flowers. The skulls might belong to Fae or other magical entities and seemed to have been culled from some otherworldly bestiary. However, Bradan saw one human cranium and guessed that this might be the drug dealer Cyrus who'd been murdered at his party and whose skull had gone missing from the morgue. There were remnants of matted hair and blood on it, so it was a recent addition to her collection.

Like his guide, the queen had sharp, watchful features and black hair, but where the man's was trimmed and straight, hers was worn in a tangled, curly mass that a silver headband couldn't control. Her mane was as wild as the foliage about her and, in fact, Bradan couldn't tell where her hair stopped and the flora began. She had rainbow-colored eyes with a gaze that could shatter a knight's plate armor. The queen didn't wear anything flowy or flowery. Instead, it was all skintight and indigo. In the warm evening, she'd tossed a cape made of leaves in a heap beside her throne.

Her throne had been placed beneath a canopy of white flower petals. It was her temple and sat beside an empty chair. She'd propped her feet up on the chair, claiming sovereignty.

The Fae ruler plucked a leaf from among the foliage draping her chair and dusted it with white powder poured from a leather pouch hanging from her neck. This was the first activity Bradan had seen her perform where she focused completely on what she did. She angled the leaf toward her nose and inhaled the powder.

Human vices have crossed over, Bradan thought.

The queen waved hugely to the assemblage, inviting them all to partake.

The moonlight's red tint deepened, painting everyone in the glade crimson.

Dispensing largesse, she tossed a big handful of white powder into the air, and Fae leaped off the ground to fly through the sparkly cloud. The crystals refracted the light in a million shades. The fairies swam through this, leaving little contrails in their wake. At first their expressions broadcast delight and they flew in graceful arcs, but then the positive energy became agitation and enervated Fae flew about randomly in disordered paths colliding with one another to fall to the ground, broken. The chemically altered beings before him turned the setting into a mad god's whimsy.

In a different time, different place, Bradan had used cocaine and the initial rush was heart-pounding, energizing, and euphoric before the rush's lingering, draining downside hit, like rolling splendidly downhill before hitting bumpy ground and rocks. The narcotic's effects on Fae was enlarged tenfold over his reactions.

While many of the supernatural creatures in the glade had surged toward the queen's gift of cocaine, others held back from the cloud of drugs still suspended before the throne. Some tried to restrain the enthusiasts from getting near enough to inhale the drug. The fault lines in the Fae convocation were based on who would or wouldn't partake in the narcotics the queen dispensed.

There are two thrones, Bradan thought. *Does the queen have a co-regent, a consort, a king? That must be the guide who escorted me here. If he's the king, are they a feuding couple? Who's usurping whose power? Has he been deposed? Will he provoke conflict by coming back to challenge her? Why bring me here? Am I in the cross-fire?*

Perhaps overhearing Bradan's thoughts, the guide motioned him and the wolf to remain amid the trees and strode boldly into the gathering.

The queen spotted him immediately. He blew her a kiss.

That's no gesture of affection; he's throwing down a gauntlet.

Out of proportion to the gesture, Bradan observed the airborne kiss sweep away the canopy's flowers, sending petals skittering across the forest floor in chaotic, white waves. Whatever deranged splendor had existed in the forest glade before the Fae king's arrival was pushed aside, furthering the malign mood.

The king walked toward the two thrones, kicking aside the petals. Again, Bradan saw a condescending smirk on his face.

Now aware of the king's presence, the rest of the assemblage paused fighting to watch his progress toward the queen.

Everyone stopped breathing.

The king turned his back on the queen to bow sardonically to the magical creatures around the glade, pulling his hat off to sweep it low over the ground, then agilely hopped onto the dais, pushed the woman's leg off the chair, and plopped himself down beside her.

Immediately, a dispute ensued in a language Bradan didn't recognize and was composed of sounds one might hear at midnight in a forest as a breeze wafted through leaves. It had rhyme and meter, but it wasn't gentle; this was the poetry of hatred.

The king's touch just before Bradan had crossed the portal lingered, and Bradan intuited the gist of the couple's verses though he wasn't privy to nuances or allusions. In the argument, Bradan sensed odd minds, apart from human reason and rules, where emotions were acted on without regard for consequences.

The queen paused midargument and sent a penetrating look right at Bradan. She'd sensed him somehow and the foliage and shadows, thick though they were, didn't hide him from supernatural attention.

The Fae king smirked as if Bradan were playing a preordained role and now he should do something spectacular like flee for his life. The king stretched his legs out, ready to be entertained by Bradan's discovery.

Is this the king testing me to see if I'm a worthy ally? Bradan wondered. *Or is he just a bastard?*

Bradan saw shock on the queen's face. Then she blew a kiss at him; the kiss was devoid of affection and as full of malignancy as the king's opening salvo a moment before. It was his final send-off.

She wants my soul.

Bradan turned and sprinted through the forest toward what he believed was the portal's location. The ever-nimble wolf rushed on ahead, looking back occasionally as if to tell him to hurry. Encumbered by his Burberry winter coat, Bradan clumsily yanked it off and threw it aside, not regretting for a second its expense. The guitar case banged against his legs, so he carried it overhead as he ran, trying to avoid branches. He'd be damned if he'd toss it aside.

The Fae didn't bother running; they flew after him, between, over, and among the trees and foliage. Indistinct in the dark forest, Bradan had the impression that he was chased through a gauntlet.

Magical creatures, Fae, water nymphs, and dryads, competed with one another to catch and extinguish him. One of them somersaulted over his head with a metallic glitter of copper-colored armor and righted herself before him. The elf maiden was incredibly fast, but he pivoted around her. The dappled nighttime illumination coming through the forest's overstory painted stripes on the maiden like a tiger's.

He splashed through the stream he'd seen earlier, half leaping, half running through chest-high water. This section flowed uphill and fought him every step. The wolf cleared the obstacle in one gravity-defying jump, snarling at the magical beings closing in.

Bradan didn't remember fording the stream going in the other direction when the king had guided them, but he plowed on regardless, conscious of packs of fairies homing in on him from above and water nymphs swimming toward him, in their element, supernaturally pretty, wearing tiaras of water lilies, their hair held in place by combs made of fish bones. They moved with predatory purpose.

He made the stream's opposite side and slipped and scrambled up its muddy bank, still trying to keep his precious Martin dry. The instrument represented his hold on London.

Dryads emerged from the trees, birthed by the trunks and branches. Bradan dodged their elongate, reaching fingers and kicked at the nearest one with all his might. He connected with a shock that sent bark, splinters, and leaves flying. The demon fell sloppy dead.

All of nature chased him, ready to rend and dismember, but their attack was wild, chaotic, and uncoordinated. The magical creatures pursued him erratically, losing focus and, if they flew, crashing onto the ground or into trees, which only served to enrage the dryads. Soon fights erupted around him in the dark forest, distracting them from him.

Moreover, he had a few friends among the throng hot on his heels—perhaps Fae who hadn't inhaled cocaine and followed the fairy king. He saw several of them grapple with malevolent Fae to push them away from Bradan. One used a silver sword to lop off branches of a dryad as its bark-covered claws ripped at Bradan's back.

Bradan caught a glimpse of the portal's purple shimmer some distance off as he sprinted forward. He would have missed it, but the king had appeared and frantically gestured him toward it.

He dove headfirst through the portal to land in a heap in Green Park's snow. The wolf arced gracefully through the portal after him.

Bradan whirled about to confront the gateway.

What chased him?

Nothing.

Trees no longer reached out to dismember him. They were just bare, winter wood.

Bradan exhaled. He had one sensation and one feeling. The sensation was of insane cold; London was arctic after time in Faerie. The feeling was rage.

"The queen didn't want to negotiate," he snarled at Tintagel.

He'd aroused the ire of supernatural creatures who'd infected his world with their savagery—as if humans weren't violent enough left to their own devices. Further, he'd been played by the Fae king, used as a pawn to taunt his rival as part of some feud for control of a magical realm of impossibilities.

The queen with her legions would come after him, but he wasn't without resources. He'd lived fifteen hundred years and planned to live fifteen hundred more.

Exhausted by his flight through Faerie, he trudged coatless through the park back toward his gallery, which he hoped would be a sanctuary tonight. The wolf loped along beside him.

Against all odds, he still carried his guitar, gripping it tight. Tomorrow, he'd compose music based on the surreally violent experience. Song was his therapy for fear, madness, and malign magic.

He needed to not die caught up in a drug-fueled Fae power struggle that had spilled into the West End.

CHAPTER 11

The Queen and the Trafficker

Green Park, London, late January, 1987

She wasn't there, then she was. She looked at Pedro with rainbow-colored eyes, but it was a glance. She seemed incurious about him. Instead, the woman stared at his briefcase. Pedro had packed a kilo brick of uncut cocaine in it. Bait.

She'd unerringly honed in on the drugs that he was sure would be part of any negotiations about partnership.

Pedro had instructed his organization to put the word out among London's narcotics underground that he would be in Green Park looking to do a deal. His men had discreetly staked out the park at exactly the spot Bradan frequented, but they'd seen only occasional well-bundled joggers breathing out puffs of steam through their scarves in the winter air.

The tactic of passively waiting wasn't working and went against Pedro's nature to directly pursue goals, but he determined to continue for another few nights before flying back to Miami. And then, success—

He didn't know who would come after the offering—probably rival drug lords accompanied by heavily armed thugs. The woman sitting beside him on a bench in snowy Green Park at midnight would have been his last guess.

It wasn't a question of who she was; it was a question of what she was—either a psychedelic vision or a demon from a dream. He wasn't superstitious, but in a life filled with oddity and excess, she was unique. Or he'd done too many lines earlier that night and his visitor was a coke-fueled hallucination. If she was real, she wasn't natural.

She'd come out of nowhere. Pedro thought he saw pointed ears poking through hair. Her skin tone was dynamic, changing from off-white to sienna. After a moment, the woman determined that coal-black hair and pale skin were how she wanted to present herself, so the color changes stopped.

It was cold. However, she wore a thin tunic over a long, sheer dress. Perhaps as a concession to the subfreezing temperature, she'd covered her shoulders with a cape made of moss and leaves. She caressed the garment as if she knew the plants composing it as friends. The cape was wild, but not warm.

Pedro felt no lust, though she was carnal. In a life spent slaking his sexual appetites untroubled by scruple or legality, now he sat meekly; used to intimidating others, now he was fearful. Pedro was a very lapsed Catholic and hadn't set foot in a church since his childhood, but he considered praying now.

Despite his visitor's sudden arrival and bizarre appearance, there was no reason to feel vulnerable. Three of his London-based crew had positioned themselves among the trees nearby. He'd never go into a business meeting with an unknown party without protection. His men's cover wasn't ideal since the trees were spaced well apart, bare trunks in a winter landscape, but as he glanced around, his gunmen weren't obvious. They were all armed with pistols and one carried a compact submachine gun under his overcoat. And they were close enough for clear shots. If negotiations went south, they'd shoot her.

Pedro carried a Beretta .45 in his pocket. He gripped it as a tangible sign that he was master of this situation.

He wondered if the woman sitting beside him had brought her own muscle. It was harder to get guns in the U.K. than in the U.S., but not that hard. In Miami, one simply walked into a store and bought them while in England one needed criminal connections to obtain handguns. However, he guessed that she didn't need firearms for protection.

With a rustle from her cape, the woman reached out and touched Pedro's forehead.

It was an intimate gesture and her fingers were light, barely perceptible.

And now he read her thoughts. He gasped. He'd been invited into a madhouse with incomprehensible images, creatures, and figures. Human perspectives were altered or absent and he was privy to memories that stretched back eons. Pedro saw vivid sights he couldn't comprehend, heard noises he didn't understand, and smelled scents that repulsed the lizard part of his brain. He teetered on the edge of a chasm before stepping back to avoid splintering his mind.

Unfathomable as this all was, Pedro sensed a recognizable theme amid the chaos: contempt for humanity's despoliation of nature. Images of her tribe venerating their world passed through Pedro's consciousness. She found London an abomination and remembered when the land had been field and forest rather than endless structures, highways, and tame patches of manicured parkland.

He also sensed ambition unchained by scruple. To the extent that human concepts of leadership applied, Pedro recognized that she was a queen or ruler in her cosmos and she had designs on his world. Her drive might even match his.

They had something in common.

The queen's touch had established a two-way bridge with his psyche, and Pedro believed she could now peer into his thoughts and memories. She recoiled from him. Her rainbow eyes blazed and her skin tone shifted abruptly to crimson before reverting to white. Evidently, what she'd sensed amazed and appalled her.

Pedro felt some pride in this.

Whereas before, she'd evidenced no particular curiosity about him, now that there was a connection and she could discern his true nature, she regarded him closely.

The peek she'd given him into her mind proved that she and her subjects had slaughtered various narcotics traffickers including some of his own foot soldiers in their efforts to acquire cocaine, but they hadn't killed Cyrus.

Who did? Pedro wondered. *Maybe Bradan did it after all, despite Marco's belief to the contrary.*

The queen interrupted his thoughts with a preemptory command that he give her his kilo of coke.

Pedro didn't hear the demand as spoken words. The dialogue was at a more visceral level and expressed as a ravenous hunger. She and her otherworldly followers had become addicted to this most human of vices, the search for ecstasy.

Ah, so that's her reason for establishing communication: to secure my drugs.

That gave him leverage—which he'd use.

He'd held his briefcase in his lap; now she held it. The change in ownership had happened so fast he'd missed it completely. So much for his bait.

"There's more where that came from," Pedro said. Would she understand? He wondered if Spanish or German would be better than English.

The queen understood perfectly. She tore the locked leather briefcase apart like tissue paper and removed the kilo.

"Let me," Pedro said. "We'll spill less."

He sensed enormous possessiveness, but she read his intentions and relinquished the narcotic back to him. Deftly he pulled a switchblade from a coat pocket. The blade clicked open and he made a tiny incision in the plastic wrapping the cocaine, then spilled out a thin stream of powder onto a large, purple leaf the queen had pulled from her cape. The blow looked like the snow surrounding the bench they sat on.

It seems some rituals are universal, Pedro thought. *She's familiar with the rites of narcotic intake.*

Believing that this was the best way to initiate the relationship, Pedro arranged several lines of cocaine with his knife blade and gallantly gestured to the Fae queen to take first choice. Regally, she plucked another purple leaf from her garment, rolled it into a perfect tube, and snorted a line. Pedro did the same using a fifty-pound note.

While he felt the drug's familiar energizing euphoria mixed with heightened sensations of his surroundings, he observed that his reaction was paltry relative to what the queen experienced. She appeared to be transported to an orgasmic state and her preternaturally intense expression softened to bliss.

More quickly than his rush, the Fae's high dwindled to nothing. Now, she regarded him, apparently weighing next steps.

Pedro gripped his Beretta again.

Will she kill me? he wondered. *Well, to business, then. I don't know whether I have an instant to make my case or until dawn. Reminds me of dealing with other cartel drug lords. Best get started.*

"I can give you and your subjects as much narcotic—rapture—as you want," Pedro said. "In return, I need an ally to rid my operation of competitors."

Just put it out there on the table.

He wondered if the business concept of ruthlessly destroying rivals would be comprehensible to her. To his amazement, this notion made perfect sense to the queen and indeed much of her incredibly long lifespan had been engaged in doing just that. Pedro became privy to scenes of slaughter and mayhem in her world as legions of Fae and other magical creatures periodically engaged in fratricidal war amid fantastical scenery. Evidently, the path to a Fae throne could be bloody.

Further, she was currently engaged in a battle with her former spouse, the king, and looking for every advantage to crush him including providing narcotics to her followers to increase their violent propensities, hence the raids on human parties or drug transactions to replenish her stock of blow and angel dust.

"Killing bystanders is sloppy," Pedro said. "So ignore the parties in favor of going after wholesalers and traffickers. Leave my operations alone, of course. And try to be discreet. The police will pay less attention."

Pedro sensed that the queen got the gist of this, though she was bemused by the function of police or why she should worry about them.

"Human civilization is more structured than your world," he said. "Think of the police as a hostile tribe. Keeping them ignorant of our affairs makes things simpler."

He handed the kilo back to her.

"As a token of good faith, keep it," he said.

This offer didn't amount to much, since the queen had already proven she could commandeer his possessions at will, but Pedro believed that gestures, even empty ones, fostered good feelings between potential business partners.

A shared image generated by the queen popped into Pedro's mind: Bradan. The Fae's anger overwhelmed the image. Bradan had evidently been dragged into the king and queen's marital and martial discord.

"I hate him, too," Pedro agreed. "He destroyed what was mine. How about a friendly competition? We'll see who can kill him first, your subjects or my men."

Pedro sensed agreement.

"We meet again here in a week to compare progress," he said. "And I'll bring along more drug. Will you know when I'm here?"

He sensed that locating him again when he visited Green Park would be trivial for her. The queen vanished with the kilo. The psychic connection faded. He missed the sensation of dipping into her disordered mind.

Besides ambition, they had dreams in common and, in these dreams, he didn't fail.

Green Park lightened as winter's late dawn brightened the east. He'd lost track of time. His uncanny dialogue with the Fae queen had lasted all night. Pedro was near-frozen from hours of sitting. He heard an early-rising runner gamely crunching through the snow along a nearby path. Where were his men? He wondered what they had seen of his eerie negotiations with the Fae royal. Likely, they'd doubt their sanity. Maybe he doubted his own.

Stiffly, he got up and approached the stand of trees where his three men had lain in ambush, all of them competent lads. One of them could replace Cyrus.

"Mickey? JT? Leo?"

They lay haphazardly in the snow, which was splotched in dark blood and splattered with viscera.

Pedro had seen more than enough death to instantly recognize its finality.

"Earth to earth, ashes to ashes."

Why not kill them cleanly instead of leaving their corpses looking like yellow and cherry-red cottage cheese?

He watched a figure lying in the snow asleep using the remnants of Mickey's torso as a pillow. The creature was a lesser version of the queen, not as intense, not as elegant, not as tall, but evidently still very lethal. And she had the same pointed ears. Pedro guessed she was a member of the queen's court, a strange and malevolent lady in waiting.

The being sensed his presence, opened her eyes, and roused herself to stretch hugely.

She gestured casually at a spot near two trees and violet light sparkled between the trunks. Everything he'd seen tonight was unnerving. Pedro guessed this was a portal to the queen's world. Tidying up, the Fae unceremoniously pitched the three bodies through the passage. They weighed nothing to her and she stepped nimbly after them. The portal vanished. The desecrated snow where the corpses had lain was now pristine except for a large indigo leaf of exotic shape.

Perhaps the queen had taken his cautions about the police to heart and ordered her minion to dispose of the mess while still making the point that he'd just allied himself with a savage partner.

His men could be replaced.

CHAPTER 12

Forty Elephants

East End, London, February, 1987

" '**E**ard you was in trouble."
It took Bradan several moments to recognize the voice on his answering machine.

"It's Mags, Forty Elephants, case you ain't figured."

The connection was wretched. The call came from somewhere very remote.

"I'm still around, sort of, though not thievin' no more. How could I?"

There was a prolonged bout of coughing like the caller had inhaled broken glass.

"You're in a fix now, it seems. The Elephants remember that we owes you a favor. Perhaps we can help, so chat when you're ready—the usual place. London's changed since I was aboveground, but the Wilton's still there. You needn't pick a time; I'll know when you come."

The voice cut out in another paroxysm of hacking.

Bradan didn't realize phantoms coughed.

The line died and the machine chirped itself to silence.

Bradan played the tape twice more to hear her voice after a century.

Mags Sutcliffe.

~

"We lived for laughs, larceny, and fuckin'," Mags said.

"Good times," Bradan said. "I remember."

It was magic when she was riding him. She did it for him, but even more, she did for herself, distracted and in her own world. "Funny styles these days. Couldn't set foot out of the house dressed as they do. Couldn't even show yourself to your man inside."

"I've seen you in less," he said.

"That you 'ave. We had something. Or am I sentimental?"

"We had something," he agreed.

"Was it love?" she asked.

"You tell me."

"Near enough."

"Mags" was the name she preferred, but to Bradan, that sounded harsh for someone with her appeal. "Margaret" he'd called her when they played together. Anyone else using her formal, Christian name risked being sliced with a straight razor. She had several of these concealed among her voluminous skirts. One of her former lovers had lost a nose by misjudging how far he could goad her. Bradan was always respectful.

They stood in the middle of the Wilton's Music Hall's stage looking out at the empty space where long tables had once seated patrons packed in for dinner variety shows. It all looked smaller now in the bare, old building, stripped of what made it fun in Victorian times—mirrors, chandeliers, and the raucous company of East Enders happy to proclaim that the city's wealthier neighborhoods had nothing on them with regard to enjoying themselves.

The hall's ornate columns supported the Wilton's second-floor gallery, where spectators had sometimes pelted poor performers with food and bottles. The place had survived fires and the Blitz, as well as Methodists who replaced music hall entertainment to spread charity and the Bible to locals.

These days, the Wilton was to be renovated. Bradan observed construction tools in the corners of the room and hoped that the laborers wouldn't efface the structure's quirkiness and character. This place shouldn't be sanitized.

He recalled going to shows arm in arm with Mags.

She could sport silk evening gowns with élan or the drab garb of an East London working woman depending on the setting; but whatever her dress, he remembered her arched eyebrows and the knowing smirk that kept the world at just the proper distance and could freeze unwanted attention in its tracks or invite a suitor to know her much better if the mood suited. Seeing the petite woman now brought these impressions back forcefully.

As always with phantoms, she was washed out, bleached of life's hues. To Bradan, this was a sin—particularly for pretty, vibrant Margaret who'd died young. However, one didn't argue with death. Muted luminescence replaced life's colors; ghosts literally glowed, but dimly. Death had taken something away and replaced it with something else; her skin was translucent, and her taffeta dress, once brilliant aquamarine, had turned palest green.

But he needed her for more than memories. He sought allies to help him fend off natural and supernatural threats.

Of course, she'd know he had ulterior motives for seeing her, as when she'd been alive and they were a couple. In Victorian London, she'd been his indispensable partner when he'd held an audience rapt with lectures on spiritualism while she'd discreetly circulated about the performance space, deftly fleecing the unsuspecting crowd of cash, jewelry, and anything else that could be fenced.

Mags had also been a member in good standing of London's preeminent all-women gang, the Forty Elephants.

There was money to burn if she and her fellow criminals had scored, hitting a snobbish shop and taking anything valuable that could be stuffed under dresses and petticoats before the women brazenly strolled out of the establishment. They'd confidently relied on Victorian propriety and hypocrisy to shield them from body searches, even by female shop assistants, despite the fact that they'd doubled in size as they waddled nonchalantly away to escape scot-free; the Elephants were more than happy to exploit polite society's sensibilities for their own ends.

Bradan had no idea why they called themselves what they did—perhaps because many of them lived in south London's Elephant and Castle neighborhood. Mags had never bothered explaining it to him.

Bradan didn't care about names. Now, he needed the Elephants as partners thanks to their criminal talents and propensity for violence. Mags might help him and bring along the others.

What would she want in return? What motivated the dead?

"They're trying to sweeten it up, the Wilton," she observed.

"A touch of squalor instills character," Bradan replied.

However, endless redevelopment schemes were forever trying to sanitize the East End and the nearby abandoned St. Katharine Docks. Despite this, the air was gritty. He felt it abrade his lungs. Even generations removed from coal-burning shipping and kitchen stoves, soot lingered. At least, he didn't smell horseshit nor did he need to watch his footing to avoid it on the streets. Progress, he supposed.

Now, besides sawdust from renovation, he smelled cumin, coriander, and kabobs wafting in from South Asian vendors outside. East End neighborhoods drew London's recent immigrants as they had in Mags's day, and in centuries before that.

He'd ask her if ghosts could smell.

"They'll try to make it fancy like Mayfair," she said with acid disapproval. "Won't work."

Redevelopment was always something that happened *to* the East End rather than evolving organically *from* it.

"Mayfair," Bradan said. "I live there now."

He knew he sounded defensive. Mayfair and the rest of the West End weren't far from where they stood as the crow flew, but the two sides of London were as distant today as they'd been generations ago.

"I know," she said caustically. "Why in bloody hell *do* you make your home in such surroundings?"

"I like the parks. So does the wolf."

"Parks always amused Tintagel," she said wistfully. "What a marvelous beast. I'd like to pat him as I used to. Nothing like him where I'm at now. Nothing at all where I'm at now. Suppose that's why it's good to come back here, though I can never stay long. Them's the rules."

Bradan observed Mags evidently lost in thought and let her reflect without interrupting.

Finally, he broke in. "I need you."

She surfaced from her reverie. "You can hardly bear to say it, can you? Always the self-reliant sort, never needin' nobody's 'elp."

"I'm glad you came," he said.

"We had a connection," Mags said. "We *have* a connection. It's what pulled me across."

The woman's demeanor sharpened.

"Mayfair." She drawled out the name with pretend patrician refinement. "You was forever wanting posh surroundings."

Ah, the old arguments! he thought.

It was as if she hadn't died and a century hadn't elapsed. Spirits came back with their personalities intact, good and bad traits. What had he expected?

"Where I live suits my current business, selling artwork," he said.

Mags snorted. She wasn't going to let his address alone.

"You kept better company once," she said. "And you was more honest in your lawlessness. These days it seems you've become what you used to laugh at, respectable and all. You've changed, but then again, you 'aven't."

Bradan bridled at her scorn. His esteem for her went a long way, but now she provoked him.

"So, have you come back to taunt me about my life's choices, or can we talk about the shit I'm in?"

Mags frowned and faced him across the stage, hands on hips. Death had drained her color, but it hadn't quenched her deep-brown eyes, which snapped at him. At last her irrepressible smirk broke through, sunshine cutting through a London fog.

"You've something you're bursting to tell, so tell it."

"A bad lot is after me," he said. "They're trying to murder me."

Mags was intrigued. "Do tell. Felt like killing you meself from time to time, but perhaps I can help you for old times' sake."

"Hope so."

"Who are they?" she asked.

"That's a long story."

"I've got all the time in the world, love. It's a condition of my circumstances."

So, he told her.

"Good thing I ain't scared of supernatural creatures, being one myself," she said when he'd finished.

～

"Well stocked for Christmas, it is," Mags said. "We all been there to see for ourselves. Perfumes, scents, all manner of clothing, even ladies 'ats on the ground floor. Much of the smaller stuff is in glass cases. We'll need to be quick-fingered."

The women stared across Brompton Road at Harrods department store, hawks sizing up a pigeon. The store was several stories of stone dominating this part of the Knightsbridge district and had bank-like permanence and impregnability, but to members of the Forty Elephants, it looked vulnerable.

If they'd dared assail this upper-crust mercantile bastion, the men's gangs from Whitechapel would have robbed it with brute force: clubs, knives, and perhaps firearms—and likely been summarily apprehended to be imprisoned or hung. However, the Elephants needed none of that. Trickery would be the order of the day.

It was noon and the road was busy with carriages and cabs. Pedestrians packed the sidewalks holiday shopping and muffled against the dank cold. Two troopers of the Household Cavalry cantered past amid the traffic heading toward their barracks, livery and red uniforms looking out of place in the black and brown business bustle. An omnibus trundled by with Charing Cross signage as well as milk advertisements. Somehow, they all missed colliding with one another and the pedestrians strolling across the road, though there were near misses.

"Good a time as any," Lilly said. "Store's busy, so we won't stand out. And I'll see to distracting the shop assistants. Pay no mind to the commotion."

"I've got the furs," Rose said. "The rest of you steer clear of that department."

"Careful, girls," Em said. "We ain't thievin' for ourselves, picking out posh holiday gifts. We need items as can be fenced to the Whitechapel or Southwark mobs. The usual drill, after we do this, spend yer shillings on gin and baubles without pulling attention to yourselves."

She looked up and down the road.

"You're dressed to the nines, so you look the part. Act the part and we'll make out like highwaymen."

With that, a dozen of the gang threaded their way across Brompton Road between the carriages with practiced ease, avoiding piles of horse dung. The street traffic was even denser in the East and South End neighborhoods they hailed from, and the drivers there were less forgiving and not above running down careless pedestrians. In Knightsbridge at least the pretense of decorum and orderly traffic flow was observed, and the cabbies sitting high in their hacks only occasionally lobbed vulgarities at the women crossing before them.

The Elephants discreetly filtered into Harrods, individually or in pairs. They'd been a cohesive group while surveying the store on the other side of Brompton; entering it, they didn't appear to know one another.

Inside, Bradan had just bought three bottles of French cognac from Harrods's wine and spirits department—an early Christmas gift to himself—and was making his way toward the front entrance. He imagined the first sip.

Mags passed him with no acknowledgment, apparently intent on a case of fine glass vases. Elsewhere in the store, a loud argument had ensued between a well-dressed woman and two shop assistants. Mags paid no mind to this, either. Bradan had never seen the Elephants in action, but sensed what was afoot and dropped his smile of recognition intended for Mags and continued toward the door.

Back out on Brompton Road, he nerved himself for the cacophony and paused in time to see a hansom cab swerve sharply to the curb and disembark a couple. The man alighted on the sidewalk and, with a show of gallantry, extended an arm to his female companion, who gripped her silk dress while taking care to keep her ankles covered, and stepped down beside him. The man peremptorily gestured with his walking stick for the driver to depart while exhaling a cloud of smoke from his cheroot. They exuded entitlement.

The woman gestured toward Harrods's front entrance with her umbrella. The man looked irritated, but gamely shrugged agreement.

This occurred as a canvas-covered dray piled with barrels misjudged the cab's intentions and collided with it. Horses from both conveyances panicked and bolted, straining against their traces and their respective driver's commands. Momentum flipped the dray on its side, smashing against the cab which also fell over. Barrels rolled onto the street and sidewalk, scattering pedestrians and carriages. One of them rolled up to Harrods's front door. Hay bales on the dray, intended as padding between the barrels, spilled out onto the street, too. The cab driver's horse broke free and galloped down Brompton Road.

With no interruption, the dray's driver and the cabbie extricated themselves from their respective vehicles and attacked each other, not bothering to argue about fault.

Far down the road, the troopers spotted the loose cabby's horse scattering traffic before it and swung round to intercept the beast. Bradan laughed. One of the soldiers had drawn his sword. What did he intend? To cut down the errant steed?

Nearer, two constables on traffic duty strolled over to manage the collision. They'd seen it all before. One of them blew his whistle. Bradan thought this was more for show than to impose order. It added to the aural anarchy, but also drew more bobbies from down the block to the scene.

Bradan moved forward to separate driver and cabbie, but saw Mags and several other Elephants burst out of Harrods running helter-skelter. Stolen items including a silk scarf dropped onto the sidewalk. The scarf fluttered away in the breeze while the thieves fell over the still rolling barrels and caromed into pedestrians, sending people sprawling. Several of the Elephants hit the pavement, spilling more of their takings. Any pretense of discretion and discipline vanished.

A man from the store raced out after them, clambering over a barrel and calling them thieves. He shouted for someone, anyone, to stop them.

The half dozen constables working to manage the cab and dray collision and help the injured paused to take in this new commotion. It took no time to prioritize stopping a robbery in progress under their noses over the mundane task of handling a traffic calamity. The Harrods manager yelling for action lent urgency to their decision as did the stolen goods falling out of overstuffed dresses and petticoats. Guilt wasn't in question.

A police sergeant quickly split his men up to pursue various women gang members.

Mags tumbled over a barrel and, before she could shake off the shock to regain her footing, a constable tackled her. Bradan saw a thin steel blade appear in Mag's hand as she slashed at the constable who'd grabbed her. His thick, woolen tunic blunted the straight razor's wicked edge, but Mags immediately took another slash at his eyes. The fight had taken a savage turn and the policeman's helmet fell to the sidewalk. Bradan guessed that if she succeeded in seriously injuring or killing the man, she'd swing for it.

A second bobby sprinted to assist his comrade with raised truncheon to crush Mags's skull.

Bradan thought of casting a spell to create a distraction, but there might be an easier way. He kissed his cognac bottles farewell.

"Sir, madam, a little assistance?"

Without waiting for the stunned couple who'd alighted from the cab to agree, Bradan grabbed the woman's umbrella and used its wooden handle to smash the neck off a glass cognac bottle. He then plucked the man's cheroot out of his mouth, flicked off the ash, and lit the brandy before hurling the now flaming liquor at the nearest straw bales. He repeated the process twice more and instantly had a series of bonfires blazing away amid the mayhem. Humans and horses recoiled from the conflagration. If the scene had been chaotic before, it now spiraled into bedlam.

The trooper with drawn sword had come abreast of the wreck only to be confronted with fire. He tried to control his bolting horse, but fell to the street and rolled away from his mount's trampling hooves.

"Mags, forget the constable. Run!" Bradan yelled.

"Shame about the spirits," he said as he passed the cheroot back to the flabbergasted gentleman and returned the umbrella to the equally dumbfounded woman.

"Merry Christmas!" he told them. "Scandalous, the training they give the mounted guards these days. They're incapable of controlling their horses. What if the French invade?"

He ran over to Mags still grappling with the constable, shoved the man aside, and dragged Mags to her feet.

Bradan ducked a truncheon blow from the constable's companion and punched him in the nose. The man went down hard.

Now they'll jail me, he thought. *Splendid start to the holidays.*

"Over to Trevor Square," he shouted. "Push through the crowd. Mind the fires."

Uneremoniously, Mags picked up the hem of her dress—not caring if her ankles showed—and ran after him as they pelted through the press and down a side street off Brompton Road to Trevor Square. Bradan glanced behind him. The crowd of pedestrians and vehicular traffic paid no particular attention to them and instead watched the three blazes combine into one huge conflagration; the barrels must have contained something flammable. The crowd hampered the police from rounding up fleeing Elephants. Lilly saw the direction they ran toward and waved to other gang members to follow.

"Don't stop till we're at the far end of the square," Bradan told Mags. "We'll wait for the rest there."

He slowed to grasp Mags's hand and steady her. She coughed continuously from exertion. They pushed into trees in a small park flanked by quietly posh, red brick townhouses lining the square.

Mags spotted other gang members trickling into the neighborhood and hissed weakly to catch their attention.

"Where's Lilly?" Em asked.

"Right 'ere," Mags said. "Look around you. We're all 'ere. No one was collared."

They crouched among the trees and shrubbery peeping out at the neighborhood, but so far, no pursuit. Everyone breathed heavily from the chase.

"We look silly sittin' here in the bushes," Mags said.

"Shouldn't have brought 'im," Em said to Mags. She stared at Bradan. "Could of gone all wrong."

"It *did* go all wrong," Mags snapped. "Fact is, 'e was 'elpful. And I didn't bring 'im. 'E was here by 'isself, buying brandy or some such."

"Peelers would have caught the lot of us if it weren't for him," Lilly added.

Em frowned.

"'E ain't joining the Elephants, for Christ's sake," Mags snarled. "Just 'appened along. You won't see more of 'im."

"You're seein' plenty of 'im," Rose said.

A dozen women laughed. Tension lessened.

Bradan tossed a mink stole to Em followed by a silver bracelet.

"You dropped them in all the fuss back there," he said.

Em nodded grudging thanks. "Not such a toff after all," she said.

~

"You stayed at my side when I took to bed the final time with consumption," Mags said. "You got me into a warm room and found a good physician."

"Who couldn't do anything," Bradan said.

"Can't hold it against 'im," she said. "I was too far gone for saving."

"The gin didn't help," he said.

"The gin didn't help," she agreed. "When you're young, you feel you can go on forever. But you can't. Life takes you down."

"I'd of died alone if not for you," she continued. "Even the other girls wouldn't come near. Not a good way to go."

"A vile way to go," Bradan agreed.

Her voice was light, as if her final moments were hardly worth a thought, but Bradan knew that she'd clung desperately to life, clawing to hold on to seconds before she died. In whatever place she now existed, he guessed that being a specter hadn't eased the pain of early death; perhaps it just prolonged suffering.

"You weren't worried about it bein' catching, the consumption?" she asked.

"No."

"Then again, nothing ever made you sick. Don't seem fair, you still bein' here."

He had no response.

"There have been others," Mags said. It was a flat statement. "Other women."

"I knew what you meant," Bradan said angrily. "How could there not be others? You've been dead—gone—a century."

She circled him on the stage. Her movements were as quiet as dust drifting in an empty room.

"I'm more than a memory," she said. "I'm here."

"You're here, but then again, not really. It's not what it was. And, before you ask, yes, there *is* another."

He paused, considering.

"Actually, there are two. One lives in Mayfair. The other, I haven't seen in a while. She's in America."

"Can't make up your mind?"

Hands back on her hips, Mags looked at him quizzically.

"Don't know how I feel about that. Least it took two to take me place."

She placed a forefinger to her lips.

"No, don't tell me of 'em. Never let a man describe his current loves to a former lover. It ain't flattering to either party. I'd like to see them for meself. They'll never know I was there. Unless I let 'em, they can't see me, mortals, 'cept you. It's a condition of my circumstances."

Bradan sensed she was ridiculing him. It was in her tone and gestures. However, something had shifted as she verbalized her thoughts, and he heard regret overcome the scorn, not at his choices but at experiences she'd never have.

"Can we talk of happier things?" he asked.

"You looked good in a top hat once," she said. "And you had grand sideburns when I was alive."

"Shaved 'em off decades ago."

"Now you look scruffy," Mags said.

"Thanks," Bradan said dryly. "Unshaved is the style these days."

"Looks unkempt."

Inspired by the setting and to break the downbeat mood between them, he burst into song, singing "Champagne Charlie," an old music hall staple he remembered as if it were yesterday. Mags watched open mouthed, then let out a storm of laughter.

He bowed and doffed an imaginary top hat.

"Cor blimey," she exclaimed. "Yer voice is still in fine form. Again. We'll do it togever as we used to."

And they harmonized for several songs, little noticing her coughing.

"I'd forgotten you sang," Bradan said. "You're quite good."

"I was in a choir as a child. Mum took me to church off and on. Naught came of it. And there was work to be done—or thievin'. Better than selling meself. I never favored whorin' to make a living."

"You'll help me?" he asked. He wasn't sure how she'd answer.

"Never in question, love. Never in question."

Bradan wanted desperately to kiss her, but didn't think that was possible. What would holding a phantom be like?

"How will you know when I need you?"

"I'll know," she said.

"And the Elephants?" he asked.

"Can't speak for the rest of the crew, but I'll ask 'em, those that passed over to where I'm at. Most of 'em didn't. They just died plain and simple. Can't say why I got special treatment, perhaps unfinished business on this side—maybe you're the unfinished business."

"That's a spooky notion," Bradan said.

"Anyway, some of 'em was kindly disposed to you. Rose, Lilly."

Mags paused. He watched the reflective side of her personality surface again.

"There *is* one favor I'd ask in return," she said after several moments.

He nerved himself to hear the bargain.

What does she want?

"I'll do anything in my power," he said. And he meant it.

"Dancing. I want to go to a place packed with people and go dancing."

They still stood on the empty stage facing the Wilton's empty hall. Mags pointed toward where patrons had once eaten and caroused away the night in raucous splendor.

"We danced out there between the tables while the music played. Others joined, even modest women, lewd and randy as goats. It was the drink, no doubt."

"There's nothing like the Wilton in London now," Bradan said. Then an idea struck him.

"But there are clubs with music, loud music, crazy loud, not like the old days. I'm in a band. You knew that?"

"I didn't," she said. "But the living can do what they like."

He heard her bitterness.

"Yes," he said. "But in this case it means we can dance on a stage in front of hundreds in a Soho club. And you can sing, too, harmonize with me."

Mags was skeptical.

"You can carry a tune," Bradan said. "That's enough to join me and the other musicians. I'll write out the lyrics for you, so you'll have the words. They're great songs, brilliant melodies."

"Ever the meek one," she said.

"You can judge for yourself when we do them."

Another thought occurred to him. "I can see you, but no one else can. Can you make yourself visible to regular folks in a club?"

"Tricky," Mags said. "Not for long."

"Then, it's a date for tonight," Bradan said. "I'll tell my band we have someone sitting in. I'll find a top hat, too."

~

The image Bradan remembered most vividly from Silicon Saturday's performance was harmonizing with Mags and the rest of the band over surging guitars, synthesizers, and amplifiers with the volume set at infinity as the crowd danced and jammed itself right up to the stage, threatening to overwhelm hulking security staff and clamber up to become part of the show. They knew the words better than the band.

Bradan shared a mic with Mags. They stood close together. She'd only briefly seen his scribbled lyric sheet before stepping on stage, but she nailed the songs, breathing in their essence and singing with dazzling effect, adding timbre and texture he hadn't realized was there when he'd arranged them.

Bradan saw that Mags looked transcendent and joyous, soaking up the crowd's energy.

She was alive for that instant.

~

"Who was the chick singer?" Suki asked. She brushed orange hair out of her eyes. "Rough around the edges with the coughing and the peculiar dress, but she had some pipes."

"Margaret Sutcliffe," he said.

"Should we know her?" Constantine asked.

The Saturdays decompressed backstage in the club's cramped dressing room, walls plastered with posters from past performances. Bradan drank from a Jack Daniel's bottle chased with warm beer while the rest of the band inhaled or smoked whatever narcotics were available. Everyone was hot from the stage lights and the intensity of their performance. Bradan played his acoustic twelve-string quietly, working on the chord changes for a new song. He wrote snatches of lyrics as they occurred to him. The tune was about love forgotten, then recalled.

"No, you wouldn't know her," he said. "She was a close friend years back, very close. Ran into her just today. I asked her to join us tonight. I thought her sound would fit in with you all."

"Give us more warning next time," Liam said.

Bradan nodded, deferring to the band's fragile democracy.

"We harmonized well together," Suki said. "She was on form, marvelous soprano, will she be back? I wouldn't mind. She left following the encore, here one minute, gone the next."

Bradan shook his head. "I'll see her again on a business matter, but she lives elsewhere."

"She was pretty," Constantine said. "And stacked. Does Del know about her?"

The musicians laughed. Bradan ignored the levity to focus on the song he was composing.

"Why were you wearing a top hat on stage?" Anu wondered.

CHAPTER 13

Art in the Dark

Mayfair, London, February, 1987

Back in his gallery, Bradan still wore the Victorian top hat. It didn't go with the Glock 9mm pistol stuffed in his waistband.

Survival trumped style.

He sat on the edge of his desk with the guitar. Packing a weapon made picking the twelve-string awkward. He put the gun on his desk in easy reach, safety off.

A melody formed on the instrument as he strummed trying to distill recent images from his crazy existence into song: phantoms, Fae, Stonehenge, beheadings, lost rivers, and lost souls. He had enough material for a dozen tunes, though they'd sound like a psychotic's ravings set to a dance beat.

Playing with the band before a packed crowd energized him and he wanted that sensation to continue. They'd made great music earlier in the evening, feeding off the club's vibe. It was better than any drug's rush.

Mags had fit right in with an instinctive sense of rhythm and harmony. Perhaps she'd spent more time in a church choir than she let on—not something to be admitted to other members of the Forty Elephants or her neighbors in a London slum. Keeping a hard surface was essential to enduring an unforgiving environment.

He'd need to be hard, too.

Bradan set the Martin aside and wandered into the gallery's bathroom and checked his look in the mirror. He tipped the hat to himself. He'd wear it for the time being.

"We'll have company sooner or later," he called over to the wolf stretched full length on an eighteenth-century sofa. The enormous beast covered the silk, flower-covered fabric. Tintagel opened one eye, then closed it. What would come would come.

Bradan pulled a spare bullet magazine out of a desk drawer and stuffed it in his pocket.

The smart move wasn't to arm himself—much good that would do against a Fae raiding party or a well-planned hit by a drug gang. Instead, he should flee Mayfair and his comfortable, but perilous life here. Nothing about that life enabled hiding. Maybe Mags and the Forty Elephants would materialize from the ether in the nick of time, maybe they wouldn't. His other spectral ally, Connie, couldn't leave the Jaguar E-type, and he'd never thought of her as useful in dealing with deadly foes. She was a Southern good ol' gal and friend, not a warrior. Even a partner as constant and unholy as Tintagel might not be able to help him.

Saving my ass is on me.

He'd bolted from Miami a few years ago and didn't want to uproot again. Leading a peripatetic life came with near immortality, but it was too soon to relocate. Silicon Saturday was developing as a band and the crowds were getting larger. London's music scene was fertile, spurring him and his fellow musicians to new creative flights. And the art gallery made him a more than comfortable living. In fact, he was rich thanks to his clientele of titled buyers.

He stared down the length of his space. It resembled a small museum with muted lighting illuminating the artwork, nothing crass or garish. He picked up the Glock and walked over to a Modigliani painting of a reclining nude. Sexual, mannered, and apparently untroubled, the woman looked back. He tried to conceive of what the artist and model would have made of an armed observer contemplating the piece.

It would take him years to re-create his gallery with its world-class art in a different place—if he ever could. Besides, whatever natural or unnatural forces hunted him—the list grew daily—wouldn't stop if he departed London. They'd track him wherever he fled.

Bradan thought he'd left the kind of life behind in sunny, savage Miami where he'd needed guns to prosper and every day brought new killings.

More than the pistol, he didn't want to resume an attitude that required, demanded, extreme violence.

Maybe I can be creative and keep killing as a last resort, he thought. *But whoever comes after me won't have those qualms.*

I'll do what it takes to survive.

So who would come after him? Presumably whoever or whatever had surgically sliced Cyrus's head off—though the killer had actually done him a solid by taking out the dealer who'd been about to blow Bradan's head off.

He suspected Cyrus somehow worked for Pedro—Inspector Young's questioning indicated as much—in which case the drug lord would certainly come after him. The lunatic wanted vengeance for Bradan's destruction of a fortune in Pedro's powder.

Or would his executioners be one of the Fae factions, the queen and her followers? Could he ally with the king? Bradan knew the Fae royal was conducting a civil war against his mate, but that didn't mean he'd be helpful to Bradan, and their last interaction had ended on an ambiguous note. Would the king consider an enemy of his enemy his friend?

Bradan was an enchanter. That must count for something. He spoke six rhyming stanzas. He got it right the first time and a six-foot-long dragon with iridescent scales materialized in the gallery's central aisle. Its saber-sharp teeth appeared able to sheer through tempered steel. It could be an addition to his art collection except that lithe, lifelike movement animated the creature. Bradan even smelled a reptilian odor. The dragon stalked the gallery's length breathing out violet fire, but none of the art suffered and Bradan felt no singeing heat.

He looked to see how the wolf would react to his creation. However, Tintagel had seen his vaporous images before and yawned hugely.

Bradan would get no respect from that quarter. The figment faded.

"Yep, a mirage," Bradan wheezed out. "It can't do anything, but maybe the right image will distract the bad actors when trouble comes, better than nothing."

He collapsed into his desk chair battling nausea. Sometimes his stomach rebelled from casting a spell. Or maybe it was just fear at being hunted.

Recovering gradually, he killed the lights and walked the length of the gallery still carrying the Glock to peer through bay windows at Half Moon Street. No need to spotlight himself for possible observers.

In the small hours, the street was quiet and dimly lit.

The whole scene waited.

Outside, a streetlight showed snow turning to sleet, bullets cascading out of the sky. The sleet smashed onto the asphalt so hard that Bradan thought it would fracture the blacktop. The scene was in keeping with January weather: bleak without a pending holiday to leaven winter with frivolity.

Bradan checked the front door's many locks and deadbolts. The entrance was robust enough to defeat casual attempts at breaking and entering, though not proof against magical assault. He confirmed that he'd set the alarm. There was a small camera with a view of Half Moon Street above the door, linked to his security service. The gallery's insurer had insisted he have it to protect the artwork. However, he wasn't confident that the service's response to a breach would be either prompt or effective; they were the same crew that had bungled guarding his Christmas party, but he hadn't had a chance to replace them with anyone better. He doubted they were armed and they wouldn't be remotely familiar with a drug gang's capacity for violence, nor would they be able to deal with supernatural threats. He mentioned neither cartel-sponsored assassins nor Fae raiding parties when they'd written the gallery's policy.

This was a night when he would have welcomed police surveillance, but he saw no sign of them on Half Moon in the wretched weather.

Face it, the gallery isn't a hardened target and neither am I.

A gray Vauxhall van nosed its way off Piccadilly and stopped in front of his gallery. It was almost invisible in the sleet, part of the storm, swaddled in black spray like a mummy about to burst its wrappings.

"Showtime!" Bradan screamed at the wolf.

The van looked too small to hold the five black-dressed men in face masks who leaped out of the vehicle before it stopped rolling. They were organic to the storm.

For a fraction of an instant, he debated shooting through the bay window at them, but the glass was hardened—yet another mandate from the insurers—and might deflect his pistol's 9mm bullets. On the upside, maybe the window would offer him some protection from incoming gunfire.

They weren't shooting. Instead, two of the van's occupants sprinted for his front door. Momentarily, he lost sight of them due to the angle, but he guessed what they were doing: attaching a C-4–shaped charge to the gallery entrance.

This was way beyond average street thugs. They were pros and they *were* coming in.

"They'll blow the door," he shouted at Tintagel.

But before the charge detonated, his Jaguar accelerated down Half Moon Street and plowed head on into the Vauxhall, slewing the van and scattering the killers. He heard the impact, crumpled metal, and broken glass. Much of that damage would be to his Jag.

"Connie?" he yelled.

She was a ghost, but could she be hurt if the vehicle she haunted got smashed?

The wreckage was right in front of the gallery, so she heard him.

"I'm all right, darling, 'cept for lots of body damage. That's fixable. You dyin' ain't fixable. I bought you time. They're doin' something to your door. Get your ass away."

What condition is Connie in? he wondered. *She sounds dreadful.*

Bradan raced down his gallery's length but an explosion hurled him into his desk. He felt heat envelop his body and splinters from the door rake his back.

CHAPTER 14

Hat Dances

His ears rang. He lay on the floor, but he felt nothing broken or severed. His art had muffled the impact. He'd reflect on that irony later—saved by his art—if he lived.

He pulled himself upright gripping the desk. The Modigliani had been tossed to the floor beside the desk. The nude regarded him reproachfully. Amazingly, the picture didn't appear damaged. Neither did his top hat which rolled to a stop next to his face. Other things hadn't fared as well and he brushed remnants of a smashed modern sculpture off him.

The gallery's alarm sounded.

"The cavalry will arrive any minute."

Even in his dazed state, he thought he sounded dubious.

"The basement, then the river," he yelled at the wolf.

Would Tintagel understand his incoherent mumbling? The wolf was way ahead of him and scrambled down the spiral staircase leading to the basement, claws clicking the metal steps.

The E-type's sudden collision with their van would confuse the hit team, and the lack of a driver would confuse them even more, but they were here to kill him and wouldn't linger investigating that mystery.

Bradan reflexively grabbed his hat, then lurched over to the stairs. His back hurt from a half dozen splinters, but his hearing was recovering. He slid down the railing, gripping the metal drunkenly and burst into his basement. Tintagel waited by the small iron door at the back to the underground passage to the Tyburn.

His attackers weren't Fae, who would have been more creative in their methodology.

Pedro's men?

Whoever they were, it wouldn't be obvious where Bradan and the wolf headed unless the killers knew London history.

He and Tintagel clambered into the culvert, and Bradan pulled the iron door closed behind them to disguise their passage and buy a little more time. There was no bolt to secure it, so once the assassins discovered it, they'd follow. He didn't want a deafening gun battle in the brick tunnel with ricochets making it inevitable someone would be hit, but there was no other escape, so he frantically slid forward.

The culvert sloped down then leveled off with flowing water up to his knees. It was pitch black excepting shafts of dim light from the street filtering through grates far above. Sleet and gutter water cascaded down in the dark-gray, hazy illumination as he sprinted along from one grimy waterfall to the next in the Stygian gloom. The water level rose with the influx of storm runoff. He could add the terror of drowning to being shot to death. At least, winter's bitter cold permeated their underworld and dampened the sewer stench. He tried not to consider what was in the water.

Bradan paused to listen. He heard the killers splashing about. They'd located the culvert's basement entrance. They must be more disoriented than he was. He'd come a little way down this culvert when he'd explored it immediately after buying his townhouse. That had been in the summer and the water level was much lower, but the stink had dissuaded extensive examination.

Despite the filth, they ran beneath London's poshest neighborhoods, most effete parks, monuments to long-gone imperial power, and the seat of modern English royalty and government. If he hadn't been fleeing for his life, he would have laughed at the juxtaposition.

Enclosed culverts fed into the main channel via black arches in his peripheral vision as he raced past. They oozed darkness into the main channel's gloom. This must be the same sensation as being trapped deep inside a pyramid surrounded by implacable stone with no way out.

The wolf navigated flawlessly; it was a beast of darkness. Bradan did his best to keep up, following Tintagel's splashing while holding the 9mm in one hand and his top hat in the other. Occasionally, Tintagel stopped to glare back at their distant pursuers with eyes that glowed brilliant orange. At these moments, Bradan knew that his lifelong ally was as demonic as anything in the realm of Fae. If he had a mind to, Bradan knew that the creature could drop him effortlessly and escape on his own. He hoped loyalty overcame self-interest.

The assassins behind him didn't know what they chased, all fangs and lightning reflexes. Bradan debated turning the creature loose on their pursuers. Tintagel might slaughter all of them—or a lucky burst of submachine gun fire could hit the wolf. The beast had supernatural recuperative powers, but enough bullets could extinguish its life force.

Bradan put a hand on the wolf's shoulder, feeling quivering muscle and tendon braced for an all-or-nothing charge to rend their would-be killers.

"Not yet," he whispered. "Connie is hurt. That's enough. We bleed them. We don't let them bleed us. So, we run. We're ahead of them. We'll stay ahead. I remember the Tyburn from years back. They don't. There's a way out ahead—somewhere."

Why couldn't they have let it run free?

He remembered when the Tyburn had been aboveground, flowing unconstrained by bricks and concrete, though even before it had been engineered into a sewer, the river hadn't been pure in many centuries, contaminated by encroaching London's human waste and the occasional body.

The two of them half splashed, half ran forward. The channel deepened and the water had become hip-deep. He guessed they weren't in a modern tributary sewer any longer and must be in the Tyburn's old riverbed bricked over 150 years ago. London history up close.

Or he wandered in Hades and he waded in the Styx.

Behind him, he heard men splashing. They weren't gaining, but if he'd hoped for confusion among the many old culverts, there was no sign of that. The assassins kept a disciplined silence until a concussive blast of submachine gun fire shredded the water behind them. Bradan watched sparks flash past him like summer fireflies from bullet strikes ricocheting from one wall to the other.

Try as he might, Bradan couldn't resist the temptation to fire two shots back down the tunnel at his trackers. His 9mm popped ear-splittingly.

I'm hitting back, he thought. *No! You've just told them you're armed and given away your position. Stupid.*

Do what you told the wolf: retaliate when the time comes.

I'm not superhuman; I'm supernatural, and not even very supernatural, so options are limited.

This was a particularly dark stretch and Bradan stuffed the gun in his waistband and extended his hand to touch the side of the culvert. The bricks and patches of concrete felt abrasive and slimy.

Are they wearing night vision goggles? They see better than me.

"Let's delay them," he whispered to the wolf. "We'll give them something to shoot at."

He kissed his sodden top hat farewell.

Bradan spoke a long series of rhyming couplets. He'd never tried this enchantment before and wasn't at all sure of the meter or wording. Nothing happened except that exhaustion hit him in the chest. He struggled to stand upright in the flowing water, and his hat now weighed a ton.

Tintagel looked at him noncommittally.

"You think it's stupid," Bradan said.

He reversed the order of two of the lines and intoned the enchantment again. This time the hat vanished from his hands to reappear some way back down the culvert atop a spitting image of Bradan making steady progress toward his would-be assassins. Even with night vision goggles, the killers would find it hard to see what approached them, but they'd think he was coming at them with his pistol.

"Ya, you wouldn't be fooled," he told the wolf. "But they will." Then he yelled, "Duck—it'll get loud."

A volley of shots buried his words. Miami memories, he recognized an AK-47's distinctive sound immediately. A war had erupted below the West End. Bradan saw his hat cartwheel into the air and jerk about as shots hit it. However, these weren't aimed, and bullets cracked and whined everywhere, smashing into the bricks and metal grates above. The eerie, disorienting Tyburn unnerved even trained killers and his now hatless image kept moving inexorably toward them unaffected by the firefight.

Bradan heard screams of pain. Ricochets must have hit at least one of the men. Someone yelled in Russian to stop shooting and the racket grudgingly died away.

Take advantage, Bradan thought. *They're hit.*

"Left at the next turn," Bradan whispered at Tintagel. "Things get narrow and there's no headroom with storm runoff adding to the flow. I've never gone this far, but I think we'll be totally underwater for a stretch. We can't worry about what's behind. Push forward."

And here it was: the deep part. Bradan felt the footing beneath him fall away so he swam, thrashing along with the current at a mad clip, being pulled underwater. The tunnel was completely dark and he gasped out a four-stanza spell as he submerged. It needed to work the first time and the image had better be waterproof. A tiny orb of incandescent light spontaneously formed in front of him, illuminating his watery surroundings. He swam in sickly, yellowish illumination and saw the wolf ahead in the black water unfazed by this submarine passage, paddling strongly forward with its tail drifting behind him. Bradan held his breath and fought off a need to retch and succumb to his spell's fatigue. He kicked himself along, using the pistol he still held to push against the brick sides of the tunnel and propel himself forward, not caring if he damaged the weapon.

The orb stayed a few feet ahead of him. It was illumination, but no guide; he'd have to find his own way through this black tunnel without suffocating. He couldn't see an end to it. The current was an ally and shoved him along, but he didn't know how long before the passage finally surfaced again. His head smacked against bricks. Instinctively, he was trying to surface.

He was out of air.

Now, surrounding him, spectral figures floated about congenially, reaching for him, inviting him to linger. The figures varied in appearance and dressed in fashions that spanned centuries. He guessed they were permanent residents of the Tyburn whose corpses had been tossed into the convenient stream to be carried out to the Thames and lost to anyone's knowledge: a barefooted farmhand victim of a highwayman's knife with his torso wounds still ragged, maids who'd died in childbirth, sickly children whose families had too many mouths to feed, some who'd died senile and old, toothless mouths lolling open.

Here, Bradan knew the Tyburn was only a dozen feet deep, but he felt like he swam over an oceanic abyss.

His vision darkened and his little, magically created orb of light dimmed.

Am I dead? he wondered. *These are fellow phantoms? A sewer isn't the way I want to go.*

The Tyburn birthed a malevolent specter. A man with a noose about his neck and his tongue flopping out grabbed at Bradan's forearm with a strong grip. A long strand of the noose's rope trailed after him until it was lost in the dark below.

The corpse's eyes were black marbles that hated him. Bradan felt utter horror at his touch.

He's long dead, Bradan thought. *Now he's a cemetery vision, but with power in my world. He must have been a criminal strung up to dangle, slowly dying, entertaining a crowd below the gallows, then the hangman cut the corpse down and tossed it in the Tyburn, less trouble than dragging it to burial.*

The specter embraced him, then deftly shed his noose and tried to loop it around Bradan's neck. Bradan squirmed aside, yanking and wrestling with the corpse. He punched the corpse's face, and the specter's visage crumpled under the blow and its eyes burst. The wraith released his hold and floated downward, more faded than ever. Bradan held the noose. He'd keep it as a ghoulish trophy.

I can see them when others can't. That means I can hit them. More coming. They won't keep me.

Other figures powered toward him out of the murk, led by a woman in a long pale-green gown, swimming right at him.

Mags!

She stroked smoothly, strongly, unencumbered by her dress. She gestured violently at the other phantoms with a straight razor. The blade left thin etchings of bubbles in the water as she sliced this way and that.

Behind Mags swam other members of the Forty Elephants, eerie and desolate, fearing nothing. They fanned out to lunge after the Tyburn's phantoms with clubs, knives, broken bottles, and their reaching fingers. They'd been in gang fights before and knew what they were about.

Phantom fought phantom.

There were scores of river specters, but they scattered before Mags and the Elephants' ferocity leaving her alone to point Bradan down the tunnel. Something, maybe the current, maybe Margaret Sutcliffe, perhaps his own efforts, brought Bradan to the end of the enclosed tunnel and its surface. The orb of light extinguished itself as he scrabbled weakly to keep himself above water.

He breathed blessed oxygen.

A narrow ledge beside the Tyburn was more inviting than a Caribbean beach as he rolled himself onto the frozen, greasy stone, out of the water, barely able to muster the energy to claw his way to safety.

Dim light from streetlights seeped downward. After the black hell of the tunnel, this was cheerier than sunlight.

Bradan observed Tintagel sitting unperturbed on his haunches observing his struggles with vague interest.

A few relentless Tyburn phantoms were gathering near where he'd beached himself and reaching after him, faces pallid blobs in the water, hands grasping at his body to pull him back into the soft, black water. However, the wolf's infinitely menacing snarl caused them to recoil and retreat to the depths.

"You hunt souls when you're in the mood," Bradan told Tintagel. "Poor sport here. Their souls are wretched."

The wolf sniffed at the dark water where the specters had disappeared.

"Persistent, some of that lot," Mags remarked conversationally. "Never know what these old rivers will spit up."

She lounged against the brick culvert wall as if she watched a music hall floor show. Her clothing wasn't wet.

"They didn't die well and they're vengeful," Mags said. She coughed for a spell before recovering.

Lilly, Em, Rose, and a dozen other gang members reclined or sat in the dark sewer tunnel beside Mags. They were dry, too. And, like Mags, they were luminescent. Fighting energized everyone. They chatted among themselves as old comrades who'd reconnected after a long time apart and remembered that they were strong together.

Rose waved in his direction.

"You helped as you'd promised," Bradan gasped out a thanks.

"I sympathize, gettin' dumped in the Tyburn," Mags said. "Now it's wastewater. Bad way to spend forever. Howbeit, they ain't gettin' you on my watch."

She looked him over. "The rope?"

"The fellow I took it from had no more need of it," Bradan said. "Can't hang a man twice."

He tossed the noose to her. She caught it, looped it around her neck pretending the rope strangled her, and capered about on the bricks to the hilarity of her comrades.

"'Tis no laugh," Lilly said soberly. "That could 'ave been our fate but for God's grace."

"No one showed me no grace," Rose said.

Mags's companions began to fade. Bradan waved at them. He wished he had his top hat to salute the women.

"Where are they going to?" he asked.

"Elsewhere."

"Silly question," he said. "I knew that."

Finally, only Mags stood before him.

"Thanks," Bradan said. "Thanks very much. Didn't know you swam."

"Couldn't before, can now," she said. "Air, sea, land, all the same to me. It's a condition of my circumstances. I can be most anywhere, but I prefer London. It's habit."

"Convenient for me," he said dryly.

They watched a thin stream of reddish water flow by virtually invisible in the gloom.

"Blood, I think," he said. "Not mine. Some of the lot that chased me are shot; they fired wildly and bullets bounced everywhere including back at them. They were pros, but I rattled them. I'm not out of it yet. There'll be others. No one could have made it through that tunnel after me. They wouldn't know how long it was. And they wouldn't be sure their weapons would fire after a prolonged soaking. They'll assume I drowned, but they'll check for my corpse. They don't get paid without my head."

"Clever trick with the hat," Mags said. "And you throw a mean punch, like back in the day. You're able to fend for yourself."

"Barely!" Bradan laughed. He tried to suppress hysterical terror.

"Weak magic, audacity, and friends. It worked this time. Will it keep working? The assassins nearly got me. The phantoms nearly got me, too."

"Then you'll be wantin' more of the Elephants," Mags said. "I'll get 'em when the need arises."

"We're close to the Tyburn's outlet onto the Thames," Bradan said. "It's probably gated, but there must be maintenance access to the street. I'll climb out."

"I'll keep you company until you're back aboveground in case our friends return." She pointed toward the water where the specters had tried to pull him under.

"Pity about your shop with all the fine pictures," she said conversationally.

"A pity," Bradan agreed. He hadn't felt anger tonight, just fear. Until now.

Now there was room for other emotions.

Rage bubbled to the surface at the thought of the wreckage the killers had turned his gallery into. And his guitar, reduced to rosewood and ash kindling.

She must have sensed his raw emotions.

"Steady on there, love. Yer still in one piece. The rest you can replace."

"Not really," he snarled. "What's gone is beyond replacing. More than that, a friend of mine was hurt when she put herself in harm's way for me. It's time I hit back."

Mags glided away from him and Tintagel leaped to his feet, fur rising on his back while staring at him.

134 PETER W. BLAISDELL

"Don't see this side of you often," she said. "Your eyes went orange for a moment."

"Just a trick of the light," Bradan said.

"You're supernatural."

"Just enough to get into trouble."

"Your friend who's hurt, that's the other spirit you keep company with?"

"Yes. She's rather dear to me."

He observed that Mags never referred to herself or other ghosts as anything other than "spirits." Maybe this softened their circumstances. Or perhaps it was her way of offering up respect for souls who hadn't received much of that in life.

"She's like you in some ways," he said. "Though not as handy with razors."

He was too tired to explain Connie's connection to his cars.

"I'll see that you meet one day," he said. "Meantime, let's get out of here. It must be morning. I'm freezing. I miss Miami. I'm always cold in London."

Mags burst into another spate of coughing before this morphed into raucous laughter that swept away glacial temperatures, mayhem, and dark magic.

"Yer hat," she said pointing at the stream. "A bit the worse for wear."

Bradan looked. He'd lost his pistol, but his tattered, bullet-riddled top hat bobbed by in the water with cheerful buoyancy. It amazed him that it floated with its many holes, a little boat braving river rapids.

Bradan stretched over the water to grab it.

CHAPTER 15

On the Case

"What do they seek in drugs, Hughes, meaning in the meaningless, wisdom in the unfathomable?"

"They want to get fucked up."

"That simple?" Young said. "Oblivion?"

"That simple," Hughes said.

They kept away, intentionally on the sidelines and discreet, observing uniformed police, detectives, and a forensics team along with explosives experts picking through the wreckage at the gallery's entrance. Bradan stood amid the scrum, but also apart, taller than most, and shielded by his aloofness. He answered questions, but didn't conceal his impatience at official proceedings.

Well, let him be bothered, Young thought. *The man is plainly guilty of something. I can't yet draw a straight line between criminal activities and Bradan's culpability, but I'll get there.*

The chief inspector would announce his and Hughes's presence momentarily and join the throng to direct their bit of the investigation, but he wanted to take in the whole scene before examining the details—it was too easy to get sucked into details, particularly for a mess like this, without having a context. He had a score of questions to put to various individuals—mostly Bradan—but he'd be better at framing them if he could make some sense of the whole of it. Also, he needed the context to respond to the inevitable barrage of questions he'd get himself. He hated it when cases rose to the level where even a chief inspector was a cog in the machine. In his experience, when that happened, things weren't solved satisfactorily. They were papered over enough to satisfy the Yard's senior leadership and placate the politicians and media. Often enough, the perpetrators waltzed off with no real punishment. However, whatever his preferences, this circus was now well above his pay grade and Security Services and the Home Office were involved, though no one had thought to inform him.

Half Moon Street was blocked off at both ends unless someone could prove that they belonged in one of its townhouses or hotels.

He'd lived in London all his life and had never paid the slightest attention to this backwater though he'd driven by it hundreds of times. Despite the relentless traffic on the nearby throughways, Half Moon Street had adopted neighboring Green Park's effete restraint, red brick or brownstone homes fronting the street, curtains closed, no building above five stories, nothing too old and quaint, but not too new, either, sort of ageless, and certainly nothing flashy enough to attract tourists, everything done with understated style.

How very British, Young thought. *Things as they should be. Change comes, but in its own time. Oscar Wilde wrote of the street in one of his plays a hundred years ago. It hasn't changed much since then. If I could afford the insane costs, I'd move here. Fat chance! Since the divorce, I've got only a few quid in disposable income.*

He didn't recall any crimes beyond the occasional burglary or an altercation between an escort and her client at one of the boutique hotels, everything hushed up with minimal fuss. Most big-time felons and petty criminals simply ignored it. Certainly nothing involving gunplay and plastic explosives had ever occurred here. And most of its residents would have been delighted that it stay unnoticed, a bit noisy, in the midst of things, convenient and a fashionable address, but not engaging with the rest of London more than it had to.

An ideal spot for a discreetly upscale art gallery—though Young guessed that Bradan would vigorously object to it being characterized as ideal now.

"It's a shambles," Young said.

At least the sleet had stopped, to be replaced by snow flurries. The chief inspector felt like he was in a holiday snow globe that someone had shaken violently to watch the flakes swirl crazily about the little figures inside.

A couple of the uniforms carried submachine guns. London cops were only armed in dire circumstances. Instinctively, Young, Hughes, and other officials stared about alertly as if last night's carnage might spring back to life.

They watched two bodies in bags lugged out of what had once been the gallery's front door. It was tough going for a dozen constables and forensics investigators to carry their macabre load and make their way through the stone, wood, and glass debris. A medical examiner hovered over the proceedings occasionally lending a hand to steady the stretchers. Young reflected that it wouldn't do for someone to trip and pitch the corpses onto the sidewalk.

"This one ain't going to be a quiet, connect-the-dots sort of thing," he said.

"No, sir, it surely isn't. But we knew that already on Christmas. It was only a question of how bad it would get."

"Rather bad, apparently." Young continued staring about, absorbing details.

"The hat," he said.

"What sir?" Hughes asked.

"The peculiar bloke wearing a hat, there, across Piccadilly at the park's edge."

The chief inspector pointed.

"That hat is identical to the one we retrieved at the Christmas party. Didn't see it as important to the crime scene, but I had it taken in anyway since it sat prominently atop a Christmas tree. Someone wanted people to see it, like Cyrus's head on the scaffolding, taunting us. Or warning us."

"Warning someone, perhaps not us," Hughes said. "Peculiar-looking fellow."

"The hat vanished from the evidence locker at the same time Cyrus's head disappeared from the morgue. Not meaning any levity, but heads will roll for that one. London police can't keep body parts in the morgue? That's not an endorsement of our competence."

"Reckon he was involved?"

The chief inspector shrugged. "Don't see how he could have gotten in, and then back out carrying a severed head with nobody noticing, but nothing about circumstances here makes sense."

"He's moving away into the park," Hughes said. "Shall I have one of the lads chase him down?"

"Do that," Young said. "In fact, send several constables. I don't know how he fits in and he may be armed. Does he know Bradan? Was he part of the crew that attacked the gallery last night coming back to check on things? Best hurry or he'll be out of sight. He's not that far from Buckingham Palace."

Hughes urgently summoned a sergeant and pointed toward the slender man in the broad-brimmed velvet hat now sauntering deeper into the park and growing indistinct in the snow.

The sergeant shouted at the mass of police by the gallery, and several uniforms peeled off to run down Half Moon and into the park, dodging cars on Piccadilly Street.

"He knew we were onto him," Young said. "Have a couple of cars swing by to assist. One can head down Piccadilly, another can work its way along Constitution Hill. Between the cars and the foot patrols, we may yet nab him."

Hughes talked rapidly into his radio while watching the man in the hat.

Young turned back to activities by Bradan's ruined gallery entrance. The scrum grew as more marked and unmarked police vehicles muscled their way onto Half Moon Street disgorging additional criminal investigators.

"I hadn't expected it would get this mad," Young said. "What's he done that would justify someone using plastic explosives to get at him? Pull Bradan back in for another chat?"

"Tempting," Hughes said. "At some point, we may have to insist he come back to your office so it looks like we're doing our jobs. I'm not sure it helps, though. He's royally pissed someone off, but if we let him stay free, he's good bait."

"Leave him loose to flush out whoever's behind all this?"

"What can we charge him with?" Hughes asked. "He seems mostly the victim. Look at him. He's soaked head to toe. Someone's got him a blanket, thank God. I'm frankly growing sympathetic."

Young looked at Hughes.

"Are you now?"

"Sorry, sir. Just saying his gallery got bombed, his Christmas thing was a disaster with a lopped-off head, and, despite his dodgy past, nowadays he doesn't really seem connected with London's narcotics trade or any other criminal doings. Besides his gallery, he's in a band, of all things. Doesn't seem to be keeping a low profile. We can't account for his every move—he's elusive—but we've had him under surveillance during some of the recent attacks, so he wasn't directly involved. He may be what he purports to be: an upscale art dealer who has somehow caught the attention of very bad actors."

"Does that seem credible to you?" Young asked. Then he interrupted himself. "He's got a bloody hat, too. It's a morning for hats."

The detectives peered over the intervening official personnel at Bradan surrounded by dozens of officials. The encircling group compressed itself about him like a python. To Young, Bradan looked like he was chilled to the bone, huddled beneath a paramedic's brilliant yellow blanket, as well as furious at standing without friends amid a hostile crowd next to his shattered gallery and home. Incongruously, he held a Victorian top hat. It was considerably the worse for wear.

"Suitable for an interview with royalty except for all the bullet holes," Hughes observed. "We'll ask him about why he's got it. And why it's all shot up."

"You know, Hughes, damnedest thing, I thought I'd seen this Bradan fellow before and I finally remembered where."

"Don't keep me in suspense, Chief Inspector."

Young noted the sarcasm in his subordinate's tone, but let it pass.

"It's daft," he said. "But he's the very image of a fellow painted by Reynolds two hundred years ago. The portrait's in the National Gallery."

"Who was Reynolds?"

"Oh, for God's sake, Hughes, what *do* they teach at school these days? Reynolds did portraits of important English folk. That's our history, our heritage. Anyway, makes no sense given the passage of time, so forget I brought it up. Coincidence, I'm sure. If anything, Bradan doesn't look a day over thirty, too young even to have been part of a cartel in Miami and then set up a thriving art business here in Mayfair."

Young felt embarrassed at mentioning the uncanny resemblance to an aristocratic figure from Georgian-era Britain. Hopefully, Hughes wouldn't blabber.

"It's time we engage," Young said. "Can't be avoided. And speakin' of the devil, there's the home secretary's chief of staff, Harry Osborn. His suit is perfect as always. So's his hair. Christ, does he want to have a go at Bradan, too, besides mucking up the crime scene generally."

He pulled angrily at his sideburns.

"Looks like Bradan's got the whole world baying at his doorstep, our chaps questioning him, insurance adjusters waiting in the wings, and not one but two beauties glaring at him. How'd they get through our cordon onto Half Moon? Wonder if they know of each other? They seem none too thrilled to be standing together. And a crew's trying to disentangle his E-type and the Vauxhall—truly a pity, hope the Jag can be put right. All that's missing is the doggie that we keep hearing about and who seems beyond the reach of Animal Protection. Friend Bradan boasted that we couldn't catch the beast."

"Just a dog," Hughes said.

They moved through the press of forensics investigators, who made way respectfully.

"Where was our car when all this went down?" Young asked.

"Got pulled away. Weather was utter shit last night as you'll recall, visibility nil. A pedestrian was hit on Curzon. Our man was sent to assist."

"I'll have a word with whoever took him off the gallery watch," Young said. "The pedestrian accident, that a distraction, do you think?"

"It would have been clever of them," Hughes said. "Anyone doing a professional hit like this with C-4 and automatic weapons would think of such things. Don't know yet, but we're talking to the woman who was struck. Maybe she saw what ran into her."

"And where the hell did the Jaguar come from?" Young demanded. "A timely distraction, was Bradan driving it, saw that his gallery was about to get invaded, and rammed the van?"

"Who else?" Hughes asked. "It didn't drive itself. However, why wouldn't he have simply fled in the car? No reason for him to go kamikaze, the wrong car to use as a battering ram, too. It crumpled like tin foil. And then what, Bradan hops out of his totaled vehicle with nary a scratch, ducks past the killers as they're about to blow his door, and makes off scot-free after a merry chase through city sewers? He's an art dealer. 'E ain't James Bond."

Young grunted. "Whatever he is, MI5's on the case, worried about domestic terrorism, near the Palace, no less. We can all sleep safe now with that lot running the show, telling us how it's to be done, posh twats."

CHAPTER 16

Miami and Mayfair

"What should I address you as? 'Your ladyship'?" Trini kept her mockery muted, but noticeable.

"I wear my titles lightly," Del said. She'd caught the sarcasm. "But I'm not careless of them. My father's family have been lords and ladies since who knows when, centuries, I suppose. My mother's family had no titles. They immigrated penniless to these green and leafy shores. But they were ambitious, worked hard, and they married well."

"Point being?"

"Point being that I know exactly who I am and where I come from. Do you?"

"I don't have titles, but I do run a very profitable business," Trini said. "I helped build it from scratch."

"How American. Something to do with cars, right? Bradan mentioned you in passing once or twice."

"I'm glad you remembered." Trini hoped she didn't sound sincere.

"We sell Bentleys and other English stuff from time to time, but nobody's too interested in that in Miami. They break down a lot. Mostly, people buy American or, if they want performance, they go with German or Italian brands like Porsche, Ferrari, and Lamborghini. How do you know Bradan?"

With no intention by either party, the two women had been waved through the police cordon together, Del when she said she was on Bradan's legal team and Trini when she said she'd be staying with Bradan at his townhouse.

"I'll let you through, miss, as you seem to know him well," a policewoman told Trini. "And since you say you've flown all the way from the States to visit, but you won't be staying in his townhouse." She gestured at the destroyed gallery entrance. "This is as bad as I've seen. Irish bombers couldn't have done worse. Doubt anyone will be staying there for a while except our lot and building contractors when we're through."

"I know Bradan because of his art and through mutual friends," Del told Trini. "He's well connected with my set."

"And what 'set' is that?" Trini asked.

"People with titles, I suppose."

"Or a lot of money if they don't have titles," Trini said. "That's what really counts."

Del ignored her comment.

Trini observed the other woman's dark mane and her skirt, sweater, and boots, everything black and stylish, but not showy. The woman didn't wear a topcoat and seemed unaffected by cold.

At that moment, Trini was conscious of her own plane-rumpled clothing. She'd come directly from Heathrow without changing to surprise Bradan. She regretted her dishevelment now as she suspected British girls—at least, moneyed British girls—tended to notice such things and would regard it as a sign irredeemably stamping one as working class and not part of the tribe.

If they were both in Miami on a Saturday night and she was dressed to hit the clubs, the tables would be turned. Nothing burned like South Beach style.

Instead, she stood freezing and rough around the edges in Mayfair where different rules applied.

Both women crowded up to the edge of the masses of officialdom questioning Bradan and picking through the pieces of his gallery. Chemists swabbed the building's door for explosives residue. Excepting the policewoman who'd granted them access to the street, they were all men, ponderous with authority in their uniforms and greatcoats dusted with snowflakes. Short of shoving their way through the masculine press, they'd get no closer.

Trini had heard that English cops didn't typically carry guns, but she saw enough to fill an arsenal around her.

Nearby, a tow truck winched the remnants of a Jaguar E-type away from a van with a grinding, shrieking scrape of metal on asphalt. Everyone jumped at the sound. Two constables raised submachine guns, stared about alertly, and slowly lowered them when no threat attacked.

She saw that Bradan looked mortified as the wreckage was pulled apart. He'd always been possessively concerned about his vehicles.

"That was his car," Del said. "Pity. A fine Jag."

"How did he survive?" Trini asked. "The driver's side is crumpled."

She waved at Bradan over the intervening men, but he didn't notice. After his sad look while watching the remnants of his car extricated from the crash site, he returned his attention to his questioners. Trini watched his expression. It was a mixture of disdain toward his interrogators and the world-weariness of someone who expected his sins to catch up with him one day— and now they had.

Still, he stood defiant.

"Thank Christ he's not hurt," Del said. "Though he seems to be soaked."

"What the hell happened?" Trini asked. "The policewoman mentioned a bomb. Or was it a gas line explosion?"

"I'm not sure what you've heard over in the States, if anything, but there's been a series of killings, slaughters really, starting with his Christmas party, pretty macabre affair. This is somehow more of the same. I don't think it's random, though nothing is making sense. He's always been cryptic about his past. The bit he's let on sounded romantic and adventurous though it didn't always sound legal. Now old enemies have noticed him."

"I know stuff about his past, a little," Trini said. "Bradan's cagey, but I did get to understand him somewhat while we lived together. He hid a lot, too. At first I was intrigued. Then, over time, it made me angry, like I was being shut out."

"I know that feeling," Del said. She seemed curious.

"You should tell me about what you know of him. It might help me defend him legally. But first, how do you know of me?"

Trini watched the snow fall.

"When he first came over to England a few years back, we stayed in touch—he mentioned you in passing once or twice. Then the calls dropped off. I was tied up on my end, too, with the business, so things lapsed more than I'd wanted, more than he'd intended, too, I think."

"He's settled into Mayfair," Del said. "He's been here a while and made new friends. Miami is a fading memory."

Del broke off to shout over the press in Bradan's direction.

"Bradan!"

He spotted them and waved hugely.

"Yes, that's me," Del called out to the crowd. "I'm his solicitor. Please make way."

She began shoving through toward Bradan like a slim ice-breaker cutting through ice floes. Reluctantly, the mass cleared a narrow path, dubious that she had any right to be here. Trini pushed through behind her.

"Can I come along?"

"I suppose," Del said. "You're here, after all. Why *are* you here?"

"I wanted see where Bradan and I stood. Call it instinct."

"Your timing is impeccable."

"She's a colleague from my firm," Del snapped when a constable tried to push Trini back. "The man who owns the gallery is my client. We've every right to be here—*both of us* have a right."

Without Del even trying, her tone was lent authority by generations of aristocratic breeding lent authority. It was a voice used to being obeyed. The pack of police, government security, and explosives experts shuffled aside, leaving them a narrow, grudging corridor to Bradan, who stood confronting senior police officials. The one doing most of the questioning tugged at his bushy, reddish sideburns.

"Thanks for getting me in," Trini murmured. "Who are all these people? They look ready to hang Bradan."

"Not far off the mark," Del said. "The best I can tell, it's police in every flavor, insurance inspectors, and MI5—that's the U.K. equivalent of your FBI—and perhaps the Home Office interested in why a Mayfair art dealer could have made enemies with the capacity to acquire and use explosives and machine guns to try to ice him."

"He lived on the edge in Florida," Trini said.

They stood by Bradan's side. He looked both relieved to have allies and shocked to see Del and Trini together.

CHAPTER 17

Pulling Rank

"Gentlemen, you've charged me with nothing," Bradan said. "I'm the victim here. As I've explained to innumerable of you over the last many hours, men broke into my gallery suddenly and violently, I don't know who they are or why they did it, but I fled through a sewer beneath my home—yes, you say you'll check, but the Tyburn once existed and still does right beneath your feet—they shot at me as the scars in the bricks below will surely show, but it was pitch dark and I evaded them, and then I climbed out through a sewer access back to street level somewhere down by the Thames. Perhaps you could spend some of the effort you're using to question me on finding out who did it. Frankly, I'm wet and cold, and I'm done here."

He pulled the blanket tighter around him.

"Liable to catch pneumonia," one of the suits said, pretending solicitude.

"That won't happen," Bradan said.

"Not worried about sickening?"

"No. I feel cold, but I won't even sneeze," Bradan said.

"Special, are we?" The suit wasn't going to let it go.

"Yep."

Trini saw Bradan's detachment transition to open anger. She sensed that Del saw this, too, because the lawyer moved forward to stand close beside Bradan and deftly, but firmly, intervened.

"My client has clearly requested that this interview break off. He's provided as much information as there is to give. You have had hours to pick and probe at his story. Bradan well appreciates that this stunning episode has occurred in proximity to the Palace, which is why he's been more than accommodating."

Del nodded familiarly at one of the suited individuals in the crowd.

"Harold, you're welcome to follow up with me off-line about next steps," she said.

The man with red sideburns broke in. "We won't be cut out of discussions about an ongoing police matter. Two men dead and possibly more in the sewer beneath us. There needs to be an accounting."

"They had it coming," Bradan said coolly.

"That's a callous remark," Young said. "Do you own a gun?"

"I'm an art dealer. What do you think?"

"I asked a question. I'm waiting for an answer."

"I had nothing to do with it, as I've already stated," Bradan said. "Their wounds came from their own weapons. Your forensics investigators will confirm that. They shot wildly, bullets bounced off the bricks. They were professionals, but something spooked them. I don't know what."

Bradan ran his forefinger over his top hat's brim. He moved to put it on, then thought better of it and simply held it.

"Chief Inspector, thank you for your perceptive questioning today," the man Del had addressed as Harold said.

He brushed snowflakes off his blond hair. The wind had mussed his coiffed do, but that only enhanced his Byronic stance. And he knew it. Unlike the other officials dressed in crumpled suits that had spent too much time in committee meetings, Harold wore a handsomely cut three-piece, and despite the weather, he didn't cover it with a shapeless overcoat. He wasn't tall, but stood straight and looked down at the others in the crowd and the world at large.

"Of course, the Yard can and should vigorously pursue this matter, but I do think at the moment we should gather our thoughts and let Bradan—"

Harold looked at Bradan with impersonal curiosity.

"I'm pronouncing your name correctly?"

"Absolutely," Bradan said.

"You're the fellow that hosted that Mayfair Christmas bash that went off the rails and thrilled half the peers of the realm? There was a body, I believe, but no head? Wish I'd gotten an invite. And now this." He pointed at the wreckage. "You *do* have a talent."

"Thrilling peers wasn't my intention," Bradan said.

"No doubt," Harold said dryly. "And an Oxford man, no less. When did you attend?"

"A while ago."

Harold nodded.

Trini guessed that Harold used his flip tone to make the point that he called the shots here. Cynically, she wondered if he saw the investigation as a political stepping-stone. Destruction and death would pull media attention.

Harold addressed Del. "Let's let your man Bradan here take a shower and get into warm clothing."

"He could tell Bradan went to Oxford from his accent?" Trini whispered to Del.

Del made subtle hushing motions.

Harold looked at the policeman with the sideburns who'd led the questioning.

"Of course, Lady Alexander and her firm will make Bradan available as needed to further assist us," he said.

"You won't scamper off?" Harold addressed Bradan.

"I'm not going anywhere, Harry," Bradan said flatly.

Trini was certain Del and Harold knew each other and had gone to the same schools. Bradan might also—somehow—be part of their world, a little club that held the levers of control in English society. Sometimes they didn't bother to hide their power, and today that worked to Bradan's advantage as connections and common upbringing overrode the chief inspector's objections.

Trini saw Bradan smile faintly as he observed Del and Harold assert themselves, and she intuited that Bradan had watched similar demonstrations of social power before in his life. He seemed to predict the players' actions.

In Miami, she'd seen him as a modern outlaw, more raffish than ruthless in a world of cold killers in the narcotics trade. Compared to building a car dealership, his life was exciting, though, even at the time, she'd known she romanticized his vocation. However, in London, he was an insider prospering in a world of money and breeding—his art masked the crass side of his life and gave it an aesthetic veneer.

Until the guns reappeared.

In Miami, she'd thought she'd known him. In Mayfair, he was a stranger.

CHAPTER 18

Oxford Accent

"A re we on the verge?" Bradan asked.

"Of what?" Trini said.

"An argument?"

"I thought we were on the verge of a relationship. Things have lapsed. That's why I came."

"It's been several years," he said.

"Where does she fit in?"

Trini looked over at Del in earnest conversation with Harold Osborn. They stood apart from the investigators, above it all. A BBC camera crew waited deferentially a little distance away, probably hoping to interview Harold, who would explain that things were under control despite appearances to the contrary and the proper authorities were working tirelessly to sort the mess.

Snow swirled around everyone, dimming sights and muffling the commotion. Evening came on, presaging a long Northern European winter night. If it weren't for the nearby mayhem, Trini could imagine that she was a character in a Dickens story where everyone had quaint names and horses stamped by exhaling steamy breath as they pulled carriages. It wasn't such a stretch to see older times around her as the flurries settled on windowsills and roofs, and covered streets and sidewalks, and gauzy lights came on inside the row houses illuminating their drawn drapes. However, she missed Miami's sun. January had never meant more than mild breezes in a city on the Caribbean's edge. In London, Trini dearly wished she'd packed more winter clothing and wondered how far south she needed to go to find a beach warm enough to wear a bikini.

Probably Dubai.

"Del's my friend," Bradan said.

Trini thought he chose his words cautiously. She wondered how he'd describe her.

"She's been a friend for a while now," he said. "She's also my solicitor. That's 'lawyer' in American English."

"I know what it means," Trini snapped. "The University of Florida isn't Oxford, but they did teach me a few things."

As they talked, Trini heard Bradan's aristocratic British accent fade. "Are you catering to my South Florida background or was that all fakery back there?"

"The accent? I'm not patronizing you. It's genuine. I went to Oxford. I try to blend in with whoever I'm with—an old habit that sometimes keeps me out of trouble. It helped today. I amplified it because I was frozen and I wanted the damned interview, interrogation, whatever it was, to stop. So, I played to Harold's tribalism and arrogance. It worked. I'd told them all I was going to say."

"You could have told them more?" Trini asked.

"It would have made no sense, doesn't make sense to me."

"Talking about sense, when could you have gone to Oxford? I've known you from our Miami days. You're not that old."

Trini saw that he became guarded. She was familiar with that.

"I'm older than I look," he said. "So you're visiting to see where we stand?"

"We'll get to that. Don't change the subject. Being a man of mystery may impress her, but not me."

"Being mysterious doesn't impress anyone, not the police, not you, certainly not Del, but I'm not trying to be mysterious."

"It just comes naturally?"

"Don't be nasty."

"Where does she fit in? She's impressive in her own way. Do you have a thing?"

Bradan's expression became even more guarded.

"Now I will change the subject," he said. His voice had been thoughtful; now it firmed. Trini knew that she couldn't pry more out of him at the moment.

"Welcome to London," he said with irony. "I'd offer you hospitality, but—" He looked toward his devastated townhouse.

"I know," Trini said. "My timing is impeccable. Del said the same. I should have called first. I wanted to surprise you. That wasn't such a terrific idea."

"You're always terrific," he said.

Trini saw Bradan glance at her breasts beneath her light sweater. It was natural and instinctual. He hadn't changed that much since Miami. He pulled his eyes back to her face.

"I'd hug you, but I stink," he said.

"Hug me anyway."

They embraced. The snow picked up, but, for a moment, she was back in Miami.

"Bradan, what's going on?" she asked, face on his shoulder. "Not what you told the police. What's really going on?"

"I'd tell you more, but you'd think I was crazy."

"I already think that," Trini said. She stepped away from him to sweep her arms wide, encompassing the art gallery wreckage and the officials and investigators still picking over the scene.

"It isn't the time to tell you how crazy," he said.

"Speaking of weird, you know her?" Trini pointed to a small, trim woman standing across Half Moon Street. She stared at both Bradan and Trini, but mostly at Trini.

"I didn't see her until now," Trini said. "She's watching me. Her dress looks like it's from a Victorian costume party, pretty, but odd, spooky."

The woman went unnoticed by the crime scene investigators who circulated around her. Disconcertingly, Trini observed that snow flurries blew right through the woman. However, it was now dark and she wasn't sure.

"Mags," Bradan said.

To Trini, his tone sounded like half a dozen reactions at once had bubbled to the surface, happiness, longing, regret, passion, exasperation, and admiration. She wondered what feelings he had for her. Time changed feelings.

"You know this Mags?" she asked. "Peculiar name. She doesn't belong here."

This last comment popped out. Trini didn't know why she'd said it.

"Mags—Margaret Sutcliffe—she belongs," he said. "She's lived in London a very long while. She's an old friend. She helped me earlier today."

Constables passed between Trini and the woman, blocking sight of her. When Trini could see across the street again, Mags was gone.

"Where'd she go?" Trini asked.

"She left," he said.

"She'll be back?"

"If I need her," he said to himself. Then he addressed Trini, acknowledging her bemusement. "I know, yet another mystery. I'm not trying to be difficult."

"This isn't just cartel shit, is it?" she said.

"That's mixed in, but that's not all of it. Not nearly."

"You don't do things by halves."

"I'd like to go back to being an art dealer," he replied. "I do music, too. That's going well."

"Get out of London," Trini said. "You left Miami under a cloud. You've got even better reason to leave London. Someone truly wants to kill you."

She watched him stare at his blasted gallery.

"Many things may happen," Bradan said. "But leaving London ain't one of them if I'm being chased out."

He looked at her.

"We'll chat tomorrow. You've got a place to stay?"

"Claridge's."

"Posh," he said. "Your business has prospered."

"Stay in my room," Trini said. "I don't snore."

Trini wanted to force the issue of his preference between her and Del.

"I remember," Bradan said. "We were incredible together. But tonight, I'm using one of Del's family flats on Chapel Street somewhere in Belgravia. It sounds discreet and it's near embassies, so it should be fairly safe."

Trini saw him observing her with a trace of a smile.

"You haven't asked," he said. "But I'll tell you anyway. I'll stay there alone. Being around friends might bring this mess down on them if it's not as safe as I think."

"Are you and Lady Del incredible together?"

"I don't owe you an answer any more than she'd get an answer if she asked about our intimacies."

"I was out of bounds," she said. "What are you planning?"

"Find my dog—or he'll find me, shower, and take a nap." He paused. "Then things get tricky. I've been trying to connect with someone who may want to help calm things down—or not. When I've tried to reach him, it hasn't gone well. I don't know his motivations. This time, I'll let him come to me."

"You're not going to tell me who that is, of course." Trini tried but couldn't keep the cynical annoyance out of her tone.

"You know, maybe I could help, but then you'd have to tell me what's going on."

Before she finished, Bradan was already shaking his head. What had she expected?

"Whoever they are, they can't be worse than the cartels," she said.

"Actually, they can," he said.

CHAPTER 19

Swans in the Park

Belgravia, London, February, 1987

Bradan whirled as a Bentley cruised past, in no hurry, snowflakes settling on its hood, contrasting with the black metal in the streetlamps. It was night and the vehicle's windows were dark, so he couldn't see inside. In the interior, disembodied, a lighter flared longer than it would take to light a cigarette and then extinguished, leaving an orange tip that blazed brightly as someone inhaled. Bradan guessed it was marijuana. The glowing tip moved languidly like a summer firefly; the smoker must be passing the joint around to other passengers.

The Bentley slowed near Bradan, getting close to the sidewalk. He tensed, ready to sprint away if a window rolled down and guns appeared, though they might simply shoot through the glass. Instinctively, he grasped for a pistol stuffed into his pants in the small of his back. However, he'd lost his Glock in the Tyburn.

The vehicle didn't stop. Instead, it picked up speed and rolled off toward Knightsbridge. In those moments, Bradan stopped breathing. He inhaled again once he saw its ruby taillights vanish.

He doubled back on his tracks and walked quickly down a side street and leaped up a townhouse's steps to stand in the shadows of its entryway, looking up and down the street. It was dark, but streetlights illuminated things well enough to spot obvious human threats, but would he notice supernatural dangers? It was ridiculous that he feared for his life in Belgravia. Here, people died of atherosclerosis and senility, or possibly tedium, not gunfire or malevolent enchantment.

After a few minutes, he resumed his search for Del's family flat, motivated by the bitter cold to leave the relative safe harbor of the doorway.

As far as he could tell, no one followed him. There were no other pedestrians and few vehicles except the now long-gone Jeep. Nighttime city sounds penetrated Belgravia, but he noticed them as muted white noise. His footsteps sounded too loud.

The buildings he passed along Belgrave Square presented a solid front to the world, no chinks in the armor and no gaps between white, four-story buildings, impressive and impassive, and not offering hospitality to a hunted man; but then, London had never been kind to those without means and power.

"Unfeeling" was the first word that came to his mind as he strode quickly along, though the residents would be bemused by that descriptor, preferring instead "grand" or "impressive." One needn't shout too loudly about privilege if an address said it all.

If he weren't being hunted, he would have laughed at the competition between Belgravia, Mayfair, and Knightsbridge for honors as London's premier neighborhood. All three of them were alike. Nowadays, ostentation replaced the neighborhoods' traditional decorum, and English money vied with Asian and Middle Eastern capital to buy the best townhouses, and the stratosphere wasn't a limit for prices.

Local or foreign, how was the money made?

Empires of sin.

Likely some of the mansions had been financed by the nineteenth-century opium trade and currently by oil investments.

He'd lived through it. The governing elites, Anglo-Saxon, Viking, Norman, through Victorian and modern times, had been plunderers. The scope of their depredations had grown to imperial scale as technology made their horizons global.

And the vices were commensurate with the wherewithal to obtain them. If they were discreet, Cyrus and his ilk would have been welcome visitors in some of the townhomes.

Careful, I can be righteous, but not self-righteous, Bradan thought. *I'm not pure. My gallery's art adorns these properties. I profit by catering to wealth.*

Belgravia might as well have been an architectural museum of expensive row houses devoid of humanity. Were there kids who played in the little patches of greenery mingled with the townhouses or pets that made inappropriate messes on the sidewalks?

The buildings he passed were properties rather than homes.

I live in the present tense. Bradan shoved aside ancient recollections. *I've enough to worry about right here, right now, without looking backward.*

With an unerring ability to find him, Tintagel materialized and fell into step beside him. If Bradan thought the wolf wouldn't tear his head off, he would have hugged the creature. Instead, he simply nodded a greeting, happy for company on a lonely, dangerous night.

The beast must have shadowed proceedings outside his gallery earlier in the day and had now trotted out of Hyde Park and planned to make himself at home in Bradan's temporary lodging. Bradan would have bought raw steaks for the beast, but

Tintagel had dined already on the park's unlucky swans, judging by bloody white feathers covering its muzzle.

"Making friends everywhere you go," Bradan remonstrated. "You need a bath."

The wolf seemed unrepentant. And full.

Gods, what would embassy security men think if they spotted Tintagel? Or him, for that matter. In his disheveled state, he'd look like anyone's idea of a terrorist or felon stalking the locals; he had no desire to engage further with the authorities tonight.

Though the police wanted him close at hand for further questioning, Del had advised him to clean up in her family's flat, then flee London. Bradan wouldn't flee.

So, what will I do?

When he found Del's family place, no surprise—it fit right in with the rest of Belgravia, a substantial address. Idly, he wondered which side of her family owned the place, probably her father's side who had manor homes sprinkled about the United Kingdom.

In the flat, Bradan ripped off his wretchedly filthy clothing and stuffed them into a rubbish bin. He'd have burned them if he could. Everything except the top hat.

He stood naked, surveying his temporary digs, and smiled at seeing one of his gallery's paintings, a Degas, above the mantel. The flat had a slightly musty smell of pipe smoke and dinners well enjoyed in good company, the smell of wealth. Wealth that bought his artwork.

Del had proposed borrowing her uncle's clothing. Bradan surveyed a closet full of suits and slacks. Evidently, the fellow had taken his best stuff to the Greek isles, but what was left looked warm and clean though small for Bradan's height. It would do. He'd be a conservative businessman tonight, good camouflage.

The shower felt fabulous in the flat's tiny bathroom. As the hot water ran over his body, and the blood and dried mud washed down the drain, he considered—

It was time to hit back, but after losing the Glock, all his remaining pistols were secreted about his now off-limits townhouse.

Did he want a gun?

That would be returning to a mode of life he'd left behind. Besides, a gun hadn't been enough to fend off the assault on his gallery, nor would it dissuade whatever Fae war parties came for him.

Instead, it would have to be weak magic, audacity, and friends that saw him through.

And more allies.

Mags and her spectral gang were formidable, but woefully outnumbered by the Fae queen's hordes. Even one on one, he didn't know who would win between a Fae and one of the Forty Elephants, though he was inclined to put his money on the gang member. Living and dying in the East End made one proof against almost anything supernatural or otherwise, though it wouldn't be an even fight. Based on what he'd seen during his visit to the realm of Fae, the queen commanded thousands.

And then there was Pedro and his crew. They were expanding into Europe and likely were involved in attacking his gallery last night. The drug lord hadn't forgotten him.

I need the king's help, Bradan thought. *Can I survive with both the Forty Elephants and the Fae king's forces behind me? My chances improve. In turn, the king may want my help against the queen. So, I'll bargain. To do that, I need a quiet moment to do a deal with him away from police, killers, and malevolent, magical creatures. I saw him near my gallery today. I'm tired of looking for him. He'll find me if he's interested.*

"Your company is appreciated," he told the wolf as he left the flat. "I need all the security I can get, and I reckon a Norse demon fills the bill–though, even for a demon, you do rather smell. Thanks for your help in the Tyburn last night."

Bradan had never seen the creature wag his tail. That was probably beneath him. Tonight, Tintagel appeared modestly appreciative of the praise.

"Off to Soho. If there's anywhere in the West End a Fae king can hide in plain sight, that's it."

Bradan walked out of staid Belgravia, transitioning through sedate, expensive townhomes to garish, neon-soaked Soho. Even on a crappy weekend night, it was busy, so it would be easy to lose himself in the crowds.

CHAPTER 20

Clubbing with Royalty

"**Y**ou look like David Bowie," Bradan told the Fae king. As Bradan turned onto Wardour Street, the Fae materialized at his side. He wasn't there, then he was striding along in synchrony with Bradan with supple athleticism.

The king smiled.

Was he bashful? Did he understand? Bradan didn't think the royal comprehended English and certainly he couldn't have heard of Bowie, but who knew? The supernatural being had the singer's mannerisms complete with an ultra-slender physique and a perfectly tailored velvet suit that subtly changed colors before settling back to its default hue, forest brown. He wore his broad-brimmed hat with élan, tilted rakishly low to hide his rainbow eyes and inhumanly sharp, handsome features.

The king smiled congenially at the wolf, but Tintagel kept his distance. Bradan sensed that the beast reserved judgment.

Grimy, urban Soho on the verge of gentrification was the right neighborhood for anonymity. Also, it was deep into a Saturday night; the king's appearance was outlandish, but few paid him any attention. Instead, passersby were on their own hedonistic journeys in search of ineffable, but cool, fun. Even Tintagel warranted hardly a second glance.

The exceptions were the prostitutes operating out of walkups with hand-lettered signs advertising "Models" and "French lessons given" who wandered outside to take in the night.

Usually hard to impress, the women gave the Fae lord a searching examination trying to determine whether he represented business or someone best left alone.

If Soho wasn't interested in a Fae royal, the king, in turn, was just vaguely attentive to the lights, crowds, and car horns.

Every bar washed Bradan and the king in sound as they strode past to be quickly replaced by the next establishment's cacophony. Little penetrated the royal's detachment beyond the occasional cool smile he bestowed upon a particularly interesting face passing them on the sidewalk.

Bradan gathered that the Fae must view humanity with the perspective of a skeptical ambassador.

Flurries fell as they approached the entrance to the club. A long queue of cutting-edge kids with every variation of makeup and clothing waited to pass muster from the club's security crew. This was a Saturday night ritual. He heard murmured conversations, in-the-know talk about music, style, and relationships. Someone remarked that it was dreamlike in the snow.

Bradan wondered if the king thought many of the folks seeking admittance uncannily resembled escapees from the Fae realm. All they needed to do was fly.

"Heard you had trouble at your gallery last night. Wouldn't think it in Mayfair."

It was Sue, one of the club's managers, standing solidly by the entrance, bundled against the night. She shaded her tone with sympathy.

"Neither would I," Bradan said. "That's why I live there."

"I was at your Christmas thing and now this?"

"Long story. I'm making enemies faster than I can count."

Bradan kept it casual, like barely surviving slaughter was all a joke hardly worth a smile.

Sue was flanked by huge bouncers, proof against interlopers trying to gain uninvited entrée. It was all part of sorting those with the requisite cachet from those who didn't. At the club, status wasn't defined by wealth but by appearance, whether one was known to the staff, and had something indefinable, but apparent when they saw it: bravery to be whoever you were as long as it wasn't boring.

The question now was whether Bradan with the king in tow could talk his way in. If he could, this was a refuge where no one would seek them.

"Constables are out and about," Sue said. "They've driven down Wardour twice since I got here, looking over the queue. There was a foot patrol, too, something serious going on. Probably your gallery thing."

"My fame precedes me," Bradan said. "Are we edgy enough to get in? We're desperados looking for a hideout. White's won't have us."

Sue laughed at his reference to the West End men's club with assorted prime ministers and English royalty as members, the complete antithesis of everything her Soho music dive stood for.

"Anyone with the bobbies after them is edgy enough to get in," she said.

The bouncers made way reluctantly for Bradan and the king as the rest of the long line of penitents looked on curiously, wondering why they got in with no wait on a cold January night. Some recognized Bradan as a musician, which dampened their hostility. The king diplomatically tipped his hat to the crowd.

"It's been a hellish month. I've dealt with police, media, my solicitor, and a girlfriend—two, actually."

"Two? You *do* get 'round," Sue chided. "I was you, I'd worry about settling with the girlfriends ahead of the authorities. Anyway, whoever you and your mate are running from, use one of the tables at the back upstairs. No one will pay any mind, and it'll be too noisy for eavesdropping. Someone trying to get past us at the door will have to be convincing."

"You're a lifesaver," Bradan asked. "Can I park Tintagel with your muscle here? He'll behave."

"Cor, mate, 'e'll take me leg right off," one of the enormous doormen said, backing away from the wolf. Two other doormen pressed themselves back against the entrance.

"Go on," Sue told them. "Just a puppy. Leave 'im be, though 'e does look a bit like a dire wolf."

"He's full," Bradan told the doormen. "Already dined on swan tonight. He'll be no trouble. Besides, with him around, no one will try to force their way in."

Bradan turned to Sue. "Chris around? I'll thank him again for letting us play here."

"He's somewhere. I worked last night, caught your set. Not our usual thing at all, but you added some funk to the synths. Who was the singer who sat in? She was from another place."

"She's actually local. We weren't too pop?"

"Your drops were spot on. I danced for your whole set."

"Praise indeed."

Bradan kissed Sue on the cheek and ushered the king upstairs to a back table. An American hip-hop group was performing. Young patrons danced, getting the vibe going early as the club began to fill. It was dark, perfect for a discreet tête-à-tête.

The music entranced the king, who waved his hands in time with the syncopated rhythm. For a moment, he observed, then he moved boldly out among the dancers and began to dance off the beat, more ballet by way of Saturn than hip-hop, but the Fae lord made it work with natural grace. Bradan marveled at the universal appeal of music.

With supreme irony, and as homage to London's swinging '60s discotheques, the club had created space by the stage for go-go dancers to undulate to the beat of whatever band played. Miniskirts and boots were the order of the day. In a concession to modern mores, the club had included male dancers, bare-chested in bell-bottoms alongside the women.

The king bounded effortlessly onto a pedestal between two dancers and meshed his movements with theirs. At first his new partners appeared stunned to share their tiny space, but the royal's otherworldly charisma carried the day, and soon the trio danced together as fluidly as three brooks merging into a river.

The Fae drew attention as women from the main dance floor clustered close to the Fae lord, unceremoniously dropping their partners who were left solo.

He's a personality that needs to be admired, Bradan thought.

The Fae lord distributed his attention impartially, dispensing cool smiles and reaching down from his perch to touch fingers with all of them, but somehow making each feel like his only focus. Some of the women's male companions took it well and admired their girlfriends spinning into the king's orbit, others looked visibly angry, and one big, tough-looking chap stepped forward to confront the king.

Bradan saw that the club's security had noted the brewing explosion. Two bouncers moved to intervene.

We'll be ejected before we've talked, Bradan thought.

Bradan pushed onto the dance floor and gently inserted himself between the king and his newfound paramours, motioning to club security that he'd deescalate things.

The king now focused on Bradan and leaped off the pedestal to dance around him before reaching out to touch Bradan's forehead.

"More of the mind-meld stuff?" Bradan shouted over the music. "I'm supposed to be impressed? You've shown me your civil war already. I know as much as I need to. I don't want to visit Faerie again. We're here to bargain."

However, his brain was catapulted from the dark Soho club saturated with the smell of beer and dancing bodies, to a fantastic, brightly lit forest filled with floral and herbaceous fragrances. The smells of the Fae realm and Soho collided, creating a psychedelic stew in his mind.

Bradan didn't know which reality he experienced as the club's walls melted into magical trees dressed in peculiar foliage and the human dancers became fairies, dryads, nymphs, and creatures that Bradan couldn't begin to identify. The bestiary combined whimsy and stark evil.

Music permeated the foliage that sounded like the Soho club before it shifted to something otherworldly.

Awing Bradan wasn't what the Fae king intended and the scene shifted jarringly like an art film that had jumped its tracks in an old movie projector with random, unnerving images flickering through Bradan's thoughts before settling on a celebration centered around a couple on a raised, blossom-strewn dais. They were deeply affectionate, touching each other everywhere, and barely able to restrain themselves from ripping off her diaphanous gown and his cape, doublet, and silk hose, and making love then and there amid the purple flower petals in front of a cheering, laughing throng of supernatural beings.

The air was supercharged with sexual energy, but propriety delayed lust, and the ceremony moved forward at a stately pace, sweeping the couple toward a climax, observed by a royal honor guard of Fae warriors of both genders in platinum armor, and thousands of onlookers, jostling for a better view.

Bradan was shocked to see Merlin presiding. His former mentor must have standing in the Fae realm to be afforded this honor. As Merlin had been dead for centuries, Bradan understood that he looked at a scene long past, peeking into the king's memory of a time long gone when he and the queen had loved each other and wed in front of a multitude.

Of course, the couple pledged eternal fidelity to each other. At the wedding's culmination, birds, Fae, and magical beings of every sort swept heavenward, and ceremony transitioned to celebration with all of nature joining.

Merlin faded into the background allowing the royal pair to take center stage, which they did, throwing aside their wedding raiment to couple acrobatically on the dais, first him on top, then her, then in every position. The queen somehow kept her flowered tiara on during the wild loving. The gathering of supernatural wedding guests needed no encouragement and took the cue to mate merrily amid the surrounding meadows and trees.

The following morning, men and women warriors washed away the night's excesses in nearby streams, laughing and splashing one another, then donned armor and satin, and grabbed serrated weapons. Then they dispersed to plant iridescent flowers honoring the royal nuptials in forest glens and along paths throughout the realm.

So far, so storybook.

Harmony prevailed—for a while.

However, over years, small disagreements between the king and queen loomed bigger and the flowers became thorny and carnivorous.

Transient infidelities, at first rare, became frequent and an ever growing number of partners beyond the marriage appealed to the king's and queen's attentions—and performed in their beds.

The cheating was mutual and retaliatory.

Bradan was conscious of time elapsing, eons, captured in big jumps in the wavering images the king showed him, as forests grew and withered, young mountains' jagged summits aged to rounded hills, and rivers dried to bare rocks, and the couple's affection dried, too.

Time crushed love.

Some of the paramours launched relationships with the king and queen that deepened beyond vengeful lust to love that rivaled what the royals had originally felt for each other. Political ambition mixed with affection as incandescently beautiful Fae women and phenomenally handsome men battered the royals' marriage vows and strained the realm's allegiances. As relations between the royals fouled, the realm's populace took their lead from the royals and divided themselves into hostile factions. Loyalty crumbled and the once unitary realm divided into competing tribes, some allied with the king, some with the queen, some loyal to no one.

Civil war prevailed.

Bradan reeled mentally from the discord in his mind, sublime images of a beautiful world mixed with coarse, inhuman evil.

Hate: easier than thinking, he reflected.

Which side is better? Don't be naïve! There aren't good or bad sides, only players at whatever game is at hand. That's as true in this magical realm as in the supposedly rational human world. History shuns black and white to paint in gray tones. The question isn't who's good, but who will help me? And what do they want in return?

There's a bargain to be struck, but I don't know what it is.

Amid civil war, the supernatural world ignored human affairs. Mortals were scorned except with regard to their vices, where Fae curiosity overcame ambivalence. Fairies flitted about feudal wine presses and breweries to sample. As generations passed and human civilization became ever more ingenious in finding oblivion, Fae tastes also evolved to include narcotics.

However, not all Fae succumbed to temptation. The king's followers disdained human vices and tried to convince their peers to forgo chemically induced mania and avoid contaminating their native world's purity. Besides, cocaine, ketamine, and opioids had an outsized effect on Fae behavior, turning mischievousness into savagery. Beings naturally erratic and governed by momentary impulse became monstrous as they chased their urges.

And narcotics were lighter fluid on the fiery civil war, burying any chance of truce.

Bradan observed scenes from this existential fight. Spears topped with pendants fluttered over lifeless battlefields. Someone had planted them as a rallying point for a beleaguered formation's last stand. Whatever esprit de corps the pendants had once signified was now forgotten under piles of magical beings' corpses and broken shields. Amid the bodies, he saw pieces of once pristine platinum armor shredded, punctured, and stained in rainbow shades by blood. These were enchanted battlefields, and besides the murder inflicted by physical weapons, other beings had died more horribly from enchantment, leaving not corpses but charred residue. Bradan tried not to see, but the images seeped around his closed eyes.

Periods of relative peace punctuated the warfare, but these were merely periods when the contestants recouped their strength and plotted more slaughter.

Suddenly, Bradan felt that he hung suspended between two worlds. Then, he was back in the club with sticky tables and shocked by the normality of it all. Bradan didn't know whether his visionary experiences had lasted seconds, minutes, or hours. However, the hip-hop group still played while the dancers danced and the images of a place far different than London faded and he was no longer a spectator to the king's disturbed psyche.

A waitress stepped up to their table with two Scotch and sodas.

"Sue said these are on the house."

The king waved the drinks away with aloof contempt.

"Thank Sue and give them both to me," Bradan said. Irony of ironies, he needed liquor to lubricate his dialogue with a puritan king and to recover from sharing a nightmare.

"Scotch isn't cocaine," Bradan said. "You're a prude."

He needed to negotiate. However, first he had to counter what he'd seen. The last word couldn't be that affection was pointless.

"Time doesn't crush love," Bradan said. "Not always."

He thought of Trini, Del, and Mags. And many others he'd loved over the centuries. Sometimes things had ended badly, but other relationships had been blazingly lustful at first and then settled into a slower-burning but still vibrant love.

Bradan sensed the king's skepticism.

"I'm seeing your side of things," Bradan said. "How do I know you're not as bad as the queen?"

Now the king had another image to share with him: Bradan was hurtled back to his Christmas party with Cyrus leering into his face and a 9mm pressing against his forehead. A shard of a champagne bottle came out of nowhere and effortlessly sheared through the drug dealer's neck and spinal cord, but this time instead of no discernible agent holding the sharp glass, the king wielded the razor-sharp shard like a sword and then vanished, leaving Cyrus's head to roll about on the floor.

"So, a quid pro quo," Bradan said. "You saved my life and you want an ally against the queen of Faerie."

He thinks I'm a much more powerful enchanter than I am.

Again an image appeared in Bradan's mind. This time, he was back in Stonehenge with his band performing for the megaliths. The fairy queen swept down to disrupt the performance. Then she shifted her attention to the wolf and flew down to taunt him, which elicited a volcanic reaction as the creature leaped up at her, missing grasping her in his jaws by millimeters. Even the queen had to retreat before a wolf-demon's fury.

Ah, that's humbling, Bradan thought. *He doesn't need me. He needs Tintagel's power.*

"We're a package," Bradan said. "If the wolf wants to help you, he will. I can try to persuade him, but, in return, we need to ally ourselves with you against the queen's crew. She's our common enemy."

There.

Put it out on the table and let the king decide what it was worth to get both of them.

There was a long pause. Bradan let it stretch and sipped his whisky. The king's normally animated expression became brooding and he tilted his hat brim over his eyes, an eerie noir detective. The dancers enveloped them, but now they kept their distance.

Suddenly, Bradan was swept back to the Fae realm. It took a moment for him to fight through the cognitive dissonance and let the image before him sharpen enough to make sense of. He expected more visions of drug-fueled revels or savage melees as Fae fought dryad fought water nymph. However, they had a forest glen to themselves. The king slouched against an oak and pointed about him. Bradan recognized the glen. It was on the Fae side of the portal where he'd entered on Twelfth Night from Green Park, a place as near the human world as one could get and still be in the magical Fae realm.

Except it didn't look so magical.

Bradan noted the tree against which the king leaned was dying, as were others nearby. Brown leaves hung from the branches and bark peeled unevenly off the trunks, leaving green splotches. Even in a world of weird flora and fauna, this was unnatural; it wasn't otherness, it was corruption and decay.

He smelled foul air, as bad as anything from London's East End docks in the days of coal-fueled shipping. It also smelled of diesel from buses and lorries. If Bradan were somehow able to see his lung's alveoli, he was sure they'd be blackened. He doubled over in a paroxysm of coughing. If he stayed here long, he'd be inhaling the equivalent of three packs of cigarettes.

A sudden squall drenched him and the vegetation. Without knowing how he knew, he sensed that the rain was acid.

Bradan looked beyond the oak, at the stream he remembered fording. Today, an oily sheen discolored its surface. This was worse than on his visit on Twelfth Night. Things were deteriorating quickly in Faerie. Somehow, this was part of the bargain, what the king wanted to present to him, so he stumbled deeper into the woods, picking his way through rotting leaves along one bank of the stream. Rain dappled its surface.

He wished he had Tintagel at his side, but the creature must still be standing guard outside the club in a different reality. He wandered in someone else's dream, the king's. And the Fae royal would yank him back to the Soho club or strand him here as he saw fit.

Bradan had no difficulty seeing beneath the dense overstory as large tears in the canopy illuminated the forest floor. The further he moved away from the portal, the better things looked, shifting from corruption to enchantment. It was strange and peculiar, but strange in a way he knew fit the Fae realm.

He saw a redheaded water nymph lounging on the creek bank in riparian splendor. She sunbathed nude on a black rock in a splash of light. Only a little of the filth downstream had reached her, but it was enough to foul her playground and she held a veil over her nose and mouth. Bradan smelled asphalt and petroleum and knew she'd once loved this place, but didn't in its current, corrupted condition. She stayed, perhaps remembering what it had once been.

Startled, she noticed him and flicked water in his direction, perhaps to drive him away. When he didn't retreat, she snarled, showing fangs, marring an otherwise charming visage. She'd been sensual and self-absorbed. Now she was focused on him and predatory. Bradan backed away as she stood up gracefully and moved after him with startling speed.

He intoned the first spell that came to mind: re-creating the image of the dragon he'd materialized in his gallery last night. The reptile was substantial and deadly with iridescent armor scales, knifelike teeth, and moved lithely, muscles bulging beneath the scales. Bradan smelled a strong serpentine odor.

It interposed itself between Bradan and the nymph, then lunged at her breathing violet fire.

The nymph shrieked and launched herself in a perfect flat dive into the stream to surge out of sight beneath the water, leaving a V-shaped wake behind her that sent water lapping into the creek banks, disturbing the reeds along the edge. Disappointed, the dragon sniffed at the water where the nymph had vanished, then faded away with a final puff of sulfurous, purple flame.

The Fae king clapped at the drama and saluted Bradan by touching a forefinger to his hat brim in his now familiar gesture as Bradan sat down on the stream bank, catching his breath, careful not to touch the reeking water.

"Glad you were impressed," he said. "You could have warned me about her."

The nymph had meant to kill him, but he reflected that she'd been right to be appalled at the creeping damage humans had done to her world. Bradan didn't know if she was one of God's creatures—probably not—but he did know that she recognized an existential threat and thought he was one of its authors.

So did the king, who stepped forward to run his hand through the stream with a look of utter disgust.

And just like that, Bradan found himself back in the club. Spent from the spell-making, he took a deep draft of whisky while the royal stared at him sardonically, then this expression shaded into anger. He pushed his hat back so that Bradan got the full force of his rainbow eyes, not whimsical and amused any longer, but angry and inhuman.

"I understand," Bradan said. "Our waste is seeping into your world through portals, and you want me to do something about it?"

The royal nodded.

"That's the one thing you and the queen agree on."

The king nodded again.

Bradan drained the whisky and stood up.

"You want to know whether I'm a worthy ally. Follow me. I'll do something right now."

CHAPTER 21

A Circus at Piccadilly

Bradan strolled up to the monumental fountain in the middle of Piccadilly Circus. Above him, atop the fountain, stood the youthful, metal figure of Anteros, the Greek god of selfless affection and vengeance for love spurned.

The vengeance part resonated with Bradan.

He'd use that as inspiration.

And the cause was good: calling out threats to nature.

Despite the rotten weather and late hour, thousands were stuffed into double-decker buses, cars, or walking about sightseeing, swaddled against the cold. Exhaust and a million footsteps blackened the snowy pavement.

Giant neon signage on buildings bordering the traffic circle blazed through the falling flakes. The garish light turned the snow into a psychedelic tapestry with ads for Coca-Cola, running shoes, and a multitude of other gaudy commercial enticements vying for attention. Bradan found it hideous and normally would have avoided this bit of the city, but if London had a center, this was it and he wanted an audience.

The magician spoke a dozen lines of rhyming enchantment. Tonight, Bradan used English for the spell, a modern language for a modern problem. No one would hear him in the racket.

He concentrated on tapping into a universal space, feeling dark matter and energy. This artistry would be hard. He might have to try repeatedly, so he'd have to hope his vigor held as he channeled power he'd never understood. Was quantum

180 PETER W. BLAISDELL

mechanics somehow at its root? Getting his spells right felt like solving multiple complex equations simultaneously to achieve the reality he wanted.

Above Bradan, Anteros held a bow and had just released an imaginary arrow. The god's black metal contrasted with the flurries. He was frozen forever in this pose, not destined to see what he hit, but calm nonetheless. However, under Bradan's ministrations, the statue became subtly animated and shifted his gaze to watch his missile arc over the intersecting street to hit the neon signage. The statue's expression changed to elation. Instantly, commercial content vanished to be replaced by a montage of images showing manufacturing plants vomiting smoke into the sky in brown plumes. This image transitioned into ocean scenes of sea mammals and birds trapped in black, oily gunk, then a nuclear plant with uranium fuel rods glowing greenly in water holding tanks, and then finally an image of Piccadilly Circus itself with vehicles and pedestrians packed as densely as ants moving round and round the traffic circle.

People stared. Some turned away to resume whatever they'd been doing before being disturbed by Bradan's images, but others watched and remarked on what they saw. Several cars swerved wildly, skidding in icy slush, and pigeons flapped into the night.

A group of young tourists sitting on the fountain's base next to Bradan passed bottles of beer and aquavit among themselves and gaped upward at the unexpected political messaging, and swore in Danish.

Bradan collapsed next to them, not caring that he sat on snow. One of the Scandinavians saw his exhaustion and offered him the aquavit bottle. He smiled thanks and took a long pull, feeling the liquor from his throat to his toes.

Above Bradan, Anteros sedately rearranged himself and resumed his original beatific expression. It was all image and vision, smoke and mirrors, but maybe that would nudge perceptions.

Or not.

For several minutes, Bradan simply sat, spent from the effort, but proud. It wasn't trivial enchantment.

The king sauntered up to join him, throwing an arm over his shoulders in a comradely fashion.

"I'm just a provocateur," Bradan said. "Nothing will change tomorrow. Hope that's not what you were expecting. To change all this"—he gestured weakly at Piccadilly's crush of endless traffic—"will take people willing to understand. Maybe, just maybe, I've made a few folks a little more aware. Meantime, your water nymph will need to find a different spot to catch her sun. I think things will take a while to clean up."

He turned to where the king had been and saw that he was talking to himself. There was no imprint in the snow to show that the Fae lord had ever stood there.

"You're speaking to no one, mate," one of the Scandinavians said with an accent. It made him hard to understand, but lent gravitas to his words. He spoke slowly in a baritone.

"No one," Bradan agreed.

"I do it all the time, as nobody will listen. My name's Sven. You can talk to me if you like."

"Thanks. I'm Bradan."

"I saw somebody standing beside you for an instant."

"Maybe it was the drink."

"No, he was real," Sven said. "As real as the images I just saw."

He looked toward his companions, who'd resumed communing with their beer after staring at Bradan's messaging.

"They don't see." He enunciated his words carefully. "They like to play."

"What do you think you saw?" Bradan asked. He wanted validation.

"I saw odd things, important things." He pointed up at the signage, which had reverted to its standard commercial content.

"You saw it, too?" Sven asked.

Bradan nodded. He passed the aquavit back.

"Nature needs to fight back." The Dane spoke reflectively and took a drink.

"Did your friends notice?" Bradan asked.

"They noticed, but they didn't really observe, which is a great shame."

"Then I guess it didn't work."

"There is oil along Denmark's western shore," Sven said. "On Fanø's beaches by where I live. The big ships flush their tanks out nearby. It fouls the sand."

"I've seen it," Bradan said. "It's disgusting. And that's only a tiny part of the problem."

Amid laughing and the sound of smashed glass, the man's companions lurched to their feet.

"There's a party in Marylebone," one of them shouted to Sven. Bradan understood enough Danish to make out the gist of it.

"Let's go."

A slender blond woman walked over and pulled Sven upright with some effort. She waved a greeting to Bradan and rolled her eyes as Sven leaned heavily on her shoulder.

"Come along to the party," she invited Bradan in English. "Should be good. The drugs are from Amsterdam, splendid stuff."

"Thanks, but I've made enough visions for one night."

"You see visions? You're high?"

Bradan shook his head.

"Visions even when you're not high? Quite the talent."

"I wonder about that," Bradan said.

"Well then, here, keep this." She handed him the aquavit bottle. "Quality liquor. It helps with visions. Also, it's consolation for missing a cool party. And, he's had enough." She gestured to her companion. "He sees things even when he's not in drink. He is quite the idealist. The rest of us just want to enjoy ourselves. Otherwise why come to London?"

In Danish, Sven protested the woman's hedonistic approach to life and losing his liquor.

"Did you see the images up there?" Bradan asked her, pointing to Piccadilly's neon signage.

"I did, yes. Messages replaced the ads. Now we're back to ads. I'm not sure what any of it means. I also have had quite a bit to drink and smoke tonight and things are rather fluid for me. Come, Sven, leave him the bottle."

She said this in English for Bradan's benefit.

"Yes, keep it," Sven told Bradan. "You need strong drink for the fight ahead. I don't know why, but I think you will have trouble soon."

"As you said, nature defends itself," Bradan remarked.

"Which side are you on?" Sven asked.

"The right side, I hope. Talk to your friends. See if you can make them more aware. Little steps at a time."

Bradan couldn't tell whether this registered on Sven. The tourists moved off toward the tube station.

He swirled the liquor inside the half-empty bottle and drank before leaning back to stare up at Anteros, who peered with dispassion at the traffic and dirty snow. The Greek god's wings and supernatural beauty made him a twin of some of the Fae.

Eventually, the wolf found Bradan and padded up to where he sat.

CHAPTER 22

Del Disenchanted

Bradan sat across from Del by a fireplace with a small walnut table and Earl Grey tea between them. He watched the wisps of steam coming off the tea. The sitting room was warm in a way that a fire makes a Victorian-era chamber feel on a midwinter day with frost on the windows and spring far off. After his recent bone-chilling experiences, he luxuriated in the heat.

It was quiet, too. The rest of London was outside battering the thick, century-old walls of the members-only club, but that existed somewhere else, somewhere noisy and uncouth; inside, civilized hush prevailed.

He wondered how much Del paid in dues.

Someone dropped a teaspoon on the floor across the room. Bradan tensed and looked about, but saw no threat. He willed himself to relax and settle back in his chair. He saw that Del noticed his agitation. He'd taken a roundabout route to the club, doubling back on his tracks several times, looking for someone following him. He'd seen nothing. The wolf accompanied him unconcerned. Bradan trusted that the creature's hypervigilant senses attuned to both natural and supernatural threats would alert him if anything were amiss and took comfort in this. Still, he was being hunted.

"It was performance art," Del said.

"What are you talking about?" Bradan asked, jarred out of his reverie.

"What happened at Piccadilly Circus last night. Things have gone a bit bonkers around London since your Christmas party—decapitations, murders, bombings—and now this weirdness. Evidently, someone commandeered the neon commercial signage on the traffic circle for about sixty seconds at midnight to show environmental messaging before the adverts came back on. Thousands must have seen it."

"Wonder who did it?" Bradan asked innocently. "A public service announcement? There needs to be more of those to make people aware."

"I don't know who's capable of that. Green protesters aren't technically sophisticated. They can barely make placards."

"Brings back memories of when we marched for green causes," he said.

"I've stepped away from causes thanks to my work with the practice. I don't feel proud of that."

"Could your firm sponsor pro bono legal support for some of the local groups doing environmental protests?" Bradan asked. "You won't make any money, but it might be good public relations for your law offices. Kind of pushes against the image of a stuffy bunch of lawyers in Savile Row bespoke suits on the side of oil companies."

"It's not a bad idea," she acknowledged. "I'll raise that with senior staff, can't say how they'll take it. I'll have to do it gently. However, it's something I should try so I sleep better at night. I told myself that as I progressed professionally, I'd use my influence to help things get better. Hasn't happened yet."

"We all make tawdry bargains," he said. "I've made any number of bad trade-offs over the years. You can't chastise yourself."

"Somebody tried to do some good last night," Del said. "I'm inspired by that."

"Guerilla theater on Piccadilly might be more effective than marches, but it takes a lot to change attitudes," Bradan said.

"Still, it was clever," Del said.

"Thanks," Bradan said thoughtlessly.

She looked at him sharply and set down her tea.

"You knew about it?"

"No, of course not," he said quickly. "I was awkward. I meant to say I support whoever did it, hope it made a splash."

"It rather did. It was in the *Times* and the *Guardian*, and probably next week's tabloids right beside the page three girl. I think it even got on television with news interviews of tourists and Londoners who'd seen it."

"Besides pro bono legal work, there's something else you could do to leverage your connections and support nature," he remarked.

"What's that?"

"Run for parliament."

During the following long pause, he heard spoons pinging against china tea sets and muted women's conversations around the room.

"You do say the damnedest things," she laughed. "I've never held any sort of office, nor wanted to."

Del paused again. "Actually, that's not true. Coming out of uni, I'd thought of going into politics, sort of a carryover from my student idealism. Parliament could have been the ultimate goal after getting experience on campaigns. There are members of parliament in the family going way back, so it's not beyond thinking—though none of them have been female. Anyway, these last few years, I've pressed all that aside and focused on law."

"Why not be an MP?" he prompted. "Might be more exciting than working in a stuffy firm till they pension you off—assuming you don't step on the wrong toes and get fired. You know people, people with money and influence. You've got that all thanks to your name and your own native talents. You also have the common touch, too, when you choose to use it. You could feel guilty about that, or you could deploy it for the right purposes."

"My, quite the evangelist," she said. "I'd have to dust off my ideals. I haven't used them in a while."

"Come on, crash the old boys' club," he said. "Government would be better for it."

"Thinking practically, I'm not known much beyond my circle. If I'm mentioned at all by the press, it's as a titled girl sashaying about to posh members-only places—"

"Like this one?" Bradan asked.

"Like this one," Del admitted. "Or shopping on Bond Street or in Knightsbridge before heading off to work at a ritzy London law office. Or, even worse, I'm recognized as a member of some dusty, aristocratic lineage that dates back to the Conquest."

Bradan heard unexpected bitterness in Del's voice.

"With the right publicity, that could change," he said.

He watched her. The bitterness faded, to be replaced by intrigue at his suggestion, and he saw that the idea might take root. Unconsciously, she straightened her skirt and touched her hair as if she were about to step behind a podium and address a crowd of voters.

"I'm indulging you here," she said. "But for the sake of argument, how would I get publicity? Hire some big PR firm from the city?"

"Sure, but maybe a little guerilla theater would be more effective. I wonder if whoever did that Piccadilly thing last night could be persuaded to help you—if they thought you'd use your office to protect nature. Certainly, they seem to have a flair for public display."

"Who are they? They sound illicit. I have no idea how I'd reach out to them."

"Leave that to me," Bradan said.

"You're more connected than you let on," she said.

"What makes you think that?" he asked, trying to suppress irony.

"Let's talk more about this again soon," he continued. "Meantime, I'm trying not to get blown to bits or beheaded. This is a good place to hide out. Quite the private club, books everywhere, and a chandelier."

He contrasted his surroundings with the seedy Soho dive he'd visited with the Fae king.

"Though I'm the only male in residence."

"No one will think to look for you here," Del agreed. "Membership is limited to women. It's probably the oldest women-only club in London, but they won't string you up for your gender as long as you're with a member. In this case, me."

He sipped tea. "It's like White's or the Carlton, but with too much pastel paint and more flowers—"

"Don't be mean, Bradan."

"—and fewer dusty old peers staring down from the walls."

"That's better."

"Must be a refuge for you in a man's world," he said.

"You said it. One needs that from time to time, not that I mind your company."

"Thanks," he said, hoping he didn't sound sardonic.

"And thanks for your help yesterday," he added. "I owe you a Modigliani if I ever get access to my gallery again."

None of Del's persuasive ability or connections had gotten him entrée, though he'd glanced through the shattered front windows and was flabbergasted to discover that most of the paintings and sculpture had survived intact.

Art had surprising durability in the face of terror.

It would probably take weeks and threatened lawsuits to gain him right of reentry. Not that he wanted to stay there and make himself a stationary target. He'd return when he'd sorted the mess he was in.

"Harry's an arrogant cunt," Del said. "But sometimes he's useful. Christ, I should keep my voice down. One of his exes or current girlfriends may well be here. There's no accounting for taste. He seems to have no end of woman admirers."

"Leveraging your connections helped," Bradan said. "It could have gone on forever."

"No," she said. "You were perfectly safe."

Del said this with the certainty of someone who knew exactly how things stood.

"Sir Harold Oswald would have cut it short with or without a push despite the Yard's best efforts. He wanted to get in front of that TV crew with a shot of him against a rubble strewn background while the light was still good—red meat for his Tory followers, rising star tackles domestic terrorism on the Palace's doorstep. If you didn't exist, he'd have to invent you. Though he'll need to be more subtle or his boss, the home secretary, will sense a rival and push him down a step or two."

Del looked him over.

"You've cleaned up well. And you smell better."

"The benefits of a very long, hot shower in Belgravia and your uncle's cologne. I've used your family's place extensively. I owe them for whatever cleaning is needed and for consuming every-thing edible in the pantry."

"Oh, don't be so middle class. You don't owe anyone anything. They never stay in that flat. Back to yesterday, I have to say, you played Sir Harry well with your imitation Oxford accent."

"It's not fake," Bradan said.

"What?" Del drawled out the question. "You went to Oxford? When?"

"I'm older than I look," he said.

He'd told Trini the same thing. He knew he was dancing right up the edge of revealing too much about who he was, but at this instant, he didn't care. He'd nearly drowned in a sewer while being chased by assassins and wraiths. He wasn't certain he'd survive the week even with the Forty Elephants and the Fae king's legions at his back. What did he have to lose?

Also, he was proud of his academic pedigree. He'd attended Oxford twice, during the late twelfth century when a quiet, scholarly, impractical life had been appealing after joining the Third Crusade's collision of cultures where slaughter, commerce, and piety smashed together. He'd attended the university again after the First World War, though he'd been threatened with expulsion for protesting loudly that ancient Greek should be kept on as an admission requirement.

Bradan saw that he'd piqued Del's inquisitorial instincts, but she didn't pursue his age. He was sure she'd return to it later.

Instead, she asked, "What's your plan now?"

"Stay alive. Stop them. Then go on leading my life. I like deal-ing art in Mayfair and doing my band thing."

"Bradan, it's been a complete roller coaster with you these last few weeks. I'm your friend and more. I can be your solicitor, too. On both counts, you owe me a little truth. As it is, my firm is none too comfortable with me representing you; your lifestyle seems more lurid than our usual client."

"I'm guessing that's British understatement."

"Things are going well for me where I work and I'd like to keep it that way, but they don't like noise. It doesn't bring them the kind of business they want."

"There probably aren't many women in senior positions," Bradan said.

"Now that's understatement," Del replied. "There are exactly three of us among three dozen senior people. Also, they've never been too keen on the Sephardic bit."

"Your mother's side of the family?"

Del nodded.

"At the risk of making another understatement," he said. "You don't get ahead by making scenes."

"You understand the finer points of corporate culture in the city's big law offices. You're charged with nothing at the moment, but the authorities can't let random heads get chopped off and a nice West End townhouse be pulverized without reacting—"

"And," he prompted.

She smiled thinly. "And you're all the Yard and the security services have got. If nothing else, they'll claim you're disturbing the peace or creating a public nuisance. They'll bring you in on something or other. If I'm to defend you, let's be a little more forthcoming. So, we'll start with who 'them' is. Who's after you and why?"

Bradan considered. Old instincts for secrecy reasserted themselves. He'd reveal the smaller lie to hide larger truths. Describing a life of crime would be more comprehensible than talking about a menagerie of vengefully magical creatures and intervening in a supernatural marital dispute. Also, there was no way he could explain that he'd survived fifteen centuries, but only looked thirty years old without seeming utterly mad.

"I lived all over," he said. "You know that, but most recently in Miami before coming to London. I had a good life—dealing art like now—but I also used planes to transport marijuana, across the Caribbean into South Florida."

He watched her to see how she took this in. Del sipped tea and looked right at him without flinching.

"I didn't know you were an entrepreneur and pilot. A man of many talents."

"Talents? Maybe, though, if I'm honest, I'm sure greed was a motivation, too. And the excitement. It was thrilling. If it helps, I didn't intend to transport anything harder than pot—which will be legal someday—so I didn't see the harm. I was good, but my reputation got me noticed by the wrong people and I wound up forced at gunpoint into ferrying a huge shipment of cocaine, tons of the stuff. Long story, but I was able to jettison it into the ocean."

"That lost someone a pile of cash," Del said.

"It's a morning for understatements," he said. "Many, many millions' worth of product went into the Atlantic."

"And I thought a little powder at your parties was as far as it went," she said.

"I barely drink these days. Those men who peddled coke and angel dust weren't invited. When one of them died—the head rolling out the window—someone higher up must have heard about it and remembered an old score that needed settling."

"You do have a way of collecting enemies. Besides psychopathic traffickers, the Yard is rather interested in you, too."

"I can't see how my Miami misadventures years back give the London police anything to press charges on now—that Young bastard tried to intimidate me by implying he'd use it some-how, but I was never arrested, let alone convicted of anything in Florida. That's all ancient history."

As he said the last line, it occurred to him—not for the first time—that much of his life was ancient history obscured by endless deceit.

"I think you're right legally," Del said. "Though a checkered past doesn't buy you credibility with the authorities."

"What about you? Do you believe me?"

"I'd say I believe *in* you. Whether I believe your stories or not, I'm not sure. Oxford?"

"I *did* go to Oxford years back," Bradan said. "I'm just well pre-served. And well educated. Those were good years at university."

"We'll leave your educational pedigree aside for the moment. Who's the girl?"

"Trini."

Bradan didn't have to ask who Del meant. Now he wished he could replace the tea with vodka.

"You've referred to her in passing since I've known you," Del said. "I thought it was over, whatever 'it' might have once been. Yet she jetted over here from Miami—surprise, surprise—to visit. She embraced you yesterday. I'd say it was a fairly warm embrace."

"It surprised me, too," Bradan said.

"Her visit or the embrace?"

Del looked at him over the rim of her china cup, prolonging the silence until he replied.

"I'll try to be forthcoming," he said.

I'm saying that, but I don't know if I can, he thought.

"I believed Trini was in the past," he said. "It burned hot—very hot—for a while when I was in Florida, but now I'm here and the relationship didn't survive four thousand miles of separation."

"She told me sort of the same thing," Del said.

"You're checking that our stories match? I like you both—a lot—and I didn't think it would come to a choice."

"Lady Alexander, not laboring away at the law offices?" An older woman stood before them. She bent to hug Del.

"To be continued," Bradan said.

"Damn right we'll continue," Del said.

The woman who'd interrupted them was dressed in an expensive-looking, cream-colored dress with a blue belt. Bradan assumed this was weekend casual for a certain set. Her brown hair was beginning to shade into gray. Probably she was at the point of deciding whether to use hair color.

"It's Sunday," Del said. "Occasionally, I take Sundays off. Don't tell my firm's senior members. Tamara, this is Bradan Badon; Bradan, this is Tamara Hancock Livingston. She does something or other for some legal business or other. I always forget what, but it sounds important."

"Patent law for Struggles and Winthrop," Tamara said. "Terribly exciting."

Bradan heard the deadpan tone and saw her exchange glances with Del, sharing the unspoken community of professionals doing work they loathed.

Then Tamara turned back to assess him.

"Couldn't place your name, but now I remember. You hosted the holiday bash where someone literally lost his head. Quite the party trick."

"It wasn't amusing at the time," Bradan said. "I'm notorious throughout London, it seems. At least I'm not boring, but I'm hoping to bring a little quiet back into my life."

"Sorry," Tamara said. "I'm sure that's not the way you want to be introduced. I spend all my time poring over patents, so I've lost my manners. You should see me when I'm in drink."

Clearly casting about for some new tack, she asked, "You're a musician?"

"It's that obvious?"

"Not in a bad way, the longish hair, a certain outlaw look. Also, I think I've seen you play on MTV."

"I peddle art mainly, but, yes, I've also got a group—pop-dance stuff."

"His music is super good," Del said. Bradan felt thrilled about Del endorsing his work.

"I didn't think you listened to that sort of music, Tamara."

"I don't," the older woman said flatly. "My daughters do." She turned to Bradan again. "You were on a music video recently. They called me over to the telly to show me. It was like a bad Fellini film."

"At Stonehenge?" Bradan asked. "That sounds like us. What did you think of the song?"

He didn't want her to believe he needed validation, but, despite himself, he wanted an opinion outside of Silicon Saturday's usual demographic. Fae enjoyed his stuff. What would a supercilious West End blue blood think?

"What I heard of it was catchy and interesting," Tamara said. "I didn't expect to like it, but I did."

"Thanks. I didn't want to create more Europop. I wanted to make something better than that, more intricate, but still danceable."

"Besides the music, you're a photogenic bunch," Tamara said. "That's got to help in the entertainment business. I suppose I should ask for an autograph. My daughters will be thrilled."

While Bradan signed the back of one of the club's tea menus, Tamara checked her watch.

"Got to leave for a lunch date with hubby. Things have hit the rocks recently. We eat together rarely, so I can't let this go if I want to keep the peace. I've taken enough of both of your time. Del, we'll catch up soon."

Tamara blew air kisses at them and then strode across the sitting room toward the entrance.

"Wow," Del said. "I knew you played as a side thing. I didn't realize you were making a name for yourself. I'm flabbergasted that Tamara heard of you. Should I get an autograph, too?"

"Just buy our CDs," he said. "Besides the gallery, my music's another reason I'm not going to be chased out of London. The Saturdays are getting a reputation."

Bradan heard a rustle of fabric behind him and saw Del's puzzled look as she stared over his shoulder.

"I'm not sure who that is," she said. "She isn't a member or I'd recognize her. One of the staff, I suppose, but unusually dressed. I'm surprised they let her come to work that way like some ghost of Christmas past. And why's she fixated on us? Another one of your many paramours?"

Without looking, Bradan knew who was behind him. He set his tea down and shifted around in his chair.

Mags.

She'd dressed for the occasion wearing her pale-green taffeta dress. Several women chatted at the far end of the room. However, no one noticed her.

Mags regarded Bradan and Del with her trademark arched eyebrows and knowing smirk. In daylight, in a well-lit room, she was beautiful, though her pale skin was nearly transparent. She'd now made good on her promise to inspect both of his love interests. He suspected she'd opine on their respective merits the next time he met her privately.

Bradan got up and approached the phantom, but she swept away toward the front entrance and around a corner into a hallway.

Out of sight of the rest of the room, she faced him.

"Won't interrupt, luv. Seems like you were getting to the 'eart of the matter about where things stand between you."

"You listened," he said, letting his irritation show.

"Only for your best interests, luv."

She blew him a kiss before fading from view.

"At least she could have brought more tea," Del said when he sat down again.

"She preferred gin," Bradan said.

CHAPTER 23

Lethal Whimsy

Weak magic was all he had.

Audacity might let him find the Fae realm's gateway unnoticed, or get him killed.

Friends might would help him—or not.

Back in Green Park, off the paths, Bradan and the wolf explored the secluded spot where he'd first entered Faerie on Twelfth Night.

"Find the portal," Bradan told the wolf.

The beast looked at him like he was crazy.

"Yes, it's mad, but negotiating didn't work, so I'm hitting back. That feels good. Maybe the king will help, maybe he won't."

The wolf looked mildly intrigued.

"But we won't wait. Time for a surprise attack. It's on us to finish the mess."

He regarded the wolf.

"Trust your instincts. If you want no part in this, go home."

Now Tintagel looked affronted at having his boldness impugned.

"I don't see the gateway. You're better at this than me. It's hidden or people would stumble on it and wander through uninvited."

The wolf began nosing among the trees.

February rain barely above freezing had melted most of the snow, leaving mud and last fall's sodden leaves. They were black litter on the ground. Hard as Bradan tried to muffle his footsteps, the mud made sucking sounds as he stepped between the trees. He disturbed the quiet glade and he believed things listened; all the more reason for urgency.

Bradan had chosen twilight for his mission because the park would be deserted in the deepening gloom and raw weather. He stared about the glade, amazed that London's most civilized park filled with prams and sunbathers in summer and well-bundled strollers in winter could take on a primal aspect tonight. The trees were normally well spaced in arranged groupings making them easy to see between—no activity in the park could be hidden—but now they pressed together into a first-growth stand.

Green Park was odd tonight.

He'd have to rely on the beast's preternatural senses to detect the gateway; the Fae king had been his guide when he'd last visited, but it was beyond Bradan to spot the whisper of violet light between two trunks on his own. Every tree looked the same. Was the portal always present and just very hard to locate, or did Fae materialize it from the ether for their convenience?—in which case not even Tintagel would be able to detect it.

If they could find it, Bradan's plan was simple: disable it and cut off Fae incursions at their source.

He'd throw magical sand in the gateway's gears.

To do that, he'd have to create the right enchantment, and he didn't know if he was a potent enough mage to do it. He had no idea what would work; he'd have to improvise. However, if he succeeded, he'd kill two birds with one stone: stop Fae marauders from invading London and halt the seepage of human pollution into the fairies' realm. Both worlds would benefit; they never should have connected to begin with.

He was certain there were other supernatural gateways scattered around the globe, but Green Park's portal facilitated two-way traffic into one of most densely populated urban areas on the planet with ill effects for everyone. In time, he would spike the rest.

Bradan could have asked for the Fae king's help. They'd parted on what he assumed were good terms after Bradan's pyrotechnics on Piccadilly Circus, but he had no idea what the king might think of severing the connection between worlds. Best do this job on his own.

Darkness came on quickly and Bradan soon couldn't see anything beyond black tree trunks closest to him. The wind blew their branches together, making clicking sounds like skeleton fingers playing castanets.

There'd be no moon tonight. Any celestial illumination was hidden by low clouds that had a bilious tint illuminated from below by London's nighttime lights. The clouds looked like the bellies of dead fish. To make visibility worse, fog covered everything at ground level, wrapping around the trunks and penetrating his clothing.

Bradan's peripheral vision registered faint, luminous figures among the trees. At first they were half hidden and blended with the mist and night, elusive and passive. Then they moved forward brazenly. He saw that he had an audience of specters of every ethnicity and age. All of them must be connected to the park in death. If they hadn't died here, maybe this was a treasured place during their earthly existence, perhaps the best memory they'd ever had.

Their contrasts jarred him, spanning millennia from Neolithic hunter-gatherers, to Viking and Norman warriors in mail leaning on spears and shields, to eighteenth-century aristocrats, to modern, summer sunbathers. He sensed the apparitions sought to alleviate afterlife's tedium by amusing themselves with the pending fight.

Even in death, especially in death, the phantoms retained their character from life. A hunter carried a small deer slung over his shoulders, game destined for a cooking fire, and the aristocrats preened and primped in their silk finery.

They kept to their own with no mixing between different eras.

The prejudices of tribe and class follow even unto death, Bradan thought.

Usually, the world of human ghosts and Fae didn't merge, ships passing in the night. Fairies had scant interest in human death or what came after. Though Fae occasionally teased living humans, how could they trouble the dead beyond the torment these spirits already experienced? And how could specters haunt beings with no souls?

Tonight was different.

And he'd be the star of this drama for everyone's jaded entertainment.

"Whose side are you on or do you care?" he asked the gathering shades.

Of course they didn't respond. He hadn't expected them to. However, he felt their malevolent interest.

"Damn your eyes," he shouted.

The fog muffled his voice. As when he'd visited the park on Twelfth Night seeking to negotiate a truce, London's sounds were deadened as if whatever happened here was shielded from unwanted attention and enchantment would be given freedom to reign undisturbed.

He was at the nexus of three worlds: the modern West End, the ghostly afterlife, and the realm of Fae. He connected the three.

The wolf yipped to get his attention. And sure enough, through the dark and murk, Bradan saw the familiar violet shimmer barely distinguishable from the general gloom. Tintagel confronted the portal like he challenged a rival and Bradan joined the beast. Behind them, he heard murmurs, and the crowd of phantoms moved closer, anxious for a better view.

The portal somehow sensed that it was being watched and condensed into a slit that stretched from the ground to the tree-tops. Bradan caught indistinct visions of the Fae realm on the other side and saw movement. They must see him standing in Green Park. The portal created a bridge between worlds and allowed a sinuous brook to flow from the Fae realm into Green Park and lap about his feet.

Tonight, the membrane was porous and formed no barrier to free movement between realms. Bradan felt warm air brush against his cheek and swirl his hair. It was always summer in Faerie. Light flooded out of the portal, illuminating the glade and contending with London's fog and darkness. The gateway breathed, inhaling the city's diesel exhaust and exhaling nature's fragrances from the Fae realm. He heard fairy music swirl through the gateway like an electric guitar's highest notes, off the fretboard, stretched out like taffy.

His senses were saturated.

The scene was surreal, sensual, and intense.

"Now or never," Bradan told Tintagel.

The wolf looked encouraging.

As quickly as he could, Bradan intoned a complex set of twelve stanzas that he hoped would disturb whatever other-worldly physics made the gateway function and decompose it into quantum fragments.

His first try made it shimmer slightly and the color shifted from violet to angry red before settling back to its original hue.

The multitude of spirits laughed at him.

Despite his exhaustion, Bradan whirled around to shout vulgarities at them. A Viking grasped his crotch and sent his tongue lolling obscenely while clutching his spear for support as he doubled over with ghostly mirth. An eighteenth-century lady in voluminous skirts giggled behind her fan and gestured to encourage a chorus of hilarity from her companions and mock reproach from her male consort as he inhaled a pinch of snuff. The sunbathers yawned as they lounged at ease among the dead leaves.

Bradan turned back to the portal, mustered his energy, and switched two of the stanzas around to create a different rhyming structure to his spell and intoned it again. This time the gateway didn't respond at all.

He threw pebbles at a brick wall.

Once again the ghostly gallery hooted and hurled insults in dialects going back centuries: Saxon, Old Norse, and Latin. Bradan understood them all. Worse, the specters began to drift away and fade into the fog and night, the ultimate insult, bored by his botched efforts. A poor performer at the old Wilton's Music Hall couldn't have fared worse.

Unlike the disdainful apparitions on his side of the portal, Bradan's attempts at sabotage had roused a wasp's nest in the Fae world. The portal undulated drunkenly and the queen arrived suddenly followed by her legions tumbling through the tall gateway in a flying, prancing, raging mass. The pack stretched the narrow portal, forcing themselves through and clawing to enter the park glade in a macabre parody of birthing.

At first, Bradan couldn't distinguish individual entities in the violet haze and fog and darkness. He only saw claws, wings, arms, and heads. These quickly resolved themselves into individual magical beings wearing elaborate, diaphanous raiment, or sturdy armor, or nothing at all. He even saw a few fairy-tale winged Fae fluttering among their fellows. They matched storybook clichés meant to amuse children—except for the eyes, which stared with carnivore intensity.

Everyone surged across the glade toward him.

The queen floated above her horde. The royal's appearance was as graceful and deranged as the first time he'd seen her. Tonight, he thought her pointed ears were more demonic than elfin.

A flower tiara perched on her head at an odd angle and she wore only a simple, silk shift blowing about her immodestly as the warm breezes of Fae collided with London's wintery, dank air. Bradan guessed she'd been interrupted dressing before a looking glass.

I'm the interruption, he thought.

He laughed at himself and at her to snap his infatuation.

Two tiny, winged beings attended the queen. They fluttered about working to straighten her crown and arrange her dress, but in their headlong rush through the gateway, they only succeeded in ripping the garment off. Now the royal attendants competed with each other to catch the shift before it hit the mud below. Grasping it simultaneously, they wrenched and tore at it until the sheer garment ripped in two with each little Fae holding a fragment of the once elegant garment. The queen murmured a curse and both the competing fairies and the silk remnants disappeared in puffs of umber smoke to the amusement of her warriors.

The queen paid no more attention to this drama and swept forward.

I had to wreck the portal fast, he thought. *Didn't happen. Now what? Weak magic and audacity failed. I need friends.*

And I have a few more tricks to play.

The wolf had sensed the coming onslaught, and, with spring-trap reflexes, leaped away from the portal, and then, with a supernaturally agile twist, reversed course midair and flew back at the leading Fae, scattering them. Some of the Fae wore ornate platinum armor, but this was no proof against Tintagel's savagery, and arcs of blood and whatever passed for internal organs among them flew about the glade. Men might struggle to fight Fae, but a primeval demon could do immense damage. Still, there was only one of him and hundreds of Fae invaders.

Their very numbers created clumsy compression at the portal's narrow mouth, and elemental blundered into dryad, Fae tripped over water nymph, all of them moving with quicksilver speed that hindered coordination.

Observing the chaos, the queen swooped low to arrange her battalion, orchestrating the action and turning the seething mob into a military formation.

She can kill me herself with enchantment, he thought. *But she'll let her warriors eviscerate me. More fun.*

To that end, she assigned two dozen Fae warriors to linger near the portal's entrance. They clearly wanted to join the fray, gesturing angrily at Bradan, but held their assigned positions from fear of their liege lord.

Reserves in case the king's forces make an unexpected appearance, Bradan thought.

A tall tree behind him exploded in flames as a fire elemental ignited the branches and residual leaves from last autumn. Despite being sodden from snow and rain, it burned in a merry inferno stretching up into the clouds. Bradan suspected the elemental's spell was meant to immolate him rather than the tree, which was part of the park flora and therefore sacred.

Bradan leaped away from the heat and used the distraction to snap off a spell. This time, he made no mistake and his magic worked, materializing a pack of vividly realistic saber-toothed tigers that promptly set upon the Fae menagerie. Saliva dripped from their mouths and he felt their breath and heard their snarls as they swept past him. However, unlike the wolf, these were mere fantasies without substance and had no power to rend their prey, so their ability to intimidate was lost in an instant as their teeth and claws had no effect on the queen's company. After momentary panic, the Fae simply ignored them.

"This will help."

A bearded man thrust a spear into his hands. Bradan saw that he'd been given a weapon by the spectral Viking who'd obscenely mocked him moments earlier.

"You cannot die without a spear in your grip," the Viking said. "Valhalla will not accept you." He pointed at the Fae. "You'll find they don't like sharp iron."

The warrior had spoken in Old Norse, but the voice was Sven's from a few evenings earlier at Piccadilly Circus. Bradan would probe that mystery later—if he lived.

Despite being a gift from a phantom, the weapon felt solid in his hands. Bradan was desperately fatigued from spell-making, but the spear's sturdy yew wood strengthened his grip and revitalized him. It had seen many battles. So had he.

A dryad was the first to get to him, pushing aside other Fae to strike and win the queen's praise. The creature was half tree, half Fae, and loomed over him tall and skeletal with brown bark. It tried to rend him with its branches. Bradan's instincts surfaced from warfare over his long life and he felt strong. He blocked the dryad's grasping, clawed hand from gutting him with his spear's butt, then reversed the weapon and stabbed forward with the point, using his shoulder muscles. The rusted iron tip gored the creature's thick wood midsection, toppling it over backward in a pile of leaves, splinters, and flailing limbs which smashed into other magical beings, momentarily clearing space before him. He heard wood shriek. Instantly, dozens more took its place and Bradan surged forward, taking the fight to them, leaping over the barky body of the dying dryad to get at the next wave of Fae warriors.

When outnumbered, attack.

As he fought, Bradan was conscious of his hypocrisy. He'd been squeamish about packing a gun and resuming Miami habits from the cocaine wars. Yet he felt butchery's visceral joy as he lunged and parried expertly at scores of magical entities closing in. He remembered times long gone when a sword or spear solved many of life's challenges; he remembered times when morality didn't get in the way of killing—it wasn't so different now. The Viking was right: The spear's iron tip ripped and tore through Fae attackers, but the queen's magical warriors simply replaced entities that he impaled or smashed with the butt end of his weapon.

Let them come!

Brute violence is ecstasy, but I'll be smart, too, or I won't survive.

Time for another trick, a distraction.

Can I work a spell and fight at the same time? Not usually.

As he stabbed, he yelled out a brief couplet.

A cloud of powder materialized about him and spread over the glade, sparkling in the portal's light. The light from the Fae side of the portal created tiny diamonds against the glade's black backdrop. It looked like cocaine, but it was no more real than the sabertooths. Nonetheless, the Fae stopped attacking him for a moment and leaped after the fake narcotic trying to inhale it. The clearing became a rushing cyclone of magical beings looking for the drug's intense rush and to hell with the lingering descent afterward.

The queen realized the ruse and waved her hand, causing his powdery vision to vanish.

Adding to the chaos, many phantoms lingered amid the fog and trees. Finally, there was action to capture their attention. Unlike humans, who usually couldn't see specters, the Fae raiders could see them, but didn't know the nature of these apparitions or whether they were friend or foe. Bradan was thrilled to see this confused the fight as they flew at the indistinct specters. In turn, most of the ghosts appeared oblivious to any threat the Fae posed. However, some took it as sport to harry the magical creatures and, since neither party was ground-bound, the supernatural conflict spiraled into the night over the park.

Bradan recognized the ghost of the woman he'd talked out of killing herself in Rosamond's Pond two centuries before. She was accompanied by the old aristocrat who'd escorted her along the park's promenade. They'd stayed together in death.

Love or lust, at least, can last! he thought.

Both enthusiastically cheered him on. The marquis drew his rapier and thrust at passing Fae, but dropped the weapon. The woman promptly picked it up and, unhampered by her gown, swept into the air lunging strongly at passing Fae with the thin, flickering blade. Bradan would take all the support he could get.

Amid his mad, thrusting battle with the spear, Bradan saw the burning tree behind him was close to falling. Its wet wood smoldered and sent out clouds of choking smoke. Its trunk had burned halfway through and what remained was charred and flaming with an orange border around blackened bark as the fire ate away at the heartwood. He dodged a fiery branch that smashed into the ground in front of him. If the whole thing went over in the wrong direction, it would crush him and Tintagel, so if it had to topple, he'd guide its fall: into the portal.

Will that smash the gateway?

He remembered collapsing the chain link fence at Stonehenge. He could attempt it here. The magical principles were the same, though the scale of the effort to push over the tree would be a hundredfold what he'd done at Stonehenge. He'd need gallons of luck. Despite his furious efforts to stab at a dozen magical entities crowding in on him, Bradan shouted out the spell, attempting to visualize the direction he wanted to guide the tree in. He pictured a giant's hand impervious to fire nudging the tree to fall toward the portal.

Bradan clung to his spear as exhaustion hit him from the magic-making and the incessant fighting. If he let go, he'd never stand again.

Above him, the tree wavered, struggling to maintain itself upright, then succumbed to gravity. The flaming inferno collapsed into the violet portal in a snapping, popping mass, falling perfectly through the slit. The queen must have determined what he planned, but whatever preventive enchantment she mustered was too late.

Bradan didn't know what to expect from the impact—cataclysmic explosions, violent fountains of energy flung about the glade—but the result was anticlimactic, though effective. The gateway quietly collapsed in on itself, the burning tree's fire guttered, and its remnants vanished. The myriad fairies and assorted supernatural entities, living and dead, were sucked back into their Fae realm, and earthly phantoms took their leave by vanishing into Green Park's fog and gloom.

The aristocrat retrieved his rapier from his mistress, sheathed his sword, and bowed deeply at Bradan. Together they faded into the trees. Bradan heard the woman's light laughter linger for a moment after the couple departed.

Bradan looked around the glade and saw that slivers of the portal remained like pieces from a shattered mirror. It might still connect worlds. Violet fragments were situated at odd angles amid the trees.

Can it mend itself? he wondered.

The queen departed last. Her hair was singed and there were sooty smears over her body. The gateway's implosion had touched her.

The royal turned and floated into the portal's remnants back to the Fae realm.

"I'll be waiting," he yelled after her.

As at Stonehenge, Bradan knew that nothing was over.

He saw her flower tiara in the mud. Its daisies still looked nice. There were other flowers he didn't recognize.

The portal remained. However, the night hadn't been wasted. He now understood that violent physical assault damaged it. More-powerful violence might destroy it.

The question was: Where could he find a weapon in London sufficient to do that?

Bradan held on to his spear for support, drained by the fight and his enchantments. He heard sirens converging on Green Park. London had awakened to eerie happenings, and city sounds were no longer muted, but emergency personnel had no clue what had gone down.

He sat in the mud and let the spear fall at his side. He felt water seep into his pants and didn't care. He wanted to lie down, but the ground was too cold.

"That must be the bloke in those trees over there."

Two constables wearing raincoats approached from the nearest path using flashlights to illuminate him. They paused for a moment to take in the scene. However, there was nothing much to see, no bodies, a few branches down and some shredded foliage. The one real token of a violent fight was a large, ragged stump, but the rest of the tree was gone.

"You'll have to come with us, sir," the nearest constable said. "You can't sit here all night. You'll catch the death. And we've got questions for you."

"You don't think that I had anything to do with any sort of disturbance," Bradan said weakly.

"We don't know what to think," the policeman's partner said. "You're the only one 'ere. Can of petrol and some matches makes anyone feel like a bloody pyro."

"Do you see a petrol can?" Bradan asked. "Or a fire, for that matter?"

"Not at the moment, but we've had reports. Is that a spear? Looks like blood or something on it."

Bradan shrugged. "See for yourself."

The constable stooped to pick up the weapon and hefted it.

"Do some damage with this, mate," he said.

"Do you see anyone damaged?" Bradan asked.

"Likely he's without a home and wanted a fire to keep 'isself warm on a wretched night," the first constable said to his partner. "The spear's for game. He's a regular survivalist."

"Surviving has been tough recently," Bradan said.

"Be that as it may, we can't have you carryin' a weapon about Green Park in the small hours. We'll need to take you in."

"You haven't a home nearby, have you?" his partner asked.

"I've got two," Bradan said, deadpan. "I'm staying in Belgravia while my place in Mayfair is being fixed."

"Two West End properties. You don't seem the sort."

"I surprise people. Listen, gentlemen, I was out for a stroll with my pet—yes, I know, bad weather for it—and I wandered off the path and slipped in the mud. So, I'm a bit the worse for wear. I haven't seen any disturbances or a fire. I don't know whose spear this is and tonight's not the time for yet more interviews with the forces of law and order."

"'Ere, that tone ain't called for—"

Bradan looked about him at the glade. His strength was returning. He didn't see the wolf.

"Tintagel!" he bellowed. "A little help."

The beast responded by wailing loudly enough for the call to reverberate throughout the park. The sound came from nearby underbrush by way of a frigid Norse hell where old gods still ruled and demons and heroes fought endlessly on twilight ice fields spilling blood that froze before it hit the ground.

Bradan used the ensuing constables' panic to slide into the trees and quickly put distance between him and the clearing. Visibility was abysmal, but he was still careful to keep the densest stands between him and the police. He doubted that anyone would try to chase him down in the fog and night with an eerie predator on the loose.

Close to the park's border and near Half Moon Street, Bradan slowed to a comfortable walk as Tintagel appeared out of the trees and sauntered along at his side.

No doubt, word of this disturbance would get back to Chief Inspector Young, but the constables were clearly shaken by the wolf's howl, so neither would be a reliable witness to identify him. Besides, what could they charge him with? Getting lost in Green Park in bad weather? There was a blackened tree trunk in the glade where he'd confronted the Fae legion, but no proof that he'd caused the destruction. And bodies of fallen Fae raiders that he and the wolf had killed had vanished back through the damaged portal. If it came up—very unlikely—he'd deny any knowledge of the spear.

He looked himself over. His muddy clothes were in tatters and he bled from several wounds. The wolf also had a gash along his flank. He spotted drops of blood on the path behind him. He supposed this might make tracking him easier, but the blood was already vanishing in the drizzle as if he'd never spilled it.

From experience, Bradan knew that his and Tintagel's cuts would heal quickly. They'd survived worse.

"My place is still a crime scene," Bradan said conversationally to the beast. "They'll have a car watching it. Won't do them any more good than it has in the past. We'll get right around them. Once we're inside, we can't use the flat's lights, of course, and the ground floor gallery will still be a wreck, but the upper stories should have survived well enough. We'll crank the heat. I'm sleeping in my own bed tonight. You've got your usual spot by the bay windows. Or take the chaise longue if you want it."

Leaning against a tree in the park's deep shadows and mist, Bradan noticed the Fae king. The royal touched a forefinger to his hat.

CHAPTER 24

Problematic Allies

Pedro had failed and it wasn't a dream.

He struggled to arrange his thoughts and plan ahead as he paced through Green Park on a sunny winter afternoon. The bad weather had finally broken and it was cold, but clear. Much of the West End took advantage and ambled along the park's paths in couples or family groups. They walked dogs or pushed strollers, and joggers squished by on the still-sodden ground, dodging piles of melting snow, puffing little clouds of mist.

The improving weather didn't dispel Pedro's bleak mindset. He'd sent Marco to accompany the Russian ex–security-service killers hired to eliminate Bradan, but Marco had barely survived to relate the disaster, wounded in the shoulder and thigh, and shaken by a nightmarish chase through London's storm sewer system plagued by mirages and echoes—hard to imagine someone as dead to perception as Marco being traumatized by a hit, even a hit gone terribly wrong. Harder still to understand how Bradan wasn't dead with his guts torn out by a burst of submachine gun fire and then a bullet to the skull to make sure. The Russians did this for a living and—he'd worked with them before—they never fucked up.

Until now.

Pedro had reviewed their plan himself and couldn't fault its simplicity and boldness: thorough reconnaissance of Bradan's gallery on Half Moon Street to understand the target, then direct, sudden action to breach the reinforced art gallery door with plastic explosives before chopping him in half with a hail of gunfire. Bad weather would help the plan, so they'd timed their attack to coincide with a nighttime snowstorm. The killers' preparatory observations had alerted them that police surveyed Bradan's flat. They would be lured away before the hit. They'd also seen that Bradan owned a fearsome dog, but bullets would finish the pet off as surely as they murdered Bradan.

The killing would be loud enough to draw scads of attention thanks to proximity to Buckingham Palace and the status of the neighborhood—members of the British elite lived close to the assault. But that was the point: broadcasting to the world and particularly local competitors in the illicit narcotics trade that crossing Pedro resulted in a messy death. Further, if Bradan's art gallery was a front for drug distribution, exacting vengeance would simultaneously rid him of an individual who'd destroyed tens of millions in cocaine dumped into the Atlantic Ocean and remove a business rival.

Everything had been thought through.

Yet they'd failed. He'd failed.

Two Russians had died. However, they were men without names; MI5 could investigate till hell froze over and never be the wiser about their identities or who'd hired them. Three more assassins were wounded, evidently from their own gunfire as they'd panicked and shot wildly in a pitch-black, stony catacomb that ricocheted bullets back at them. Marco had suffered the same fate. Bloodied and terrified, they'd managed to retreat back through the gallery, dragging themselves to Half Moon Street where they'd been picked up by a backup vehicle before the police arrived in force. Survivors recuperated in an inconspicuous flat in Uxbridge under the care of a doctor Pedro had hired.

As someone who prided himself on being a business strategist, he planned for success, but prepared in case the wheels fell off. The Uxbridge flat had been used to coordinate the hit and now served as an infirmary and safe house. Money kept the landlord happy and quiet.

Bradan had survived without a scratch to be the defiant hero of the attack. There were a thousand media pictures of him amid every flavor of police investigator imaginable along with various high government officials.

If Pedro had wanted loud, he'd certainly gotten that by bringing the Miami cocaine wars to Mayfair. His sole satisfaction was that Bradan, despite being the victim of this assault, was now also suspected of involvement in London's burgeoning narcotics trade thanks to his checkered past in South Florida.

Pedro could have waited for the Fae queen to work her dark arts. However, maybe she didn't exist and he'd imagined that night in Green Park in a cocaine-fueled dream. Everything about that episode was weird in the extreme. Still, the corpses of his three bodyguards had been real before they'd been unceremoniously dumped into some hellish netherworld to vanish from this earth.

Assuming the peculiar supernatural creature he'd chosen to partner with was real, she'd been no more successful than he'd been, or at least she hadn't come to claim the keys of coke as spoils for dispatching Bradan.

So, eliminating Bradan and cornering the United Kingdom's market for narcotics were no nearer than they had been when he'd flown into Heathrow on a Concorde several weeks back. The flight had taken just three hours. That was efficiency. He needed to emulate that efficiency.

In his business, failure was inexcusable. Since he was the top of the reporting chain in his organization, no one could fire him. Still, word had gotten around to competitors in other cartels that he was working to expand his European footprint starting in London. Not making progress toward that goal so he could broadcast triumph to his peers risked his credibility and would inevitably be taken as weakness. He could expect emboldened rivals encroaching on his operations and working to eliminate him.

Pedro looked about at the park's fields and trees bordering the paths. To him, it was far too chilly to sunbathe, but with the English, one never knew, though he saw no one braving the elements in summer clothing today. At that moment, he didn't miss Miami's beaches—they were simply a typical feature of that city—but he did miss the girls who hung out there. In Green Park, every woman was swaddled in layers of coats, scarves, and gloves. It gave them an androgynous quality, but he'd be back in Miami on the first Concorde he could book once Bradan had been removed and his nascent European drug distribution organization was on firm footing. For that to happen, he needed the Fae queen's help, problematic ally though she was.

Pedro walked toward the glade where he'd met her. Individually they'd failed, but if they combined forces, synergy should allow them to finally kill Bradan. That required coordinated effort and another meeting. It had been a good strategy when he'd first met her, and it was still good now.

He didn't know whether she'd sense him, but he'd brought along several baggies of uncut, pure coke in a satchel as a lure.

Somehow Fae senses could cross between worlds in search of their preferred vices.

The drug lord had no bodyguards. They hadn't protected him last time. The queen was capricious. However, he expected broad daylight and the sheer numbers of passersby to inhibit her violent tendencies if negotiations went south today. He did carry a gun. It was a tool of his trade. He felt undressed without it.

Pedro saw her ahead of him amid dozens of park visitors walking along the path. Amazingly, she'd muted her outré clothing tastes and wore a black leather jacket over a dark-blue sweater and a forest-green woolen skirt. She'd also swirled a tan scarf around her neck and let the loose ends float behind her in the breeze. A beret covered her pointed ears. The ensemble made him think that she'd stepped out of an upscale women's boutique on King's Road. Her brown suede boots looked expensive and remained spotless despite the mud and pools of standing water along the path.

He remembered that her hair color and skin tone were fluid last time, but today in the sunlight, her pale complexion stayed fixed and blended in with the locals' sun-starved skin. Completing the façade of a West End resident out for walk, the royal had concealed her rainbow-colored eyes behind stylish sunglasses. She'd kept the tiara of exotic flowers, but held it at her side in favor of wearing the beret. The crown drew no more than an occasional glance from passing Londoners; it was impolite to notice too much about one's fellow city dwellers.

All in all, Pedro thought that she'd studied what West Enders wore and determined to blend in. He guessed this might be the same approach that an actress would take in adopting the mannerisms of a person they wanted to mimic. Or she might be a zoologist studying an exotic species.

The drug lord couldn't spot any retinue or guards accompanying the queen. She did lead two young girls, one on either side of her. He wondered if they were daughters. They could be twins. Both were small, dark-haired, and wore umber-colored frocks covered by coats. They were reasonably well behaved, albeit very curious about their surroundings. Periodically, they fussed over the queen's dress and scarf.

Though Pedro prided himself on excellent eyesight, the queen had spotted him before he'd noticed her. She gracefully strode in his direction.

A park bench sat beside the path with an older couple taking in the passing parade. The queen subtly gestured to the two children, who raced over to the bench and then stopped in front of the couple and stared at them. At first, the couple paid no attention, but then gradually became visibly discomforted by the girls' fixed glare.

Pedro's inclination would have been to remain unobtrusive and seek out another bench, but eventually the couple got up and walked off, looking back anxiously at the kids. Victoriously, the two girls planted themselves on the bench and made way for the queen, leaving no room for Pedro who stood before them.

She removed her beret and replaced it with the tiara. Somehow, this complemented her other clothing.

He recognized that the queen wanted to present herself as his liege lord, sitting while he was forced to stand. Stifling irritation he tapped his satchel—no seat, no drugs, a simple bargain. She could wrench the satchel from his grip as she'd done a few nights before, but Pedro guessed that she'd expended some effort to blend in and didn't want to create a scene. The queen grimaced, but gestured to her two charges to shift out of the way to make space for Pedro next to her.

For a moment, they sat together like other couples out for a day in the park with the kids. The girls fidgeting close beside them were the product of a happy marriage. Pedro fought back laughter.

To complete the image of marital bliss, he could throw his arm around the queen, but he could guess the reaction this would provoke and checked his impulse.

He was a drug lord sitting beside a demon plotting an execution.

He glanced at the two girls. Outwardly, they were normal enough, perhaps a little too perfect. And their eyes gave them a malign depth beyond their childish demeanor.

In a field behind their bench, two teenage boys in T-shirts braved the wet ground to toss a Frisbee back and forth. They stood far apart and threw strongly, sending the disk in long, flat flights that smacked into their partner's hands. The recipient would flip the Frisbee over and send it back fast and straight. They taunted each other to move further apart to make the throws more challenging. They were a picture of exuberance.

The queen looked disinterested. However, her girls leaped off the bench and raced over to join the teenagers. With a supernaturally spry bound, one of the girls jumped into the air and floated momentarily to perfectly position herself to intercept the Frisbee before deftly catching it midflight. Her partner, only a step behind, also leaped into the air to hover and grasp the disk, attempting to wrench it out of the hands of the other girl before their struggles tore the tough plastic in two, sending them both falling to the wet ground.

Pedro watched, amazed, to see the battle conducted midair. The teenagers also gaped at the competition and several passersby stopped on the path. The queen looked on serenely, but noting Pedro's bemusement, she snapped her fingers and the two girls returned to the bench, each triumphantly holding a raggedly torn half of a Frisbee.

Pedro saw immediately what must be done to manage the situation and stifle any attention they'd drawn to themselves. He strode over to teenagers, both of whom were angry at losing their toy and completely baffled at the girls' eerie athletic ability. A hundred-pound note to each quelled their anger even if it didn't dispel their disbelief over what they'd observed. As Pedro passed over the money, he explained that both girls were training at a young age to become Olympic gymnasts and were already displaying precocious abilities to defy gravity. He didn't believe this would be convincing, as the queen's girls had literally floated for several seconds as if they'd deployed invisible fairy wings. However, it would have to do and it gave the Frisbee players a rational explanation for what they'd seen. He guessed they'd cling to it—and the money.

If he hadn't been already privy to the altogether strange Fae world, he'd have doubted his senses, too. Things that were inconceivable a week ago seemed normal now.

Pedro ignored the small cluster of walkers who'd witnessed the girls' supernatural abilities from the path. They'd been too distant to be sure what they saw and would eventually discount it as being some kind of illusion.

Returning to the bench, he sat down next to the queen. The girls presented him with the torn Frisbee pieces. Pedro surprised himself by being touched. He awkwardly held the useless fragments while the girls looked on expectantly.

"What?" he asked. "I can't fix it."

The queen plucked the pieces away and instantly it was whole again. She presented it to the girls, who bolted off to where the teenagers had been and, after a few clumsy tries, were soon flinging it in perfect, straight casts that covered half the length of a soccer field, much further than the older boys had done.

As before, the queen reached over to touch his forehead.

This was at once an intimate act and one of shared psychosis.

His first impression was of a damaged portal that now made commuting between the Fae and human worlds difficult. While she'd made the passage with the two kids in tow, ushering all of her followers through was now cumbersome. Somehow, Bradan was responsible for this circumstance and the scenes she showed him confirmed that far from waiting like a cow for slaughter, Bradan had initiated a bold attack on the gateway between worlds, felling a burning tree to crush the portal. Further, the queen suspected that Bradan had sought out the king as an ally.

Pedro sat for a moment digesting this information. He realized that Bradan had magical abilities—probably that had made him the outstanding marijuana transporter he'd once been in South Florida—though Pedro sensed that the queen ascribed his recent successes in attacking the portal to chance rather than advanced magical skills.

Now, the drug lord sensed some confusion from the queen. Bradan had alliances with beings who were wholly outside of her comprehension. Whether they helped, hindered, or had no role in his efforts to defeat the queen and Pedro, she didn't know.

It took some moments for him to understand the images she laid out for him, shades and shadows among Green Park's trees when Bradan had sabotaged the portal a few nights ago. What came after human death meant nothing to her. This was a collision of the afterlife with the fairy netherworld.

"Ghosts," Pedro said. "Phantoms, spirits. I don't believe in them, but then again, I didn't believe in your world, either, until a few days ago."

He saw one of the shades shove a spear into Bradan's hands, which Bradan then used to devastating effect on Fae warriors. Bradan was more capable than he'd imagined—and had more friends. There were many players in this game and overwhelming Bradan was turning into a frightful challenge.

Pedro wasn't sure which of his management strategies applied here. None of the Harvard Business School's case studies covered these circumstances, so he needed to expand his thinking about how to smash Bradan and achieve his goals.

Cocaine clarifies things, he thought.

At the moment, no walkers were near. Of its own volition, his hand opened the flap on his satchel and pulled out a plastic bag of cocaine. He laid the satchel flat on his lap and cautiously poured two thin lines of powder onto its surface. He wasn't sure what overdose looked like in a fairy, but he didn't want to provoke cardiac arrest in the queen—assuming she had anything resembling a heart—or a burst of homicidal rage from her, so he frugally poured out the drug. The queen and her followers were capable of berserk flights of violence when under its influence as the massacres over Christmas showed, but she'd kept her temper when he'd first met her a few weeks ago and they'd partaken together, so he felt confident sharing. Besides, he needed the narcotic.

This was becoming a familiar, convivial ritual between the two of them. Pedro wondered whether it garnered him any respect from the queen.

Dispensing with ritual, the fairy queen grabbed the bag from him and inhaled an enormous amount of powder.

Instantly, she threw aside her hat and sunglasses. She was no longer an incognito royal. Her rainbow eyes blazed crimson and she turned on him. He thought she would rend him limb from limb. The two dark-haired girls must have sensed their ruler's towering anger and stopped tossing their Frisbee to sprint over to defend their ruler by attacking Pedro.

Pedro reached for his gun though he knew it wouldn't protect him; he believed he could empty its entire clip into her with no damage. However, in her eyes, the crimson fire guttered to embers and the drug lord sensed a massive struggle within her culminating in a semblance of returning sanity.

Now she stared at him with rainbow eyes that were otherworldly, but not mad.

The queen waved away the two girls. They hovered nearby in case she changed her mind, but he sensed that the storm had passed, leaving her energized and more commanding than ever, but in control of her impulses.

She held onto the baggie of coke.

The queen touched his forehead again, maybe to assure him that she wouldn't slaughter him. Also, she searched for something Pedro knew she'd never find: his soul.

He sensed that this elevated him in her opinion. She relaxed and leaned back on the bench. The rage had blown through and she removed her tiara and set it on the bench beside her, replacing it with the beret, which she took some time arranging to cover her ears. She put her sunglasses back on.

"That was you when the gloves come off," he said. "I'm glad we're on the same side."

Now she communicated anger that he would consider her a peer. From her perspective, he was a subject, albeit one from the human realm and a useful source of narcotics.

Pedro grew angry. He was nobody's minion. His whole purpose in expanding into England was to avoid coming under the thumb of other cartels. The Fae royal should know that he wasn't under her thumb, either.

The queen must have detected his pride and arrogance. By tacit agreement, they stopped short of contending for superiority and focused on cooperating against mutual enemies.

"I'll give you additional cocaine," he said. "The more berserk you and your followers are when we next meet Bradan and whatever friends he's able to muster, the better, but we need to harness that rage."

He sensed that she proposed luring Bradan into her realm to dispatch him.

"He'll never go for it," Pedro said. "We'll have to defeat him at the border between my world and yours. You came close to crushing him a few nights ago in this very park before he managed to disrupt the fight by sending a tree into the gateway. He knows he's had a series of close calls evading both my men and your raiders. It's only pride that keeps him in London when he'd be better off fleeing, but he's good at leveraging his friends, and that's made him stubborn about staying."

An image came to him of Bradan's pet slaughtering her followers in their fight in Green Park and Pedro understood that what he'd supposed was Bradan's pet must be a demon of uncommon capability.

Nothing is inconceivable in this looking-glass reality since meeting the queen, he thought.

I've seen his beast before. Now that's the kind of follower I need, savage and incapable of defeat. It tore my Dobermans to shreds in the Bahamas when he transported powder for me a few years back.

"Bradan's beast is formidable, and if Bradan has allied himself with the king, he'll be stronger than ever," Pedro said.

He felt the queen's anger at the mention of her former lover and co-regent.

"So, we've both missed getting him," Pedro said. "That can't happen again. Here's what I propose . . ."

CHAPTER 25

Blues for an E-Type

Hackney, London, February, 1987

Bradan surveyed his Jaguar E-type in a million pieces all over the shop floor in Hackney. Other wrecks had mostly been left outside in the elements. However, by paying extra, he'd secured the Jag a spot in the garage. At least Connie would be warm and dry—assuming that she'd survived. He didn't know how it worked with ghosts that haunted cars. Did they become unattached if their vehicle was massively damaged?

The wolf nosed about sadly before curling up on the cold concrete floor beside the wreckage.

"Connie?" Bradan whispered.

He kept quiet. No sense having the Punjabi shop owner think him daft because he talked to a pile of debris.

During the ensuing silence, Bradan noticed only the sounds of mechanics working on the cars and neighborhood noises beyond the garage.

"I hope they don't get me confused with the other cars."

She sounded tired with a ragged edge to her voice, but the Southern drawl was intact.

"There's every heap on God's green earth in this dive. My luck, the mechanic guy will stick a VW engine in me."

Bradan wanted to embrace her, but wasn't sure which piece of twisted metal most embodied his ghostly friend. He settled for kissing the E-type's windshield, which somehow had survived the collision.

"Don't get weird on me," she said. "We're still at the just friends stage."

"Ranbir's supposed to be the best for servicing E-types," Bradan said. "Anu from my band recommended him. They're related somehow, think he's her uncle."

"I'm starting to come back together," Connie said. "So, I guess he knows his business. There's other spirits like me here among the scrap and wrecks."

"I thought you were unique."

"Nope. Plenty of us hang on to whatever car or truck we died in. A fair number of the wrecks about this place met bad ends on the roads. Least I've got company at night."

Bradan looked around the small garage where his Jaguar had pride of place in the middle of the shop floor with other vehicles in different stages of repair jammed along the perimeter. Outside, more cars waited on a lot for Ranbir's team of mechanics to tend to them. Rolls of barbed wire atop a tall chain link fence that would have done credit to a prison surrounded the place. He hoped it would be enough to dissuade local gangs from breaking in and making off with his car. Even a wrecked E-type was worth a bundle for parts.

To his uneducated eye, the Jag's frame was unbent though the hood was crumpled and had been removed and propped against a wall. Both front tires were flat and splayed out away from the frame. The engine was a mess.

"Yes, it looks bad, but we can fix it. My body man, Stalin, is terribly good with that end of things. I do the mechanicals."

While Bradan had checked out his Jag, the shop's lead mechanic, Ranbir, had wandered over to join him.

"I'm afraid I'm going to have to revise my original estimate higher," he said. "Parts are hard to come by. It's a special automobile. It deserves attentive care."

The mechanic's accent and speech patterns would have done credit to Oxford dons.

"Whatever it takes," Bradan said. "Give me an updated quote. What about the crumpled fenders and hood?"

"The body is where your auto received most of the hurt. May I ask how this happened in Mayfair? Hard to believe that one could drive fast enough to do so much damage unless you were on a motorway beyond downtown London. Usually, it's minor dents for accidents around town."

"Long story," Bradan said.

"You're the art fellow whose gallery got blown to bits."

"That's me," Bradan said curtly.

Ranbir took the hint and didn't press further.

"I am not a curious sort," he said. "As long as you pay your bills and your adventures don't bring the authorities down on our ears, I'm happy to fix your car. And here is Stalin to brief us on progress for your E-type's body repairs."

A thin, intense fellow with contempt in his eyes, a black goatee sharp enough to cut glass, and a balding pate, joined them. He looked more like Vladimir Lenin than Stalin.

He shook Bradan's hand with a crushing grip as if trying to wring out any capitalist tendencies.

A radio sitting on a tool bench played pop music. The weather was as bleak as Bradan's mood and seeing Connie in pieces only made him more morose, but he brightened as he heard Silicon Saturday's song from the Stonehenge MTV video played. It sounded good despite the noisy setting and the radio's tinny sound.

"I like it," Connie quietly told him. "I hadn't heard it until now."

"Stonehenge seems an age ago," Bradan said. "That's when this all started."

Oblivious to the exchange, Ranbir and Stalin considered his Jag and murmured to themselves.

"That's my song," Bradan called to the mechanics. He couldn't keep the pride out of his voice. After recent disasters, he had to brag about something even if it was to garage staff intent on overcharging him for his car's resurrection.

"Yes, Anu is my niece and she is in your group," Ranbir said. "She says you're a creative fellow. Well done on writing such a popular song."

"Music is for people's instruction," Stalin said. "Not enter-tainment. That is waste."

He had a Russian accent and dropped articles like they were bourgeois luxuries unneeded for speech clarity.

Ranbir looked tolerant of his colleague's comments, but also embarrassed.

"Why insult our customers?" he asked. "They keep food on our tables and a roof over head. My niece is studying medicine, but she plays for fun—in this chap's band."

"Music can be for whatever we want it to be," Bradan said. "I count Rimsky-Korsakov as an inspiration, especially his use of fairy stories and folklore in his work."

"Russians can be silly, too," Stalin said reluctantly before changing the topic. "Side panels will have to be replaced com-pletely. But most of the rest, I deal with using blow torch."

At the mention of "blow torch," Bradan sensed Connie cringe.

The three of them stood like doctors examining a patient in an ICU bed.

"It's a crime when a car this beautiful and with so much soul is damaged," Bradan said. "I'll return the favor when I get a chance."

"If someone is at fault, let the authorities and insurance adjusters deal with it," Ranbir said.

"Revenge is good and pure," Stalin said.

"No sense in getting into a blood feud," Ranbir said. "We had those in villages in my birth country and there is never a good outcome."

"I'll side with pure vengeance," Bradan said.

Bradan realized he was letting his anger get the best of him. Worse, he was openly talking about his plans. Seeing Connie in this state surfaced emotions he needed to check to stay cool-headed enough to confront the next round of narco assassins and Fae demons. Rage was satisfying, but surviving to win was better.

"I feel honored to work on it," Ranbir said. "For no good reason, I think of this vehicle not as an inanimate object, but as a 'she.' It has a feminine personality. When the Jag's body is repaired, this car will be all curves. Stalin, what do you say?"

"Bollocks," the body man said curtly. "Just metal."

"I will do professional repair on your car," he continued. "Artistic job, but I don't approve of such vehicles. Public transportation should be used by citizens. Not this. Your vehicle is frivolous and costs many times annual salary of a laboring man."

Ranbir made shushing motions at Stalin.

"If everyone used public transportation, we'd have no business. Any car entering these premises will be given the utmost care."

Ranbir ran his hand over the crumpled roof. "When I'm here late at night working on the vehicles, I don't feel alone now that your Jaguar is here. Very curious."

"It has personality," Bradan agreed.

"You are a lucky man. This car belongs in a film."

Bradan sensed Connie purr at the flattery. No one else noticed.

He stared about at Hindi movie posters taped to whatever spot on walls wasn't hung with tools. Instead of undressed pinups, stars from the past—Rekha, Shabana Azmi, and Smita Patil—vied with current starlets, everyone alluring, yet chaste, and ready to burst into song. Keeping the filmi posters company, Bradan saw a huge poster of Karl Marx in shades of bright red and black glowering at the movie actresses, though he presumed Marx would have been sympathetic to the honest labor done by Ranbir, Stalin, and their mechanics. A Russian flag flew over the shop, presumably a concession to Stalin. However, someone had subverted any political messaging by leaving Christmas lights strung up around Marx well past the holiday season.

"There's one thing that is proving a bit of a challenge," Ranbir noted. "Somehow the electrical system—never this model's strong point—refuses to be repaired. It keeps shorting. I've tried everything."

"Tell him to replace the original distributor cap with a new one from a dealership," Bradan heard Connie whisper.

Bradan repeated the suggestion to Ranbir.

"It cannot be so simple," the mechanic said. "I've done that already."

"He's using aftermarket parts," Connie said. "Has to be factory rebuilt. Otherwise the connection is faulty."

"Do you have a Jaguar rebuilt?" Bradan asked.

Ranbir nodded. "I was trying to save you money as you're already spending so much."

"Since I'm already spending a ton, do it and damn the cost."

"As you wish. How do you know so much about specialized details of repair? Perhaps I should hire you on as a mechanic for my shop."

"Just a good guess," Bradan said. "If you have the part, can you do it now? Let's see if she's right—let's see if *I'm* right."

Ranbir rummaged through a rack of parts and found what he needed.

"Bless me, it worked," Ranbir exclaimed after attaching the distributor cap and starting the engine. "Stalin, our customer Bradan solved the mystery."

"I'll let you all take the credit," Connie whispered to him.

"I'm grateful," Bradan told Ranbir and Stalin. "This car is more than transportation to me. We've been through a lot together. It's rolling art."

"The masses would disagree—"

"Well said, Bradan," Ranbir cut in smoothly.

CHAPTER 26

Russian Armor and English Houseboats

"Come, Bradan, let me show you what is true soul in transportation."

Stalin gestured outside through an open garage door before threading his way between the packed vehicles in various stages of repair.

Bradan followed, wondering what was up. He'd rather the Russian focused on repairing the Jag instead of explaining Marxism's relevance for automotive maintenance.

"Ideology is an anchor in a changing world, I suppose," Bradan remarked.

"Marxism explains everything we can observe about us. Anything else is magic and fairy tales."

"I believe in magic and fairy tales," Bradan murmured to himself.

He marveled that the lot could contain such a mass of cars. The further from the garage they moved, the more rusted the cars became. He had a sense of traveling back in time past vehicles that had been dropped off decades ago and then abandoned, here a couple of black cabs from the 1950s, there an ancient Silver Wraith Rolls-Royce with its Spirit of Ecstasy ornament still atop the massive hood. Near the Rolls sat an archaic double-decker bus moldering with red paint so faded it was light pink with an equally faint ad for "National War Bonds for Victory" on the top deck. An ad for Barclays bank flanked the war bonds promotion. Time had forgotten this place or, at least, modern London wished to ignore it. Hence, the yard was relegated to working-class Hackney with its endless reddish-brown brick row houses.

A nineteenth-century, black steam locomotive kept the bus company. The engine was coupled to a tender loaded with coal. A dusting of snow contrasted with the coal.

Piles of wrecks of indeterminate make and vintage sat behind the bus and locomotive, stacked one atop another such that their weight compressed the bottom layer into slabs of rotting metal. The piles, taller than Stonehenge's blocks, towered over the garage, ready to collapse onto it in the next winter storm.

Bradan sensed their history. Some had been towed here after horrific crashes, some simply needed repairs they'd never get. Connie was right: However they had arrived, each had a story and a few had attached phantoms.

The yard reeked of tar, petrol, and oil. Bradan tasted the air on his tongue and stifled his need to retch. He saw sludgy pools of rusty water leaching into the muddy ground near the wrecks. If she'd seen it, the water nymph would have attacked him and Stalin out of hand.

"Can this be cleaned up?" Bradan asked.

"Where is money?" Stalin asked. "Besides, I do not want corrupt city officials inspecting my property. What harm is mess doing?"

"A lot," Bradan said. "God knows what toxins you're putting into the groundwater."

The mechanic shrugged. "I do not believe in God, but if there is a god, he knows big companies make worse shit than me."

"But you can do something about your yard," Bradan said.

"Plainly, you care about *your* causes as I care about *my* causes. A little spilled oil is a small price to pay for keeping my mechanics employed. Nobody else will help them."

The Russian stopped.

"Ah, here is what I wanted to show you."

A squat, ominous tank sat near the bus and locomotive. In contrast to the other vehicles, it was in good shape with clean, olive-green paint. Its cannon pointed directly at them. It looked like it could withstand all manner of bullets and bombs, and, indeed, Bradan saw deep gouges in the frontal armor. However, no assault had penetrated completely. He noted a red star on its turret and the broad treads that had carried it across snow, steppe, and tundra, and into Berlin in 1945. It was a sinister antique, and the snow on its armor didn't soften the menace.

"This machine kills fascists," Stalin said.

"Does it kill demons?" Bradan asked.

Stalin looked at him. "This isn't joke. I brought you here to show you what real vehicle looks like, something that protected comrades, unlike your trivial sports car."

"I wasn't joking," Bradan said. He approached the tank.

"Can I touch?"

Stalin shrugged. "You can't hurt it."

Running his hands along the sides, Bradan sensed thirty-five tons of implacable strength, very different from the sensations of fleet elegance he got from his E-type. He also sensed spirits of the soldiers who'd driven it across Eastern Europe and into Germany.

"T-34," Bradan said. "This one has an 85mm gun, very effective."

"Ah, you know it."

"One of them saved me."

"You are full of bad jokes today," Stalin said.

"I'm not mocking you. I flew an American fighter in the Second World War. I got shot down by anti-aircraft fire over Germany. It was near the end, so your countrymen were advancing fast when I crash landed on a farm road a few kilometers from Dresden. My plane was damaged, and I thought I could use the road as a runway, but it was too rough and the landing gear collapsed. The plane skidded into a field. I was in an area contested by retreating Germans and oncoming Russians. A panzer detachment spotted me as I climbed out of the cockpit and fired machine guns, but the shooting attracted a Russian tank company with T-34s and they chased off the Germans. The plane was a loss, but I was never so happy to see Russians."

For a moment, Bradan was back in a field hugging the mud, terrified as machine gun and rifle fire zipped around him, kicking up clods of dirt and grass, and shards of rye against his cheek. He smelled manure used for fertilizer.

When he'd soared above the land battle moments before, the farms were abstract, geometric patterns in brown and green below. Sometimes he saw tiny flashes of light from gun and cannon fire and knew that fighting raged, but he looked down like a god detached from the carnage. However, the fight was visceral and immediate as he lay in the field.

Why were the Germans working to kill him with such fervor? Their war was lost. Probably, they hated American pilots who'd turned their homeland to rubble. Certainly, they expended bullets copiously firing at him until the first round from a Russian tank hit their positions. Then it turned into a firefight with Bradan in the middle, forgotten. Russian Red Army and German Wehrmacht ordnance smashed into the ground beside him and he heard shrapnel zipping over him as he lay prone on the cold ground clenching the dirt and cow shit. His presence was the excuse for them to savage each other.

The small arms fire was loud, but the tank cannon discharges deafened him. He felt their concussions in his chest. Periodically, one of these shots punched through a rival's armor to detonate in a thunderous blast as one of the steel beasts blew apart followed by secondary explosions as their ammunition cooked off. Weight of numbers finally carried the day and the Germans pulled back. One downed American flyer was not worth so much effort.

In a minute or after several hours, Bradan didn't know which, the Russian mechanized infantry found him and pulled him to his feet, at first not sure whose side he was on and ready to shoot him out of hand, but he pointed to his crashed fighter as he brushed off the dirt from his flight suit, and they realized he was American when he spoke.

"You were somewhere else for a moment," Stalin said.

"They let me ride in a tank back to their camp," Bradan said. "To amuse us all, they showed me how to aim and fire its cannon—not easy to aim, but not impossible, either—and shoot off a few rounds at German positions. After a couple of shots, I was getting better, but wasting their ammunition, so we stopped.

"We drank vodka from the bottle that night. One of the officers had been saving it till they had an occasion. Rescuing me was the excuse—though Russians need no excuse for vodka."

"You like vodka?" the Russian mechanic asked. Respect shaded his tone. "This speaks well for you. It's true liquor unlike Scotch, which doesn't burn when it goes down."

"I hate vodka, but at that moment, nothing tasted better. I made it back to my air base in France eventually. They thought I'd died. We all had good champagne to celebrate. I cut the bottle tops off with a cavalry saber. The things you do to forget being shot at. The war didn't last much longer. I survived."

"There is a question here," Stalin said. "My father fought in that war as a tanker. He's dead of old age and drink. And how old are you?"

"That would take some time to answer," Bradan said.

He didn't like outright lies, though he did it to protect himself if he couldn't think of a clever evasion. He slept better if he could get away with half-facts, and he occasionally volunteered tidbits of his past, taunting the world to see beneath the surface. How close could he dance up to truth's edge without compromising his identity?

Only phantoms like Mags or Connie knew him for what he was: ageless. And leading a life of deception.

Stalin as a good Marxist was too literal to spot the chinks in his cover, especially if Bradan employed judicious misdirection.

He patted the T-34. "Does it still run?"

"I tend it carefully," Stalin said. "If you knew how, you could drive it off the lot this very minute, though I won't let you."

"Why would I take it anywhere?" Bradan asked casually.

"It is dear to me. I have kept it in good repair out of respect for my father. Do not tell anyone, but it has munitions for the guns. I am not sure if the shells still work, but they came with it and I could not find a way to safely dispose of them without risking the destruction of half of Hackney. It was a gift from a Russian general to a British officer when they linked up as the war ended—silly gesture. In return, the Britisher gave the general a jeep filled with a dozen cases of French Burgundy.

"The Brit packed the tank on a transport ship and sent it across the Channel. No one knew what to do with it once it arrived. No one wanted reminders of war. The British military man had only accepted it out of politeness. The Russians were still England's friend as the war ended. It wouldn't do to rebuff their gifts. Eventually, I bought cheaply and it wound up here."

He brushed away snow and hoisted himself up to sit on the tank's fender.

"My name is not Stalin."

"I guessed," Bradan said dryly. "Sounds impressive, though."

"The comrade meant well. He saw needs that had to be addressed. However, there were excesses."

"What's your real name?"

"Dimitri. As a child, my family called me 'Dimka.' Russians love informal names."

"Dimka sounds less aggressive than Stalin."

"We live in a world that needs strength to confront it. Keep calling me Stalin."

The Russian stood up and bent to kiss the red star on the turret. Then he climbed on top of the tank and hauled open a hatch.

"Come. I show you. Get inside with me."

Bradan was curious to see what he remembered.

"Will I fit?"

"You are tall, but stoop a little and it may be possible."

Stalin dropped down through the hatch out of view. Bradan clambered up after him, stepping on a tread and then the tank's deck. There were two hatches on top of the turret. The Russian had used one. He squished himself through the other to join Stalin, scraping his forearms in the process.

Bradan's first impression was one of compression. The metal cab was tiny and designed with no thought to ergonomics; the crew's comfort was completely secondary to their utility for destroying enemies of the state. Bradan barely fit and he imagined himself being battered around the interior if the tank were moving toward the front over broken and shell-torn terrain.

Bradan's second impression was of death. This machine and the men manning it had taken life and some of them had themselves died while doing it.

"It has soul," he said. "A dark soul."

He sat almost on top of Stalin who, now that they were piled into this tiny space together, smelled of garlic, ethanol, and marijuana. Directly in front of him was the breech of the cannon. The weapon was huge and divided the turret's interior in half. He sat on one side, Dimitri on the other.

"Those are the shells?" Bradan asked.

He pointed to a haphazard stack of projectiles lining the turret in racks or scattered about on the floor. Bradan tried to imagine what loading the cannon would be like in battle with enemy armor-piercing rounds hitting the T-34's sloped sides.

"Yes. I will show you how to put one into the gun."

The mechanic levered the cannon's breech open and, with enormous exertion, reached to grab a shell and lurched up with it cradled in his arms.

"Don't drop this," he said.

He shoved it into the cannon.

"Christ!" Bradan said. "Can you take it out?"

"No need," the Russian said. "These have been here since forever. They cannot still be live. My father showed me how to load and fire when he lived. I feel I owe my father to show you how this was done even if we cannot shoot. This makes the experience more real to you. Too bad the shell won't work or I show you that the projectile can pierce four inches of armor and travel a mile and a half."

"If you're wrong about the shells, we're in the middle of London," Bradan pointed out. "There's nowhere you can fire this thing without hitting something, causing God knows what destruction."

"You talk of God too much."

Stalin squinted through the gunsight's reticle.

"In my imagination, I have struck this blow many times for workers like myself, people who cannot buy a pretty car like yours and then wreck it like a toy. I know nothing will come of it in this junkyard with an old tank, but it is good to dream. What better thing than to pretend to hit a symbol of capitalism: an ad for a bank."

Three things happened simultaneously: the cannon fired with a flat, deafening blast, the barrel recoiled into the turret, and the thirty-five-ton vehicle rocked back on clanking metal tracks.

"What did you fucking hit?" Bradan shouted.

He thought he said this, but he wasn't sure as his ears still rang from the cannon's concussive discharge. The smell of propellant filled the tank turret.

"That cannot have occurred," the Russian said.

"It did," Bradan said. "Was anyone hurt?"

He surged out of the hatch and stood atop the turret. The cannon had been pointed directly at the Barclays bank ad on the side of the old London double-decker. There was now a neat hole punched through the ad.

"Was the shell armor-piercing or high-explosive?" he yelled down at Stalin.

"Armor-piercing, I think."

"Then it will keep going through buildings—or anything else—until it hits something really, really thick."

Bradan jumped off the tank and ran around the bus to see the exit hole on its opposite side where the tank round had continued straight through not even noticing the bus's thin sheet metal. He visualized the trajectory and saw that the shell had penetrated into the wall of wrecks beyond the bus.

Ranbir looked cautiously out of the garage along with other mechanics.

"What has happened?" he yelled.

However, nobody was anxious to come outside and examine the damage.

"What happened?" Ranbir repeated.

"Ask Stalin," Bradan shouted. "His tank still works. What's on the other side of the bus?"

"Wrecks and vehicles waiting for repair. Some of the wrecks are piled high, scrap metal after too many seasons outside. After that, it's a clear path to the Regent's Canal, nothing in the way."

"There are boats on the canal?"

"Sure. Lots of them. They're houseboats with people living on them."

"This gets better and better," Bradan snarled. "Somebody's bound to have noticed—neighbors, police, whoever. If constables show up, act puzzled, and don't mention the tank. Perhaps they'll think it was one of your cars backfiring. They've no right to enter your yard without a warrant. That should hold them till I get back."

"How do you know so much about police procedures?" Ranbir asked.

"Lots of recent practice."

"And why are you helping?" Ranbir asked. "This is Stalin's doing. Let him sort it."

"I've taken a liking to Stalin's tank. It packs a punch. I might have a use for it, so it would be a shame to have it confiscated."

Without waiting for the mechanic's reply, Bradan sprinted out of the garage's lot and raced down Queensbridge Road toward the canal. Within seconds, the wolf had caught up with him. Pedestrians leaped out of their way, helped along by Tintagel's snarls. Bradan thanked God this stretch of the street was relatively straight so the cannon's shell hadn't hit any buildings.

At the canal, he vaulted over a metal fence and took in the row of narrow houseboats tied to cleats on a path flanking the canal.

At first nothing seemed wrong. A dozen boats lined his side of the canal gently tugging at the lines securing them to the grassy embankment like old dogs too lazy to loose themselves from their leashes. A few swans drifted past the boats, leaving little wakes in the green algae.

The boats were all long and narrow with deckhouses that served as the owners' homes stretching the length of the craft. They were cramped but cozy, and English individuality rendered every boat as variations on a theme. Some of the craft were neat and tidy while others looked bohemian with potted plants haphazardly positioned on the roof of the boat. Most of them had eccentric paint jobs.

It all looked untroubled by random Second World War tank fire until Bradan realized that the boat nearest him had a neat hole cut through the wall of its deckhouse. Directly across the canal, on the opposite side, there was a deep gouge in a concrete embankment where something had hit the shore at enormous velocity. A large section of the surrounding concrete and dirt had crumbled into the water. A bicyclist stopped to peer at the destruction. However, aside from the punctured houseboat, no people or residences were worse for wear.

Bradan walked over to the damaged boat. A gangway led onto a ramshackle vessel painted in psychedelic, paisley hues amid which were environmental slogans in fat lettering. Solar water heaters covered part of the roof. Portholes dotted the length of the craft.

Bradan clunked aboard and across a tiny rear deck to a door leading into the deckhouse. A nautical bell flanked the door, which Bradan rang feeling like he'd stepped onto an eighteenth-century frigate.

The bell's clangs sounded loud enough to wake the dead. There was a very long pause before two pairs of brown eyes peeked out at him from behind a door that cracked open. Through the sliver, Bradan saw a young couple. Pot and a warm, inside-on-a-winter-day smell of sex, fried food, and beer oozed out of the cabin. Bradan also smelled paint.

"This is a bad time," a man said.

"I gathered," Bradan said. "But it's important. Your boat is damaged."

He tried to think of a more absurd introduction, but couldn't. However, the couple now looked mildly intrigued.

"I heard something slam into us a little while back, boat rocked, but I thought it was the dope being strange with my brain," the woman said. She smiled languidly.

"We were distracted at the time," the man said. "Jesus, are we sinking?"

"Not that bad, but your craft's been holed," Bradan said.

There was a long pause. He let his words sink in.

"Good that we're still floating," the fellow said. "Don't want to be bailing."

He stared at Bradan.

"You're in Silicon Saturday. Saw you at Glastonbury last year. We have one of your CDs. And you just put out a video—kind of a weird vibe, but interesting. I'm Andrew, by the way."

Now that Bradan had been identified as a performer and a celebrity, the door swung wide open. Bradan reflected that music unlocked barriers. He'd been adopted into their family temporarily.

The man was bare-chested wearing jeans. The woman stood beside him in a paint-stained Judas Priest T-shirt and panties.

"I'm Naomi," she said. "Chill dog, isn't it?"

She shook her brown-blond hair free of her T-shirt collar as if she'd pulled the shirt on hurriedly when he'd rung.

"Can I pat him or her?" Naomi had a West London accent with broad *a*'s that stretched forever. She might be living on a Hackney houseboat, but she came from money. An accent invariably identified one's class.

"It's a him," Bradan said. "Tintagel is his name and it's his call about being patted. Sometimes he's okay with it, mostly not. About your boat-"

"Creative name, Tintagel," she said. "Why? It's a castle in Cornwall."

"It's now a ruin in Cornwall. It was important to both of us—once."

"Come here, Tintagel," Naomi said.

She reached out slowly and stroked the wolf's neck. Bradan waited for the beast's eyes to blaze red, but they didn't, and Tintagel tolerated her caressing touch—an unusually relaxed reaction.

"Where's the damage to our boat?" Andrew asked.

"Something passed clean through your living quarters," Bradan said. "You must have heard a ripping sound like the air being torn apart," Bradan asked.

He didn't elaborate on his description of the sounds of being on the receiving end of incoming artillery fire. These kids didn't need to hear about that.

"Have a check," Bradan said.

Finally becoming alarmed, the couple stepped away from the door. Andrew returned a moment later.

"Punched clean through," he said. "You were right, mate. A few feet further forward and whatever it was would have shot us in bed. As it is, our kitchen and some of her paintings are smashed up. They were hanging on the wall. Now, they're fragments. Other than that, nothing."

By now, Naomi had returned, too. "It's not nothing that my artwork is wrecked. This is our home and my studio. How would you know to ask us about damage to our boat? Did you see something? What hit us?"

"I saw the hole from shore," Bradan said. "Listen, I've a huge favor to ask: Can you cover the gaps—yes, both of them, on each side of your boat—maybe use plants or clothing or something, and, if the police happen by, don't mention the damage? Don't mention me, either."

They stared at him blankly.

"We probably should report it," Andrew said after a moment. "This is criminal. We could be dead. Will anything else hit us?"

"No."

Bradan hoped to hell Stalin wouldn't fool around in his tank again. He could think of better uses for the T-34.

"I think five hundred pounds should cover damages." Bradan pulled out his wallet and passed five hundred-pound notes to Andrew.

"Generous," the man said.

"You have more art?" Bradan asked Naomi. "Besides what was destroyed."

"I've got a ton of stuff I haven't sold yet. Want to see?"

"Another time," Bradan said. "Will you sell me your best work? Does a thousand pounds seem a fair price?"

"You're having me on," she said.

"Really, I'm not. I have a gallery in Mayfair—"

"The one that got blown up?" Andrew asked.

Bradan sighed. "Yep."

"Sure, I'll sell you a painting," Naomi said. "That's in return for not tattling to the constables?"

"You catch on fast," Bradan said. "There's a story behind all this, but you'd find it silly and fantastic."

"Don't you want to see what you're buying? A thousand quid ain't small change."

"You choose. Give me two of your works if that seems fairer. At the moment, I'm in a rush, so I'll buy them right now."

He counted out ten more hundred-pound notes.

"You've just made fifteen hundred pounds for keeping quiet."

"Cheers, mate," Andrew said. "We'll catch your next London show."

Bradan jogged back to the mechanic's shop carrying Naomi's paintings one under each arm. He didn't think he could sell them, but he consoled himself that besides covering for Stalin he was making good on his bargain with Merlin: near immortality in return for supporting culture, even badly done art.

Back at the garage yard, as he'd feared, police cars parked at the shop's main gate and Ranbir and Stalin argued with four bobbies. Bradan stopped where he had a good view of the proceedings and crouched behind a parked car. Far back in the yard, he saw the tank's cannon poking out from among the derelicts. He didn't think the police were positioned so they could see the T-34, but if they managed to bully their way into the yard, they'd spot it. Sure enough, the constables now moved past the gate. Two entered the garage and began questioning the staff. The other two inspected the vehicles in the outside yard. Ranbir looked on forlornly while Stalin shouted about his rights and getting a solicitor.

Bradan watched the police move ever closer to the tank. He spoke eight stanzas. This should be a simple piece of enchantment—but one never knew—and watched the T-34 transform into an ice cream truck in pristine white paint with blotches of brown making the entire vehicle look like a giant scoop of cookies and cream pulled from the freezer.

"A little more rust, not so new, it's got to seem that it's been sitting on the lot for years in rainy weather," Bradan said, feeling fatigue sweep over him. He sat down on the bumper of the car he hid behind. Rarely, he tried tweaking the spell on the fly. Usually, it didn't work. His exhaustion worsened, but in a flash, the new ice cream truck aged before his eyes with stretches of rust, some of it eating clear through the vehicle's side panels. Even the tires lost their showroom patina and dulled. One of them went flat. The entire image merged seamlessly with the aging fleet that Ranbir and Stalin tended.

One of the constables strolled past the truck, giving it no more than a passing glance. He spent more time examining the old double-decker bus, but paid no attention to the neat hole drilled through the bank ad. Stalin trailed the constable and stopped dead in front of the where the T-34 sat. He stared at the ice cream truck.

Maintaining the image sapped Bradan's energy as much as creating the work in the first place, and he sweated in the cold watching the bobbies complete their leisurely circuit of the premises. Finally, the four policemen gathered to compare notes, then casually waved at Ranbir before climbing back into their cars and driving off.

Bradan let the spell lapse and the ice cream truck reverted to a tank. He waited fully ten minutes to catch his breath before trudging slowly into the garage. He realized he still carried Naomi's paintings.

"If I could let Stalin go, I would," Ranbir told Bradan. "But he is part owner of the shop. What damage did the cannon do? Is Hackney in ruins?"

"Your neighbors are really lucky, especially a couple in a houseboat. It was almost a disaster for them, but they're fine and I don't think they'll talk to anyone."

"Ah, well, that is good at least. I have never felt comfortable with his metal monster parked in our yard, so unprofessional. It must be illegal. How the constables did not see it and question us further, I don't know. This has disrupted our entire day and we'll be late in getting your car together. I will charge you only half the usual cost for the repair work on your Jaguar."

"Thanks," Bradan said. "By the way, I've a gift to make to your shop."

"And what would that be?" Ranbir asked.

"Two paintings. Hang them next to your film posters or beside Marx, my gift to the masses."

"I think I must thank you." Stalin joined them. "Though I don't know for what I thank you. Yet the bobbies missed my tank. Somehow you helped. I know it. My tank changed into an antique truck for a moment."

Ranbir looked at his partner like he'd gone crazy.

"What in the hell are you saying? It's the vodka and dope talking."

"I know what I saw, an ice cream van," Stalin said. "And I know what the police didn't see, my tank. I owe you."

"You do," Bradan said. "And I need a favor in return."

"What?" Suspicion radiated from the mechanic.

"I want to sit in your T-34 again. I'll show up after hours, say around midnight this Saturday."

"Why?"

"For the memories. It's a cool vehicle, takes me back to other times, other places. I'll bring along the vodka and weed. What's the harm? We won't go anywhere. I can't drive it."

Bradan wandered back into the garage and stood next to his E-type's scattered parts.

"What happened?" Connie asked. "Sounded like a bomb went off."

"Close," Bradan said. "It was a tank cannon."

"Whatever it was, it sounded dangerous. So, why cover for this stupid shop? Who ever heard of a mechanic spouting communist bullshit? Let the authorities haul it off for scrap."

"I need it."

"What!?"

"Connie, can you drive a tank?"

CHAPTER 27

Entreating an Enchanter

Tintagel, England, February, 1987

"I knew their marriage would never last," Merlin remarked.

"Then why marry them?" Bradan demanded.

"So they'd sleep with me," the enchanter said.

"What!"

"Don't be so shocked."

Merlin sat on a boulder and gathered his cloak about him against the cold. His gray beard whipped about in the wind. He looked like a mystic tonight.

"I never thought of you as a prude," Merlin said. "They married to bring their realm together and they owed me because I helped. Among the Fae realm's capricious creatures, no one else had my gravitas to perform the nuptials. That gave me standing among all their combative tribes. Ironic, since I'm sort of human."

Bradan sat down beside the wizard. The enchanter was steeped in knowledge about the Fae. Bradan had asked him back to tap that knowledge.

It felt good to speak ancient Celtic again. Bradan was rusty, but the language was poetry and gradually the old intonations and cadence came back to him.

It was a night for ancient things and there wasn't a better place to commune with long-gone Merlin about stopping a supernatural war than the ruins of Tintagel Castle. It had been Arthur's rude sixth-century fortress on the edge of a world beset by threats.

The night was arctic. Bradan expected winter to defer to the wizard. However, even Merlin, usually able to bend the elements to his needs, faced a glacial wind blowing off the Celtic Sea.

The wizard stared out at the ocean.

"At first, they loved each other, but it was a political alliance, too. Anyway, it worked for a while. Peace prevailed in the realm and the three of us frolicked together for months. Exhausting, I must say. I'm won't be coy to protect your sensibilities: The queen had a magic cunt. Ah, the pleasures of being a wizard."

"Motivation to bless their marriage," Bradan said acidly. "Good that you had fun."

"Now you're being sarcastic. Just to show you that I'm not selfish, I had another motive, too: I hoped the king and queen's relationship would last, though I didn't think so. Rarely people— or in this case, Fae—surprise me. I want to be surprised. I'm like you: a romantic, though you try to cover it with cynicism."

"Nothing is forever," Bradan said. "Sometimes a relationship is over in an eyeblink."

"That's the cynic speaking," the enchanter said. "Not your real feelings. I distinctly heard you tell the king that time doesn't crush love."

"You overheard? How?"

"I'm Merlin."

Like the wizard, Bradan watched the Celtic Sea. That name sounded evocative and romantic. However, he knew the locals never referred to it as such. It was simply a frigid body of water that had carried raiders and pirates to their shores a thousand years ago and nowadays brought tourists in search of a past that never was.

Will English spring ever come? Bradan wondered.

"I argued with the Fae king," he said. "I couldn't let him have the last word. I was on the side of romance."

"Sometimes that's the losing side," Merlin said.

"Now who's cynical?"

"Speaking of romance," the enchanter said. "You've gotten yourself into a jam with women."

He laughed. "Reminds me of when I was still interested in that sort of thing. Is that why you've called me back, for advice on your entanglements? I'll place no wagers on what's best for you."

"I'm not in a horse race," Bradan said angrily. "I'll sort that one myself—or try, anyway. Do you think about love now?"

"I wish you hadn't reminded me. Yes, I miss it dearly, but I'm not in a place where it matters."

The wizard shifted to face him. "Why *did* you bring me back?"

He'd been fanciful and mocking. Now, there was flint in his voice.

"I don't want to be here. I made that clear when we parted company many, many centuries ago."

"You shouldn't have married them," Bradan said. "They're at each other's throats and I'm caught up in it. It's spilled over into this world."

"I'm not the cause of their troubles—or yours."

"No? It seems that way."

He'd used an old minstrel's ballad from revels in Arthur's court that he'd plucked on his guitar and sung with heartfelt emotion to call Merlin back from whatever space the enchanter had retired to after a long life in old Britain's hinterlands. It could only have happened at Tintagel, a space the wizard revered, catalyzed by music's magic. However, Bradan felt exhausted by the effort and now doubted the wisdom of resurrecting Merlin—they'd reverted to the mentor-student relationship they'd once had. Merlin would never treat him as a peer.

It was a measure of Bradan's desperation that he'd sought the wizard's advice, but what would a being suffused with Dark Ages moral principles make of his current circumstances?

The wolf approached to sit on it haunches beside them. It yawned. Diplomatically, the beast had sensed their tension and located itself halfway between them, honoring both equally with his presence.

"Ah, and here's the wolf," Merlin said conversationally. "That's one relationship that has lasted. I believe you named him after this place, Tintagel."

"He seemed to approve."

The light was magical and perfect. It was dusk and clear with a rising half-moon illuminating sparse grass, rocks, and ancient structures reduced to piles of rocks vaguely defining their perimeters. He remembered when these were more impressive fifteen hundred years ago, but even in its heyday, Tintagel had been a rough-hewn outpost when Arthur was its lord and they'd fended off Saxon raiders and Irish pirates while trading for wine and olive oil from the old Roman Empire's distant south.

Tonight, Tintagel was a place of shadows set against an indigo sky fading to black. Bradan was on the temporal edge between what had come before and whatever came next.

Excepting the wizard and the wolf, Bradan had the place to himself. He got up and walked to the cliffs overlooking the breakers. Moonlight lit the waves. Memories merged with what he saw below.

It was a long drop to hard rocks and he didn't tempt fate by getting too close to the edge.

He hadn't been here in centuries. He'd heard that it had been turned into a national park, so he'd stayed away, fearing that it had been civilized and explained beyond recognition and stripped of its character, but excepting a few informational placards, and a distant visitors center, it was as wild and eerie as ever.

"Bad things are happening in both the Fae and human worlds," Bradan said. "I'm trying to keep the realms from colliding."

He reached down and grabbed a handful of soil.

"We're wrecking this place. Looks like dirt, but who knows what's in my hand, heavy metals, plastic, or poisons washed ashore from across the globe. There's too much of everything, cities, roads—things you couldn't imagine from Roman Britain—but most of all, there are too many people."

"I know some of this," Merlin said. "That's the reason I left and why I passed responsibility on to you. It would take a younger man to come of age with the changes I knew were happening. It's beyond my simple magic. What I did was based on understanding nature and aligning my spells with the environment around me, seeing the trees, breathing the air, feeling a creek's water pass between my fingers. And then doing my enchantment."

"How do you know what's happened since you retired?"

"I know because I'm Merlin."

"You've been here an hour and only seen Tintagel."

"It would sadden me to travel about. Here, I look at ruins, barely foundations that were once stone drinking halls, and

ramparts, and homes. In its time, this was the place for knowledge and prosperity. Now, there isn't anything left."

"Some help you are."

"I'm part of nature. You shouldn't have brought me back. If I
were to join the fight, it would be on the Fae side."

"Which Fae side?"

"Either! They hate each other with blood lust—they're quick
to war on each other; it's easier than thinking—but both the
king and queen and all their subjects detest humanity even
more. And they've a right to. Our waste and our vices, they're
spilling over into Faerie."

"Guilty as charged about the waste," Bradan said. "As for the
vices, that's their own fault."

"You're trying to do something about the waste? I sensed
what you did a few days ago with your illusions."

"People noticed." Bradan let pride color his tone.

"A few people noticed," he corrected himself.

"Do you think it did good?" Merlin asked.

"A little. I amused a bunch of drunks. Then they went off
to chase drugs from Amsterdam—probably none of that means
anything to you—but one man listened. It also made the media
the next day—probably that doesn't mean anything to you,
either, but these days, it's how you get the word out."

They looked inland away from the surf and sea.

"Even here on the edge of nowhere, you can see lights from
Cornish towns," Bradan said.

"I remember it as pitch black at night once the cooking fires
were put out," the enchanter said.

"There's nowhere in my world today that's pitch black,"
Bradan said.

Merlin threw an arm over Bradan's shoulder.

"I *am* sorry," he said. "You've resurrected me for no purpose. Except to hear that I'm a randy old goat who used ritual and magic to serve my own sordid needs—which you knew already."

"I thought you'd have insight about defusing a war," Bradan said.

"Ha! You want insight. You've come to the wrong mage."

"You were my teacher." Bradan tried to stifle the accusatory tone that crept into his voice.

"You once faulted me for being clever," Merlin replied. "But not wise nor smart, or words to that effect—no, don't apologize. I'm long dead, after all, or something like that. Truthfully, I'm not sure what I am—retired, as you say—but I can't stay around here indulging your curiosity about things I've left behind. 'Mess' I believe you rather quaintly called the situation here. Well, you'll have to get yourself out of it."

"That's your lesson for me."

"You're on your own."

"Not even some hints?" Bradan asked.

Above, a jet flew toward the stratosphere, leaving a luminescent contrail marring the perfect, velvety purple-black sky. The plane's sound disturbed the quiet.

The wizard glanced upward without interest.

"You expect me to be curious about what's happened since I've been gone," Merlin said. "I'm not. Eras come and go and mine is long gone. This is your world, not mine. Even if I wanted to help—and I don't—it's all beyond me. Back in my day, all I could muster was parlor tricks. The big enchantment took time to prepare and, often as not, didn't work, or not the way I'd intended."

"What did work?"

"You know the answer."

"Weak magic, audacity, and friends," Bradan said.

"Bravo!" the enchanter said. "It seems I taught you something."

Bradan sighed and leaned on his guitar case.

"You brought me back with music," Merlin said. "As long as I'm here, play me something I haven't heard. I enjoyed your epic poetry accompanied by a lute so many generations ago."

"My guitar sounds as pretty as a lute," Bradan said.

Bradan strummed his instrument, feeling the tactile sensation of the icy metal strings against his fingers and its wood against his palm. As at Stonehenge and Green Park, the cold bothered the Martin's splendid pitch. However, once in tune, it produced a powerful tone that floated out over the Celtic Sea sustaining the notes endlessly, amplified by the wind. The cold sharpened their bell-like clarity.

"You played at Stonehenge," the wizard observed.

"You knew that from one chord?" Bradan asked, unsurprised. The enchanter had phenomenal intuition. Sometimes he'd display it when he was trying to impress an audience skeptical of his powers. Other times, Bradan suspected it was simple hubris.

"I just knew," Merlin said. "Music is magic. For good or ill, the right melody awakens ancient things, as you discovered at Stonehenge. I'm one of those ancient things that would rather not have been awakened. Music can also quiet rage if it's good enough. You discovered that at Stonehenge, too, when the warring Fae set aside their animus to dance."

"I've worked on this piece for days—" Bradan began.

"Don't explain, just play. Your song either works or it doesn't."

Bradan played, inspired by remembered love for Margaret Sutcliffe and by his complex feelings for Trini and Del. His guitar's sound merged with nature's voices, the surf and the wind.

He sang, too, sometimes swapping modern English for old languages of his childhood. He hadn't written it that way, but the archaic words fit this setting and he accommodated them into the tune's rhythmic structure. It was a new piece; where he forgot words, he hummed.

Bradan performed for himself and the enchanter, but he had another listener.

Out at sea, dancing on the wave tops, he saw a woman. She was magical, of course. Otherwise how could she have avoided sinking or being pulled into Tintagel's rocks, or freezing in the cutting, winter blast coming down from the Arctic and gaining speed as it flew across the North Atlantic?

The figure was as naked as an animal and as natural as he remembered her from the riverbank in the Fae realm. She flung her red hair about in the wind and his guitar's melodies. Periodically, she dived gracefully, disappearing beneath the black waves before surfacing again in a fountain of seawater. She was way below him, but he observed her bare her fangs at him showing that she wouldn't be trifled with. Bradan also saw brilliant green eyes reflecting starlight. She was a mixture of sensual, sinister, and whimsical.

"You have a listener," Merlin remarked. "A child of nature."

"A water demon," Bradan said. "We've met already. We didn't hit it off."

"Obviously. She means to kill you tonight. She still might. I'd keep playing if I were you. She does seem to like your music."

"I'm out of verses."

"That's not good. I'm sure you've got something up your sleeve. You'd better."

Bradan improvised several more parts to the song to extend it and then shifted seamlessly into the piece Silicon Saturday had performed at Stonehenge. Without a backing band, it sounded thin.

He remembered playing as a folk minstrel four centuries before on midwinter nights in smoky inns with badly ventilated fireplaces to a group of travelers and local tradespeople, soldiers, too. Then, he'd had no amplifiers and silicon chips or backing musicians. That audience had also been hard to impress, as warfare and rapine were endemic to the times and distracted his listeners, so he'd relied on only his voice and the melody to hold them. Tonight, this worked and stripped the song to essentials and made it pure.

Bradan knew the demon judged. What verdict would she come to?

The wind picked up. Mid-song, he stopped and looked out at the sea. As he'd performed, it had turned choppy and now the breakers hit Tintagel's rocks hard, sending the spray high up the cliffs. He tasted sea salt in the air. Clouds he hadn't seen before pushed toward land from the west, coalescing into a black shelf heading right at him. However, there was time for one more song before he had to race for shelter to avoid soaking himself and the guitar.

He didn't play to forestall the nymph's attack or to amuse Merlin. He played because the gathering gale's energy was too good to miss and he channeled it into his song. He played outside the chord changes and imported exotic scales he'd learned over a peripatetic life. He remembered particularly the acid rock he'd played in psychedelic San Francisco during the Summer of Love when he'd fronted a band in the Haight.

He sent his twelve-string's chimey harmonics off into the ether between the human and Fae realms.

To hell with Merlin and the demon. The music was his magic.

He finished.

Everything froze.

Rain hit.

And thunder shook the rocks.

Bradan frantically packed his guitar into its case. He'd need it again soon. He doubted the case would protect his precious instrument from this torrent, so he spoke a rhyme in an archaic Celtic dialect. If the spell worked, he'd just rendered the Martin twelve-string safe from water damage for the next hour or so. He knelt in the drenching rain trying to catch his breath.

Through the torrent, Bradan saw the water nymph laugh and wave before disappearing into the water.

He'd entertained her.

And survived.

"You're on your own," Merlin said. He faded into the storm.

"I have an idea about how to stop a war," Bradan shouted through the storm at the wolf, his only audience now. "And save ourselves. Maybe we can take it from a boil down to a simmer. Won't be easy."

CHAPTER 28

Band Practice

Soho, London, February, 1987

"What are we rehearsing?" Anu asked. She arrived after Bradan at Silicon Saturday's upstairs Soho studio. She sat on a flimsy folding chair by her synth on a small table. The place had sparse furnishing and no curtains. The band never stored their instruments and amplifiers in the room when they weren't practicing to avoid having them stolen. Their studio had been broken into thrice since they'd rented it, but there was never anything for the thieves to take. One had written "Silicon Saturday rules" on the wall. Bradan believed they were being satirical.

Neon light from the signage of neighboring sex shops and music clubs washed through the room, daubing the room with spectacular colors. It was nighttime, so the effect was particularly surreal.

Surreal suits my mood, Bradan reflected.

The Saturdays had done what they could to improve the room's acoustics by covering most of the bare, concrete walls with blankets, but nothing about the place could match the sound quality of even a rudimentary recording studio.

However, the Chinese restaurant on the floor below never protested or even noticed their late-night, building-rattling practice sessions nor had they complained about the ever-present smell of marijuana. Local prostitutes or passersby on the sidewalk below walking home from a pub heard their rehearsals and occasionally stopped to cheer or jeer up at their flat, but as the Saturdays' musical cohesion improved, the ratio of cheers to jeers swung in the band's favor and fewer beer bottles were hurled at them. These were tough crowds to entertain, but in the spirit of edgy artistic license, the Saturdays would fling open the windows and perform impromptu concerts for the demimonde until constables arrived to break up the party and issue citations to the band.

It inured them to the most hostile crowds and it was good PR.

Bradan hoped listeners wandered off to buy their music.

As things started to happen for the Saturdays, they'd debated whether to set up shop in more respectable digs above Bradan's gallery, but his prim Mayfair neighbors would have flipped at the volume. Besides, the band was supposed to be a democracy, and relocating rehearsals to a building Bradan owned would have been perceived as his effort to unduly influence their musical direction and business decisions. Further, practicing in gritty, trendy Soho was authentic to what they wanted to present themselves as.

So, they stayed.

"We'll rehearse our usual set list," Bradan answered Anu.

"You written anything new?"

"I've got something. I'm not sure what."

"Something for the band?"

"A different audience. It has to be perfect. This crowd, they can be troublesome if they're not impressed."

"Worse than the crowds we get on the street below?"

"Maybe."

"Mysterious," she said.

Anu wound a strand of black hair around her forefinger. The hair bit into her flesh.

"Before the rest of the crew arrive," she said, "I've got kind of an off-the-wall question."

"Shoot," Bradan said.

"Seems totally absurd," she admitted. "But Uncle Ranbir said the police wanted to search the garage yard after Stalin pulled some daft stunt with his pet tank and a mirage or something happened that hid the tank and fooled the authorities. That saved everyone lots of trouble, but it's all bloody supernatural, don't you think? You didn't have anything to do with that?"

"Your uncle's a fine mechanic, and he has an absolutely brilliant imagination."

Every once in a while, someone gets close to the truth, he thought.

"Next you'll ask if I can see my reflection in a mirror," he said. "I can and I have no mystical talents. I sell art and play music."

"It seems utterly bonkers, Bradan. Maybe my uncle has been sharing Stalin's vodka, though he's never been much of a drinker. That's not all. I'm still not sure what happened at Stonehenge. First, we were merrily playing along with that crazy director, Damian, egging us on, then it all went pear-shaped. I thought I saw creatures fluttering about us and dancing a wild roundelay to our music. It was a frenzy. Even your dog went mad."

"The light was weird," Bradan said. "Who knows what we saw. The stones affect folks differently especially on a solstice twilight. And everyone was high. Perhaps it was all an opium dream."

"But that's just it, I wasn't high. The rest of 'em were, but not me. I never use drugs."

"You lost your glasses," he said.

"Yep. It was impossible to see clearly after they fell off. Anyway, forget I said anything. You write great music."

I can't let her believe she's losing it, he thought. *It ain't cool.*

"I wasn't high at Stonehenge, either," he said. "I thought I saw things, too. When I looked at Damian's raw footage, there were some insanely weird effects in the background, things flying around. I told him not to edit it out of the final cut. It makes for a better video."

He saw that she wouldn't be sidetracked.

"Look, Anu, it was a creepy night. I don't know what we saw. It seemed like things were there, then they weren't. Anyway, we made stellar music."

She shrugged. "That's what counts."

The keyboard player absently noodled a few chords on her synthesizer. Her sense of music was excellent. Bradan knew she'd been trained in classical piano, but had given that up to take on studying for a more practical career in health care. Playing with the Saturdays was her way of assuaging her creative instincts.

She looked at him across their rehearsal room.

"Your friend—Mags or Margaret or whatever—I saw her leave the stage after she sang with us at the club and wander off to a quiet, dark corner backstage away from the spotlights. I think she thought no one paid her any mind. Then she disappeared into thin air."

"This was our gig at the club on Wardour?" Bradan asked. "As you say, that club is dark. Ask the rest of the band or anyone in the audience, they all saw Mags, as did I. She did leave in a hurry, had to be somewhere, but if you want to meet up, I'll ask."

Careful. Let's not make promises you can't keep, he thought. *I've no idea how this particular apparition would feel about being trotted out just to prove she's no ghost. She won't see the humor in it.*

They were interrupted as the other musicians clumped up the narrow stairs to arrive in haphazard order, Liam carrying his precious Gibson Les Paul guitar in its black case; Suki lugging her Fender Jazz bass and with a cool-looking black leather jacket tossed over her shoulder, hussar style; and Constantine, last of all, holding two sets of drumsticks and complaining about how the U.K.'s weather was way more wretched than San Francisco's, even on that city's worst days, but he was wearing shorts.

The five of them then made several more pilgrimages down to the band's van and Liam's Ford Cortina to haul assorted amplifiers and Constantine's drum kit to their rehearsal space.

As they set up their instruments, shoved the amps into place, and plugged in, Bradan idly played the opening chords of "Dancing in the Forest." It was for himself more than the Saturdays. He sang, too.

"Interesting words," Constantine called over to him from his stool behind a mountain of drums. "Sounds kind of political, more so than your usual stuff, but pretty."

"We *are* political," Bradan said. "We're a pop-dance band, but we also say things that need saying, especially about environmental causes. That sets us apart."

"Hear, hear," Liam said. Bradan thought the guitarist didn't try to muffle scorn.

"It's about saving nature," Anu said. "You want us to work it through with you?"

"It's personal," Bradan said.

"It's a dance jam," Suki said. "The bass part writes itself."

The room rumbled as she plucked out the tune on her instrument. Bradan felt the deep, subsonic notes in his chest as the windowpanes rattled. She was right. The added electric instrumentation turned his wispy folk song into something that would get any crowd on their feet.

Liam sent cutting chords over Suki's rhythm and Anu joined with her synthesizer. Not to be left out, Constantine hammered out the beat on his drums. Bradan's wispy, allusive tune grew big enough to fill a stadium.

"Fuckin' spectacular," someone shouted encouragement from the street below.

"Let's do our regular set list," Bradan shouted over the impromptu jam.

"Bradan, why are you holding out on us?" Liam asked as things quieted and the instruments tapered off into a disjointed silence.

"When we formed the group, we all agreed that the rest of us had first right of refusal if any one of us came up with something good. You can't just run off with it on your own without seeing if it works with the Saturdays."

"You think it's good?" Bradan asked. He felt flattered. Liam was the band's most savage critic of new material.

"Why don't you tell us about it?" Anu asked. She seemed intrigued.

"I'll play it later tonight, outside. I think there's even a moon out. It'll be magical."

I must sound crazy, he thought.

"That's eccentric, even for you," Suki said.

"You going to play electric?" Constantine asked.

"Maybe, if I want volume."

"Where's the power coming from?" the drummer wanted to know.

I wonder if the king can help with that, Bradan thought.

What he said was, "I'll think of something, or maybe just play acoustic. It'll be quiet and beautiful."

"A folk minstrel thing?" Suki asked. "Kinda quaint. Who's going to watch you on a frozen night?"

"It's good for my soul to play alone once in a while."

Pass it off as an eccentric musician thing where I need to recharge my creative batteries, Bradan thought.

"I'll find a spot near my flat over in Green Park," he said. "There's a glade I like. I don't think anyone will watch. Let's get back to rehearsing our set list."

Take the hint, he thought. *You'd want no part of what I'm planning. It's just like any other gig except for the audience of supernatural warriors from rival Fae tribes out to slaughter one another. One side outright hates me and the other is ambivalent about me at best. And there'll be cartel assassins thrown in for good measure. My song might create harmony. Or it doesn't, but it's my only move.*

Music as magic; I'm naïve.

The tank may help.

"Bradan, are you in trouble?" Anu asked.

"No more than usual," he said.

CHAPTER 29

Saturday Night with the Saturdays

"Bradan's in trouble," Anu said.

"He's shook," Constantine agreed. "I've known him for years. He's a strange dude doing strange things, but this is as worried as I've ever seen him."

"He's not askin' for our help, thinks he doesn't need us," Liam said. "Whatever this park thing is, it's on him, just another of his many secrets."

"I think he's planning a publicity stunt with the song he played for us," Anu said. "He wanted to keep us out of if the police arrive, but let's show up to support him—or post bond if he's arrested. That park isn't big. We can find him. We'll hear him playing."

"I grant you, the tune he did was solid," Liam said. "But he didn't want to include us, so screw him. Pass the joint."

The drummer hit a rim shot, startling everyone. "I'm with Anu. If he's in trouble, we should help. We got to stick together to make the band work."

Silence met him.

"No one's interested," Suki said.

"*You're* not interested," Anu said. "Perhaps the rest of us want to talk about it."

"Why the fuck are we talking?" Liam asked. "Who's the audience supposed to be in the dead of winter at midnight?"

"Swans," Suki said.

She took a long drag on a joint, held the smoke in her lungs.

"I've had my share of bizarre experiences with him," Liam said. "They don't end well. Playing Stonehenge was fuckin' terrifying. Thought it was just the drugs dazzling my brain, but we all saw the same bizarre shit. And that was before the police showed up. Plus, someone's trying to kill him. His art gallery got blown to bits. And his Christmas party, son of a bitch, I don't want my head lopped off. And who was that Mags babe that he just invited into our set with no by-your-leave from the rest of us?"

"That actually worked," Suki said. "She was peculiar as shit, but a terrific singer."

"There's something in it for us," Anu replied. "If we play even one song, it will be publicity like you wouldn't believe. We've done amazingly well over the last year, but if we want to really cut through all the competition from other bands, we need to do something insane. Damian's video at Stonehenge pushed us along. What I'm proposing will get us more attention."

"So self-interest makes this all okay?" Liam asked. "We'll wind up with a huge fine, in prison, or both. You're usually the sensible one. Never get high, always the cautious sort. You keep the rest of us in line. This seems like the maddest thing ever."

"Pass me the joint," Anu said.

The other three stared at her.

"Pass me the joint," she demanded. "It's bonkers, but it gets our name out—and may help Bradan with whatever he's gotten himself into."

Looking dubious, Liam gave Anu the marijuana. She took a tentative toke and coughed out smoke.

Liam laughed.

"You like him, don't you?" he said.

"As a friend," Anu said angrily. "I don't have to hop in bed with him to help him. This band's been good to me. It's creative. We're saying something and I'm happy with my royalty checks. The rest of you are, too, far as I know. I'm getting a flat in Uxbridge and I don't need family money to make that happen for the first time ever in my life."

"I'm paying my bills, too," Constantine said.

"The Amesbury police are still after us for trespassing at Stonehenge," Suki said. "We're lucky they haven't chased us down in London to prosecute."

"We turned that to our advantage," Anu snapped. "Don't be a bunch of wankers. Our press releases can play it up, Stonehenge and now a London park at midnight. We'd be total outlaws."

"We'd be totally arrested," Suki said.

Constantine said, "Anu's right. I'm for being a rebel."

"Fuck no," Liam said. "This is a joke? It's tonight. How do we set up in a West End public park in two hours? We'd never get permits. No power, either."

"We have a generator," Constantine said. "Never gave it back to Damian after the Stonehenge thing."

"We're really doing this, Tiny?" Liam asked. "Is it decided, then? Let's put it to a vote."

"What happens if it's a tie?" Constantine asked.

CHAPTER 30

In the Belly of the Beast

Green Park, London, February, 1987

"We hit something," Bradan said. He listened to the tank's metal tracks crunch against metal.

"We crushed that car," Stalin said. "Did you hurt my tank?"

"Not bloody likely," Bradan said, peering down from the turret at the T-34's victim.

The tank had crumpled a parked Morris Mini Cooper, slewing the wreck onto the sidewalk and into a shop front.

It was past two in the morning and the back streets of Hackney were mostly deserted. Bradan looked up at the dark windows and wondered what residents would make of the bizarre scene: an ice cream truck that had crashed into another vehicle to the accompaniment of cheesy cartoon music.

Disguising the T-34 as an ice cream van was a natural move. It had fooled the constables in the car repair yard and he'd carried the deception over for this madcap dash through nighttime London en route to Green Park.

Consistent with a visual disguise for the tank, he'd created an aural accompaniment reasoning that ice cream trucks usually announced themselves with tinkling music, but after hearing it on repeat, the tune was driving him mad.

"Who or what is driving?" Stalin demanded. "I'm asking you again. The steering levers have moved by themselves ever since we left my yard. I don't believe anything that is happening tonight."

"There's more coming. Have some vodka." Bradan passed a bottle to the mechanic.

"I am so high, I'm floating. You encouraged me to smoke two fat joints back in the yard."

"That I did. And I recommended drinking half the vodka, too. Here, have the rest now. If things don't make sense, vodka helps."

Through a haze of ethanol and dope, Stalin appeared stunned by events after he'd reluctantly let Bradan clamber back into the T-34's turret earlier in the evening. Likely, the Russian assumed that since Bradan couldn't drive the tank, nothing untoward would happen.

Bradan didn't mention that the next time the 85mm cannon fired, he'd be pulling the trigger, not Stalin. No need to panic the man.

After midnight, Connie had migrated from the shattered E-type to Stalin's tank. Bradan didn't know she was there until the tank's V-12 engine spontaneously started in a cloud of diesel smoke and, after a few tentative mechanical sounds, the T-34's gears grated into place with a loud, rasping thunk. The tank lurched into reverse. Bradan sensed a string of ghostly profanity before they came to a shuddering stop, then, accompanied by more gear grinding, they'd rolled forward, out of the yard, picking up speed, narrowly missing the yard's gate, and moved out onto Hackney's streets, and into the night.

Bradan stood out of the commander's cupola on top of the turret holding on for dear life. Tintagel perched beside him, adroitly moving to match the pitching rhythm of the T-34.

The Russian swayed drunkenly and almost fell out of the turret.

276 PETER W. BLAISDELL

"How?" he slurred.

"It's a fairy tale," Bradan replied.

"It's a ghost story," Connie corrected quietly into his ear.

As soon as they'd cleared the yard, Bradan recited the spell disguising the war machine as an ice cream van and off they went toward Green Park. The tank moved surprisingly quickly over city streets, and Bradan felt the cold wind pushing past him. He felt invincible riding atop thirty-five tons.

Then they crashed into the Mini.

The ice cream van was just image. The reality under the image was that a tank did enormous damage if it collided with something. Connie hadn't yet mastered the art of driving the beast through narrow streets jammed with parked cars.

Bradan hopped off the tank, leaning on a fender for support. He looked at the Mini Cooper. It was a squashed bug and a total loss with one of the Russian tank's treads sitting atop the crumpled car and all of its windows shattered, leaving glass strewn across the pavement. Tintagel leaped gracefully to the sidewalk to sniff at radiator fluid spilling from the wreck.

Bradan let the ice cream van illusion lapse and the olive-green T-34 reappeared with its sinister 85mm cannon pointed down the street.

He felt like he'd run a marathon and stumbled over the finish line. He needed to recuperate to wash away the crushing fatigue entailed in maintaining the illusion. He'd have to risk passersby seeing them, but there was little traffic and few pedestrians this late on a cold night, and he'd intentionally chosen badly lit side streets, so the risk was tolerable.

Stalin half climbed, half fell off the turret and threw up.

"Too much smoke and vodka, never a good combination," Bradan remarked.

"You encouraged me," the Russian said.

"Never take a magician's advice."

"What?" Stalin said.

A few lights went on behind curtained windows on second and third floors, but nobody called down at them. Someone must have heard the sounds of rent, crumpled metal. However, it was the kind of neighborhood where folks tended not to pay close attention to unusual sounds that didn't directly impinge on them. Nor did they call the police.

"Should we stay here and let someone know about the car?" Connie asked.

"Can't," Bradan shouted over the engine. "We need to get to Green Park soon. Insurance will cover damages to the Cooper. And I'll come back to pay for any costs above that."

"If you survive," Connie said.

"If I survive," Bradan confirmed. "Did the crash hurt?"

"Didn't feel it," she said.

"Three inches of armor keeps the world at bay," Bradan observed.

"'If you can drive a car, you can drive a tank,'" Connie said. "You promised me that. Hate to tell ya, it ain't true. This thing is almost impossible to manage even for me. It's worse than handling a tractor in a muddy farm field back in Mississippi— did that when I was a kid growing up. Glad the Russians didn't design my daddy's tractor."

Bradan reached down and grabbed the Russian and pulled him back up the turret.

"You won't want to miss what's coming," he said.

The wolf leaped aboard.

"You bring a musical instrument. Why?" Stalin asked. "This is beyond silly."

"Silly," Bradan agreed.

Rolling forward again, Bradan stood out of the tank's hatch and watched the street ahead. To a viewer, it would look like he sat on the roof of an ice cream van, a curious sight, but less crazy than riding a Russian tank through central London.

It thrilled him.

Until he remembered what he faced.

A collapsing tree hadn't disabled the portal, but the T-34's cannon would be more potent. If one shot didn't do the job, he had dozens of rounds of armor-piercing and high-explosive shells. This antique was the most destructive weapon he could lay his hands on.

However, it would be vulnerable to magical threats, so he'd count on his modest skills with enchantment and the Fae king's help. He'd also use his music as a pretty distraction.

"We have company," Connie said.

Bradan saw the Fae king lounging on the ice cream van's hood as if he owned the world.

"He saved me once for his purposes," Bradan said. "He's with me—I think, but he's got his own game. How this plays out, I don't know."

The king snapped his fingers and, overhead, a formation of his followers materialized and circled about the ice cream truck, flying close to marvel at this strange contraption. Did they see the tank beneath his illusion? They danced in the air anticipating the coming battle. Bradan intuited that they were eager to get on with it, but fearful.

"An escort," Bradan said.

He felt like a shark trailed by a school of pilot fish. The king's followers had grown into legions. Among them, he recognized the water demon he'd seen on his tour of the king's Fae realm and again at Tintagel. She blew him a kiss. Water was her natural element, but she flew gamely along with other Fae of every variety.

They reached Green Park's entrance by Half Moon Street.

"Let's go," Bradan shouted. "They started it, I'm finishing it."

The purity of his rage and purpose held off his fear for a few heartbeats. He'd ride that as long as it lasted.

"Good you're angry, sugar, but what's the plan?" Connie asked. She sounded tense. Bradan heard the ghost's voice as if she spoke next to his ear despite the tank engine's diesel growl.

"There *is* a plan, right?"

"There's a plan," he said. "Whether it works or not—"

"As many friends as you've got, they've got more," Connie said.

"I've got you," he told her. "I'll drop the disguise. You're back to being a tank. Music may calm them like at Stonehenge."

"Didn't the Fae queen almost kill you at Stonehenge?"

"I'll have to play better. Let's find the portal."

"And then?"

"And then, war."

CHAPTER 31

The Band Plays On

Fear started in Bradan's gut and moved into his chest, shoving aside anger but not his purpose.

If there's a sacrificial lamb tonight, it's me.

The king clapped his hands once and the portal appeared. It was always there, but imperceptibly faint, connecting worlds that were joined at the hip.

Bradan pressed his eye against the tank's telescopic gunsight. Decades of grime obscured his view through the primitive optics and he felt like he peered down the wrong end of a telescope. Despite that, he saw the portal's luminescent haze dead ahead, contrasting with the black trees.

He pulled himself halfway out of the turret to see better.

Tintagel took this as his hint to leap off the rear deck, sniffing about, sensing slaughter.

"Kill the engine," Bradan whispered to Connie.

The diesel growl guttered, the glade went quiet, and the park appeared dark and empty, but the tank's noisy approach must have been noticed.

Bradan intuited that the king's legions hovered amid the trees behind him. However, except for tinkling vocalizations on the outer boundary of his auditory senses, he didn't hear them.

Are they afraid of the coming fight? he wondered.

Usually, he could see across the park from this central spot, but tonight the glade transformed itself, and the trees became hostile and ancient. Having the Fae present shifted things as their realm impinged on London. As he'd noticed before, proximity to the portal deadened the city's familiar sounds. The border between realms influenced both realities for the worse. The foliage packed together forming an impenetrable mass with a dense overstory. In the daytime, the green space was open and too civilized to host mayhem, but tonight, he no longer recognized the familiar species of sturdy, English trees that kept to themselves except when needed to give summertime shade to park visitors. The glade had become an arena for blood sport cut off from the rest of the city.

Bradan sensed that he teetered on the edge of a space truly unknowable to him or any human. He'd sever that link now.

He dropped back into the turret and adjusted the gun's elevation, lining up the first shot perfectly.

Stalin watched him.

"I'll shoot," the Russian said quietly.

"The first shot's mine," Bradan replied. "I started this somehow. I'll end it—I'll *try* to end it. Just load. You can fire soon."

He thought he'd hesitate—the Fae, savage and morally apart from mankind, could still teach his species respect for nature. However, suffocating the chaos that free transit across the portal allowed was the right thing to do, the only thing to do.

Adrenaline and fatigue made the decision for him and he pulled the trigger lever. He gripped the gunsight, holding on, mentally and physically bracing himself for the cannon's concussive noise and jarring recoil.

Nothing happened.

Had the queen sensed his intent and worked some enchantment to stymie the gun from sending an armor-piercing shell blasting out of the cannon at 2,600 feet per second toward the portal, faster than thought, faster by far than the fleetest Fae?

There was a backup firing mechanism—the Russians thought of everything when they'd designed this crude killing machine—a lanyard hanging on the side of the breech like an eighteenth-century ship's cannon.

Will it work?

Will it snap?

Bradan yanked the lanyard and the T-34 rocked back, recoiling from the blast.

That kicked things off.

The Fae queen and her armies boiled out of the portal and fell on the king's forces surging out from behind the tank.

Bradan tried to track the shot's effect through the telescopic sight, but the muzzle flash had fried his night vision, so he pulled himself through the hatch for a better view, dodging a grappling pair of Fae trying to wrest the life out of each other, fingers clinging to necks. They collided with the turret and fell to the ground.

Through the dancing spots in his vision, he saw nearby leaves and branches blown down from the muzzle blast. Magical creatures had been knocked indiscriminately about, buffeted by the concussion.

As his vision cleared, he saw the portal still intact, but it wavered. Violet and reddish tendrils drifted about the central slit. Fae from the queen's armies made their way through, but they struggled. Whatever magic enabled the portal's function had been hurt.

"Another round," Bradan shouted to Stalin. "Armor-piercing and then high-explosive, as many as it takes to finish things right here, right now."

Fumbling drunkenly, the Russian loaded another shot into the cannon.

"You are a dictator," he yelled.

"Damn straight. I'll finish this with fire."

Bradan recentered the gun on the portal.

He noticed that the king now sat in the cramped folding chair for the tank commander watching intently the teamwork between Bradan and Stalin.

Is he helping? Bradan wondered.

Stalin signaled another round chambered. The king made a small hand motion sending a spritz of sparkling dust motes into air around the T-34's trigger.

Has he reversed whatever spell blocked the cannon from functioning earlier?

Bradan pulled the trigger and the cannon blasted another round toward the portal. He nodded thanks to the king, who clambered out of the tank to rejoin his legions.

Bradan continued to madly fire as Stalin loaded shells and the portal became more tattered and faded with every shot.

The tank's metal turret was his cocoon, but Bradan poked his head up. The scene before him was more horrific than any he'd witnessed when the king had guided him through the Fae's civil war. Gory, hacking creatures now packed the glade. Their delicate appearance wasn't compatible with such savagery. One hurled a spear with enough force to impale three of his opponents. A sprinkling of fairy dust cast by a tiny, floating woman wiped away a whole squad of her enemies.

Bradan couldn't discern who was who; the king and queen knew. They floated above the trees on opposite sides of the glade directing their respective forces.

What did spilled Fae blood look like? Rainbow-colored puddles that mixed with the muddy snow. He saw it spattered about the clearing symbolizing an entity's life force seeping away. The blood was as alien to Bradan as the beings who bled, but it none-theless represented grievous wounds or death.

The queen's forces were doing their damnedest to attack the tank, but the Russian beast had so far been impervious to fire and spell though it was now dented and gouged. The king's enchantment must be countering any spell powerful enough to really harm the T-34. Bradan yanked himself back into the tur-ret as a large branch snapped from a nearby tree and bounced off the tank. Wood—even magically propelled—was no match for steel armor.

Nobody's winning. Actually, everyone is losing.

The dead were piled in mountains.

Tintagel stood beside the tank raptly following the carnage, eager to join the fray, agnostic to which faction he tore to shreds.

"It's their fight," Bradan yelled at the wolf. "Leave them to it."

Bradan saw the water nymph who had threatened him streamside in the Fae realm and then danced to his music on the coast. She was in the thick of the conflict. He surprised him-self by being relieved that she'd survived so far.

Bradan remembered being caught between the Russian army and German Wehrmacht as ordnance smashed into the ground beside him. Now as then, he was the excuse for savagery.

A fumbling midair group of Fae clawed and stabbed at one another then lost momentum and slammed into the tank. The impact dented the T-34's sloped frontal armor and rocked the thirty-five-ton vehicle backward.

"Shoot the sons of bitches," Connie yelled. "They've tried to kill you since Stonehenge."

"*Some* want to kill me. Not all of them."

"What now?"

"Play my guitar."

"Fuckin' crazy," Connie said scornfully.

"Music, it's the one thing they all like," Bradan shouted.

"Bad idea, sugar. Hide in the tank. Keep blasting their gateway."

"Violence isn't solving this. They'll listen to me. Even an angry truce stops the slaughter."

"What works?" Connie asked. "Small magic, or audacity, or friends?"

"And the music."

Bradan nerved himself and lurched out of the turret. Stalin gaped at him as Bradan frantically uncased his guitar.

"Keep firing," Bradan yelled. "You'll have to do it all by yourself."

The Russian looked dazed from the mystical violence exploding around him. The cosmos was tearing itself apart before his eyes.

Bradan strummed the opening chords of "Dancing in the Forest." It was a bold song and he'd planned to stand boldly, using the tank's rear deck as his stage, the minstrel confronting chaos with melody, but instead he crouched behind the turret dodging flying spears, arrows, and cartwheeling bodies, the tune interrupted by his efforts to hide from death.

The tank fired again at the portal. Bradan clung to the turret, then resumed playing. His guitar sent forth beautiful notes. He played as well as he ever had and the song was more sublime than at Tintagel Castle. However, there, nature had been wild but sympathetic. The surf and sudden storm propelled the song and the raw coast inspired him to improvise over the song's melodies. Even Merlin's sardonic reaction and the demonic maiden dancing on the wave tops were goads for his flights of fancy.

But tonight, he made thin gruel. It was impossible to hear the twelve-string's incandescent tone or his voice. Bradan's lyrics were intricate and playful, but it was dandelion down in a storm, and the Fae paid no attention. Playing folk minstrel in a war wasn't working, and his musical magic didn't dampen blood lust. It had been an arrogant, whimsical notion to think that he could defuse a war that had gone on since time immemorial.

A bolt of light hit the tank's turret beside him, melting the steel and deeply gouging it. He felt heat and heard Connie shout in pain. Whatever protective spell the king had cast sheltering the T-34 had faded.

Faintly at first, but gaining volume, Bradan heard a keyboard echo the melody that he plucked on his twelve-string. The overdriven synthesizer thickened the sound and made it propulsive and danceable. He recognized Anu's assured touch turning his little folksong into a dance jam. And now he heard Constantine's smashing symbols and drums overlaid by the squall of Liam's guitar adding sharp edges and pure chords to the song's melody. A lush, fat bass line pushed the cadence—Suki working her magic. As the separate instruments all synchronized into a cohesive sound, the volume climbed gigantically.

And now he fronted a band.

Silicon Saturday had joined the party.

Bradan heard the band's amplifiers, everything needed for an outdoor concert, overwhelming the rude battle's cacophony.

"I'm tripping balls," Constantine shouted at him.

The Fae aren't bothering to hide from us, Bradan thought. *The musicians see them.*

"What are these things?" Suki screamed back.

"Play," Bradan yelled. "It's *really* bad if the music stops."

Don't question what's happening or the house of cards collapses. Don't let modern skepticism mess with the vibe.

Where is the band? How did they set up so quickly?

They'd positioned themselves as far from the portal as possible. He saw amplifiers and speaker cabinets randomly arranged amid trees. The Saturdays had equally haphazardly situated themselves amid the greenery, standing on moss, beneath low branches, appearing organic to the setting as if they'd become magical entities themselves. Constantine played his full drum kit, double kick drums sitting unevenly on the damp ground and a dozen cymbals canted at unusual angles, and a gong suspended from an oak branch. He hunched over his kit, apparently trying to blot out medieval viciousness and magical dementia. This was the antithesis of a controlled studio environment, and only the drummer's mastery of percussion allowed him to not only keep the beat but work in complex cross rhythms at once tribal and cosmic.

What do they think they're seeing?

Fleetingly, Bradan wondered how the Saturdays kept their composure amid the mind-bending, enchanted disorder all about them. Maybe months of playing from their practice studio with the windows open to raucous strangers in Soho had inured them to any assault on their senses.

With renewed energy, Bradan sang above the surging synthesizer, percussion, and guitar. Amazingly, his unamplified voice carried over the instrumentation.

Will anyone listen?

Will they think we're intruding on their war and attack us?

Ironically, considering their slaughterhouse setting in the park glade, his lyrics spoke of gaiety and timeless love in the modern world and the beat carried the day with sheer volume tumbling the Fae about.

The battle's clamor dwindled, buried beneath song. Magical beings stopped killing one another. Some Fae still grappled with their opponents, but the rabid energy left their tendons. Fighting became embracing. They weren't warm embraces. Hatred couldn't be discarded easily. But they weren't trying to kill one another—or him.

At first the combatants watched the musicians impassively, some sitting on tree branches, others leaning on magical weapons, or simply floating in air, but then, as at Stonehenge, they danced. Some used the beat, others moved to their own rhythm. At first, the warring tribes pirouetted among themselves, sticking together, insular and tribal. Then the boundaries diffused and the groups blended like different-colored liquids merging to form a solution of uniform hue. Perhaps they remembered their common culture: They were all Fae and nothing like humans.

Bradan had to hand it to Silicon Saturday, when they laid down a dance groove, they knew their business. Soon everyone danced on the ground or in the air with their dented armor, gauzy robes, flowery tiaras, and battered weaponry. Some linked arms with enemies they'd just tried to slaughter. Everyone mingled except the king and queen, who remained aloof and watched the revel from opposite sides of the glade, not hiding mutual contempt.

Do they hate each other so much? Bradan wondered.

The song ended.

"What next?" Liam shouted at him.

"Play our club set in order," Bradan yelled urgently. "Keep going."

Whatever magic they worked was based on momentum, to not give the warring parties time to reflect and fight again or turn on the band.

The Saturdays roared through their songs.

And then Bradan saw that exhausted Fae danced, limped, walked, or flew with torn dragonfly wings toward the portal entrance to vanish back into their realm. The gateway was tattered, but it sufficed to transport them home in small bands or individually. Many helped injured comrades. A few still carried lances and spears topped with ragged pendants.

The portal was a shadow of itself so the fairies queued up in a line that meandered through the park. Eventually the glade emptied save for the two royals, the Saturdays, the Russian, and the wolf.

Fae bodies shimmered and dissolved into rainbow puddles like water on neon-lit, city sidewalks after a shower.

The queen looked over the glade. If this was peace, it was barely reconciliation.

She turned on her heel and sailed through the portal. As she entered, she bestowed a look of incandescent fury at Bradan.

No parting threats or curses, Bradan thought. *But I've been warned to leave.*

CHAPTER 32

Vodka Is the Answer

The king left last.

He'd done this at Stonehenge.

Bradan watched him saunter across the glade stepping respectfully over rainbow pools before bounding through the portal's remnants. He moved as agilely as a ballerina.

Now on the other side of the fractured door between worlds, his image floated hazy and distorted. Bradan observed him touching his hat with a forefinger, a salute. Or maybe he did no such thing and turned away and vanished into his Fae realm without a backward glance.

However, the king's broad-brimmed velvet hat sailed through the portal at the same instant the Russian tank's cannon split the night with a concussive blast that knocked Bradan off his feet. He felt something smack him hard in the chest. As his vision cleared, he saw the king's hat next to him. It still felt warm and Bradan guessed this was from royal body heat.

He placed the hat on his head. It fit perfectly.

The portal was now utterly gone. The T-34's last shot had been the coup de grace.

The wolf surveyed the battle scene and wandered over to pee on the spot the portal had occupied. Then it moved away into the trees. The beast appeared as exhausted as Bradan felt. Probably, he would curl up somewhere and snooze.

"I did not fire the cannon," Stalin shouted.

"No need to yell," Bradan said.

Everything supernatural was gone—except him.

Silicon Saturday let the music dwindle to silence. Constantine set his sticks down on a snare drum. The other musicians stared at Green Park's glade. It reverted in an eyeblink from a wild, alien forest to manicured greenery. London's sounds flooded back into the park.

"Let's go," Bradan said. "Sound doesn't carry well sometimes hereabouts, like it's been dampened. Still, someone will likely have heard a bit of the noise from all the shit that just went down and constables will arrive eventually. Anu, give me your hand."

With enormous effort, he gripped the keyboard player's outstretched hand and pulled himself to his feet. He motioned tiredly for the band to follow and put distance between themselves and the battlefield. He focused on making it to a distant park bench that looked more inviting than any feather bed he'd ever seen. Arriving, he sagged into it and propped his Martin against the armrest. Then he lay down. He barely had energy for breath, but managed to tilt the hat over his eyes. Every bit of strength had been leached out of him. He knew from hundreds of fights big and small over his long life that he'd gradually recover, but at the moment he couldn't muster any emotion whatever.

Stalin followed him, looking back at his tank.

"I know it wasn't you," Bradan said.

"Who was that fellow who disappeared into the trees?" the Russian demanded. He still shouted.

"Quiet," Bradan said. "Let's not get arrested."

Bradan tilted his hat just far enough so that he could see. In the distance, the glade filled with police, first two on horses, their mounts skittish about entering the glade, then a half dozen cars disgorged constables in body armor carrying automatic weapons, then oceans of officers inundated the park.

"A visitor from somewhere else," Bradan said. "He fired at the portal."

"How?"

"I don't know," Bradan said. The bench was too far for the police to pay him any attention at the moment. However, they'd spread their dragnet soon. He'd leave before that happened. No one would be able to connect the now quiet pastoral glade with whatever calls the authorities had received describing mayhem in the West End. Right now, the only tangible evidence of peculiar events was the tank, its cannon barrel still hot. The park's trees had reverted to their normal British, civilized foliage with nary a primeval oak or sprig of magical flora to be seen.

He noticed a smear of rainbow-colored blood on his pants.

"Why?" Stalin asked.

"He wanted to close a door," Bradan said. "I did, too. It's almost morning. Sorry about your tank. Can't get it back to the garage yard even with Connie driving."

"Who's Connie?"

"She drove it here."

"Leave it," Stalin said. "It is possessed. Let the police have it."

"Wise choice," Bradan said. He felt relieved. Trying to mask the armored vehicle with an image on a return journey to Hackney was beyond him after the night's exhausting events. Besides, police would have clambered over the T-34 by now, and have erected barriers around it. He'd never be able to free it from their grasp. If Chief Inspector Young were involved in trying to resolve tonight's confusing events, he'd be hard pressed to explain the presence of a Second World War relic in Green Park.

"They can't trace it to you," Bradan said.

"They'll see damage to Mayfair," Stalin said. "Buildings must be in rubble for miles around."

"Nope. All the shots went into the portal. They didn't touch one bit of London."

He saw that the Russian looked utterly baffled.

"Have more vodka, the people's drink. I'll have some myself."

Bradan grabbed the bottle from Stalin and took a long pull. It burned on the way down.

"What are you?" Stalin asked.

"There's not enough vodka in your bottle to explain."

The band members straggled over to his bench. The musicians carried their instruments like itinerant Renaissance minstrels. They looked stunned.

Before the inevitable barrage of questions, Bradan sat up with enormous effort and faced them. He forced his lassitude aside.

"Long night," he said. "Go home. Thanks for your help. You played brilliantly. It all worked out better than I'd hoped. The police will impound our stuff, but we'll get it back soon, maybe pay a fine for disturbing the peace, probably not. Not that much sound went beyond the park. I have a good solicitor and no one actually saw us play—no one who will talk to the cops anyway. We'll claim ignorance about how our amps and generators wound up here in the middle of the night. They could have been stolen. We'll rehearse new songs Monday evening in our Soho space. What we played tonight belongs on our next album. You'll all get writing credits and royalties."

Money tends to blunt curiosity, he thought.

"You'll go home, too?" Anu asked. She looked shocked, but worked to keep it together.

"Once I get up the energy," Bradan said.

"Creatures took our equipment from the studio and arranged it here," Suki said. "How?" She looked as shocked as Anu, but her composure frayed.

"Magical roadies," Bradan said. "Must have been the king's tribe."

"What happened?" Constantine asked. "Don't shit us, what happened?"

"You haven't taken enough drugs for the story to make any sense at all."

CHAPTER 33

Devil's Hour in the Park

"Look at it this way, you got to blast away with a tank cannon before I kill you. That counts for something, anyone's wet dream."

Bradan recognized the voice immediately and his hatred came just as quickly.

Pedro said, "I don't know what I saw a moment ago across the park, but you were a big part of it—fine music, by the way. I'd wondered how you transported product so skillfully for us in Miami, how you got out of some very bad situations without the feds grabbing you. Now I know. You're some sort of magician or shaman. Say a spell and impossible things happen. Nothing too big, though. I've observed you and the fairy princess and she's much more capable than you—"

"Queen," Bradan corrected.

"—the queen or whatever, she was can work real wonders. She's deadly when the mood strikes."

Pedro held a shotgun pointed at Bradan's gut.

"Nice hat," he said.

He leaned against a tree.

"Hers?" Pedro asked. He didn't seem curious.

"Her ex's," Bradan said.

"Nice hat anyway. Let's get to business. At end of the day— love how Brits use that expression—at the end of the day, you dropped a planeload of my product into the Caribbean. It was a big plane, so I lost a lot. From a strategic perspective, if I let that go, it sends the wrong message to competitors. So we have to make things right."

From Miami, Bradan remembered the drug lord's even, modulated tone slightly inflected with an accent from somewhere in South America.

"I can't get your coke back," Bradan said. "You forced me at gunpoint to fly it into the States."

"This isn't a chat. Marco has a blowtorch. We'll start with that if you've no objections. From there, we'll see where it goes."

Bradan saw a small, pointed blue jet flare behind Pedro. Marco held the torch connected by a hose to a small dolly with two tanks of gas. They'd come prepared.

Bradan watched a half dozen other men behind Marco. None of them paid particular attention to him. Instead, they'd set up a rough perimeter using what cover the trees and shadows provided and scanned the surrounding park. Professionals. This was a job. But they were tense and carried their guns openly. Even Marco kept looking about at the dark trees. Torturing Bradan was an afterthought. However, Pedro focused on him and waved Marco over with the lit torch.

Bradan watched the blue flame approach. It was tiny, but it stood out in the dark. He imagined what it would do to him.

"Police are near," he said.

He knew Pedro and his crew were aware of the crime scene in the glade. Bradan played for time. The wolf should arrive. And if he were to work any sort of spell to avoid dying, he needed time to recover from his exhaustion.

The drug lord looked at the commotion in the glade.

"Not that close," Pedro said. "They may search the park, but it will take a while. And we'll make sure you're not noisy enough for them to hear."

"Why are you here?" Bradan asked.

Stall. I need time for weak magic, audacity, and friends to help me.

It was cruel that he'd brokered a truce between warring Fae tribes only to be caught by Pedro. He'd jettisoned that past, but it confronted him now. He wondered if any of the drug lord's men had been among those who had stormed his gallery. Had they witnessed the chaos in the glade? Professionals or not, they had to be shaken by what they'd seen. He'd use that.

"This is pure, nihilistic violence," Bradan said.

"That's better than violence for a cause?" Pedro asked.

"I'm here because she needed product," he added. The drug lord patted a small suitcase. "Which I can't give to her. I missed the party thanks to you. Strange creature, beyond strange, calling her 'sane' or 'insane' doesn't apply, human descriptions don't fit."

If he weren't about to die, Bradan would have been impressed by the drug lord's lyrical description of his erstwhile partner.

"You've thought about her," Bradan said.

"I always like to understand who I'm dealing with. She could do anything, lethal as hell, so she'd have made a perfect business ally. Nothing would have been beyond us. However, you've thrown sand in the gears again. You dismissed her."

"She dismissed herself. And you've had too much powder."

"I had some, sure, but nothing controls me, not drugs, not anything."

"We should leave," one of Pedro's men called over to them. "Constables heading our way."

Bradan had recovered his stamina, so using the approaching police as a distraction, he intoned the spell to materialize a dragon image. He'd done it twice recently, he knew it worked, and it was all he could think of, nothing fancy.

The dragon with iridescent scales appeared next to Bradan. It could be his pet except for the butcher-knife teeth lining its mouth. As before, the beast breathed violet fire.

It whirled and faced Pedro. Marco leaped backward, tumbling the gas canisters off the dolly and setting his coat afire as the torch touched it. The big man rolled on the ground trying to put out the flames.

"Don't shoot!" Pedro yelled to his men. They'd all aimed automatic rifles at Bradan's apparition.

"It's not real. I'll show you."

The drug lord extended his hand at the dragon like he intended to stroke a German shepherd. The magical creature lunged at him. Even knowing his image, Bradan was still impressed by the realistic bunching of its muscles as it leaped. The image became less impressive as it passed right through Pedro. The dragon immediately whipped around for a second try. One of his men fired a burst at the mirage. The weapon was silenced, but still audible.

"Stupid to shoot," the drug lord said. He pointed at the dragon. "It's nothing, absolutely nothing. Not even a warm bath. Let it come at me again."

Almost immediately, the image began to dissipate and vanished altogether, leaving a final burst of violet flame to mark its passing.

Alerted by the gunshots, but unsure of their precise origin, police in body armor moved in their general direction. Bradan saw them spread out in a long line.

Time to confuse things further, he thought.

Consciously, working to ignore the fatigue brought on by materializing the dragon, Bradan again resorted to enchantment he knew worked and intoned a spell while sailing his hat at Pedro's men. Propelled by his enchantment, it zipped at them like a magical Frisbee, smacking the closest gunman hard in the face before ricocheting into the next closest. All discipline vanished and Pedro's men opened fire on the hat, sending it cartwheeling about in the air, but still making the rounds, targeting each of the killers.

Shooting at it didn't help and immediately the men had to dodge their own bullets.

In the distance, Bradan heard yells from the police and saw them fanning out in their direction. Flashlights probed ahead of them, moving forward methodically, not sure what they were getting into, not taking chances.

As Pedro stared at the chaos, clearly dumbfounded, Bradan stepped closer and hit him as hard as he could on the chin.

God, that felt good. After fifteen hundred years, I've learned how to throw a punch.

The drug lord stumbled backward and sprawled on the grass.

"You've got 'em on the run, you 'ave, but we're happy to lend our services."

"Mags," Bradan shouted. "A sight for sore eyes."

"Yer doin' bloody well with the hat alone. And yer knocked that bloke cold."

"Can't keep it up, running out of strength."

A half dozen of the Elephants materialized beside Mags. Bradan recognized the same crew he'd seen by the Tyburn. They looked even more eerie and wickedly competent tonight. In the darkness and shadow, the women glowed. They held an assortment of clubs, knives, and broken bottles.

Clubs won't do any good against automatic weapons, but then they're ghosts.

"Lay 'em out," Mags shouted at her companions. The Forty Elephants needed no encouragement and, holding their skirts high, raced at Pedro's gunman with supernatural agility. Bullets didn't affect the apparitions, and within seconds all of Pedro's men were prone on the ground bleeding and concussed.

"Don't kill them," Bradan yelled.

"Whyever not?" Mags asked. She flipped open a straight razor. "They was about to do you. And they destroyed your home."

"We'll leave them to the police. I'm sure they'll hire the best solicitors, but there's enough cocaine to send Pedro here away for a long while regardless of his legal defense, given his record in the States. The rest of them will be jailed if for no other reason than they've got illegal firearms."

Bradan reached up to catch his hat, which had returned to him like a boomerang. It had many bullet holes, but was intact enough to put on his head.

"Yer 'ard on yer hats," Mags said.

Bradan stooped to roll over the drug lord. "Tie him up. Have any rope?"

"I 'appen to have some on me. Saved it from our escapade in the Tyburn. Think it was part of someone's noose."

"Suitable for this lot," he said. "We'll leave them for the coppers."

Police flashlight beams probed nearby.

"Good luck with the two ladies," Mags said. "Seen 'em both, like 'em both, so I'll play no favorites and I'll bet on neither horse. But you do have a job sorting things out."

"It lapsed with Trini and I met Del. Then Trini reappeared. They're both incredible. Any advice?"

"Don't fuck up."

With that parting shot, Mags and the Elephants vanished.

Bradan got ready to run, leaving Pedro and his men hog-tied with the suitcase opened plainly displaying the narcotics.

"Stop a moment," Pedro said. Even helpless, he was preemptory.

"That's all you get," Bradan said.

"Who are you?"

"I keep hearing that question."

"So what do you tell them?"

Bradan shrugged. "Lies."

They both looked back at the glade.

"There's nothing the authorities can link to me," Bradan said. "No bodies, no real damage to park property. Sure, a lot of mysterious pools of odd blood, but those are vanishing as we speak. The forensics teams won't be able to make heads or tails of it even if they collect enough for lab analysis—I'd love to see *that* report. There's the tank, of course. That's a mystery they won't be able to solve, a relic with live ammunition not far from Buckingham Palace—awkward to explain how it got within firing range of the royals—so they'll eventually find a happy home for it somewhere in a remote, dusty, military museum and hope the story fades."

The wolf sidled up to Bradan. It had been snacking on swans again. It sniffed disdainfully at Pedro like it couldn't be bothered to tear his throat out.

"I saw things," the drug lord said. "I'll tell people."

Bradan shuddered with pretend anxiety. "Should I be scared? Lots of people saw things, a drunk Russian mechanic, my band of wasted musicians, and your lot of cartel thugs. Gosh, with so much choice, who will they believe? And you, wanted in at least two continents for more felonies than I can count. Bringing up demons and magic will look like a ploy to lighten your sentence based on an insanity plea."

Bradan thought he spotted Chief Inspector Young among the approaching policemen. He'd have to flee.

"But since you've asked," he told Pedro, "I'll tell you not just who I am, but what I am. It won't help you, but it's a rare treat to talk honestly."

Bradan tried to summarize fifteen centuries of hard living in a few sentences.

It felt good that he failed.

There was too much to say.

Especially when he was being truthful.

"All you can do is small magic," Pedro said.

"That's what you got from my biography?" Bradan asked, incredulous. "Nothing else?"

"You're right. It *is* a nice hat," he added and left.

CHAPTER 34

Two Romances, a Phantom, and Incidental Enchantment

Magic didn't solve romantic dilemmas. And immortality didn't make him wise about love.

Bradan *did* know love was a sublime mess and that it was brilliant until it wasn't.

Poets described—very prettily—love, but their fancies didn't fit his experience: Love faded languidly or fractured suddenly. Or it burned until his partner died while he lived on. That was hardest of all.

He also knew that, as often as not, love was just animal lust usefully harnessed. If the parties adored each other, good, but feelings weren't the point.

When love didn't exist, one settled for affection or pragmatic accommodation.

Merlin would call him cynical. However, he'd also agree.

Whatever love was, Bradan believed in it and, over his long life, romantic relationships defined him.

I'll meet Del and Trini, he thought.

How will that go?

Not magical.

∽

"I'm returning to America," Bradan said.

Del looked surprised.

They were back in her club. Bradan had suggested this. His feelings wouldn't get overwrought. The club's rules wouldn't allow it.

Tea sent steamy tendrils into the air between them sitting across a small table from each other. The settings were perfect with tiny lavender flowers on the cups. Bradan thought the rising steam—diaphanous though it was—separated him from Del.

This morning, he'd have preferred something stronger than Earl Grey.

Outside, he saw freezing rain and sleet hitting the club's windows. Spring wasn't arriving in March.

I won't miss this weather for a second, he thought. *But it doesn't make leaving easy that Del's smart and pretty. How does she manage a perfect balance of understatement and exuberant femininity?*

Primary colors, pastels, every hue worked with her. Today, her skirt was wine-red and her blouse was mauve. She'd tossed a business-appropriate black jacket onto a nearby chair.

"I thought you weren't going to be chased out of Mayfair," she said.

"Nobody's chasing me," Bradan replied, angry at her suggestion that he was fleeing.

"I've addressed issues and things are settling down. The random slaughter has stopped. Psychotic folks I once did unwilling business with in Florida will be locked up for a long while in English jails. But I've been through too much to hang around."

He thought about the Fae queen. "I don't think they'll be back, but who knows."

"Where did 'they' go?" Del probed.

"Far away."

"And who are 'they'? Witches, ghosts, and hobgoblins?"

She saw he wasn't going to answer.

"Damn it, Bradan, you've been coy about these insane events since your Christmas bash. You owe me more. We've been together for three years."

Del waved away an attendant trying to pour more tea.

"There won't be further bloodshed at my parties or gallery openings," he said.

"The police?" she asked. "Are they still after you? Or are you going to be coquettish about that, too?"

"The chief inspector wants to interview me about the cartel kingpin they nabbed in Green Park, but for a change I'm apparently not a suspect, or at least not the primary one."

"Bring me along," she said.

"To the States?"

"No," Del laughed. "I've visited, love it, but I'd never live there."

She'd just answered his unasked question.

Bradan felt like Del had kicked him in the gut, but then he'd never expected her to jettison a successful and titled life to follow him around on his nomadic journey. However, hearing her say it buried any shred of hope.

"I meant you should invite me to interviews with the authorities," she said.

"Of course," he said, working to get himself back on track. Then added, "I'm a loose end Young can't account for. He may try to tie me together with Pedro."

"That's his name, Pedro? You knew this kingpin?"

"In another life."

"I'd never appreciated just how many lives you've had until the last few weeks. Putting on my solicitor's hat, is there anything that links you to his drugs business in the U.K.?"

Bradan sipped cold tea. "The fellow's making all sorts of wild allegations, but they'd have to believe I was some sort of immortal wizard for any of it to be true."

"I'm becoming more sympathetic to this guy's ravings," Del said.

"That's all they are, ravings," Bradan said firmly. "The fact that he's a cokehead doesn't help his credibility."

"I'd heard," she said. "Harry Osborn claims this guy had literally kilograms of narcotics on him in the park. Evidently, he planned to meet someone there. Can't imagine who. And it seems an odd spot to transact that kind of business."

"An odd spot," Bradan agreed innocently. "Not to mention the Russian tank misplaced nearby."

"You heard about that? Harry told me they're trying to keep it quiet since it potentially threatened the Palace. How did you come to find out?"

Bradan hid a smile. The truth was so peculiar, nobody would believe it.

"Hard to hide a tank," he said. "I suppose it must be connected with Pedro's narcotics business."

"See, Bradan, you know more than you let on. This is just another example of your secrets."

"I found out harmlessly enough. I took an early morning run through the park. They'd cordoned off a big patch of it, but from a distance, I saw them examining it."

The lies came so easily. This one was even plausible.

"By the way, have they found the head yet?" he asked.

"From the guy that had it chopped off in your flat? Harry's more connected than I am with the Yard, but he's said nothing to me."

"Thinking ahead to better days, it seems a good time to go home," he said.

"Isn't Mayfair home?"

Bradan thought for a moment. "I'm not sure where home is. I've had a lot of them including Mayfair, but this is a chapter closing, and maybe the important thing is knowing when to find another home."

"We have a good life here," Del said.

"We did."

"That's past tense."

"I'm fed up with London," he said flatly.

His feelings came out in a rush with none of the nuance he'd intended.

"Doesn't sound like there's a lot of room for me to persuade you to stay."

"Not being with you will be almost impossible," he said.

"I'm flattered, I suppose."

"Del, considering the last few weeks, it's time to leave. I'm not being chased out; I'm doing this on my own terms. I'll keep my gallery going here. It's doing well and the staff can handle day-to-day."

"You'll be back occasionally?" Del kept her tone casual, but she leaned forward.

He sipped his tea. It was now cold.

A group of women across the room waved at Del. She smiled and waved back.

Bradan used the distraction to whisper a quick spell. His tea instantly became hot. He drained the cup. For several moments, he felt as weak as a kitten and leaned back in the chair.

"I'll visit," he said. "I can't sever ties with you completely. I just can't."

"You once had a gallery in Miami?" she asked.

"Yep."

"And Trini lives in Miami?"

Del parachuted the question gently into their conversation.

"That's no secret," Bradan said. "I didn't say I was going to Miami."

He paused.

Just get it out there, he thought. *I don't gain anything by being coy. Sometimes secrecy works. Today, it won't. And it isn't fair to her.*

"But I probably will," he said. "I'll get my old gallery going again. Former customers reach out to me all the time, so I've got a clientele. I'll be international with locations in both London and the States. Music-wise, my band wants to get bigger. Having a base in both the U.K. and the States helps that, too. Miami isn't perfect for a pop group trying to make their name—L.A. would be better—but there is a scene in South Florida."

"And she's there," Del said.

"And she's there," he agreed. "But if she weren't, I'd still make the move. I used to love London, but I have bad history here. I'm provoking things if I stay."

"'Provoking things'? Well, aren't we being mysterious. I've always hated that about you, Bradan. Since I've known you, there's been a big hidden part."

"I'm not fond of hiding things, either, but it's part of the package."

"I knew it would come to a head when she showed up," Del said.

"Trini traveling to London has nothing to do with it," Bradan snapped. "Getting shot at, having my gallery destroyed, seeing heads rolling about my flat has everything to do with it. And that's not the half of it."

"There's more?" She stared at him hard. "I can see you're not going to tell me. Admittedly, even the bits I know, you've had a rough go of it."

"You'd leave, too."

"Perhaps. It's still a lot to take in over one tea."

Del looked out the window and frowned as the rain hammered the panes. Then she smiled, appearing to change gears.

"On another note," she said. "It seems you've worked your magic."

The remark astounded Bradan. She suspected he was different and unusual, but what had she really known about the supernatural side of his life?

"The *Times* ran a piece on me yesterday, something along the lines of 'Socially prominent city solicitor with strong environmental message sets her sights on parliament.' I could have done without the 'socially prominent' bit, but it's generally rather gratifying."

"Great news. Wonder what prompted the story?"

"Bradan, you're not a bad actor, but the smirk gives you away. It was another series of ads at Piccadilly. I actually saw one of them, well designed and eye-catching."

"Congratulations," he said. "I can't think of a more capable legislator. We're both trying to do right by the environment. If you're elected, you'll be positioned to actually make things happen. Of course, I had nothing to do with the ad."

Yet another untruth, but this one is a white lie.

"Somehow, I get the feeling that this is a parting gift," Del said.

"There will be other chances to help you," he said.

And he hoped it was true. He didn't want to lose touch completely.

~

"I'm returning to America," Bradan said.

Trini didn't look surprised.

"Smart move," she said. "I thought Miami could be crazy, but London is out of control. Saw contractors working on your gallery on the ground floor. They've still got a lot to fix. Those guys who hit you really did a number on it. Aren't the British all about restraint?"

She stood in his foyer.

He was back in his flat. He regretted seeing her here. The thoroughbred atmosphere of Del's club muted emotional outbursts. In his flat, alone with Trini, things could go ballistic. He'd wanted to meet her at an upscale restaurant, but she'd arrived unannounced at his front entrance.

Usually, he admired direct people. Not this afternoon.

She looked past him at the flat. "Great space, high ceilings, and French doors leading to a balcony. And, my God, the paintings. It could be a museum."

His home didn't feel like home though the artwork and furniture were all there. The London police had done a good, but not perfect job, of tidying up after themselves. However, there was residue of the forensics workup of the crime scene. The wolf nosed about, sometimes scratching at the floor here and there, troubled by signs of official investigation. The place smelled of lab chemicals, other people's sweat, and Young's sandalwood cologne. If he used his imagination, he still detected fragrances from his Christmas party's wine and fine spirits, but the other odors almost buried them.

One smell that couldn't be buried was the copper tang of bloody death. That would linger.

Bradan had set his top hat and the Fae king's broad-brimmed velvet hat on a coffee table. They were both considerably the worse for wear, but he kept them for the time being. Even the vilest of times deserved mementos.

At the outer edge of his perception, he intuited that Cyrus's apparition lingered. Violent death sometimes created a durable stain on the ether, but this didn't disturb Bradan. The wolf would chase off the dealer's shade. Tintagel had once roamed with a pack that hunted souls after ancient battles, and those warriors had been made of sterner stuff than Cyrus.

It would take a while for his Mayfair digs to feel like his again.

Really, it never would feel like his again. And he didn't need it to. He was leaving. Connie in the E-type was already on a freighter to Florida.

He'd have a cleaning crew come through tomorrow. It would take time to organize his move, so he'd scrub away as much of the last few months' residual awfulness as possible to make the flat temporarily livable if not homey.

Bradan heard a power saw five floors down where contractors repaired his damaged gallery. He hadn't bothered to tell them about his basement or the lost Tyburn below that. What were they supposed to do about bullet holes in an obscure part of his building no one would see?

His notoriety had increased interest in purchasing expensive art pieces from the gallery. As during the aftermath of his Christmas party, violence and death lent his business cachet. His clientele had a macabre sense of values. But he'd monetize that and reopen next week.

A neighbor had sent a stiffly worded letter suggesting that Half Moon Street would be much better off without him.

Fuck him.

"The chaos in the West End is partly my fault," he told Trini.

"Trouble chases you," she said.

He nodded regretfully. "So much for leading a quiet life in England away from the bad blood I stirred up in Florida. But I've dealt with things here."

He felt proud that he could say this, but also ambivalent. It sounded like something a narco-trafficker would note matter-of-factly after eliminating a business rival.

"You asked Lady Adela to come along to the U.S." Trini didn't frame this as a question. It was a statement.

Bradan shook his head. "I didn't ask. I knew she'd never leave her life. Why should she? Here, she's got a title and a growing career with one of London's biggest legal firms. I've even heard she's planning to run for parliament on an environmental platform."

"That's noble of her. So you're out one aristocratic girlfriend."

"Cold."

"Sorry! I didn't mean it the way it came out. She seemed kind of neat."

"Well, you're here," Bradan said. He waved her into his flat.

"I'd offer you something, but I just got permission to return this afternoon, and I haven't restocked the kitchen or wine room, so options are limited. Sorry about the chill. I've only now turned on the heat, place feels like a morgue. Haven't checked the kitchen yet, but I may be able to make a pot of tea. Does Earl Grey work?"

"Coffee, if you have it, or we can just sit and talk."

He wandered into his kitchen. He heard her move about his place examining the art and then open the French doors and walk onto his balcony. He remembered standing there with Del on Christmas Eve. The memory stung.

The cupboard was almost bare.

"All I've got is a bottle of brandy," he called to Trini.

"Whatever."

Bradan skeptically pulled out the brandy. It was cheap stuff he used for cooking. If he was going to argue with Trini, they might as well share quality liquor. He recited a spell and the brandy metamorphosed into Hennessy Paradis Imperial, a top-flight French cognac.

He knelt on the floor for a while, recovering.

"Bradan, you okay?" Trini called from the balcony.

"Give me a moment," he said.

The better the liquor, the greater the alchemic effort needed to create it from a lesser brand. Magic exacted a price proportional to the outcome. However, he liked good cognac and he needed spirits to fortify himself for Trini.

Slowly he stood up.

"Let's chat," he said, emerging into the main room with two glasses and the bottle.

They positioned themselves opposite each other on nineteenth-century, Restoration-era chairs with a small coffee table between them. He set the cognac bottle on the table beside the hats. The afternoon sun turned the liquor amber. It was an elegant bottle, but it separated them nonetheless.

This won't be a "chat," he thought. *Will it be confrontation or rapprochement?*

"I was expecting bloodstains on the chairs," he said. "But everything looks okay."

Trini leaped up and inspected her chair before reseating herself.

"Someone died here?" she said. "Del mentioned a murder on Christmas Eve."

"They lost their head, literally."

Bradan surprised himself by not feeling one way or the other about Cyrus's gory demise—except relief that the dealer had been killed before he could take Bradan out. Bradan had seen a lot of death in his long life, but the last few weeks had massively compressed the violence into a short period. Well, it had been a war. He didn't consider himself callous despite Chief Inspector Young's appraisal. However, his psyche was good at protecting itself from dreams that would otherwise drive him mad.

"My furniture is clean," he reassured her.

"Interesting hat collection," Trini said. He saw that she stalled before jumping into the deep end. She reached out for the top hat and placed it on her head, adjusting the angle to peer out at him from beneath its lowered brim.

"My grandfather wore one at formal government functions in Havana during the pre-Castro regime."

She pulled the hat off and looked it over.

"Bullet holes? It has history."

"Not in a good way," Bradan said.

He looked her over, remembering their embrace by his shattered gallery. He thought of her intelligence and her musical passion; she'd been renowned as a Cuban-style guitar player in Little Havana's Latin club scene. He also remembered her sensuality and hanging out on South Florida's beaches from Palm Beach to the Keys. No one looked better in a bikini when they'd hit the sand before crowds arrived and it was still cool dawn with the sun just rising and damp air blowing up from the Caribbean.

Trini still had the same unaffected smile and dark eyes he remembered. Her eyes were wonderful. So were her breasts beneath a heavy forest-green sweater. She'd bundled herself with a dark-gray scarf and wore jeans over boots. She'd shopped for winter clothing since arriving in London.

"I never know what to expect from you, Bradan."

"That's not my intention," he answered. "I like consistency. I'd be fine with an ordinary existence. Being in a band is as much adrenaline as I need."

She toyed with the hat, poking her fingers through its many holes before putting it back on. The vintage black silk top hat shadowed half her face including her eyes, but he plainly saw her frown.

"We have things to say," he said. "Let's say them."

"I followed you over here not knowing what to expect," she said. "I told you I wanted to see where things stood with us. I didn't know how settled you were in Mayfair. You might have met someone and I didn't expect you to be celibate—"

"Good to know."

"Don't be sarcastic. I had a couple of relationships in Miami once we'd stopped communicating regularly."

"Anything serious?"

"Nothing that's lasted. Seeing you with Adela—'Del' seems too casual for her—but I guess that's the point. Everyone has cute nicknames over here if you're from a certain set. Seeing you with her, it looked serious. Whatever you have, I'm intruding."

"Del's just her name," he said. "To your point, I'm not over her, but I *am* leaving Mayfair, so that's brought things to a hard stop."

He paused.

"I'm fortunate beyond words to know two unbelievable women. It's unfortunate that I know you both at the same time, so, if you're willing, let's see where things go with us. If this is all too much drama to deal with, I understand, and we'll part on speaking terms. Maybe we'll cross paths in the future. Who knows?"

He saw that she wasn't quite ready to leave things on this note.

"Your band," she said. "Silicon Saturday, it's mostly synth-pop dance stuff from what I've heard?"

"It's dance-oriented, but we're more than that. It's global, it's R&B, it's whatever it is. If we're playing for the right crowd, it's kind of magic."

Trini tilted the top hat back. "If the group is shifting to the U.S. and you start doing gigs there and recording, I'd like to sit in. Maybe you can incorporate a Spanish guitar and my vocals into the mix. I like your lyrics. You're poetic when you talk about love and nature."

~

"I'm still reeling from talking to them," Bradan said.

"And yer expecting sympathy?" Mags asked. "The dead tend not to be understanding of the living's problems."

The apparition had never directly admitted that she'd died. She did now.

He was packed and ready to go, but he'd made time for a stroll with her in Green Park before heading to Heathrow.

He scanned the paths and trees and saw no sign of Russian tanks or sinister entities from other realms.

Above, the sun traded places with plump, puffy clouds. It was April in London and not raining. There was just a hint of spring warmth, but already runners swept past in shorts and tank tops.

Usually, spirits were invisible to the living, but Mags was one apparition who occasionally allowed herself to be seen as she had when she sang with Silicon Saturday in Soho. Today, she walked at his side visible to one and all, ignoring the occasional stare from passersby at her long Victorian-era dress and pale visage. The runners gave them a wide berth. They were probably also apprehensive about the massive wolf pacing along beside Bradan and Mags.

"I'm not expecting anyone's sympathy," Bradan said.

That wasn't quite true, but Margaret Sutcliffe was rarely the shoulder to cry on, and it didn't appear to be a day to look for her softer side. However, her bracing observations kept him honest.

"I'll survive," he said.

"We 'ad a wager about who you'd wind up with," Mags said conversationally.

"The Elephants bet on who I'd keep my relationship with, Trini or Del?"

He was angry, but also intrigued.

"Who'd you pick?" he asked.

He'd never observed color in Mags's features, but now her cheeks turned rose.

He laughed.

Is she embarrassed?

The color disappeared quickly.

"Told you I 'ad no horse in this race. Like 'em both despite one being from posh society and the other being a Yank, so I laid no money on either of 'em."

"Who'd the rest pick?"

"Wouldn't you know, split down the middle. We needed a vote to decide the issue, but I wouldn't be the tie-breaker."

"Them's the rules?" Bradan said.

"Them's *my* rules," she replied.

Bradan already knew the answer, but he asked anyway. "You listened to me talking with Trini and Del?"

"Usually yer good about spotting me, but things must 'ave

been a bit dodgy when you was speaking to 'em, and you didn't pay me no mind at all, didn't notice a thing. I admit to being rude, but yer good sport to watch, I give you that. 'Alf expected one or the other of 'em to gut you with a razor. If I was in their place, I might 'ave done it, but you appear to 'ave lived to tell the tale. Drink some gin to celebrate."

They strolled companionably for a while, getting closer to Piccadilly's traffic and racket.

"I could have played it better," he said.

"The women?"

He nodded. "But then I'm only supernatural, not super-human. And not very supernatural."

"You did stop a war, and that fucker, Pedro, has naught but a cold cell for comfort 'cause of you."

"Thanks," he said. And he meant it.

"That's as much sympathy as yer gettin' today," she said. "I must leave you now."

Mags looked about, appearing to savor the park before departing to wherever she went. Her expression darkened as she turned to the busy thoroughfares.

"I never thought of it much when I was aboveground, but being dead tends to change one's perspective. We're wrecking the place. Keep doing your bit to help."

"I will," he said. "And I'll come to London from time to time to visit. I'd like to see you in America, too. Can you cross an ocean? Just once in a while?"

"Not easy, but never say never." And with that she vanished.

Just off the path, a couple, bodies intertwined, sprawled across a blanket on the grass. Their radio played a Silicon Saturday song.

THE END

If you enjoyed this fanciful tale, please rate and/or review it on Amazon, Goodreads, or other book review sites. If a review sounds like work, even a complimentary sentence would thrill the humble author! Or just rate the book (hopefully well). Thanks and please read my other stories.

The Lords of the West End is part of a series of modern fantasies that can be read in any order or all by themselves. If there is a chronological sequence to the stories, it starts with *The Lords of the Summer Season* set during San Francisco's "Summer of Love" in the 1960s, followed by *The Lords of Powder* set during Miami's cocaine wars in the late 1970s. This is followed by *The Lords of the West End*, which occurs in London during the mid-1980s, and finally, *The Lords of Oblivion* set in today's San Francisco.

I can be reached at: blaisdellliteraryenterprises.com. I also have Instagram and Facebook pages, which you're welcome to follow.

AUTHOR'S NOTES

It's hard to understand your own writing. And, of course, it's the reader who decides whether the writer's mad visions work. So, feel free to skim or ignore altogether what's below. Nonetheless, rushing in where angels fear to tread, I'll make a few points about themes, characters, plot, and setting for *The Lords of the West End*.

Themes

First, entertaining readers is my main goal. Hopefully, thematic elements enrich the experience, but don't impede the story. Otherwise, literature becomes polemics. Having said that, *The Lords of the West End* centers on an existential conflict between nature, represented by Fae and their realm, versus human technology and cities with their potential to corrupt nature, represented by London and Miami. Green Park, Stonehenge, and Tintagel Castle are at the border between these two forces, the liminal spaces where the novel's drama unfolds.

Another theme is the power of music and, more generally, creativity to affect outcomes. Bradan's tunes and also his magic represent this. Sometimes the copious consumption of drugs described herein amplifies creativity; sometimes it prompts the characters to run amok. So, while creativity is two-edged, ultimately it's a positive force in this story.

A big part of the novel is the related notions of secrets, history, and memories—or perhaps secretive memories. Bradan, being an almost ageless, near-immortal magician, has a closet packed with skeletons. He's become adept over the centuries at lying to hide this past while allowing only the wolf and two phantoms, Connie and Mags, to truly know him. They keep secrets. He holds the rest of the world at bay including girlfriends, band mates, and the police, all of whom suspect, but can't prove, he isn't who he purports to be. Naturally, this massively stresses his relationships. Bradan is acutely aware of this, but sees no choice if he's to protect his livelihood in a skeptical and hostile world, though he occasionally slips and dances right up to the edge of divulging what he is before rescuing himself with yet another lie. Ironically, the one person he finally reveals himself to is a drug lord out to kill him, because he knows this criminal will never be believed if he talks about Bradan.

I also touch on romantic choices (see the Del Versus Trini section below). I hadn't intended to. It's good, maybe even inevitable, that a fantasy novel include some romance. Even the chaste *Lord of the Rings* does so. And current romantasy has taken romance and upped the spice quotient considerably (e.g., Clare Sager's books). However, while I respect this subgenre's sales, in my books, I've focused on action, drama, and ideas. But romance can be dramatic, and love is a wonderfully complex idea. So, *The Lords of the West End* bowed to the inescapable and included Bradan's messy love life.

Del Versus Trini

Why is Bradan forced to choose between two stellar love interests, Del and Trini? The women are mostly a study in contrasts, but they share more qualities than either would admit. Bradan first meets Trini in *The Lords of Powder* and that story ends with a seemingly ardent future ahead for them, but life intervenes when Bradan moves to London to escape enemies in Miami, causing things to lapse between them. Bradan then meets Del in

London. I originally intended Del to be a minor character in *The Lords of the West End*, emblematic of casual and careless wealth, unconcerned about issues beyond her class, but she evolved into a more appealing character (to me anyway). Bradan falls for her, too. Then, to everyone's surprise—certainly Bradan's—Trini arrives unannounced in London and friction ensues. Moreover, at the story's conclusion, circumstances force Bradan to choose which relationship to carry on. Obviously, the women have an equal say in what transpires.

So . . . why? I had three reasons: 1) To create ongoing romantic tension amplifying all the other pressures Bradan faces in stopping a supernatural civil war, defeating cartel assassins, and keeping his identity secret; 2) because other books in this series have Bradan and Trini marrying after events in *The Lords of the West End* conclude, and I felt I couldn't change what was promised in previously published books; 3) I wanted to be a contrarian and ignore some of the tropes of fantasy romance by injecting ambivalence and some heartache into Bradan's relations. Rest assured, Trini and Del—and Bradan, too—go on to lead reasonably happy romantic lives following *The Lords of the West End*.

The Forty Elephants

Bradan's old and dear friend, Margaret (Mags) Sutcliffe, was a member in good standing of England's premier all-woman's criminal gang, the Forty Elephants, who successfully pilfered England's most prestigious stores from Victorian times to well into the twentieth century. Part of the fun in writing fantasies is the author can include real individuals or organizations that rival the wildest flights of fancy. The Forty Elephants meet this criterion in spades! For a further look at this fascinating band of miscreants, readers are encouraged to check out various YouTube videos available on the internet.

Shooting an MTV Video at Stonehenge on the Solstice

I wanted a whimsical, over-the-top opening to this novel, and Silicon Saturday playing Stonehenge seemed a cool way to kick things off. Setting the date on the winter solstice added a mystical element that foreshadowed some of the novel's themes, nature versus urbanity and time's passage. After all, this is a site where archaic humans built a monumental structure to determine an important date in their calendar, the shortest day/longest night of the year. Today, Stonehenge is open to visitors on the solstice, but in the mid-'80s, the authorities prohibited tourists on this date—presumably for fear that the site would be "overrun." I can find no records of a temporary chain link barrier erected to enforce this ban, but it doesn't seem unreasonable that it might have existed, giving Bradan a chance to demonstrate his modest magical skills by surmounting the fence and allowing his band and the MTV video crew access to the site.

1980s Pop Music

The 1980s English musical scene was crammed with different pop subgenres. Bradan's band, Silicon Saturday, is best described as "synth-pop" (short for synthesizer pop) which, as the name implies, centered tunes around synthesizers sometimes complemented with guitars and percussion (either human or machine made) as well as vocals. Many of these groups leveraged the rising popularity of MTV to market themselves, and some of these videos show real ambition. Damian, in *The Lords of the West End*, is a tongue-in-cheek send-up of one such video director. A complete listing of 1980s synth-pop musical groups is vastly beyond the scope of these notes and runs the risk of transgressing the somewhat blurry lines defining just what made a band authentically synth-pop. Suffice it to say that Bradan's band competed with, was influenced by, and, dare I say, influenced groups including Spandau Ballet, Soft Cell, Duran Duran, Visage, New Order, Tears for Fears, and Depeche Mode. No doubt, I'm leaving out aficionados' favorites. For those interested in what these bands looked and sounded like, check out videos from Visage, "Fade to Grey"; Spandau Ballet's "To Cut a Long Story Short"; New Order's "Blue Monday"; and David Bowie's "Blue Jean." Most of these exist in several versions. There are hundreds and hundreds of others.

Haters may say this music was superficial. However, it wasn't ephemeral and current artists have been influenced by it. Also, the tunes were fun to dance to.

London's Green Park

Several scenes from *The Lords of the West End* occur in Green Park. Anyone who's visited this pleasant, well-manicured spot in central London will be flabbergasted at my descriptions of specters and Fae commandeering it for midnight battles among densely packed trees that more closely resemble a primeval wilderness than a staid city open space. Mea culpa. I've used poetic license to alter the park's appearance to make it more mystical and eerie when magic is at play. One feature of the park's history that isn't a fabrication is Rosamond's Pond, which had a notorious reputation as the final resting place for lovelorn suicides during the eighteenth century.

Russian Tanks in London

A vintage Russian T-34 tank plays an important role in *The Lords of the West End*'s climactic scenes. This isn't a daft figment of the author's imagination. In fact, a T-34-85 *did* sit on Mandela Way in the Bermondsey district south of the Thames. Evidently, it was acquired by a scrap dealer and sat for several years in an otherwise vacant lot before being removed for refurbishment in 2022. While it was on public display, it became a local landmark and was painted in varying shades that only occasionally matched its original olive-drab combat coloring.

London's Lost Rivers

Like any number of oddities in *The Lords of the West End*, London's underground "lost rivers" are real. I made liberal use of the Tyburn, but, in fact, there are at least a dozen others running beneath the modern city, mostly unnoticed, but occasionally revolting at their entombment and pushing out to the surface. Besides their dramatic possibilities, these waterways seemed emblematic of the conflict between urban spaces and nature. Building on this leitmotif, rivers appear in Faerie, too, though there, they're allowed to flow free.

Whether the Tyburn actually runs beneath Bradan's fictitious Half Moon Street address, I'm uncertain, but its course is fairly near and hopefully the reader will forgive a smidgen of authorial imagination in bending local geography to the novel's needs. For more about these intriguing aspects of London's past, check out Peter Ackroyd's *London: The Biography* or simply do an internet search for "London's lost rivers."

ACKNOWLEDGMENTS

Many thanks to Shikha, Shraya, John B, Eric G, and Carolyn for thoughtful input. Of course, any mistakes are mine.

ABOUT THE AUTHOR

Peter Blaisdell lives in the greater L.A. area. He has a Ph.D. in Biochemistry and has conducted postdoctoral research in microbiology. On the literary side of his life, he's written a series of modern fantasies: *The Lords of Oblivion*, *The Lords of Powder*, and *The Lords of the Summer Season*. *The Lords of the West End* now belongs to this series. Each of these novels can be read on its own.

Peter Blaisdell has also published *The Jinn and the Two Kingdoms*. This is the first in a historical fantasy series featuring the jinn, Thiago.

The author can be contacted at blaisdellliteraryenterprises. com

Printed in Great Britain
by Amazon

61336882R00194